THE CAPE AGULHAS

To Jane
Love Mike xx

M.J. McMullin

ISBN: 978-1-913012-58-8

Dedications

*There are a lot of people to whom I am very grateful for having given me
the opportunity for not only being able to write but to allow me to be able
to complete this book.*

*So, this book is dedicated to my loving wife, Jeanie, without whose support
this book would never have got written, let alone published, twice.*

*And especially to the Doctors, Nurses, Physiotherapists, HCA'S the
ESD team and all the staff of:
Twyford Ward, Royal Hampshire County Hospital, Winchester.*

*Without your help, I wouldn't be here to be able to finish this book,
let alone complete a second edition.*

To my sons, you knew your Dad could do it.

Michael McMullin

Contents

Acknowledgements	vii
About the Author	ix
Chapter 1	1
Chapter 2	15
Chapter 3	27
Chapter 4	44
Chapter 5	52
Chapter 6	62
Chapter 7	69
Chapter 8	83
Chapter 9	92
Chapter 10	109
Chapter 11	122
Chapter 12	136
Chapter 13	148
Chapter 14	159
Chapter 15	168
Chapter 16	179
Chapter 17	187
Chapter 18	196
Chapter 19	205
Chapter 20	217
Chapter 21	229
Chapter 22	237
Chapter 23	246
Chapter 24	260
Chapter 25	273

CONTENTS

Chapter 26   284
Chapter 27   292
Chapter 28   301
Chapter 29   316
Chapter 30   331
Chapter 31   341
Chapter 32   356

Glossary of Terms   362

Acknowledgements

In the first instance this book is a work of fiction, I have however made reference to certain products and properties in order to retain a sense of reality. I wish to acknowledge the following people and organisations for their guidance, advice and permissions for the use of products and premises.

Firstly, my profound thanks go out to Rhoda for proofreading this edition of the book, without her help and experience, there would be a lot more mistakes. Thank you!

Heartfelt thanks to James Barke, Managing Director of Boats.co.uk for his agreed assistance in the promotion and marketing of this book and for permission to use the reference to the Kawasaki products.

https://www.boats.co.uk

Ollie Taylor, Marketing Manager for Williams Jet Tenders.

https://www.williamsjettenders.com/

Louise Morley. Manageress of the Royal Naval and Royal Albert Yacht Club.

http://www.rnc-rayc.co.uk/

Robert Heiland, Marketing Manager. Cayago AG. Bad Salzuflen, Germany.

https://seabob.com/en/cayago-ag/

José Garcia and Pilar Candil. Restuarante José Garcia, Malaga, Spain.

https://www.restaurantejcg.com/

I have also made mention and reference to a number of organisations and manufacturers, some of whom I have made numerous attempts to contact, others I have not. I have also attempted to maintain every individual product description to the best of my ability and have not knowingly made any disparaging remarks in relation to any product or property.

MJ McMullin

About the Author

Michael John McMullin was born in Red Ruth, in the county of Cornwall, England in 1947. Both parents had served in the armed forces and had spent time in East Africa which was where they met and got married in 1945. In 1948, Mike and his parents emigrated to East Africa, before he could speak English his prime language was Swahili which he still speaks to-day, although maybe not quite so fluently.

Eventually the family moved south to what was then Northern Rhodesia and now Zambia, where from 1960 to 1964 Mike attended Hillcrest High School in Livingstone, home of the Victoria Falls. From a very young age he developed an affinity with all animals and reptiles and maintains that to this day.

In 1966 Mike moved back to the UK in order to complete his Master Divers Certificate at the then British Underwater Centre in Dartmouth. Dissolution followed and just after his eighteenth birthday, Mike joined the British Army and served for twelve years in a number of guises. In 1973 he met and married his wife, Jeanie, together they have two wonderful sons, two gorgeous daughters in law and four delightful grandchildren. After leaving the Army, he served for ten years with an English provincial Police Force after which he qualified highly within the UK transport industry where he gained extensive knowledge not only of the UK but Europe as well.

Mike's interests include photography, wildlife and a passion for flying. In 2019, he retired from his photographic business and started writing at the beginning of 2020.

In August of 2020, Mike suffered a stroke disabling his left side, since then he has persevered to complete the original version of *The Cape Agulhas* but now this the second edition of the book containing references to a mostly completed first prequel (*Ingwe*) despite his disabilities.

Currently he is working on both the prequel and sequel (*The Sins of Our Sons*) to this book.

In addition, Michael has written two short stories, *Animal Justice* and *Rusty*. These, he hopes to be able to publish along with some other short stories under a single cover at some time in the future.

CHAPTER 1

British Airways flight BA2713, an Airbus A320 made her approach into Malaga on finals coming into land from over the sea. Bruce Williams was occupying seat 5A which was just forward of the aircraft port wing in the Club Europe section. The vibrations emanating from the stresses that the aircraft were going through, were evident throughout the jet as she made her short finals with full flaps and the undercarriage down. The plane flashed over the short stretch of beach, where a large number of motorhomes appeared to be parked haphazardly on the hardstanding, then disappeared under the port wing. A second later, there was a soft bump as the wheels made contact with the asphalt runway. Immediately, two things happened at the same time. The vibrations increased as the air brakes on top of the wings were deployed, the twin engines went into reverse thrust slowing the aircraft quite violently. This only lasted a few seconds and then the pilot allowed the aircraft to run out to the end of the runway before turning to port and picking up the taxiway that ran parallel to the runway.

Williams collected his bulky bags and cleared Spanish customs and passport control without any problems, then making his way out through the busy terminal building following the signs for Salida and Taxies. Struggling with the bags, he made it to the first taxi, a white Hyundai i40 saloon car. The undercover area was filled with the sound of revving engines, squealing tyres on smooth asphalt, the honking of horns as well as the smell of exhaust fumes. This caused Williams to have to stand signalling for the driver to open the boot of the vehicle, eventually and seemingly reluctantly he got out of the vehicle, opened the boot of the taxi and assisted Williams with his luggage. The laptop and large camera bag got placed with care onto the rear passenger seat, the bulky suitcases and hand luggage having taken up all the boot space in the vehicle.

"Where you want to go?" The driver asked in passable English.

"Paseo del Muelle Uno, in the port area please." Replied Williams.

"Ok, Signor!" The driver replied pulling out sharply from the pickup area and immediately braked violently to avoid a collision with another taxi. A tirade of Spanish abuse followed, directed at the other taxi driver who seemingly wasn't at fault.

The 25-minute drive through the bright sunlit streets of Malaga contrasted with the rainy grey roads of the UK that he had left some four hours previously. Shortly the taxi brought them up to the beginning of the marina, the journey had passed with very little conversation apart from the driver asking, "Where on Paseo del Muelle Uno you want to go to? You have a boat, you go on a cruise ship perhaps?"

"I have a boat, moored just opposite the Restuarante José Carlos Garcia." Replied Bruce. "Or at least that's where she was when I last saw her ten days ago."

As the taxi entered the Paseo del Muelle Uno, the driver slowed and Bruce peered through the windscreen, he could see the 82-foot Princess motor yacht further down the quay. She was moored stern on to the quay with a smaller cruiser on her starboard side and the pontoon to her port side. A tight knot formed in the pit of his stomach, his lifestyle was about to change forever. He had just invested a large sum of money into the boat that had been a very good deal from Bruce's modest point of view. The taxi pulled up close to the stern of the 82-foot cruiser, the chrome and polished gelcoat glinted in the early February Spanish sunshine. On the cockpit deck, James Barke stood dressed in slacks, a white shirt showed through from the blue lightweight windcheater with the Boats.co.uk logo that he wore.

It had been ten days ago since Bruce had last seen the big Princess 82 and that was when he had first met James Barke.

As the taxi came to a halt, James Barke from Boats.co.uk with offices in Cala d'Or, Mallorca, at Wallasea Island in Essex, Poole in Dorset and now in Malaga, Spain. Straightened himself up from where he had been leaning on the rail and approached the opening from the port deck onto the pontoon. Business was beginning to pick up since Boats.co.uk had taken over from Ellis Marine.

James Barke had first met Bruce Williams some ten days previously collecting him from Malaga airport and had brought him down to see the *Cape Agulhas* at the Malaga marina and his mind went back to that time when they had first met.

James remembered that it was very apparent that Bruce Williams had walking issues as he had a pronounced limp on his left side. He was about five foot, nine inches tall, with a full head of collar-length dark brown hair and a neatly trimmed beard. Both the hair and beard were tinged with grey, giving him a distinguished look. At the same time, he gave off a distinct aura of confidence as he had limped towards James and introduced himself. It was the piercing blue eyes that caught James's attention and the smiling, friendly demeanour as he extended his right hand to greet him. His handshake was very firm, indicating that he had great strength in his upper body. As he spoke, he sounded confident and there was that slight accent that James had confused with either antipodean or South African. Once the introductions had been completed and from the initial conversation, it was apparent that he was also very definitely an intelligent and a 'no' nonsense person. They made their way to the taxi ranks very much at Williams' reduced speed, he appeared to be travelling very lightly on this first visit with what appeared to be a laptop case and a lightly packed overnight rucksack.

Standing on the quayside, Bruce himself recollected their first meeting when he had flown out from England on that January morning. James with that wonderful constant smile stood over Bruce at about six foot one, the firm handshake returned equally, the full head of mostly grey hair neatly trimmed with a fashionably short back and sides. He further recalled how the conversation and events of the day had progressed. Once ensconced in the taxi and on their way to the marina. James had asked, "So Bruce, what have you got in mind for the use of such a big cruiser, perhaps some charters or something along those lines?"

"No, I suppose that I am having a late midlife crisis." Replied Bruce, repositioning his light luggage on his lap. He continued with a wry smile. "I lost my wife in a traffic accident about two years ago." Bruce's features softened at the recollection.

3

The image of the huge truck hurtling down the autobahn hill in the opposite direction with the bend at the bottom then failing to make the bend as the truck flew over the dividing crash barrier and slammed into their motorhome travelling on the opposite carriageway. Bruce had drifted in and out of consciousness during the ordeal, his first recollection had been of his dead wife, Lucy, lying on top of him, her once beautiful face now bloody and unrecognisable. The second recollection had been during the time that he was being pulled from the wreckage, the incredible pain in his left leg and arm, he had screamed in agony then passed out again. Then it had been a series of conscious periods through operating theatres and repatriation flights more operating theatres and argumentative threats with surgeons that he was going to keep his leg and more pain during the lengthy recovery process.

"So, I sold everything we had owned together and bought a bungalow on Hayling Island. I decided that I still hated the UK weather, but I couldn't afford to be without the security of a UK permanent address." Bruce paused briefly, almost as though he was choosing his next words with care. Then he continued. "I have always had a penchant for the sea and to own a live on boat, it was something that didn't appeal to my late wife. We caravanned, motor homed and enjoyed part winters in Spain when we could, just something that I feel that I don't want to go back to." He paused briefly before continuing. "I guess that something like the *Cape*." He said referring to the name of the cruiser. "Is something that meets with what I have in mind for my future. To be able to meander at will staying in warmer waters and at the same time having my children and grandchildren out to spend time with me as well!" He turned to face James, almost seeking an understanding of how he saw his future unfolding.

"Yes." Replied James. "The *Cape* should suit you admirably." He smiled. "Have you had any experience with motor cruisers before?"

"Actually." Replied Bruce. "I managed to charter a 70-foot Princess out of Plymouth last December for two weeks, she was partly crewed and the whole emphasis was to teach me boat handling, navigation and how to use the various instruments. We did this on a day-to-day basis, Plymouth Sound and the waters of that part of the English Channel in December are pretty inhospitable, so I suppose in some ways it was a really good school for learning boat handling."

"Great, that is fantastic." James responded. "Is this why you are looking at this particular make now?"

"Partly, I have to say that the 70 was wonderful in rough seas and the stabilizers were brilliant. However, I would say that despite the sea handling abilities of the 72 and the 82, I don't have any intention of sailing in other than perfect conditions where I can. However, having said that, I am not naïve enough to realise that weather can't blow up anywhere or at any time and that forecasters are not infallible." His mind went back to the disaster in October of 1987, when Michael Fish got it all wrong. "However, I want to know that the boat I have will take bad weather in her stride."

"Wise idea. What about a crew?"

"To be honest, James, it is something that I have considered but not something that is immediately important to me. I am pretty confident that I will be able to maintain the boat and sail her from port to port without any assistance from any crew. When I was doing my short course back in the UK last December, the skipper was a slave driver to some extent and made me work on docking procedures and manoeuvres. The video cameras are a huge help, but then he would switch the cameras off and made me make judgements from the lower helm by referring to obstacles relevant to parts of the outside rail. We spent a lot of time picking up various buoys solo and from a variety of approaches."

"Crikey!" Exclaimed James. "It sounds as though you had a very comprehensive course in a very short time."

"Oh yes. We would set off in darkness, starting at six in the morning and not returning until eight in the evening, obviously, again in darkness and often with sleeting rain to boot. I have already made enquiries locally with regards to completing my RYA Masters." Bruce paused. "So, tell me about the *Cape*?"

The taxi turned onto the Paseo del Muelle, and James gave the driver final instructions. Bruce looked ahead down the road and caught sight of the *Cape Agulhas* with the distinct line of her flybridge masts, enclosed satellite domes and radar scanner. Even then as they approached, he had to admire the lines of her upper decks. His heart skipped as the taxi came to a halt and he got out of the vehicle and stood briefly admiring the boat while James paid the taxi driver.

"Well? What do you think?" asked James, pushing his sunglasses up onto his forehead. He turned sideways with a beaming smile. "Like you, this will be my first time on this boat, but I have been on them before and they are absolutely beautiful."

The smile was infectious and Bruce smiled in return. "Awesome! She is a bit wider on the beam than the 72 isn't she." Bruce noted the Red Maltese flag flown from the stern mast and the courtesy Spanish flag flown from the short starboard burgee.

"Yes, not much though, only 25 cm. Now shall we get on board? Hopefully, my chap will have some coffee on the go, but if you prefer tea, that can be arranged as well?"

"No, coffee will be fine, thanks." Bruce replied gratefully. His experience of other people making tea made this decision very easy.

The narrow passerelle had been extended from the stern, allowing easy access to the aft deck and a crewman offered to take Bruce's laptop and rucksack making it easier to cross on the narrow walkway. Bruce stepped onto the cockpit of the boat and took in the beautiful teak decking but noted that it could have done with a good clean. Having retrieved his baggage from the crewman, he nodded a grateful 'gracias' to him. His eyes looked forward through the saloon and beyond to the large eight-seater dining table and beyond that towards the lower helm. James came on board behind Bruce and spoke briefly to the crewman in Spanish.

"Come and sit down." James ushered Bruce into the sumptuous 'C' shaped port sofa with the round coffee table in front of it. Several documents had been distributed onto the table. As they waited for their coffee, James explained.

"I am going to come clean with you Bruce. As you know your communications and todays appointment were all set up by Ellis Marine, Boats.co.uk have just taken over Ellis Marine and this is literally my first day here in Malaga having flown in from Mallorca last night." As James sat back on the sofa Bruce couldn't help but notice the black socks with what appeared to be brightly coloured cherries. "The program that I have set out for today Bruce, is as follows, as long as you approve of course. We will have our coffee then starting from the flybridge, we will make our way down through the boat finishing with the engines and crew quarters in the stern." Bruce nodded with approval and James continued. "After that, I suggest a light lunch across the road there at Restaurante José Paulo followed by a short trip out of the harbour and down the coast. Please, at any time, feel free to lift, open, ask or change anything you like. Will that be alright?"

"Yes, of course, absolutely fine."

The coffee was served whilst Bruce perused engine, generator logs and registration documents, questions arose surrounding discrepancies in the engine running logs with over a thirty-hour difference between the two main engines. In the past three years servicing intervals had been missed on both the Onan generators and main engines, similarly, fuel filter changes. Bruce asked as to when she had last been lifted out of the water and the last anti-fouling, no record of this was indicated. James had not got the answers to these questions, but a series of very terse phone calls ensued. Coffee was concluded and the tour of the boat began. Following the telephone conversations, James added, "I'll have those answers for you by close of play today Bruce."

As they gained the flybridge via the starboard stairwell, Bruce commented. "I noted that she is Maltese registered. Would there be any financial reason for not changing her registration to somewhere like the UK?"

"No, not really, other than of course if you were to employ any crew, the fact that the boat is UK registered would mean that you and they would have to comply with terms and conditions compliant with UK employment law. Most UK registered owners use the zero-hours, self-employed contracts to get around it, others opt for something like Panamanian or Bahamian registration."

"Hmm! I think that if the sale were to go ahead, I would like to have her registered in the UK."

"I would happily arrange all that for you if you so wished."

Bruce pondered this and continued to the upper helm position located at the front and centre of the flybridge. The white leather seat was showing wear and tear and a lot of green algae as well as salt staining. "I would say that this seat hasn't seen a weatherproof cover for some time."

Embarrassed, James exclaimed, "Ahh! Yeah, look Bruce we are talking a few aesthetics here." Some rapid Spanish to the accompanying crewman followed, James was very unhappy. He then continued addressing Bruce. "This is something we can take care of Bruce either replace the seat or recover it."

The inspection of the flybridge continued. Bruce moved aft and lifted the grill lid on the wet bar located on the starboard side and left it open, it seemed that it hadn't been cleaned since it had last been used, leaving the lid open. Bruce opened the large fridge for the wet bar and stepped back with the smell that came out from within, again he left it open. Continuing aft Bruce inspected the lockers housing the cushions for the deck furnishings. He found that the furnishings were damp and mouldy, once more, he left the access covers open so that James could see for himself. Bruce moved right to the rear of the flybridge, the area that housed the hydraulic crane that was capable of lifting a 5,000 lb tender right out over the beam. The crane jib was in the stored position and like everything on the flybridge it was showing signs of neglect with rusty coloured stains on the white paintwork and the weather cover was missing.

During the rest of the tour, several things came to light, a lack of cutlery, glasses, no sheets, duvets, blankets, a musty smell in the master cabin and the crew area. Televisions missing from the cabins. Bruce was shaking his head as he went through the engine room and looked at the twin Caterpillar engines. Engine rooms should be immaculate. He noticed a slight fuel drip from one of the fuel filters, so with a grunt, he got down so that the offending fuel filter was at eye level. Straightening up, he mentioned to no one in particular. "Cross threaded. I might suggest that this is seen to before we go out on our trip this afternoon." It was however heard and noted by James. More phone calls from James resulted.

As Bruce and James went ashore for lunch, two vans appeared, four people boarded the boat, two went straight into the engine room through the crew quarter access. Entering the restaurant Bruce, selected a table from which he could continue to have a good view of the comings and goings, on what he had already decided was his boat. They ordered lunch, Bruce went for a cheese and tomato tostado, James opted for a club sandwich.

Opening the conversation, James asked. "So, what are your feelings so far Bruce?"

Bruce paused for about ten seconds between mouthfuls, considering his answer before replying, then turning towards James, the penetrating blue eyes looked straight into his. "James, being very fucking honest with you and I know that today has not been down to you or Boats.co.uk, but if a manager from Ellis Marine had been sat in your place right now I would have told them that I feel like I have been treated as an idiot. Judging by the way things have gone so this far, I would have to ask. Did Ellis Marine really want to sell me this boat or not?"

James felt a chill run down his spine, the faded Rhodesian accent was more apparent with this mans' suppressed anger. At that moment, words failed him.

"Now I realise that this is not down to you, so forgive me, but I have just flown out from the UK and spent time being shown a boat that was supposedly prepared for sale. Yet it is apparent that no one has made any form of an effort to make the boat presentable." Pausing briefly to stir his coffee, he continued. "The advert reads that everything is in pristine condition, and I have to say that if anyone is expecting me to part with what the asking price is, then you can forget it. Quite frankly, James, as I said, I feel that someone has been wasting my time. I love the boat, the spec is exactly what I want but seriously, I can find another one somewhere else."

James looked pensive. Right now, the sale of the motor yacht was rapidly going southwards. "Okay, look Bruce, I do apologise unreservedly. We can make adjustments on the price and of course, a lot of the faults can be rectified." He paused briefly and then continued. "I will give you my personal guarantee that I will take charge of everything. The truth is as you are aware, we have three other offices and as we have just taken over from Ellis Marine, who incidentally ran the advert, after having been asked not to, prior to the takeover. The manager here is about to be sacked as a result of this morning's catastrophe and several other unrelated incidents. However, as he is also the only skipper available, I'll have to wait until later to do it. If you understand where I am coming from?" He finished with a wan smile.

The skipper, despite his experience, yet not with this boat, whilst conducting the exit manoeuvre from the berth, had clipped the next-door boat with the starboard rear corner. Fortunately, not causing any damage to the next-door Pershing, but it did graze the *Cape Agulhas's* gelcoat. That was his first mistake as Bruce indicated the error to James. They were making their way out down the harbour approaching the cruise liner that was docked, maintaining a four to five-knot speed the twin nineteen hundred horsepower Caterpillars barely idling. Earlier, Bruce had gone up to the flybridge, where the skipper, suitably attired for a late January, Spanish sun sparkling afternoon, was piloting the big cruiser down the starboard side of the lane. He glanced sideways at Bruce and addressed him in heavily accented English. "I take the boat out, do some fast running, then I let you drive. Okay? This boat is rubbish."

"Oh! How is it rubbish then?"

"Because it smell and then there is theese and that, you know. You know my Eenglish not so good."

"Okay!" Replied Bruce. "In the meantime, I'll go below to the lower helm." He nodded in acceptance of the statement and the offer.

Bruce went below to the main deck. James was sitting on the 'C' shaped sofa with a mobile phone pressed close to his ear and was seemingly getting frustrated with the conversation he was having. Bruce continued further forward and settled himself into the lower helm seat and leant back with his arms resting comfortably on the armrests taking in the various instruments. He noted that none of the navigation screens were switched on. Almost as an afterthought, he got back out of the seat and started to prowl around the helm station, taking in a rack at the back of the pilot area, which would normally house the courtesy flags of countries that the boat might visit. The rack was empty. He stepped over to the chart table, normally motor yachts of this size would not have a chart table on the pilot station. However, a previous owner had instigated a chart table and chart locker being built towards the port side of the pilot station. There were no charts displayed. In anticipation, he opened the top drawer of the chart desk, it was empty. He opened all the drawers in turn with similar results. Some instinct prompted him to open the top drawer again, there seemed to be a space of a drawer depth between the top of the top drawer and the top of the chart desk. Bruce opened the top drawer fully and felt up underneath the top of the chart desk, there was a piece of wood filling the entire top of the drawer space, indicating the probability of a space between the chart drawer and the top of the chart desk. For some reason, this immediately intrigued Bruce. He closed the chart drawer just as James joined him on the pilot station.

"Ah! There you are Bruce." He exclaimed brightly. "I have got some very good news for you. I have just had a word with the vendors, and they have agreed to a substantial reduction in price given the problems and discrepancies that we have encountered. I can arrange for a full complement of cutlery, sheets, duvet covers, towels etc. I will also arrange for the boat to be lifted sometime soon for a full service and filter changes at our expense." Pausing, he glanced up at the courtesy flag locker. "I'll also make sure that you have got…...!" At that point, the boat lurched forwards violently as the throttles were thrown wide open. Thrown off balance James disappeared backwards down into the main salon with a shout of. "Fuckin' hell!" As his voice faded away. Bruce was fortunate and hung onto the chart table until the boat steadied up on the plane at something over thirty knots which didn't seem to take too long at all. James came struggling back up to the helm station. "That's fuckin it! He's done for now. Bruce, do you think you can take over the boat?"

"I'll give it a go." Bruce responded, as he moved as fast as he could after James and gained the flybridge just as James was ordering the skipper off the helm. Bruce took the helm and slowly brought the throttles down to idle and the gearboxes into neutral. Pushing the command button on the throttle quadrant, he disabled the flybridge control. The *Cape* was wallowing in her wake with the gentle swell of the sea as Bruce briefly took in the view from the flybridge. They were still in the outer harbour where there was a maximum ten-knot speed limit.

James addressed an annoyed Spanish skipper. "Get your fuckin' arse below. Now!" Turning to Bruce, he asked. "Bruce where will you helm from?"

"Lower helm position." Bruce replied. "It's too bloody cold for me up here and quite apart from which getting up and down those stairs isn't that easy." Bruce made his way down the stairs, followed by the Spanish skipper and James taking up the rear. Bruce noticed the access doorway to the crew area and engine room had been left open. Changing his route, he made his way towards the offending access and made sure that it was firmly closed, then made his way back to the lower helm position.

Bruce was just in time to hear the final part of James's tirade at the skipper "You will now fuckin' well stay there until we dock, then you'll get your sorry arse off this boat. At eleven-thirty am tomorrow, you will report to me at the office to face a disciplinary. Is that clear?" The Spaniard turned his head away and gazed out through the stern in an attitude of 'don't give a shit'.

"Fuck! Today is just going from fuckin' bad to worse." James exploded. "Apologies for the language." He concluded as he took a seat in front of the chart table.

Again, realising that none of the electronics were on, Bruce did a quick visual check that he was not impeding the passage of any other vessel. He switched on the Raymarine chart plotter and radar and watched them come to life and then from the two available screens selected what he wanted to view. Neither of the two VHF radios were switched on. Again, he took a quick visual glance around to make sure that there was no other shipping around and then a glance at the radar display, confirmed the same. Bruce reached up to the radios and after a quick examination turned them both on, he tuned one to the international maritime frequency.

The second radio was already tuned to 134.4, the frequency for Malaga Ports. No sooner had he switched it on when he heard. "*Cape Agulhas, Cape Agulhas* this is Malaga Ports, this is Malaga Ports do you receive, over?" Came the weary heavily Spanish accented request.

Bruce keyed the transmit button. "Malaga Ports, this is *Cape Agulhas*, receiving you five by five."

"*Cape Agulhas*, your pilot was exceeding the ten-knot speed limit and has failed to respond to our radio calls, over."

"Ports, apologies for the delay in getting back to you we were just conducting some trials and we will be returning to port in about forty minutes to one hour. We will be happy to meet with you for a full explanation when we return to port, over."

"*Cape Agulhas*, roger that, I look forward to your excuses."

Both James and Bruce looked rearwards to the skipper and shook their heads in disbelief. The Spaniard just turned his head away and resumed his gaze out over the stern.

"Are we good to go James?" Bruce asked.

"Yes, absolutely Bruce, you seem to know what you are doing."

Bruce selected the command button on the throttle quadrant and with a glance around engaged forwards and started to open the throttles. Checking the engine temperatures as he did, clearing the outer harbour markers, he again slowly opened the throttles until they were at twenty-five knots. No words were spoken, Bruce just enjoyed the feel of the boat under him as he put the *Cape* through various manoeuvres and at different speeds. At thirty knots, the twin Caterpillar engines growled in unison, but not so loudly that Bruce and James couldn't continue in conversation. She was exhilarating to drive, almost like a huge sports boat, however, when Bruce brought her speed down to twenty-two knots, the twin Cats purred as she provided a very comfortable and stable cruising platform. At the same time, Bruce checked the computer for fuel consumption and discovered it was also probably the most economical speed and would provide a more than reasonable range for the boat. Bruce had made up his mind, he was head over heels in love with the *Cape Agulhas*, despite her faults, most of which could be easily remedied. He was determined that they were going to spend the rest of their days together.

Fifty minutes after taking over the helm, Bruce picked up the radio microphone and pressed the transmit button. "Malaga Ports, Malaga Ports, this is the Motor Yacht *Cape Agulhas*, over."

"*Cape Agulhas*, go ahead, over." Replied the same heavily accented, pissed off sounding controller.

"Malaga Ports, this is *Cape Agulhas*, permission to return to berth 146 on the marina please, over." Bruce continued glancing at James for confirmation of the berth number. James nodded in confirmation.

"*Cape Agulhas*, this is Malaga Ports, permission granted. Do you require any assistance, over?" The question was full of sarcasm. James looked at Bruce, questioning him silently.

Bruce replied. "Malaga Ports this is *Cape Agulhas*, negative, thank you. Out!"

Bruce brought the *Cape* back into port and docked at 146 as though he had been sailing the big cruiser since she had been built. Standing on the quayside were a couple of uniformed men, one the Harbour Master, the other a very stern looking Captain from the Guardia Civil.

"I'll handle the shore party Bruce. That, was impressive boat handling by the way." Volunteered James.

There had followed a ten-minute period of terse discussions between James and the two uniformed officers of authority, during which the hapless skipper had been summoned ashore and was then sent on his way. During this time, Bruce had gone through the *Cape* shutting down engines and electronics, coupling in the shoreline and turning off the generators, finally doing a check on the engine room as he lovingly patted each of the big Cat engines which were still warm to his touch. He smiled inwardly. 'Rest now my beauties, we'll be playing soon enough.' Bruce thought to himself. He was still wondering as to why the Spanish skipper had warned him off the purchase and as to why the manager had failed to make the boat presentable for sale? But the skipper was the manager or soon to be ex-manager.

Finally, the day had been concluded with a lot of haggling and was finalised with a bottle of Champagne which appeared from the Restaurante José Paulo, delivered to the boat personally by the owner, José.

CHAPTER 2

The ten days had passed all too swiftly for Bruce Williams, it was now Friday the 7th of February, 2020 and he was now looking at his new home. He briefly recalled the argumentative discussions with his two sons about the suitability of his decision. The discussions with his bank, the money transfers and the endless phone calls to and from James Barke and more arguments with his health insurance providers. The boat survey had concluded favourably, which had probably proved to be the last stumbling block.

Whilst the taxi driver unloaded the luggage from the boot of the vehicle, Bruce Stood on the quayside with the early February sunshine warming through his leather jacket. The scent of the Mediterranean ocean, the sound of the occasional gull and a quiet jingle of a halyard rattling against a mast further up the quay. The *Cape Agulhas* sparkled in every place possible. She looked like a totally different boat to the one which he had docked two berths up only ten days previously. The gelcoat on her hull and upperworks glistened in the sunlight, with the darkened windows adding an air of mystery. The Maltese flag of registration had now been replaced by the Red Ensign, which was fluttering gently in the breeze. Now she was moored stern on to berth 144 but also with a pontoon on her port side. Mooring fees had been paid for up until the end of February, courtesy of Boats.co.uk. At the end of February, the *Cape Agulhas* would then be taken out of the water and have a full external inspection carried out on her hull, propellers, rudder gear, drive bearings and a full antifouling service carried out. The twin Caterpillar engines and Onan generators would also be serviced. In the meantime, he was going to get to know his new love intimately.

James extended his hand. "Welcome aboard Captain." he said with a huge smile on his face. During the course of transactions over the ether, they had become firm friends, with a mutual deep respect for each other.

"Hardly a Captain." Blushed Bruce as he handed baggage through the port rail access from the pontoon.

"Come aboard and sign your life away." Joked James. "We have changed the port of registry to Portsmouth, as you asked and I think that you will find everything else in order. By the way, this is Sergio he will now be my right-hand man here in Malaga." James indicated the smiling Spaniard next to him. Williams shook his hand.

"Where would you like your luggage Capitain?" Asked Sergio. "Master cabin?"

"Uhh! No, thank you. Forward VIP please, thank you."

He followed James into the salon where paperwork was spread out on the coffee table. Another of the Boats.co.uk employees was also on the deck at the galley end and was preparing coffee which was subsequently served. Bruce and James went through all the various pieces of paperwork, including the change of ownership and post-sale arrangements.

Upon conclusion of the paperwork, Sergio joined Bruce and James at the table as they sipped their coffee.

"Okay!" said Bruce, "I have had one or two ideas that I would like to discuss as modifications." The other two nodded in acceptance, so Bruce continued. "The first thing that I would like, is to have the crew cabins aft converted into a workshop come storage area for some diving equipment, leaving the heads and shower where they are and installing a dive compressor and filling station. Then, of course, there is still the matter of a tender?"

James looked across to Sergio for the answers, who replied. "This is not a problem Capitain, we have a Zodiac with a twenty-five-horsepower engine, nearly new, I think it has only twenty hours, maybe, I can bring this over on Monday for you. Would that be okay?" Sergio's English was excellent.

"Okay!" replied Bruce. "In addition, I have drawn up a list of equipment that I would like to acquire through your chandlery, including dive cylinders, wet suits, fins, goggles, life jackets, three handheld VHF radios and chargers, a CF Moto quad bike and a Sea-Doo wave rider. Very pistol and cartridges, two safes, one for the pilot station and one for the forward VIP cabin." He handed the list over to Sergio.

"This is not a problem Capitain, we can discuss storage and mountings on Monday. Is this okay?" Replied Sergio.

James chipped in. "Bruce, would you mind if I made a couple of suggestions in respect of your choice of Seadoo and quad."

"Not at all, please feel free to do so, after all you have been in this industry for a long time." Bruce leaned back in the sofa.

"May I suggest that you possibly consider the Kawasaki Ultra 310LX it is considerably better and more reliable than the Seadoo and we can get it shipped out straight away. After all it was Kawasaki that invented the jet ski. Back home, I have got a picture of the Bee Gees on one, long hair, beards and all.

"Great, we'll go with that. And your second suggestion?"

"Why not consider the Kawasaki Brute Force 750, I don't think you will regret it. It has got a fantastic off-road capability as well and again we can get that shipped out straight away along with the STX."

"Fantastic! I'll go along with your ideas James. Thank you."

James sat forward. "So, what are your plans for the immediate future?"

"My thoughts are to get to know my new home as best I can, chill, enjoy some sunshine and just get settled in generally." Concluded Bruce. "I have got a lot of reading to do as well." He exclaimed, indicating the owner's manual.

When the three men had departed, Bruce stowed all the paperwork concerning the boat in one of the forward lockers in the pilot station, leaving the owner's manual out on top of the chart table. At the same time, he noted that someone had placed a local chart indicating all the channels for the harbour. As well as the local coast down as far as Marbella to the west and Nerja to the northeast.

Needless to say, there did not appear to be, nor would he have expected to find any groceries on board, so sourcing the whereabouts of the local Lidl and Mercadonna shops on his iPad was not too much of a problem. He then sat down and set about preparing a comprehensive shopping list, primarily including wine, beer, whisky and milk, but also including other possibly more necessary items. Notwithstanding that Spain came to a standstill on a Sunday, he knew that most shops would be closed. Having experienced Saturday shopping in Spain in the past, he concluded that as much as he disliked the necessity of having to shop, Bruce was of the opinion that the sooner he got it done, the sooner he could relax. But not until he had had some lunch.

Ensuring that the boat was locked up, he went across to the Restaurante José Paulo, where he ordered a Club Sandwich accompanied by a glass of cold crisp white Pinot Grigio. Bruce was served by a smiling José who insisted on calling him Captain Bruce and who constantly sent his attractive eldest daughter over to make sure everything was okay. Enjoying his Club Sandwich, Bruce was sat at a terrace table with a wonderful view of the stern quarter of his boat, it was his boat. He now owned a boat, the realisation that *The Cape Agulhas* was now his, began to sink in as he sat and admired her. He noticed the reaction of passers-by strolling down the marina quay who turned their heads in admiration of the boat on her berth and inwardly, he felt pride swell in his chest. 'That's my boat.' he thought.

Bruce had noticed a young man with a taxi who seemed to spend quite a bit of time hanging around the restaurant, so when he had finished his lunch he went over to speak to the driver. With a combination of Spanish and English, Bruce established that the driver would drop him off at the Lidl store and then pick him up an hour later from outside the Mercadonna shop which was very close to the Lidl's store. True to his word, Ivan picked up Bruce from outside the Mercadonna store and ignoring the 'no vehicles beyond this point' sign pulled up onto the pontoon next to the *Cape* and helped him offload the taxi onto the deck of the boat. Ivan received a generous tip for his efforts and left Bruce with one of his cards saying. "You telephone me anytime Captain Bruce, I come. Okay?" Bruce just smiled, this 'Captain Bruce' bit was very amusing, the Spanish emphasis being on the 'i' between the 'p' and the 't'.

The fact that Bruce had previously asked for the change of berth to the one with a pontoon alongside was to make access to the deck easier. Notwithstanding that he was still very much in the recovery stages from the last surgery to his left leg following the fateful accident two years previously. So, rather than having to lift heavy goods over the stern of the boat and to negotiate the narrow passerelle, Bruce had requested the empty berth next to the pontoon. Which was just as well as he had just offloaded something that felt like a weeks' worth of groceries and alcohol.

Bruce stored the provisions in the galley area behind the pilot station. He continued making notes regarding things that he had missed like, barbeque equipment, but then he realised that he hadn't looked in the grill area up on the flybridge. This prompted him to open the rear salon door and make his way up to the flybridge where he opened the grill lid.

"Wow!" He exclaimed, it looked brand new. He opened the storage cupboard under it and saw that there were brand new barbeque tools and cleaner, all set to go. Outstanding, he thought thinking of the generous sirloin he had picked up earlier. 'I'll see what the weather does over the weekend'. He thought closing down the grill and replacing the weather cover over it and then continuing around the fly deck, he checked the rest of the weather covers on the flybridge. Briefly lifting the covers from the twin imitation leather seats at the helm station, he noted that the seats had been beautifully cleaned and refurbished. He leant over the front rail to the right of the helm station and spent some time gazing out across the marina. Traffic was light as a twenty-foot sailboat was puttering up the marina on her single-engine. The mainsail loosely furled, she was making for either a mooring or a berth further up the marina. The Trans Mediterranean ferry opposite was gearing up, ready to make her way across to Morocco. The sun was beautifully warm on his body, even this early in February and it was winter. When he had left the UK another storm for the south and west had been forecasted with snow on the high grounds and flooding elsewhere. 'I am well out of it.' He thought to himself. There was a very gentle swell under the boat as the small wake from the sailboat passed under the cruiser, up here on the flybridge it would have been more noticeable. Not feeling in any rush to have to do anything, Bruce remained on the flybridge enjoying the sun and the warmth on his back and shoulders. He continued to watch the sailboat as it went to pick up a mooring to which a tender had been made secure. He grinned inwardly as the skipper of the boat missed picking up the mooring twice. That prompted a thought for Bruce. A boat hook, did he have a boat hook anywhere because he hadn't seen one. A last look around the flybridge, making sure that everything was secure, weatherproofed and covered. He made his way down the companionway to the main deck.

As he walked back in from the stern of the boat, Bruce was aware of the hubbub sound from the passers-by, then realising that anyone walking along the quay would have an almost uninterrupted view of the inside of the salon. It meant that the lounge and dining room were visually invaded. So, he closed and locked the rear salon doors, which like the windows were constructed from strengthened smoked glass allowing the occupier good views to the outside of the boat, but prevented anyone from being able to see in. Making his way forward to the foredeck, he opened up various lockers looking for signs of a boat hook. 'Nothing!' He concluded. He made a note to have the issue addressed on Monday when Sergio delivered the tender. Thinking. 'I'll have it mounted onto the foredeck railing so that it will be easily to hand when I need it to pick up lines or buoys. The tender.' He continued thinking. 'He looked forward to having a play with that and the Kawasaki jet ski as well come to that.'

Bruce spent the rest of the afternoon unpacking his clothes and equipment that he had brought out with him. The ample space in the bathroom allowed Bruce to store his personal effects in such a fashion that no personal items were left on display. Yet, his adequate toiletry equipment only took up a small amount of the available space in the cupboards. He had remembered to pack a small travel hand and shower wash pack, these he placed on the washbasin and in the shower cubicle. He carried on exploring the other cabins at leisure. The master cabin was huge, it took up the full width of the boat with unusual-shaped windows. The two guest cabins to port and starboard, one consisting of two singles and the other a double, were more than adequately comfortable. His decision to occupy the forward VIP cabin, he felt was suitably justified, especially as a single person. The thought of occupying the master cabin left him with the feeling that he would really feel lost in a cabin of that size, anyway he thought, it would be nice to be able to let a guest have the use of it instead. He thought of his two sons and their respective families. So, he finished off by making up his bed in the forward VIP cabin, one less job to have to contend with before he went to bed that night.

Bruce made his way back up the companionway dropping the blue Steiner Marine 7 X 50 binoculars off at the lower helm and putting them on the front of the helm position. Then making his way aft, descending the starboard stairs to the aft swim deck, he went through the access to the crew accommodation and utility area. Here he examined with interest the functions of the washing machine drier. Again, he took the time to familiarise himself with the positions of the light switches, then into the engine room compartment. Once more, he made a mental note to himself to ensure that ear defenders were also to be added to the shopping list for Monday.

Making his way back up to the swim deck, Bruce closed and locked the access hatch, noting that by this time dusk was beginning to fall. Checking his watch, he saw that it was gone a quarter past six. 'Right!' he thought to himself. 'That has now got to be time for drinky poos.' As he made his way back up to the main deck, he noticed that there had been a significant increase in foot traffic and the *Cape* was getting even more admiring glances from passers-by, some had stopped and were actually staring at the boat remarking to each other on various aspects. This was something that he certainly wasn't used to or had even considered but having said that, he thought on reflection that he had certainly done a lot of it himself in the past. To some degree, it had given him some inspiration and had provided easy research, along with the many hours spent on YouTube, of course. Bruce made his way up the starboard walkway onto the main deck and went into the salon via the door from the lower helm, making his way aft to the salon he examined the ice maker. Satisfied that it was going to donate ice. Bruce retrieved a tumbler and fixed himself a gin and tonic then settled himself back at the dining table with the owner's manual and carried on going through it. It was about eight o'clock when he realised that he hadn't eaten.

Grabbing a piece of chicken from out of the fridge, Bruce chopped it up into small pieces, fried it off in olive oil, garlic, and onion. Then he added some pre-cooked mixed Mediterranean vegetables and served it up accompanied by a second glass of Rioja. Once he had washed up, Bruce left the plates and utensils to drain on the side of the sink. Then locking both doors that gave access to the sides of the boat and taking the remainder of the bottle of wine, he made his way down the companionway to his cabin.

No television signal was available, another thing to have to address on Monday. So, he opened his Kindle and continued with the Edward Rutherford story that he had been reading. Then it was a quick shower followed by time spent rubbing Bio-Oil into his scars and moisturising his legs and arm with an Avon product before getting into bed. Sleep didn't come easily that first night on the *Cape*, the gentle movement of the hull in the harbour swell was a movement that Bruce wasn't used to as yet, no matter how soothing it was. This and the number of things going through his crowded mind made it impossible for his brain and body to transfer to the state of sleep. When finally, sleep did come, it was fitful and he was restless. Eventually, the deep sleep came at about five am and he didn't wake up until nine am with the sun streaming in from behind the blind on the port side of the cabin.

Grabbing his towelling robe, Bruce went up to the main deck and into the galley. First priority, he thought! 'A brew'. It had gone ten am by the time he had got dressed, breakfasted on cereal and had a second mug of tea. Bruce had already decided that the prospect of spending a day tied up alongside with very little to do with the boat was a situation that he didn't want to have to endure. What he really wanted was to be able to get to somewhere where he could sunbathe in relative privacy and that was certainly not going to happen as long as he was tied up at the marina.

The crash and subsequent surgery had left both Bruce's left leg and left arm with horrendous scars from the wounds. As he was very conscious of this, he felt that he did not want to expose the results of the injuries to viewings by members of the general public. When asked by his grandchildren, he had referred to the damage as him having had a fight with a crocodile, but it was alright now, as he and the crocodile were now the best of friends. It was a lot more difficult explaining where grandma was.

Taking some kitchen roll from the galley, Bruce went aft and into the engine room, dipping the necessary oil levels and checking the filters, he completed the daily pre-running checks, then moved forward to the lower helm he started one of the Onan generators, checking the throttle settings and then started the Cats and listened to them burbling gently. Then making his way forward to the foredeck, he prepared the port anchor removing the safety pin. This was a procedure he had adopted from his lessons in

Plymouth, where he was told, that this precaution added a substance of safety. In the event of an engine failure, all that was required was to release the anchor to retain his position. Until he could get power back to the boat.

All instruments switched on and operating, CCTV cameras switched on, radio permissions granted and Bruce slipped the stern, fore and aft mooring lines and left them loose on the deck. There was a gentle onshore breeze at about 2 knots, clearing the berth, Bruce turned to starboard and then rotated the *Cape* through one hundred and eighty degrees using the engines and turning the big cruiser within her length. Nosing up into the wind, he put the engines in to neutral. Following this, he gathered up the fenders, stowed them and then coiled and stowed his mooring lines. Checking all the time to make sure that he wasn't drifting too far to the north and that he wasn't endangering himself or another craft. Finally, he replaced the safety pin for the anchor so that it couldn't be dropped by mistake. Back at the lower helm on the main deck he slipped the throttles forward and just letting the engines idle to give the boat way until he cleared the marina. Then he increased his speed up to 4 knots until he reached the outer harbour wall on his port side, then slowly increased speed out towards the open sea. Bruce gradually turned the boat to port and brought her around to a north, north-easterly course at a steady twenty-two knots, in so doing, following the coast up towards Nerja. The *Cape* felt wonderful under him. However, a degree of trepidation suddenly washed over him as he realised that for the first time, he was sailing solo. That there was no one else to hand should, or if anything were to go wrong. It was an utterly surreal feeling, much the same as his first solo flight so many years ago. He was alone, thinking that maybe if he did have a crew member on board, things might be safer. Although, in himself, he felt fully confident. His course in Plymouth had made certain that he was more than competent to handle the sixty-ton vessel on his own. Bruce started to bring the *Cape* in closer to the shore, keeping an eye on both the continuously moving electronic chart and depth gauge. He had decided to head up towards the Playa Perros Rincon De La Victoria. It appeared on his chart and Google Maps of course, that he should be able to put the anchor down offshore and where he could chill for the remainder of the day without being overlooked by passers-by. Within forty minutes of leaving the marina, Bruce had the *Cape's* anchor down onto a sandy bottom about 300 yards off the beach. He had turned off the two main engines, switched off the main generator, but not before powering up the small seven point five KVA generator. Setting the drift alert on, as the *Cape* snubbed upon her anchor chain and came up nose into the light onshore breeze. Bruce went below and changed into his shorts and then made his way up to the foredeck where he got himself comfortable on the sun lounger. With his eyes closed and drifting in and out of sleep and with nothing much on his mind, he found himself able to relax for the first time in many weeks. He could feel the warmth of the sun eating into the scars at the same time he could physically feel the healing process of the ultraviolet light on the wounds in a strangely penetrating way.

The rest of the morning passed swiftly, Bruce decided to make himself a sandwich and pour a glass of juice for lunch. He did this intending to give himself a break from the sun. He had taken his sandwich up to the helm position and was casually sat on the helm seat, looking over to the port side when he looked at the chart locker beneath the chart table. Recalling the intrigue that the chart locker had raised in him some eleven days earlier, his mind suddenly focused on it. Putting the sandwich down carefully, he went over to the chart locker and opened the top drawer. Noting with interest that now the drawer had a collection of charts in it, this time he pulled it out to the stops and felt up at the top of the drawer space. Sure enough, the top of the drawer space was covered, he pushed upwards gently, the piece of marine ply moved upwards marginally. It wasn't fixed. Intrigued, he lifted the entire drawer out over the stops and placed it on top of the chart table. Reaching up, he felt up around the top of the cavity. Bruce couldn't reach the far end of the space, so he removed the next drawer down and peered up into the cavity. He needed a torch. Going below, he retrieved a torch from beside his bed and made his way back up to the main deck.

Before continuing, he finished the sandwich and washed it down with the remains of the juice, placing the used utensils into the galley sink. Then turning his attention to the chart locker, he shone the torch into the cavity. Going through his mind, Bruce had been thinking, that it might make a nice 'hidey-hole' for a weapon of sorts. He could see that the piece of plywood in question was held in place with three dowels, reaching up inside the front of the drawer, he found the fourth dowel, it felt loose, so he removed it allowing it to sag marginally. Supporting the piece of plywood with his left hand, he reached inside and removed the remaining three dowels and allowed the piece of twelve-millimetre ply to drop down onto the charts that sat on the third drawer down.

There were four charts, one of an area in the Aegean Sea, one of an area of the Adriatic and two of various areas of the Mediterranean which he didn't recognise. The charts were relatively large-scale indicating depths in metres. Each chart was marked with a single red cross and on top of each chart were written very precise coordinates, also in red. No doubt that the coordinates related to the crosses on the charts. All the charts also indicated a relative proximity to a coastline. He looked at the back of the charts and again examined the cavity under the top of the chart table, there was nothing there to suggest the origins of the charts or any reference to the marks on the charts.

The satellite phone rang with a shrill ring causing Bruce to jump. One of the big Tracvision satellite dishes provided satellite telephone facilities, another provided TV facilities throughout the *Cape* via an AV system. Recovering quickly, he picked up the phone, not having realised that it was even working. It was Sergio, letting him know that the Tracvision facilities and accounts had been opened. Also asking if it would be possible for Bruce to go over to the chandlery on Monday morning instead of the previous arrangements made the day before. Sergio needed to discuss the tender, as well as getting Bruce sized up for his wet suit. He further needed to speak to Bruce about the quad bike as well. So, it was settled that Sergio would arrange to have a vehicle pick Bruce up at about ten o'clock on Monday morning.

Putting the phone back in the holder, he turned his mind back to the charts that he had discovered and wondered why anyone would want to hide them away. More importantly, what was the significance of the markings, all the positions given were all offshore and they were all in relatively sheltered coastal waters. His mind went back to eleven days previously when the Spanish skipper warned him off buying the *Cape*. Was this what he was after? There was also no doubt that he had found a suitable hiding place for any article that he wanted to keep away from prying eyes. He made a note of the coordinates on his cell phone and decided that he would put the charts back where he had found them. A pirate treasure indeed. 'Maybe I should get a *Jolly Roger* flag and fly it from the bargee'. He smiled to himself.

Sitting on the sofa at the back of the main deck, Bruce contemplated what he was going to do with his immediate future. He was very keen to acquire his RYA Masters, but it was going to be necessary to build up his sea miles first. He could always do the occasional run up to Cartagena via Adra or even pop down to Gibraltar for a visit, notwithstanding cheap whisky and other duty-free goods at Morrison's for example. The idea made Gibraltar a must-do soon requirement.

The *Cape* was going to be lifted out of the water, so she would be out for at least a week to 10 days whilst her hull was examined. Engines and generators serviced and modifications made to the crew room. As he didn't relish the prospect of a hotel or living aboard in a chandlery, this would be an excellent opportunity to return to the UK and collect the rest of his clothes and numerous items which he wanted for the *Cape*. Including new televisions for the salon and his cabin. Coffee machine, a goodly quantity of PG Tips and Kenyan coffee, the rest of his cameras and drone, plus anything else he could think of in the interim period. One thing, he decided, was that first thing on Monday once his business with Sergio had been completed, he was going to find a fishing shop and get himself some fishing gear. It would be perfect to be able to sit out on the swim deck and fish for his supper, but only if he caught anything, of course.

Checking his watch, he saw that it was 15:55, so he decided that he would return to the marina for the evening. Going below, he changed back into his slacks and set about preparing to start the engines and raise the anchor. The onshore breeze had freshened by a couple of knots, looking out to sea towards the African coast, he could see a long dark line on the horizon. That was a sign of bad weather coming in.

CHAPTER 3

Coming back into the marina, Bruce was grateful that he had decided to get back to port, an onshore breeze was going to make it tricky getting in alongside his berth. He would have to be quick getting the beam secured thank goodness he didn't have to pick up a bowline as the onshore wind would rapidly push the *Cape* off the pontoon. Tensioning between the bow and crossed stern lines would help to keep the big boat straight once in at the pontoon.

Slowly, arriving back at the marina, the sun still shining, Bruce took in the beauty of the scene that met him and especially the colourful Centre de Pompidou at the end of the marina. The people sitting outside various restaurants and cafes and naturally folks out for a stroll admiring the various boats in the marina. He also noticed that the Trans Mediterranean ferry was in port and discharging her cargo and passengers from Melilla, the small Spanish enclave on the coast of Morocco. In the background the ruins of the Castillo de Gibralfaro loomed. Families were walking up and down the quayside, even two Spanish Police Officers were patrolling on their Segways. That's when the idea struck him that what he needed was a little electric scooter. This would enable him to get around locally, allowing him to get himself down to the shops or do a bit of local exploring. Then he turned his mind towards the upcoming berthing procedure.

He went in and past his berth, turned the *Cape* into wind, getting his lines and anchor ready for docking, then made his way back to the aft control point. There was a nice gap for his berth as he nosed the boat up past the berth, then screwing the stern around all he had to do was to get some rearwards momentum going. He was parallel to the pontoon with sufficient way on to see him into the berth. Bruce operated both stern and bow thrusters together, causing the *Cape* to move sideways alongside the berth. Once the boat had gone back as far as it needed to, he gave the engines a bit of forward thrust to bring the *Cape* to a standstill. Taking his beamline from the deck, he looped it around the bollard on the pontoon and tied it off to a cleat. Then returning to the aft control point he gave the stern thruster a little nudge. Just to keep the stern in whilst he went ashore with the two stern lines. Bruce was about to step ashore when Wonder Woman appeared saying, "Give me those stern lines skipper, I'll sort them out whilst you stay on board. Do you want them passed back?"

"Err! Yes, please." Bruce responded. Moving aft he waited for the lines to be passed back to him so that he could tie off on the aft cleats, once that had been done, he moved forward and picked up the bowline and made that fast. Wonder Woman was stood on the side of the pontoon looking down at him. She must have been at least six foot tall, or possibly six foot one. She was truly the spitting image of Wonder Woman with that distinctive face of an angel but perhaps a little older. Her below shoulder length, jet black hair was tied back harshly into a single broad plait, the bright hazel eyes looked directly into his. Bruce's heart skipped a beat.

"You really didn't need me at all. That was some neat docking skipper." She volunteered, "She is a beautiful boat. Is she yours?"

"Got her yesterday, I thought that I would take her up the coast for some privacy for the day." 'What the hell am I telling her that for?' Bruce thought to himself.

"Yes!" She replied looking around the quay and at those on the pontoon, "I can understand how you feel. A bit like a goldfish bowl." She smiled. Wonder Woman was thirty-five to thirty-six years old, casually dressed in jeans, an open-necked shirt and a hoody top that was unzipped, with casual slip-on trainers on her feet. "Are you by any chance looking for crew?" She added.

"Well!" Bruce responded, looking up to her, his heartfelt as though it skipped another beat. Admittedly the pontoon on which she was standing was marginally higher than the deck Bruce was on. "I would suppose that it would all depend on what sort of work you are looking for and what your qualifications are?" Wonder Woman nodded. "So, I'll tell you what, why don't you step aboard and make yourself comfortable in the salon." Bruce's mouth was dry as he indicated the access from the deck. "Whilst I close down and hook up shore power, then we can discuss what might suit us both. My name is Bruce Williams by the way." He proffered his right hand. "Welcome aboard the *Cape Agulhas*."

She took Bruce's offered right hand in hers, "Charlie, Charlotte Hope." She introduced herself. The grip of her hand was warm and dry but very firm for a woman. She stepped onto the deck and kicked off the trainers that she had been wearing on the pontoon. As she stepped past him and for the first time, he smelled the delicious faint aroma of her body scent, he knew he would never forget it from that moment on.

Bruce initially made his way forward and secured the anchor, then making his way aft, he checked his lines and fenders and plugged in the shorelines, finally making his way back into the lower helm and turning off the idling engines. Bruce went back into the salon, where Charlie was standing looking around and taking in her surroundings. "Oh please, do take a seat. Can I get you anything to drink, tea, coffee or a beer?"

Charlie turned smiling, "Would a beer be alright, or is it too early?" she replied.

"It has to be six o'clock somewhere." Bruce responded, making his way to the fridge in the galley and taking out two tins of Alhambra lager. "Glass?" Bruce inquired.

"Err! Yes, please, if it is not too much trouble." she replied smiling.

Bruce put the two tins on the table and then got two tumblers out of the sideboard storage drawer. He poured most of the first tin into a glass then sitting down, he offered it to Wonder Woman, Charlie. "There you go." He poured the second tin of Alhambra for himself and proffered. "Cheers, Charlie!" He followed this by taking a lengthy pull of the lager, an action which he instantly regretted as he felt the wind gather itself into an almighty belch. Which, somehow he managed to marginally suppress. "Pardon me!" Charlie smiled. "Right!" Bruce continued, "Have you got a CV or some sort of resume with you?"

Charlie rummaged very briefly in the top of her handbag and produced some folded paperwork which she handed across the table to Bruce. "Thank you." he said.

"Now, before I go into your history and carry out a formal interrogation." He smiled and then continued. "Why don't I tell you what I have got planned for the boat and if you still think that you want a part of what I have in mind, then we'll press on. How's that sound?"

Smiling, Charlie replied. "I think that is fair enough."

Bruce told her about some of his past circumstances and then some of his current circumstances, during which Charlie nodded and passed comments appropriately. Then he got to the point of the present time, continuing to tell her about the additions and modifications that were going to be made to the boat. Also informing her that he anticipated the *Cape* being out of the water for one week to ten days.

"Wow! That does sound reasonable." Replied Charlie. "What sort of time scale are you placing on all this and will you be taking on any charters?"

"Time scale-wise. I haven't yet placed any sort of time provisions on my life. I will be taking every day as it comes. I have no plans to take on a six to ten-foot swell, just because I can. Storms blow or the weather is bad, then I stay in port. If I spot bad weather coming up, two things will happen. The first is that I have a boat that will cope with a trans-Atlantic crossing in the winter and the second is that I will run for cover at thirty-five knots. When the weather is nice, my intention will be to moor on safe anchorages most nights. The other thing is that I left the UK to get away from the weather, now all I want is sunshine, so I have no intention of going anywhere where it gets cold unless I have to." Bruce shifted in his seat and took a swallow of his lager before continuing. "In respect of charters, it is not something that I have planned for as yet or ever." Bruce concluded.

Charlie sat up in her seat, took a lady-like sip of her lager before saying. "I think that you may like to take the time to read my CV. It sounds to me that what you have got planned is going to be right up my street. Which is of course if you want to employ me?"

Nodding in agreement, Bruce picked up the document from the table where he had put it down before commencing his statement. He took a pull of his lager and sat back on the sofa to start reading the CV.

The CV read.

Charlotte Samantha Hope: DOB 14/10/1981

Personal Statement:

I am a highly motivated, tenacious and conscientious person, with the ability to encompass any requirement and fulfil it to the end. Whilst remaining very much a 'team player', I retain the capacity to work independently. I can communicate eloquently, both verbally and in writing. These qualities, together with the highest of moral and personal values and an old-fashioned sense of loyalty, are my core values.

Her work history included a self-employed Seamstress, Captain in the British Army, the self-employed crew on two charter motor yachts as a deckhand lasting no more than six weeks on the last yacht, being *Octopus*. Her qualifications included three A levels, Level Three City and Guilds as a Seamstress qualification, an Instructor with the Professional Association of Dive Instructors and a Royal Yacht Associations' Professional Certificate of Competence for Offshore Powerboat.

Languages, French, Italian and Spanish.

It took Bruce less than three minutes to skim the CV, he then went over it again, at the same time, he mentally formulated the questions that he was going to put to her. He started, "So what is your current state of employment?" He asked.

"Unemployed, at the moment." She replied, "My last job was as a Deck Hand come Chefs Assistant on *Octopus*, which came to an end when the boat was sold. The new Russian owner wanted a crew that neither spoke nor understood Russian. I have spent the last few months bumming around Spain and the last six weeks in Morocco. I had just got off the ferry, saw the marina and thought to do some dock walking."

"Do you speak Russian?" Bruce inquired.

"No, I don't nor do I understand it." Charlie smiled. "I turned down his romantic advances towards me though."

"Okay! Any takers so far from any of the other boats?" Bruce asked.

"No, To be honest, yours is the first boat that looked as though you might be big enough to require a crew. Having watched you come into the marina and then docking, you don't need a crew though. Do you? You had everything figured out before you came anywhere near your berth." She replied with a look of curious admiration.

"I don't know about that, I was docking in a very light breeze and not having to worry about dropping an anchor or pick up a bowline to keep my bow straight." Bruce responded. "So, how current is your PADI qualification?"

"Oh, absolutely up to date, I will probably need to do a refresher sometime in 2021, but I can do that anywhere in the world."

"So, how about the languages? Do you get confused between Spanish and Italian at any time?"

"Yes, at times." She replied laughingly.

"British Army, and an ex-Rupert?" Bruce looked at her with interest.

"Yes, I was with the Queen Alexander's Royal Nursing Corps. I did seven years with them starting as a private and then applied for a commission. I saw service in Iraq and Afghan."

Bruce's attention was drawn away as the sound of big boat engines being used excessively within the confines of the marina. "Excuse me." He said as he got up and looked forward through the front windscreen. A fifty-foot Beneteau Swift Trawler was in the marina, the pilot was over-revving to compensate for the movements, almost as though the pilot was in a hurry. She was flying a French flag of registration but no courtesy Spanish flag. Every time the pilot operated the throttles, a burst of black smoke plumed from the exhausts at the back. Bruce moved forward into the helm area, all the better to watch the proceedings. By this time, the onshore wind had picked up quite substantially, as Bruce was aware of the sound of the wind rattling the rigging of the nearby sailboats, as well as a small chop, was apparent in the outer harbour.

Charlie moved up next to Bruce at the lower helm, "Mind if I join you to watch the fun?"

"No, not at all." Bruce replied with a wry smile. He was aware of her height and the presence of her proximity to him. Again, he was aware of her distinct scent. It was difficult to discern. She smelt fresh without the smell of an obvious perfume. Bruce felt very comfortable being close to her. They watched as the Beneteau came to a halt about five berths up from the *Cape*, where Bruce knew there was a large double berth free. The pilot then started his reverse manoeuvre for the berth, more engine bursts. On the stern, a crewman appeared. Bruce recognised him immediately. It was the past employee of Ellis Marine/Boats.co.uk, the same skipper that had lost his job some eleven days earlier and who had had his marching orders from James Barke. Bruce pointed the crewman out to Charlie and briefly recounted the incident to her as they continued to watch the docking attempts of the Beneteau.

Bruce suddenly asked. "Seven years, Charlie? It seems a strange time for a length of service in the Army. I always thought that it was six, nine or twelve years of service that someone served." He turned marginally towards her in anticipation of the answer.

"Good question." Charlie turned and faced Bruce directly as she replied. "I was wounded in Afghanistan. A piece of shrapnel from an IED got me in the lower abdomen."

"Oh, Christ!" Bruce reacted. "Sorry, I didn't mean to pry or anything. Are you okay now? I mean, are your activities restricted by not being able to lift anything for instance?"

Continuing to watch the docking entertainment, Charlie replied. "No, as long as I don't have to lift dead bodies anymore." She smiled sadly.

Bruce smiled back at her. "Well, Charlie, I feel that I am a pretty good judge of character and you come across as being an okay sort of person. I didn't get up this morning with a view to hiring any crew today. But if I were to take you on, in the first instance, when would you want to start? Secondly, what sort of wage would you be looking to earn?"

Charlie had turned away slightly but then again swung back to face Bruce directly. "To answer your questions, I would like to start as soon as possible and secondly, assuming that there is no charge for food and accommodation, I would settle for four hundred pounds a month. But as you are going to convert your crew quarters to a workshop space, where will I berth?"

Bruce pondered the question and the answers. "You may use either one of the port or starboard guest cabins. I have taken up residence in the forward VIP, I would like to leave the master cabin free so, the other two are available." Charlie nodded as Bruce continued. "Four hundred pounds a month is acceptable, as for starting, we can make that effective now. If you have no further plans?"

"That is very generous of you, boss, thank you. I accept." She proffered her right hand, which Bruce took.

"Right! Where is your gear and do you need a hand with it?"

There were more engine revs and then a loud bump followed by cursing in Spanish as the Beneteau ran into the Spanish sailing yacht that it was trying to berth next to. Bruce laughed, Charlie smiled ruefully and in reply to the question she said. "No, thank you, I haven't got very much, I left it up at the terminal. Uhh! Do you mind if I ask you a question, more of a bye your leave?" Bruce nodded in assent. "But you know when you go back to the UK?" Again, Bruce nodded. "Would you mind very much if I came with you? My folks live in Gosport and it would be nice to be able to pick up some more gear from home. I would pay my way of course."

"That's no problem, Charlie, there should be plenty of room and we could share the driving." Bruce replied, walking her out onto the deck. "Hang on a second." He said, just spotting Ivan lounging by his taxi outside the restaurant.

"Hola Capitain." Greeted Ivan, "You are well?"

"Yes, thank you, Ivan." Bruce replied. "Look, can you take this young lady where she needs to go to, wait for her and then bring her back here please, Ivan?"

"No problems, Capitain.". He shot around the vehicle and opened the back door for Charlie. "Hola Signora."

"Hola!" Replied Charlie, as she squeezed into the back seat of the taxi. Ivan sped off up the road in the direction of the terminal almost opposite where the *Cape* was moored.

José and his daughter were outside making adjustments to the menu of the day. So, Bruce ambled across the road to inspect the new menu and enquire as to whether he would need to book a table for the evening. He assumed that the meal quantities that he had on board wouldn't be sufficient for two people for the weekend. The conversation followed politely for the next five minutes, when suddenly, José's daughter, Maria exclaimed. "Signor Capitain! A man is going on your boat."

Bruce whirled around, just in time to see the displaced skipper and seemingly now the new crew member on the French registered Beneteau, just about to let himself in through the open door to the galley. "Oy!" Bruce shouted. "Get off my boat." He crossed the road and regained the deck of the *Cape*. "What are you doing here?" He questioned the man.

"I leave some stuff on the boat." He replied belligerently.

"What sort of stuff?"

"I leave some charts in chart locker."

"No, you didn't." Bruce responded angrily. "I checked the chart drawers, while you were taking us out of the harbour, there were no charts in any of those drawers. The only charts in there now are those that Boats.co.uk have replaced. Now, get the fuck off my boat and don't come back." Bruce stepped back, the anger showing on his face and with his fists clenched, fully prepared for anything that was to come. "Go on! Vete a la mierda!" (Fuck off). Bruce raised his voice and hiked his thumb towards the pontoon.

Taking in the presence of José and Maria, who had followed Bruce across the road and who were taking in the exchange between the two men. A couple of other people had stopped to see what was going on as well. The Spaniard trespasser thought twice about escalating the situation, so sullenly he stepped back onto the dock and made his way back towards the boat he had come in on, watched by a very angry Bruce.

"He is a very bad mans." José finally commented, with Maria nodding her head in agreement.

"How so?" Asked Bruce.

"He is a thief and we think he has done people smuggling from North Africa." Maria continued. "One night, he tries to make the love with me, I say no, no, no and he just keeps trying, then my father he comes and this man he goes. I think his name is Pedro. Before he works at Ellis Marine now, I think he is on the French boat that does underwater charter over there. I think he is a bad driver too." Maria concluded by flouncing her head up.

Bruce nodded. "It was certainly entertaining to watch them docking this afternoon." The conversation followed on for a short while as he discovered the owner of the French registered Beneteau was someone from Holland and again apparently not the nicest of people. They were still in conversation when Ivan brought Charlie back to the boat with her luggage, a very large haversack which seemed crammed and a large holdall, equally jam-packed.

Leaving Charlie to sort out her luggage, Bruce went to pay Ivan.

"Ivan, when you took the Senorita to collect her luggage, did she speak to anyone?"

"Si Capitano." Ivan answered not wishing to look Bruce in the eye. "She speaks with a man. I teenk he English, he hair it goes back like these." Ivan motioned with his hands indicating a swept-back hairstyle.

Bruce was surprised. "Muchas gracias Ivan, esto se queda entre nosotros, si." (This stays between us, yes.) Bruce handed a ten euro note to Ivan.

"Capitano! The Senorita, she ees not happy with the hombre she spoke to when she collected her bags. The Senorita she is very angry with this man." Ivan added, almost as an afterthought.

"Gracias, Ivan." Bruce turned and returned to the boat. Back onboard the *Cape* Bruce helped Charlie below with her luggage and helped her choose her cabin. She opted for the port cabin with the two single bunks. He rummaged around in one of the cupboards and found the linen for her bed.

"Right." he said. "I'll leave you to settle in as best you can and because this skipper hadn't anticipated company for dinner and didn't get sufficient provisions. I am afraid we will have to dine out. So, we'll go across the road to José's this evening for dinner. I trust that is okay?"

"Fine boss. Yes, thank you."

"If you want anything just help yourself, Charlie. If we muster at about nineteen, thirty in the main salon, I'll give you a quick tour of the boat, but we will do an in-depth tour tomorrow or Monday, depending on how energetic I am feeling. Okay?"

She smiled in response. "That will be fine, thanks."

Bruce made his way back up to the salon and put Charlies' glass in the sink disposed of the two empty tins, getting another Alhambra from out of the fridge, he had just sat down with his fresh beer. 'So!' He thought. 'What the hell is so important about those charts? He knows where they are, doesn't he?' Swiftly he put his lager down and retrieved the four charts, rolling them up, he made his way aft into the engine room. Looking up into the engine room roof several inspection hatches provided access to the between deck voids. Reaching up, he undid one of the hatches and slid the charts into the void, closing the hatch. Back on deck, Bruce secured and locked the engine room door and returned to the salon. He checked his watch, it was a quarter past six. Bruce was finishing his lager and going around switching on lights.

"Ahoy! Eenglish!" Came the holler from the dockside. 'He really must put that chain across the access for the pontoon.' Bruce thought as he sauntered out of the galley door and stood on the deck. On the pontoon stood a tall blond-haired man with a pair of sunglasses tipped back onto his unkempt hair. He was about forty years old and with what looked like a physique that could certainly do with some exercise. He was wearing a white T-shirt which sported the logo 'Diving Van de Niekerk' and a picture of a fast cruiser, certainly not the Beneteau he had been piloting earlier. He was also wearing a pair of sports shorts that came down to his knees and flip flops.

"How can I help you?" Bruce inquired politely.

"My name is Pieter Van de Niekerk. I want to charter your boat." The accent was Dutch. "I do dive charters and I need to use a bigger boat for some very important customers. I want to look in your boat. Okay?"

"No!" Replied Bruce putting his hand up to stop the advancing dutchman from stepping onto the deck. "This boat is mine and is not for charter, not to you or anybody else for that matter. Besides which she is not registered for charters. So that is the end of the matter." Bruce concluded, not raising his voice.

"But I just want to look in your boat, I am interested maybe I buy." He looked around for the maker's plate. "Okay?" He persisted.

"No! Absolutely not." Bruce was only aware of her presence because of the reaction in Van de Niekerk's eyes, then he caught the whiff of her fresh feminine scent as she silently came and stood next to him. "You are the second person in the last hour that has tried to board my vessel without any good reason. The first was your crewman, Pedro over there." He pointed at the man standing unobtrusively in the falling shadows of the early evening. "So again. No." Bruce concluded.

"Listen man." The Dutchman persisted. "He tells me that he has left some charts in your boat, these charts are his, you must let him have them, hey. They will not mean anything to you."

"Van de Niekerk." Bruce's Rhodesian accent came to the fore as he pronounced the words. "This man of yours, whilst working for Boats. co.uk, was piloting my boat out of the harbour some eleven days ago. I checked the chart locker for charts, there were none. Check with James Barke he was with me at the time. The charts that are in there now are those that have been supplied to me by Boats,co.uk, therefore there can't be any charts belonging to anyone else other than me. Is that clear enough for you?"

"Can we just check?" Van de Niekerk persisted.

"What part of 'no' do you not fuckin' understand Mr. Van de Niekerk?" Again, Bruce's accent came to the fore, as he continued "Do not come around here again and do not attempt to board my boat again. That goes for you and your man over there. Understand?" Bruce had started menacingly towards the deck access to the pontoon.

Van de Niekerk turned and started to saunter away, with the parting comment. "Or what old man? Are you going to set your pet Amazon on me? Hey!"

Bruce turned to look at Charlie. "Pet Amazon?" They chorused, bursting into laughter. Bruce continued onto the pontoon and put the chain across the pontoon access from the marina side. There was a no entry sign written on it in Spanish were the words 'Sin Entrada'.

Back onboard the *Cape*, Bruce went back into the salon "Pet Amazon, indeed." Bruce said again, shaking his head as he picked up the remainder of his lager.

"What was that about boss?" Charlie asked.

Bruce checked his watch. "Quite a long story, so why don't I tell you once I have had a shower and we do the quick boat tour?"

"Okay." she replied. "I'll have my shower at the same time. "What are you wearing tonight?" She asked.

"Just a pair of jeans and a shirt." He replied casually. Bruce made a point of checking to make sure that all the access doors from the deck were locked before going below to his cabin.

Thirty-five minutes later he emerged from his cabin freshly shaved where applicable, beard and moustache tidied, he had even added some Jean-Paul Gautier after shave lotion. Something he hadn't done for a very long time. He was wearing a long-sleeved blue cotton shirt, blue denim jeans and a black leather jacket and carried in his hands a pair of loafers which he deposited next to the galley deck access. Going back to the lower helm, he switched all the *Cape's* external and flybridge lights on, including the underwater lights. It was exactly half-past seven when Charlie came up the companionway, wearing jeans, a pink blouse over which she had a Moroccan shawl draped around her shoulders. Her jet-black hair was loose but held in place by a gold hairband. This latter item gave her the Wonder Woman look. She looked stunning. Bruce was so tempted to say. 'Ahh! My Wonder Woman Amazon!' But refrained, reminding himself that he was old enough to be her father. Instead, he said. "You look nice."

The boat tour started at the flybridge. Bruce couldn't help but admire the scene from the flybridge, especially with the underwater lights on. Then there were the twinkling lights around the marina, harbour and the ruins of the castle overlooking the city. However, as it was blowing a good ten to twelve-knot breeze. The time spent on the flybridge in their stockinged feet was very limited. They decided to leave the engine room until the morning and so returned to the lower helm on the main deck. Bruce went through various aspects on the bridge and then moved aft to the galley. He showed her the fridge and freezer and explained that he was thinking of putting in an additional freezer in the utility area. Then further aft to the dining area and finally explained the remote for the fifty-five-inch TV that came up out of the rear of the sideboard. Where all the glasses, dishes and cutlery were stowed in the soft-close drawers and then finally back to the pilot station. Bruce sat down on the short sofa facing the chart table and drawers and Charlie perched herself on the pilot seat at the helm.

"Okay!" started Bruce. "I was sat in the same place as you are now just over eleven or twelve days ago when I spotted the chart table. This is not standard on this boat or even any other yacht of this size. One of the previous owners did a lot of charters and being a bit of the old school, I guess, had this chart table put in so that he could carry paper charts. Now, the first thing I noticed was that there were no charts, someone had 'legged it' with the charts. But then I noticed that just above the top drawer there is a piece of plywood, meaning that there was a gap between the plywood here and the bottom of the chart tabletop there." He opened the drawer and offered her the opportunity to see for herself.

"Oh, yes!" She exclaimed.

"Well!" continued Bruce. "This afternoon, I took out that piece of plywood and found four charts in the void here. But!" He added hastily. "They are no longer there. I have secreted them somewhere else for the moment. Now, come to think of it, the *Cape* was brought over from Mallorca to here because there was a very interested supposed customer who wanted to see the *Cape*. This customer turned out to be a bit of a 'tyre kicker' or a 'fender basher' so to speak. Following this, Ellis Marine had her moved to a mooring buoy, pending further enquiries. During this time, she was broken into one night. Just food for thought in respect of our visits this afternoon."

"Wow!" Exclaimed Charlie. "Is this for real?"

"Yes." He replied. Nodding his head. "Now, we had better make tracks for dinner. I could do with a glass of something alcoholic and something to eat." All the unnecessary lights were turned off, except for the underwater lights. They looked really 'cool'. All the doors were secured and Bruce set the alarm remotely from the fob attached to the keyring as they made their way across the road to the restaurant.

Maria showed them to a large table where two places had been set, however, Bruce noticed that there were six chairs. Previously, Bruce had also noticed that the family had sat at that same table. Bruce introduced Maria to Charlie who then magically produced menus. A bottle and a half of house red and the three-course 'Menu de Dia' later when Charlie asked. "Boss, these charts, did you get a look at them at all?"

"I certainly did but they didn't make any sense to me at the time and still don't. They are all coastal charts of islands, two in the Mediterranean, one in the Adriatic and one in the Aegean Sea. All the charts had a red spot marked on them with coordinates written in red at the top of the chart. Now just in case, I have gone bananas, the coordinates don't bear any resemblance to the marks on the charts. The references, however, do relate to two of the charts that I looked at this afternoon and the other thing is this. All those charts appear to have been published in 1947."

"Yes, so not long after cessation of hostilities of the second world war." Commented Charlie.

"Could be a point there. All this area of the Mediterranean, Adriatic and Aegean Seas were under Nazi German control at one time and we do know that a lot of looting took place by the Nazis during their time of management in the area." Bruce continued. "What has really piqued my interest now, is that those two goons on that French Beneteau know about those charts and are keen to get hold of them for themselves. What I am hoping is that they are unaware that I and now you, know about those charts. I am almost expecting to be burgled and have the boat broken into in the future."

"Boss, I have a plan." Charlie leant across the table in a conspiring manner.

"Ahh! Charlie. Would it be all right for you just to call me Bruce? Please." She smiled in return, marginally embarrassed. "Absolutely, no problem."

"Okay, so what is this plan that you have?" Bruce inquired.

"An Uncle of mine works at the Admiralty Offices in Taunton. He could make us up a set of similar charts but with different information on them. You put the fake charts back in the void of the chart table, leave the boat unlocked so they don't break anything getting to the chart table. They then think that they have stolen the correct charts and that should let us off the hook."

"Sneaky." Bruce commented. "Okay, but this will only work if they don't already know where or what the charts relate to or for that matter the significance between the coordinates that are written down and the marks on the charts. So, we will have to work out what the significance of the coordinates and the marks relate to before we can set up the false information. They would also have to be similarly shaped islands."

The conversation ended with the arrival of José and Senata, José's wife. Bruce stood up and following the small talk as to whether or not the meal had been satisfactory, they all sat down and a fresh bottle of the house red was produced by Maria and glasses re-charged.

There had been a middle-aged couple dining at one of the corner tables not too far from where Bruce and Charlie had been seated. He appeared mildly familiar to Bruce, throughout the meal he had been trying to work out where he had seen him before. The couple had finished dining and were now getting up. They came straight to the table occupied by the four of them.

There was an exchange in rapid Spanish with José and Senata, then the man leant forward, proffering his right hand. "Senor Capitain, I am Capitain Miguel Garcia, I am with the Guardia Civil, I see you have now bought a fine boat. This is my wife, Clarissa." His English was very good. "José is my brother."

The penny dropped, Bruce recognised him from the post-encounter with the skipper. He was one of the two uniformed officers on the quay. Bruce leaned forward and took the offered hand, a good firm handshake. Bruce introduced Charlie, but not as a crew member. Clarissa didn't speak very much English, so Charlie conversed with her in Spanish. The evening was spent in amiable company with considerably more wine being consumed. So, it wasn't until half-past eleven when Bruce and Charlie got back to the *Cape*. The wind had picked up considerably, just as they got back on board so, the rain started. The AEMET weather forecast was for rain and high winds to continue during the next day, but Monday was due to be fine again with the temperatures getting better as the week wore on.

They made their way into the salon. "Do you drink Scotch?" Bruce asked. "I have some Glenmorangie."

"Lovely!" Charlie replied. "I'll get the water." She volunteered.

Whisky's poured, they both lounged on the sofa. "That was a lovely evening, thank you." Charlie smiled her appreciation.

"No problem." Bruce replied. "As your employer, I now have a duty of care for you." Bruce smiled at her. "By the way, will you be okay about a contract until I have time to draw one up and print it? I don't have a printer here at the moment."

"No, I don't have a problem with that." Charlie replied.

They spent the rest of the evening in conversation discussing the state of the world and general bits and pieces. Bruce discovered that Charlie was a very keen cook and wanted to take over all galley duties. This was something that suited Bruce down to the ground, although there were times when he did enjoy cooking. They planned to spend the next day on board, given that the weather forecast wasn't brilliant. They discovered that they shared many interests over a wide range of topics including music and singing. Charlie played the guitar and she would bring that back from the UK, Bruce played keyboards and a ukulele rather badly. It was gone one o'clock in the morning by the time Charlie made her way down to her cabin. Bruce switched off all the unnecessary lights, checked the doors were all locked and made his way down to his own cabin.

CHAPTER 4

Bruce slept soundly waking refreshed just before nine am. Thinking to himself that he didn't deserve to feel that perky after the quantity of alcohol he had consumed the previous evening. Dressing quickly, he made his way up the companionway to the smell of fried eggs and bacon coming from the galley. 'God! That smells good.' He thought.

Bruce was greeted with a cheery. "Morning Capitan! I was just about to go below and give you a knock." Charlie greeted him.

"Wow! Certainly, smells good. Would you like the table set?" Bruce asked.

"Nope, all done." She replied.

They decided they would spend the day as a day off and with only the necessary chores to have to be done, Charlie officially had the day off. However, she had insisted on being allowed to run the galley as far as food for the two of them was concerned. Charlie had even decided that they did not need to go ashore for an evening meal, as she felt that there were more than enough supplies to feed them both for the next two days.

The weather had worsened overnight and with daybreak, the continuous rain had changed to heavy showers. After breakfast and between the showers, Bruce retrieved a light slicker from below and did a round of the *Cape*. He made sure that the moorings were fast and none of the lines had loosened during the night. The deck was wet but not slippery, he used the access from the pilot station to the starboard deck to minimise the making of any mess inside the boat. Whilst on his rounds, he stopped for an inspection of the engine room and checked the heating controls and aircon system. Whilst in the engine room, Bruce recovered the mystery charts from their hiding place, rolled them up and put them up under his slicker. Locking the engine room and crew room access door as he left.

Returning to the salon, Bruce placed the charts on the dining room table and unrolled the first chart. It was one of the ones in the Mediterranean Sea. No sooner had he put the charts on the table than he was joined by Charlie, her interest piqued. He looked at the almost teardrop-shaped island and saw that it was called S'Espalmador, going forward to the pilot station, Bruce switched on his laptop computer. 'Google Maps could help.' He thought. The island showed up as being one of the islands belonging to the Balearic group of islands just off the south coast of Ibiza. Charlie went to the plotter and having got it initialized, put in the coordinates that had been written down on the top of the chart.

"Oh wow!" She exclaimed. "These coordinates relate to a lighthouse at Cabo Berberia on the southernmost point of that island, which is exactly due east of that point marked on that chart."

Bruce brought the chart up to the chart table and put it on top. Retrieving a ruler, he placed it on the chart and drew an imaginary line between the lighthouse marked on the chart and the point marked on the chart. Bruce looked but couldn't see anything between the two points. Charlie spent another twenty minutes flitting between the chart plotter and the chart whilst Bruce made the tea. Still, Charlie came up with nothing. "Let's have a look at one of the other charts, shall we?" Charlie suggested.

Bruce moved to lift the chart from the chart table and lifted it high as Charlie placed the next chart on the table. As the chart was lifted, the light coming through the windshield was blocked out. This resulted in a tiny pinprick of light shining through from the back of the chart. Bruce nearly missed it. "Hang on!" He exclaimed.

"What is it?" Charlie questioned.

"There was a pinprick of light, like a small pinhole on the chart, hang on I can't see it now." Bruce was excited. "Have you got a magnifying glass, Charlie?" He asked.

"I am afraid not."

"I know!" Bruce exclaimed. "I have got a torch in my cabin, if I put that behind the chart, it might show through, on the other hand, it is an old chart." Bruce continued holding the chart up to the light from the windscreen. "It might be something unintentional, or it might not be."

Charlie volunteered to get the torch from Bruce's cabin on the basis that she was quicker on her feet than Bruce was. It was her first visit to the forward VIP cabin and her first thoughts were what a plush cabin, very masculine and tidy to boot. She retrieved the torch and got back up to the pilot station. "Just a thought." Bruce commented. "But if we go below, we can black out my cabin and then we should be able to see anything obvious with the torch behind the chart."

"Great idea." Replied Charlie, immediately turning around and heading back towards Bruce's cabin. Bruce had stopped to pick the other charts as well and followed Charlie down to his cabin. Charlie had already closed the blinds and switched on the cabin lights when Bruce made it into his cabin.

"Right! Let's give this a whirl." Bruce switched off the cabin lights and held the chart up in front of Charlie, who turned the torch on. "There it is, there it is, it is very close to where the lighthouse is marked on the chart." Bruce exclaimed.

Charlie leaned around the chart. "Oh, God! Yes!" She exclaimed in excitement. Her arm touched Bruce's unintentionally as she struggled to maintain the light behind the chart and at the same time, peer around at the chart to see the result. Her breath was warm and sweet on Bruce's cheek as he became very aware of her proximity. The pinprick of light showed through at a point just to the west of the lighthouse. But on the trajectory of the line between the lighthouse and the red mark on the chart. That had to be more than a coincidence.

"Okay, dokey then. Let's have a look at this one, shall we?" Bruce said as he switched on the cabin lights and exchanged the charts. This one was the chart of a tiny island in the Adriatic Sea called Modra Spilja. The point where the tiny red mark was located was at the north-eastern point of the tiny island and the coordinates referred to the north-westernmost point of the island. Again, Bruce switched off the cabin lights and held up the chart so that Charlie could stand behind it with the torch. It didn't take long as Bruce exclaimed. "I just don't believe it. Right smack bang on the track between the coordinates and the red mark, almost halfway between the two points.". They swapped places so that Charlie could clearly see for herself, not that Bruce minded Charlie's proximity. They passed the rest of the morning examining the remaining two charts and achieved similar results.

Charlie made them a sandwich and they had an Alhambra each to wash the sandwiches down. During which the speculation started. After lunch, Charlie on her iPad and Bruce on his laptop struggled to find any references to the two islands.

"Bruce?" Charlie asked. "What experience if any have you with diving because I remember you saying yesterday that you were going to get some diving equipment and have a compressor installed in what is now the crew quarters, but that was before I arrived on the scene?"

Bruce looked up from his laptop, where he had been scouring the internet for any indication or reference to treasure or anomalies related to the islands. He had discovered that any form of treasure search, related to the travel industry and even entering searches relating to missing ships and aircraft revealed nothing. He shoved his reading glasses up onto his forehead and rubbed his strained eyes as he got up and stretched. "Yesss! Many moons ago, I qualified as a Master Diver, at what was then the British Underwater Centre. However, I dare say that equipment has come on a long way since then. I had intended to do a course locally, just to get me back up to speed again. But then, guess what? You came along, so my little PADI diving instructor, you now know who is going to be bringing me up to speed."

Charlie smiled. "That will be fun, I will get to tell you what to do then."

Bruce returned the smile "Just treat me gently, it has been a long time."

They continued into the evening discussing, in essence, the next day. Bruce had been having doubts about the Zodiac tender. It was a great little run around and easy to access a beach with, but it didn't have much of a capacity for carrying people, equipment and stores. Bruce was beginning to consider something in the range of four metres, but park it on the aft swim deck, which could be submerged, to facilitate launching. He had started to look at and despite having researched the standard RIB with outboard configuration. Nothing other than the Williams 435 was coming to mind. He discussed this with Charlie and between them, they agreed on the 435 as probably being the best suitable boat as a tender. Considering that it also had a swim platform on it, which made recovering a swimmer, skier or diver more practicable.

Charlie had gone below to take a shower and go to bed. Bruce had finished his last night walk around the *Cape,* again checking that the mooring lines were secure and on his visit to the engine room, he had replaced the treasure charts as he and Charlie now referred to them. The wind had died down and it had stopped raining. The clouds were dispersing and in some areas of the sky, Bruce could see the odd star peeking out. The quay was quiet and José's restaurant was in virtual darkness. It was quiet with the infrequent sound of the odd rigging line rattling against a mast and the occasional sound of lapping water against a hull. The dock and marina were also in silence. The boats on mooring buoys sat quietly, moving gently on the very slight swell that came in from the harbour mouth. They were dimly lit by the lights shining out from the quayside. Bruce quietly stepped onto the pontoon and strolled briefly along the quayside admiring the lights from the castle above the city of Malaga. The harbour was in silence, seemingly he was the only person awake in the marina, or so he thought. The figure in the shadows had been unseen as he cupped his hand around the cigarette and drew a lungful of smoke before exhaling quietly through his nose. Bruce had smelt the smoke, the hairs on the back of his neck had risen in a sense of warning. The smoke had a very unusual scent to it, sweet, roasted, almost like Turkish tobacco. He turned back to the *Cape* very casually but not looking at the area from which the wind was blowing the smoke. Sauntering back to the pontoon, he stepped over the chain prohibiting access. If the watcher had seen Bruce take the charts into the engine room earlier, they would know that the charts had been discovered and were now being secreted in the engine/crew room area. However, realising that he might be observed, Bruce had carefully disguised the charts into a pile of laundry destined for the washing machine and had gone about his activities in a seemingly blasé manner. Just in case someone had been watching the boat. Bruce was now really interested in those charts, it was more than apparent to him now that they were also of value to someone else. Value to most people usually meant monetary. Especially to the likes of his newfound friend, Van de Niekerk.

Bruce opened the salon blinds, exposing himself to the quayside through the smoked glass windows and poured himself a glass of single malt. Making his way back towards the stairs, he turned the salon and stair lights off, pausing momentarily at the top of the stairs. Bruce turned back towards the darkened salon and sat down on the sofa to watch the area of the shadows from where he had smelt the smoke. To anyone on the outside, he was invisible. He didn't have long to wait, probably only five minutes before the unmistakable figure of Van de Niekerk emerged from the shadows and made his way back up the quay towards his boat. Satisfied at what he had seen, he shared the tranquillity to himself, taking a sip at the Glenmorangie whilst he pondered the situation.

He smelt her before he saw or heard her. Charlie appeared at the top of the stairwell. "Bruce are you okay? Why are you sitting up here in the dark?" As far as Bruce could tell in the darkened salon, she was wearing what appeared to be a very short towelling robe.

"Come and sit down, but don't turn any lights on. I thought that you had gone to bed." Bruce replied. "Would you like one of these?"

"What is it?" She asked.

"Glenmorangie with just a trickle of water."

"Not the nectar of the glens. Yes please!" She sat down on the sofa just as he got up to pour the drink in with only the barest of light. He put the whisky tumbler down in front of her, retrieved his glass and refreshed it before returning to his original place on the sofa next to Charlie.

"Charlie!" Bruce started. "I think that these charts mean something to someone and I mean a lot of something. I have just seen Van de Niekerk skulking in the shadows. He doesn't know that I have seen him, so whether it is him or he is working for someone else, I have no idea." Charlie remained sitting still, half-turned towards Bruce on the sofa. "Now, I don't want to scare you, but I think that these characters will stop at nothing to get what they want. And I am not planning on letting them have those charts. Legally, I suppose they are mine as I bought them as part of the fixtures and fittings with the boat." He paused and took a sip of whisky, continuing. "Having given some thought in reference as to what these charts and the secrets that they may give up. I seriously don't think that they refer to a sunken pirate treasure. But I do think that they relate to something of high monetary and easily disposable material. I also think that the material I am referring to has been relocated to the position of the pinholes on the charts and these characters weren't the originators of these charts either. But they do know about the existence of them. How much they know is anybody's guess." Charlie shifted her body on the sofa, turning further towards Bruce and placed her left arm across the back of the sofa, almost touching Bruce's shoulder. "Until we have a good look to see what the 'treasure' is if that is indeed what we are both speculating about?" Bruce shifted awkwardly on the sofa, swivelling a little more towards Charlie. "What I am saying Charlie, is that we have just met, we don't know each other and it has been a bit of a whirlwind over the past twenty-four hours. The last thing I want is for you to come into harm's way."

Charlie touched Bruce's shoulder. "Bruce, that was a very touching little speech and please don't take this the wrong way but for the first time in a long time, I think I have found someone to whom I can relate. You've told me very little about yourself, but I would say that you have probably spent some time at Hereford. I had a fiancée who was with 'B' Squadron and died when the helicopter he and the rest of his section were in, crashed in Iraq. At the time we were three weeks off getting married."

"Oh my God! Charlie, I remember the incident." Bruce turned towards her and took her left hand in his, shaking his head in anguish. "I am sorry. That must have been tough for you?" Bruce remembered the accident vividly. It was most of 'D' Squadron that had gone in to recover the bodies. They had parachuted in from a height of 500 feet with just their belt kit and 'weapons hot'. That had been Bruce's last operational jump. The Taliban had claimed that they had shot it down however the last transmission from the pilot indicated a gear box failure.

She shook her head "No! It's okay now, honestly, thank you. What I mean to say is that I understand people like you, you are genuine and unless you don't want me here, then I fully intend to keep to my side of our bargain and carry on working for you."

Bruce shook his head. "No! Not working for me, but with me. That is how we did things in the good old days and that is how I have done things since, now I hope to be able to carry that on in the present day here on the *Cape*."

CHAPTER 5

Monday dawned bright and sunny. The wind had dropped to a two-knot gentle breeze and Bruce was on deck by eight am dressed in a pair of sand-coloured sports trousers, a blue short-sleeved T-shirt with a collar and a long-sleeved hoodie with a zip up the front. He made his way into the galley and put the kettle on before going out to check the mooring lines. As he left the lower helm to go out onto the deck, he saw Van de Niekerk and Pedro on the Beneteau leaving the marina. They were going a bit too quick for the marina, in which the speed limit was four knots. They both looked over to the *Cape* and shot what Bruce interpreted to be a filthy look. Bruce didn't react but carried on with checking the lines. The passing of the Beneteau had set up a small wake that gently rocked the *Cape*. Bruce went up onto the flybridge to ensure that they hadn't lost any of the weather covers, but he needn't have worried as they were all there, securely tied down. Making his way back down to the main deck, he slipped into the galley, just as the kettle was coming to the boil, so he made two mugs of tea. He was just finishing as Charlie appeared at the top of the companionway.

"Morning!" He greeted her. "Sleep well?" he inquired. She was wearing a pair of similar slacks, only in blue with an almost matching T-shirt and cardigan.

"Sort of." She replied. "I couldn't get those 'treasure charts' and Van de Niekerk out of my mind."

"Well, they have just put out, that is what has caused our little 'wibbly wobbly'." He smiled at her.

They had some muesli and toast for breakfast. As the transport from Sergio wasn't due until ten o'clock, Bruce took Charlie on a full tour of the boat, starting down in the engine room. They went through the functions of the two generators, the water maker, the main engines and oil levels. Then the controls for the engine room systems including levels of freshwater, automatic fire suppression system, wastewater and sewage levels. Then Bruce took Charlie into the crew quarters and the utility room and pointed out his intentions for the conversion to a workshop, dive station refill and storage area, indicating that the heads and shower would remain. Bruce had taken all the cushions from the fore sundeck and flybridge areas and had stored them in the crew quarters for safekeeping. He also indicated the area that he had mentally reserved for the storage of foul weather gear and life jackets for when they weren't in use.

From there, they made their way back up to the flybridge. Bruce went through the various controls and indicated the intended storage points for the Quad Bike and the Kawasaki jet ski. The jet ski would be just for fun. Whereas the Quad would be necessary as a means of transport to allow Bruce and or crew to get to places for shopping and sightseeing. José was outside his restaurant with Senata arranging the tables in preparation for the days business. They waved and shouted "Hola's!" to one another before continuing down to the main deck and making a second cup of tea. It was nearly ten o'clock, Charlie went below as Bruce went around the boat securing the engine and crew space access and doing final checks of the mooring lines. Just as Charlie reappeared on deck, so did a Seat minibus appear on the quayside. They made their way across the quay and got into the minibus with a friendly driver. The journey wasn't a great distance, only some three kilometres but it did take nearly twenty minutes to get to the other side of the docks where Sergio was there to greet them at the chandlery and Boats.co.uk berths.

"Capitano Bruce, you have a good weekend. Yes?" He enquired eyeing Charlie at the same time. Bruce introduced them but again intentionally failed to mention that she was his new crew member.

The morning progressed with coffee and bartering. Charlie had gone off with Sergio's female assistant to inspect and order all the diving equipment, foul weather gear and radios etc. It transpired that there was a Williams 435 available however, it was at the Cala d'or depot of Boats.co.uk. They were interrupted only once by Charlie and the assistant to get Bruce's sizes and very quietly Charlie asked.

"Bruce, how much do you want to spend on this gear and what sort of quantity are we talking about?"

"I think that we should go for three sets of the dive equipment, one for spare. Cost isn't the issue here. With your knowledge get the best that there is. Our lives and comfort are priceless."

By the end of the morning, many things had been agreed upon. The Williams 435 would be on its way on the evening ferry to Valencia and would then be brought down by road to Malaga, it would be in Malaga by close of play on Tuesday. On Wednesday, Bruce and Charlie would bring the *Cape* around from the marina to Boats.co.uk, where the jet ski, Williams and quad bike would be loaded onto the *Cape* and where the correct deck mounting equipment and straps could be fitted. At the same time, Sergio's architect would look at the modifications for the crew quarter conversion.

The three fifteen litre Faber cylinders, Sunto Dive computers, BCD's compressor and all the rest of the diving equipment would be ordered and placed onboard the *Cape* once the refurbishment had been completed. As would the two safes and the Very pistol with the appropriate cartridges. However, the life jackets, radios, boat hook and the rest of the equipment that Bruce had ordered would accompany them back to the *Cape* where the driver would take the appropriate tools to mount the boat hook on the foredeck railing for him.

Before departing the chandlery, Sergio took them across the road to a small restaurant and treated them to lunch. During a lull in the general chit chat of conversation, the two girls had gone to powder their noses. This allowed Bruce to ask Sergio. "When I first met James, he told me that the *Cape* had been brought over from Palma for a prospective customer. Would you happen to know who that was?"

"Si!" replied Sergio. "The customer he was Van Noikerk or something, I think he was Dutch."

"Van de Niekerk." Bruce corrected him.

"Yes, yes that was his name. Pedro, he was the boss then, flew to Palma to bring back the *Cape* for Van de Niekerk. I don't think he really wanted to buy the boat. I don't know why?"

"When Van de Niekerk didn't buy the *Cape*, she was put on a mooring where someone broke into her one night. Was anything actually taken that you know of?" Bruce asked.

"No! Not that I know of." Replied Sergio.

"What about the Police?"

"Pedro, he says not to involve the Police. My Cousin, he is with the Police Nationale, in the marine division, I tell him though!"

"Great! Well done for doing that." Bruce sat back as the two women arrived back at the table.

"Bruce?" Sergio asked. "When the *Cape* is out of the water at the end of the month what will you and Charlie do? Go to a hotel?"

"No! We are planning to hire a vehicle and return to the UK for a week or so, pick up some personal belongings etc. before returning."

"But Bruce, you don't have to hire a vehicle, you can use our bus there and back. Which ferry will you use?"

"Ahh! Very probably Bilbao to Portsmouth." Bruce replied.

So, that was settled, they had their transport to and from the UK. All Bruce had to do was to arrange the ferry crossing. Following lunch, the recent purchases were loaded into the minibus and they were returned to the *Cape*. Fernando, the amiable driver had parked on the quayside and helped them to offload the goods and then set about fitting the boat hook.

Bruce placed the three VHF radios in their chargers and plugged them into a socket at the base of the chart table. The chargers were placed in a small recess in front of the chart table almost as though that was where they had been designed to go. Two of the crew savers were put in an easy-access storage cupboard on the pilot station, then Bruce and Charlie took the remaining four aft to stow in the crew area. One of the crew cabins was a double single bunk configuration the other crew cabin consisted of a single bunk and hadn't got any cushions stored in it. It was to this cabin that Bruce led Charlie.

"This bunk bed should lift we can stow them in here out of the way for the moment." He said to Charlie as he lifted the mattress base. Bruce looked in astonishment at the gleaming red Sea-Bob that was taking up half the available space. It was the top of the range, an F5 SR, still in some of its packaging. This baby was capable of an underwater speed of up to twenty knots and a battery life of one hour with a quick recharge time of one and a half hours. On the downside, it weighed just under seventy pounds and if you wanted to buy one it would set you back a cool £12,000. It was one of the ultimate rich boys' toys.

"Oh my God!" Exclaimed Charlie. "I have always wanted to have a go on one of those, I have seen them on *Octopus* but we were never allowed to play with them."

"Well, on this boat, you will be positively encouraged to play with all the toys." Bruce replied, looking back at her over his shoulder and smiling. He had been thinking of putting one on his shopping list but truthfully hadn't been able to justify the expense. No matter, he wondered if Boats.co.uk had known about the presence of the Sea-Bob. They probably did.

As they made their way back up to the main deck to see how Fernando was doing, Bruce's left calf went into spasm. He stopped and grunting with the cramp-like pain he grabbed the rail for support. Charlie turned around with a look of surprised concern. "Bruce, what is it?"

"My calf muscle is cramping." He grunted, the agony showing on his face.

Charlie turned around and went to grab him under his arm to support him. He felt the strength in her arms as she supported him taking the weight off his left leg. "Right, let's get you sat down." As she manoeuvred him through the open stern salon door and got him onto the sofa. She returned and closed the door. "Right, let's have a look at this leg." She pulled the loose-fitting slacks up to his knee and was visibly appalled at the scaring. The scars were healing well, but from her medical expertise gained in the Army, she could only imagine the damage that had been inflicted to the bone, flesh, muscle, nerves and blood vessels. She gently applied pressure onto the calf and very gently started to massage the calf, prompting further grunts from Bruce.

"Charlie, Charlie I will be okay. Honestly, I have probably just overdone it a bit today with all the running around. I'll be fine, honestly." The agony showed clearly on Bruce's face.

"Now then, Captain, not only am I your chief galley and deckhand, your Diving Officer, I am now also your Chief Medical Officer as well. So, you just lie back and let someone help you for a change." She gently admonished. "How is it that you didn't lose your leg and how much more damage is there?" She asked with obvious concern on her face.

"Some." He replied. "The femur was fractured and they discovered some other problems at the same time. I refused to let them take my leg." He almost whispered. "That feels better, thank you, Charlie." Charlie continued to massage the calf for a short while until she felt the cramping spasms dissipate. 'That calf muscle is going to ache for the rest of the day'. She thought to herself.

Fernando had poked his head around the access from the galley and had said his goodbyes. Charlie was making a list of stores that they had and then she returned to where Bruce had continued to sit with his left leg resting up on the sofa.

"Bruce, how were you planning on doing your re-supplying? Shop every few days?" She asked.

"Do you know what, Charlie, I hadn't even thought about it. Yes, I suppose shop every few days, I imagine. Of course, that until the crew area is modified and I can get another freezer in there, the only one we have is the small one in the galley."

"So, Wednesday we are taking the *Cape* over to Boats.co.uk, any plans for tomorrow?" came the question.

"Yes." he replied. "What about we take the boat out and give her some exercise, practise some drills and then spend some time in the sun?"

"That sounds like a fantastic idea. But it does mean that I need to go and do some provisioning for us. Otherwise, I am going to be redundant in the galley. Then we'll be eating across the road or somewhere else."

"Are you happy to do that?"

"Yes, but you are to stay here and rest that leg. Deal?" She was back in a hospital somewhere, gently admonishing a patient in the nicest possible way. Continuing but in a more business-like tone. "In the past, I have learned that it is much easier to do large provisioning procedures with victualing companies. The way it works is that they source the goods for you from wherever you specify, then they deliver them to the boat. Or if you are moored offshore to a jetty or wherever you specify. I have known deliveries to a beach before now."

"That seems like a really good idea. But is there a big difference in the cost?" Bruce inquired.

"No, not really, because the victuallers or suppliers will have a substantial discount with the stores but then they will possibly put a five per cent levy on for their effort."

"I think that is a great idea, Charlie. I hate shopping at the best of times. We'll have a look at that idea when we get back from the UK."

Bruce sent her below to his cabin to get the debit card from his wallet. "You use this card for anything you need and I mean anything at all. If there is something that you want, need, or feel that we should have, then please, just feel free to get it. Will that be okay?" He had placed a heavy emphasis on the word 'anything'.

After a quick visit to the heads, she went off to get hold of Ivan and his taxi. Bruce went forward and fired up his laptop. He needed to do some fund transfers to cover the shopping trip from earlier in the day. Whilst the laptop was open, Bruce spent some time checking and replying to his emails. He had just completed that and glanced at his watch. It was four pm. He was just about to go into the galley to put the kettle on when his attention was drawn to further down the marina with the heavy throb of powerful marine diesels. The Guardia Civil patrol boat was manoeuvring in the marina. Bruce went out on deck for a better view and then noticed that there were two uniformed Guardia Civil officers on the pontoon. There was no doubt where the boat was heading to berth. It was on the other side of the pontoon from the *Cape*. One of the two shore party had turned and had acknowledged Bruce's presence on his deck. They exchanged nods. Bruce was just about to go back into the galley when he caught sight of Charlie returning with the provisions ably assisted by Ivan.

"What's happening here?" She inquired quizzically.

"New neighbours. No more nude sunbathing." He smirked.

She punched him gently on the shoulder following the quip. He recognised the man who was giving the orders from the bridge of the boat. It was Captain Miguel Garcia and he was about to berth the fifty-five-foot patrol vessel named *Rio Jenil* on to the other side of the pontoon. "Ahh well." Bruce mused, "This should put an end to Van de Niekerk's evening stealth activities." He helped Charlie aboard with the groceries and the clinking bottles of wine.

Having finished his docking procedures with his five crew members, Miguel came over and shook Bruce's hand as they exchanged pleasantries. It appeared that the usual mooring point for the *Rio Jenil* was currently undergoing repairs, so her temporary berth had been re-allocated alongside the pontoon next to the *Cape*. For security reasons, there would always be a minimum of one sailor on board and awake. Bruce went back into the galley and passed on the good news to Charlie, then he went into the salon and was playing with his iPod. Bruce had earlier found a cable enabling him to connect the iPod to the sound system. He selected Andre Rieu as The Last Rose of Picardy boomed through the boat. Hastily, he turned down the volume in the salon, only to become aware that the classic was booming out from below decks and the flybridge as well. He paused the music and looking a bit bewildered, he looked at Charlie and said. "Someone has maxed the volume controls right through the boat."

Charlie was laughing. It was a beautiful warm laugh of fun. "Oh! And I like Andre Rieu too." Bruce went out of the stern salon door closing it behind him and went up to the fly deck. Finding the AV volume control, he minimised it and then with a wry grin at the smiling sailors on the pontoon, made his way back below and repeated the process in all the cabins, including the crew area and cockpit speakers. Returning to the salon, he tried again. Andre Rieu was now being piped into the salon speakers at a moderate level, followed by George Ezra and others. Accompanied by the music, Bruce went forward and sat down at the computer to start booking their return passage to the UK. Charlie came forward with two mugs of tea.

"Charlie, would you want an inside or an outside cabin on the ferry?" Bruce queried.

"Where would you prefer?" She responded.

"From experience, definitely the outside of the boat, it's not so claustrophobic and they have two side by side bunks as against one above the other on the inside cabins of the ship." Bruce replied. "Unfortunately, they don't do single cabins, so you will have to have a double to yourself."

Looking over his shoulder she said. "Hang on! That is an additional cost of sixty-five pounds for a cabin. If it's alright with you, I am more than happy to share a cabin with you. I am sure that you will behave like a gentleman." She nudged his shoulder playfully with her arm.

"Who? Me? Never!" He retorted, nudging her in return.

They spent a pleasant evening. Charlie had produced grilled pork cutlets accompanied by potato gratin and runner beans, followed by Spanish strawberries and ice cream. They washed and dried up together and then watched a film on TV. Bruce did the routine night rounds, noting the armed guard on the pontoon. He bade him a 'Buenos Noches' and made his way back into the salon. They both then made their way below to their respective cabins. As they reached the accommodation deck, Charlie turned to Bruce.

"Bruce! I would like to have a look at the rest of your injuries if you don't mind?"

"Yep! No problem, Charlie." He replied with a smile. "I'll give you a shout when I have had a shower."

Fifteen minutes later, wearing a bathrobe, Bruce tentatively knocked on her cabin door. "I'll be with you in two minutes." Came the response from behind the door. Bruce returned to his cabin via the salon with two glasses, the bottle of Glenmorangie and a small bottle of water. He was just returning to his cabin as Charlie came out of hers. She was wearing the pink towelling robe, which was far too short, with her hair trussed up in a white towel. Bruce poured the two drinks and then got on to the bed and modestly exposed his legs up to his covered crotch.

"Those knees look swollen. Is that normal?" Charlie asked. She was standing to the side of the bed. "Budge over." She requested and sat down on the bed. Starting at his left foot, which was slightly swollen as well. She moved her hand, gradually feeling into what passed for muscles. Finally, she got to the scar where the surgeons had pinned his femur.

"When was the last time they cut you open?" she asked.

"Just over five months ago." Bruce replied, reaching over to his whisky and taking a sip.

"Are you in any pain now?" Charlie's robe had ridden dangerously high up her thigh. She really had beautiful legs.

"No, not at the moment. Discomfort some, but I wouldn't call it pain as such." Bruce's eyes were inexorably drawn towards the top of Charlie's leg.

Quickly he averted them back to her hazel-coloured eyes. They were lovely too.

She was smiling. "Typical macho mano reply. I have heard that so many times. Are you taking anything for the discomfort?" She mimicked the word discomfort.

Bruce smiled in return. "No, just the bio-oil and the whisky, not together of course."

"Okay, let's have a good look at your left arm?" Charlie reached over to the bedside table where her drink was. Bruce's eyes were drawn towards the exposed cleavage as he took the damaged left arm out of the sleeve of his robe, again managing to avert his eyes before Charlie noticed. "So, what happened here?" She felt up and turning his arm outwards looked at the puckered scars on the inside and outside of his arm.

"Don't do things by half, do you?" Charlie was feeling the tight muscle under his forearm. "I think that you have mended extremely well but what I would suggest is that at least once a day, you let me give you a massage. Where there has been so much damage to the nerve ends, the muscles have got tense and won't relax. This will slow down your healing process. A daily gentle massage will start to relax those muscles and will help the healing process. What do you say?"

"Uhh haa!" Bruce nodded in agreement.

"After all, we need to have a healthy, fit skipper so that we can go finding a pirate treasure." She laughed as she pulled Bruce's robe back down over his legs.

CHAPTER 6

They were both up and in the galley by nine o'clock. The patrol boat from the other side of the pontoon had already put out. The noisy engines had woken Bruce up as his alarm had gone off. Breakfast over, Bruce and Charlie started the routine of getting the *Cape* ready to leave the berth.

It was still quite cool with a temperature of only about fourteen degrees. But the forecast promised temperatures of twenty-two degrees by midday. Charlie was wearing a pair of the fashionable black skin-tight leggings and a body warmer over a long-sleeved shirt, her hair was contained in a bright red snood. The new red Crewsaver life jacket seemed to sit comfortably on her body. As they slipped from the berth, Charlie moved aft, keeping an eye out for the distance from the pontoon and hauling the fenders inboard as the *Cape* passed the end of the pontoon. Bruce concentrated on keeping the boat in a slow straight line as he glanced out of the starboard side to check his clearance from the boat to their right. Plenty of room, getting back to the helm, he made a small adjustment to the wheel, the portable VHF crackled into life. "Stern clear." Came Charlie's voice, he acknowledged the call then using the engines, Bruce manoeuvred the *Cape* to starboard, turning her so that they could go into the pool and secure all lines and fenders. That done, Bruce returned to the helm and Charlie to the bow standing by to secure the anchor with the safety pin, ready for sea.

"Secure the anchor please Charlie." Bruce said over the radio.

"Roger that!" Charlie replied. She turned and bent straight legged to secure the anchor. Bruce involuntarily took in a sharp breath. The outline of just about every physical attribute of those enclosed legs was delightfully exposed. Turning his mind to taking the *Cape* out of the Marina and into the dock area, Bruce was suddenly intrigued by Charlie. She had picked the boathook out of its clips and using it as a mock rifle, she went through a series of immaculately performed British Army rifle drills including, some left and right turns. The display only lasted about twenty seconds and it was concluded by a mock salute to the bridge. Bruce found himself in fits of laughter. Following the conclusion of the little display, people onshore applauded loudly, accompanied by whistles and shouts of 'encore'. Realising that she had had more than Bruce as an audience, she scampered back along the deck and entering the pilot station, she impulsively hugged Bruce. Suddenly realising what she was doing, she released him. "Oh my God! I am so sorry. I am just so excited I just needed to do that." She enthused.

Bruce smiled at her. "Please don't be. I enjoyed it too, here take the helm." He said, stepping away. "Have you ever driven a boat before?" Bruce asked.

"No, nothing this big, just a dinghy with a little outboard on the back. Oh my God! This just so different to when I was sat here whilst we were on the berth, the movement is so subtle and incredible."

As Bruce moved around behind the helm seat so that he could be near the throttles, he said to her. "Okay, so when we are moving this slowly, it is sometimes easier and the boat becomes more responsive to steering with the engines. At the moment, we have equal revolutions going to both engines, the rudders are amidships, so if we want to move to starboard, we put the starboard engine into neutral." He took her right hand, she willingly allowed the contact, placing it on the throttle controls and using her little finger and the ring finger he pulled them gently back until there was a click and a little electronic 'bleep' indicating that the starboard engine was in neutral. "Now, we can increase the speed of the port engine." He moved the lower part of her hand at the base of the index and middle finger marginally moved the port throttle forward. The *Cape* responded. Bruce kept his hand on top of Charlie's hand until their course had come around by five points of the compass. "Now we have come around to the course that we want, we resume our engines to what they were to keep us going straight." Bruce moved her hand and fingers on the throttle controls again. "Everything is done almost in slow motion and especially at low speeds. We are driving a sixty-ton boat and we don't want to have it getting away from us."

Bruce continued to allow her the helm. They planned to go up the coast for a while, then they were going to exercise picking up mooring buoys and simulating man overboard procedures for a while. Then find a sheltered cove to have lunch and spend some time sunbathing on the foredeck. Bruce had allowed Charlie to bring the *Cape* up to twenty knots and was encouraging her to keep a straight line by a combination of picking a point on the horizon and watching the digital compass. At the same time watching, their position on the chart plotter. After ten minutes and continuous 'Whoopsies.' As the *Cape* was brought back on to her course of thirty-five degrees. "Charlie, there is a very easy way to do what you are doing of course." She glanced quizzically sideways at him as he moved around to her left-hand side and switched on the autopilot. "Autopilot! You can let go now."

"Oh great!" She said. "I am dying for a wee." Heading towards the day heads as she spoke.

The *Cape* was cruising at twenty knots, there was a two to three-foot swell running following Sunday's bad weather, but she hardly moved in response to the sea. The *Cape* was equipped with two automated stabilisers and they did a fantastic job of keeping her steady. Charlie came out of the heads and offered to make tea. Bruce readily accepted and brought the *Cape* to a new heading of four zero degrees, angling his course direction towards Nerja, some twenty nautical miles up the coast from Malaga.

As they had finished their tea, Bruce brought the *Cape* to a standstill and together they went forward to the bow. Charlie's experience on boats had been more in respect of waiting and kitchen duties and was very limited in the way of deck duties other than docking. So, Bruce instructed her on the procedures associated with the recovery of a mooring buoy and the method of guiding the pilot by arm and hand signals. As well as by the use of the radio and then the technique of taking the buoy with a boat hook. When they had spent forty minutes practising this Bruce, decided to move on. Charlie was proving to be a superb sailor and Bruce was more than confident that they could pick up a buoy in just about any condition. The next subject was far more important than picking up a mooring buoy and that was the response and recovery to a 'man overboard'. Again, Bruce brought the *Cape* to a halt and explained the method of marking the position on the chart plotter, knowing the heading and speed that they had been travelling in at the time of the incident. Then again giving the helmsperson similar guidance from the bow and finally walking the roped swimmer to the swim deck at the stern.

Again, using a fender as a person, they practised this for another forty minutes and were just about to call it a day for the afternoon when the fast-moving contact on the radar plotter heading straight for them manifested itself into view. The speed didn't diminish as the gap between the two boats closed until the Guardia Civil patrol boat came to within one hundred yards. Bruce considered the arrival of the authorities. Then it dawned on him, the antics of the *Cape* over the past two hours must have seemed strange to anyone watching on a radar plot or from an aircraft for that matter.

"Hola, Capitain Bruce." Hollered Miguel laughingly. "The people onshore think that you were up to no good my friend."

"We were just doing man overboard drills." Bruce laughed in return. "This is the man we were recovering." He said, holding up the offending fender.

Miguel and the crew laughed and waved as Miguel shouted. "Adios, a' la Fuego." The patrol boat shot forward, heading towards Malaga.

Bruce turned the *Cape* back towards the area he had found on Saturday whilst Charlie started the sandwiches and coffee. It was only twenty minutes later that they dropped the port anchor and tucked into their lunch. After lunch, they both went below to change, Bruce into his shorts and Charlie into a high waisted red bikini but with the top of the outside of the leg cutaway, emphasising her long legs and gorgeous thighs. The bikini top exposed a good three-quarter of her ample breasts, with the cups being joined at the base by a thin strap. Having retrieved the two cushions for the foredeck sun lounger, they spent the next hour and a half lying side by side on the foredeck.

Again, enjoying the sensation of the sun on his body whilst he was lying on his back. Not only the healing powers of the ultraviolet and deep warmth but he could also feel the sun warming his crotch and found himself wondering if he was going to be able to control himself as the days went on. At the same time, he couldn't help wondering why a woman like her wasn't married, he remembered about the engagement of course but that was some time ago now. Would she soon meet someone with whom she would fall in love and then leave him with a void to have to fill? Again! She came across as quite a touchy, feely sort of person and wasn't shy of making personal contact, which he loved.

Charlie was lying on her stomach, raised on her elbows reading her kindle. Being self-consciously aware of the increasing size of his penis, Bruce turned over onto his stomach as he did, so Charlie looked across and smiled at him. 'Shit! Did she know what affect her presence was having on him. Did she realise that he was getting a hard-on?' Which was very much a novelty anyway. Ever since that first moment four days ago, this woman had some sort of strange influence on him. Was he being senile in thinking that a beautiful young woman like her could possibly have any feelings of attraction for a man twice her age? A mental image of Victor Meldrew from the BBC sitcom series 'One Foot in The Grave' flashed across his mind. 'I don't believe it!' Oh, and that massage she had given him in the afternoon and again yesterday evening. Oh, Wow! That was something else.'

Another question arose in his mind. Of course, what to do about it but who was the man she had met at the terminal when she picked up her luggage. The man that had swept-back hair, the man with whom Charlie was not pleased to see according to Ivan. A past lover? She had not mentioned him, nor had she seen him again as far as Ivan had noted. He decided to let the question lie for the moment.

Bruce, lying on his stomach, with his head twisted towards Charlie took in the absolute beauty of the profile of her face as he studied her, Charlie, in turn, was engrossed in the story she was reading and seemed oblivious to his stare for the next few minutes. In a serene sense of security, comfort, warmth and the picture of Charlie's face firmly imprinted in his mind, Bruce fell asleep. When he awoke some one hour and five minutes later, he was on his side facing Charlie as he opened his eyes, she too was on her side facing him. She smiled warmly at him. "Did you have a nice sleep?" She asked.

They or probably he had inadvertently moved closer together, her breath on his face was sweet and clean. Pausing for five seconds before replying to the question. "Oh yes! It was beautiful." In his mind, he wasn't referring to the sleep but to the dream he had been having. Charlie continued the enigmatic smile, the desire to reach out and touch her was almost overwhelming for Bruce. But the fact that his right arm had gone to sleep under him gave him the excuse to break his improper reverie.

Charlie offered to make tea and as she knelt in front of Bruce collecting her phone and kindle, the 'V' of her crutch was two feet from Bruce's face. Briefly, he glimpsed the perfect outline of her womanhood through the thin gusseted spandex material. This did nothing to improve Bruce's mental or physical disposition. Deciding that he should find something to take his mind off the disturbing effects that the afternoon had produced, he went and found the operation instructions for the Seabob under the crew bunk. He spent some time inwardly digesting them. Once he had done that, he lifted the Seabob out onto the bunk and familiarised himself with the controls and the SD card access, which digitally recorded the film from the onboard cameras. Noting that there was no card in the camera, he retrieved a spare from his camera bag and inserted it ready for use. Venturing out to the swim deck, Bruce sat down and put his foot in the water, considering taking the Seabob for a quick try out. It was cold. That did it. There was no way he was going to go for a swim without a wet suit, in water that was only thirteen degrees and would almost certainly cramp his left leg again.

"You'll regret it if you do it." Came the remark from the deck above him.

Bruce looked up into Charlie's smiling face. "No need to worry, that's too cold for me without a wet suit." Bruce laughed. He shivered as he felt the first chill of the evening coming in from the sea. "I think that it is time that we started to make back for port. What have we got on the menu for tonight chef?"

They returned to the Malaga marina and berthed the *Cape* back onto the pontoon. The *Rio Jenil* had arrived ahead of them, one of her sailors, already on the pontoon slung the short, barrelled machine gun across his back and took the stern lines from Charlie. Once they had finished tying up, connecting shorelines and shutting down engines and generators, they both brushed and hosed down the *Cape's* decks. For Bruce, it was a labour of love. For Charlie, it was to be with someone she loved.

The task of deck cleaning ended with both of them soaked from the ensuing water fight that they had with the hoses, much to the entertainment to people ashore and their neighbours on the *Rio Jenil*. Early showers and a change of clothing before dinner followed.

Charlie's chicken fricassee that she served was absolutely superb. Served with a well-chilled Chablis, Bruce's taste buds had run wild. The meal finished simply with grapes and a small piece of cheese. Following dinner, they decided on a gentle stroll down the quay as far as the Spanish Navy sail training ship, the *Juan Sebastian de Elcano*. She was a four-masted barquentine, beautifully elegant and at 320 feet long she was the third-largest tall ship in the world.

As they turned to make their way back, Bruce commented. "I would love to get a picture of her out on the ocean with all her sails out."

"That would be fantastic if you could. We may try to keep an eye on her movements." Charlie slipped her hand into the crook of Bruce's right arm. "Hope you don't mind." She added.

"Not at all." Bruce smiled sideways at her. Bruce's chest swelled with pride with the thought of the envy that other men would have when they saw this beautiful woman on his arm. Then his ego dipped as he considered that she would probably be deemed as his daughter. They stopped off at José's for a couple of glasses of wine. Bruce took up a seat where he could admire the *Cape*. Charlie sat next to him, rather than opposite him as they continued with conversations regarding sailing boats against powered cruisers, music and other trivia as they watched the world go by.

'Does life get any better than this?' Bruce thought to himself.

CHAPTER 7

Wednesday morning dawned a beautiful warm Spanish spring day. At nine o'clock they slipped their moorings and moved the *Cape* over to the Boats.co.uk chandleries wharf. There they were greeted by a beaming Sergio and another man. He was introduced to Bruce and Charlie as Max, originally from Germany, he was the Marine Consultant for Boats. co.uk. True to his word, Sergio had received the Williams 435 that had arrived on a road trailer and was parked on the wharf as was the black Kawasaki, Brute Force quadbike and the distinctive ebony and lime green Kawasaki 310LX that was just having the silver coloured cover removed. A mobile crane was being manoeuvred into position, ready to start the lifting and fitting operations. Bruce and Charlie went over to the Williams 435 and had a good look around her, noting that she had already had the title *T/T Cape Agulhas* stencilled on both sides of her bow. Bruce released the two catches under the helm position, tilting it forwards giving him access to the engine compartment and allowing him to admire the compact 150 HP Rotax engine with the integrated fire suppression system. Moving forwards, he lifted the forward seat cover and looked into the spacious splashproof storage locker. Then taking his mobile phone, Bruce went to the stern and easily found the hull number. Using his phone, he photographed it so that he could register it for warranty purposes.

Sergio took them over to the 310LX jet ski where he went through some of the included extras, amongst which was the Bluetooth stereo system. With it were two lime green and black buoyancy aids with 'Kawasaki' across the left breast. Charlies eyes gleamed. She didn't ask any questions and just murmured appropriately at the right time. Rather than getting in anyone's way, all four of them boarded the *Cape* and went around to the stern and into what was going to be the workshop come, dive storage area.

Charlie excused herself to go and make coffee. Once Bruce had outlined his plans to Max, he started making copious notes and took measurements with a laser device.

"So, Max. What do you think, is this a feasible project?"

"Bruce, everything is possible. I noticed that all your Aaah, how can I say, accessories, are powered by petrol. Is this correct?"

Bruce and Sergio looked at each other, surprised by the question. "Ahh, yes!" Bruce confirmed. The question had taken Bruce unawares.

"Ah-ha!" Max looked at Bruce with a grin. "I am pleased that I have been able to surprise you, Bruce. But I am going to suggest that we could also install a one hundred litre fuel bladder, complete with an integrated pump in here." He indicated a space to the side of the accessway. "This will enable you to fuel the jet ski and Williams and do away with cans and containers. The bladder can be refilled at any of the normal marina refuelling points."

Bruce looked at Sergio and Max. "That's a great idea, but how does it fit in with fire requirements and legislation?"

"That should be no problem at all, you will just need to contact your insurance company and inform them. We issue you with the necessary certificates and hey presto." Max said reassuringly. "Teutonic efficiency at its best."

"Right! Well, let's go with that idea as well." Bruce concluded.

Charlie poked her head around the access door. "Bruce, coffee in the salon, or would you like it here?"

"Salon, please. Charlie. Max, have you seen enough here?" Bruce asked.

"Yes, yes, thank you." Max replied. It was just as well that they had decided to vacate the area as Sergio's men were in the process of craning the Williams 435 down to the swim deck. Once in the salon, Max ensconced himself at the dining room table, opened a large sketch pad and started drawing furiously. Nursing their coffees Sergio, Charlie and Bruce stood in the cockpit and watched as the two men placed the support mounts for the 435 and secured them.

"Sergio?" Bruce asked. "Just a thought, but I hope that the swim deck will lower sufficiently to float the 435 off the cradle?"

"It should do." Sergio replied. "But we will check before you go." There followed some direct communication with the two workmen in rapid Spanish, who responded with nods and si's. Sergio went down to inspect the work that the workmen were doing.

"Bruce turned to Charlie. "Excited?" He asked.

"I can't wait. Do you know when our wet suits will be ready?"

"No! Good point." Just at that moment, Sergio's mobile phone rang and removing it from his pocket, he answered it in Spanish. The conversation was seemingly brief.

"Bruce, Charlie. If you come with me, we can check sizes on wet suits." Sergio looked Charlie up and down with a grin. "We had to make some adjustments for you Charlie."

Charlie responded with a tight-lipped smile. Following Sergio, they made their way into the chandlery where they were again met by Sergio's female assistant. They tried on the wet suits, Charlie's was made by Cressi in blue and black, Bruce's was an Osprey, also in blue and black, both were perfect fits. However, both men couldn't help but admire the picture that Charlie presented in the skin-tight neoprene. Packing up their wet suits, they also collected masks, snorkels, fins and weight belts, which they took back to the *Cape* with them.

The guys that had been working on the swim deck were ready to check the launching of the 435. Bruce powered up the main generator and moved aft to the control panel for the swim deck. "All ready?" He asked. Charlie had moved and had taken up the bowline. One of the workers had taken the stern line on the 435. As the hydraulics pump whirred and the deck moved out slightly from the stern of the swim deck. It then submerged itself as the Williams 435 magically floated free.

"Well, that seems to work well." Bruce commented and then operated the deck back inboard with the 435 settled back on its cradle. He broke out a freshwater hose and rinsed down the deck and the hull of the tender. "One down, two to go."

Bruce and Sergio went up to the flybridge, between them they decided on the best places to mount the two accessories that were to be stored on the aft of the flybridge. The quad bike at that moment didn't have a weather cover, but Sergio had taken the dimensions and had then sent specifications off to the sailmaker housed next to the chandlery. The Kawasaki 310LX jet ski, on the other hand, came complete with a beautiful silver and black, heavy-duty, weather cover. It left no one in any doubt as to what was under the cover.

Bruce and Sergio spent the rest of the day organising the stowage of the 310LX and quad bike. Charlie was allowed to borrow the Boats.co.uk courtesy minibus and spent the afternoon shopping, returning to the quayside just before four o'clock. The cover for the quad bike had been finished and was now adorning the four-wheeled machine. Then it was time for a gentle meander back to the marina and the pontoon.

Following the evening meal, Charlie was curled up on the sofa watching the television whilst Bruce was at his laptop at the chart table. Charlie had refilled their wine glasses and had come up to the pilot station with Bruce's wine. "What's happening Bruce, you are very quiet tonight?" She sat down on the helm seat and faced Bruce across the bridge.

Bruce paused from staring at the screen of the computer. Sat back and pushed his reading glasses up onto his forehead rubbing his eyes. "To be honest, I don't think that what I am looking for is going to leap out to me from Google. I am still trying to find the significance of the coordinates of the pinpricks. The other puzzle is the date that the charts were published, which I don't think is that significant. Because it is plausible that those charts could have still been in use well into the eighties or nineties even. Anyway, we can speculate to our heart's content but until we get to the respective areas and can see for ourselves, we might as well keep on guessing."

Charlie nodded her head in understanding. "So, plans for the morrow?" She enquired.

"Yep! Been giving that some thought as well. The weather forecast is for absolutely brilliant weather tomorrow, so how about we have a bit of a play and just have some fun with some of those toys we have just acquired?"

"Oh, what! Yeah! I won't be able to sleep tonight."

Bruce smiled at her. "Then how about on Friday, we take a run down to Gibraltar, fill up with duty-free alcohol, see some of the sites and come back on Saturday?"

"Are you paying me for this? Seriously are you paying me to have fun?" She asked, sounding bewildered.

"Well! I guess so – I am having fun and it is nice to share it with someone." Embarrassed at suddenly realising what he had blurted out. Bruce turned away from her and was looking out towards the pontoon and the *Rio Jenil*. The starboard door from the pilot station to the deck was ajar behind Charlie. As much as seeing the reflection, he sensed the change in the doorway. He whirled around, coming to his feet at the same time. Van de Niekerk was reaching in behind Charlie putting his left arm around her throat. In his right hand, he held a pistol.

Threateningly he said. "Not a word English bastard, or this bitch gets it." He hadn't shouted, being more than aware of the armed guard that would no doubt be very close to the other side of the *Cape*. Charlie had automatically reached up with both her hands to Van de Niekerk's left arm in an attempt to reduce the pressure on her throat. "Keep still bitch. You, English, get me the fucking sea charts. I know that you have found them, they mean nothing to you, hey." Van de Niekerk wasn't quite into the pilot station but was leaning in from the deck. As he pulled Charlie around the helm seat, he twisted the pistol towards Bruce. A nine-millimetre Russian Tokarev with a silencer on it. It was pointing at Bruce's chest. As Charlie was pulled around the helm seat, she suddenly pushed backwards with all her force. This sent Van de Niekerk staggering backwards, out onto the deck, but as he did so, he swivelled around sending Charlie's head crashing into the side of the doorway then flying over the railing into the dark marina, with a splash, semi-conscious.

Van de Niekerk turned and fled back towards the stern. Bruce rushed to the side of the *Cape* and peered over the rail for any sign of Charlie. All he could see was the disturbed water where Charlie had gone in. Glancing briefly to his right, Bruce was aware of Van de Niekerk running towards the back of the boat. He heard someone shout 'Parada, Parada' in Spanish as he reached into the control panel and turned on the underwater lights, then throwing his glasses off his forehead. Without a moment's hesitation, Bruce leapt over the rail and into the marina as the sound of two of rapid shots rang out. Bruce hit the water feet first. He was shocked by the sudden coldness and ignoring the jolt, Bruce started to search for any signs of Charlie. With a mixture of relief and concern, he almost immediately saw Charlie. She was just a few feet below him, seemingly lifeless. Pulling strongly with his arms in a breaststroke action, he reached her and grabbed the back of her hoodie, pulling her towards him and enabling him to get his right arm under her armpits. Swimming with all his might in a side stroke action and kicking vigorously with his feet, he broke the surface of the marina with a gasp a moment later.

Bruce started to swim around the bow of the *Cape* towards the pontoon. His progress was understandably slow as he progressed towards the bow, he started shouting for help. Rounding the bow, Charlie started to shake her head, then she coughed wretchedly and moaned.

"It's okay! It's okay! I've got you, I've got you, you'll be okay, just stay still." As Bruce was trying to reassure her, he was aware that his reserves were rapidly ebbing away, plus he hadn't realised as to just how unfit he was. There was the flashing of torch lights, then the lights on the *Rio Jenil* were switched on. Bruce got Charlie to the short ladder on the end of the pontoon, facing her around towards him, he got both his arms under her armpits and was then able to hold on to the pontoon ladder supporting her. Charlie was semi-conscious. Bruce looked up to the pontoon, two men were kneeling on the deck of the pontoon. They reached their arms down and took Charlie under her armpits, hauling her out in one straight heave. One of the men, who he now recognised as one of the sailors from the *Rio Jenil*, helped Bruce get up the ladder and out of the water. Charlie had been laid down in the recovery position and was now struggling to sit up.

Bruce went and knelt in front of her and tried to examine the back of her head for damage. She was sobbing as she put both her arms around him as he held her head to his chest and hugged her.

"You saved my life. You saved my life, Bruce." Bruce couldn't find any blood on the back of her head or any words, realising how close he had come to possibly losing his own life. He shivered from the cold and the shock of the event that was now setting in. One of the sailors from the *Rio Jenil* had got a couple of survival blankets and put them around the shoulders of the soaked couple.

In next to no time, there were sirens and blue lights all around them. Up, on the quay, another Spanish sailor was standing guard over a writhing prone figure with the barrel of his machine carbine pointing menacingly at it. Bruce continued to shush Charlie, still holding her head to his chest and rocking her gently sideways. An ambulance came screaming to a stop on the quayside at the end of the pontoon. There was a brief hasty exchange in Spanish between the two crew and the Guardia Civil sailors, whereupon the ambulance crew ran down to Bruce and Charlie. Charlie vomited, narrowly missing everyone. As she wretched again, Bruce held her forehead until she stopped.

Bruce tried to explain in English to the female ambulance attendant what had happened to Charlie, she nodded understandingly, producing a torch and having a close look at the back and side of Charlie's head. Charlie, beginning to recover, again and in her fluent Spanish, explained what had happened. There were several exchanges between Charlie and the medics as she started to get to her feet. The medics started to walk Charlie towards the ambulance. Bruce followed on closely behind, pulling the survival blanket tighter around his shoulders. His attention was now drawn to the guarded figure on the ground as he made his way over to it. Van de Niekerk was losing blood from a bullet wound to his right thigh.

Addressing the sailor, Bruce smiled at him and said. "You missed. You should have shot him in the fucking head." Bruce gesticulated with his thumb and forefinger the act of shooting Van de Niekerk in the head. The sailor nodded with a wry, nervous smile. He was quite young and had probably never fired a weapon in anger before. Bruce was just about to launch a kick at Van de Niekerk's injured leg when there was the sound of a person running up behind him.

Bruce turned around. "Bruce! Are you alright?" It was Capitain Miguel. "I hear one of my men has shot an intruder from your boat. Is Charlie okay?"

"Aah! Yes." Bruce turned and patted the sailor on his shoulder in a conspiratorial manner. The young sailor returned a weak grin. "I really have to say that I think if your guys hadn't been around, then we would possibly not be alive to tell the tale."

"What was that all about? Do you know him?" Miguel asked, putting a conspiratorial arm around Bruce's shoulder as they made their way back towards the rear of the ambulance, just as another police vehicle arrived. Bruce explained how he came to know of Van de Niekerk and the circumstances of the evening's occurrence. "So, have you found these charts to which he refers?"

"No, no! I haven't the faintest idea what he is talking about." Bruce lied. He didn't feel comfortable about it, but as the charts didn't just refer to Spanish waters, he didn't feel too bad about it. They returned to Van de Niekerk, who by this time was having a pressure dressing applied to his wound by a male medic. Bruce bent down to Van de Niekerk and very quietly spoke to him, very slowly and pronouncing each word meticulously, his Rhodesian accent very evident. "Van de Niekerk, if ever you come anywhere near me, or any of mine again for whatever reason, I will bend you over and fire a very pistol right up your fuckin' arse. Do you understand?" Turning to Miguel, he continued. "Miguel, when he was on my boat, he had what looked like a Tokarev with a silencer, have your guys found it?"

There was a rapid exchange in Spanish between Miguel and his crewman. "No, Bruce, no pistol." Miguel looked perplexed. There followed another brief conversation in Spanish between Miguel and the crewman, with a second crewman joining in the conversation as well. "In the morning, I will send divers to search in the marina. He got straight onto his mobile phone and had a brief conversation during which he looked at Bruce once. "Bruce, can you leave your underwater lights on for a half-hour please, my divers can be here in thirty minutes."

"No problem." Bruce replied. Miguel turned back to the crewman who had shot Van de Niekerk and patted him on the shoulder. He looked gratefully at Bruce. "I take it that you need proof that he was armed to justify your man's action for having shot Van de Niekerk?" Bruce asked.

"It would help." Miguel admitted. "But here in Spain it doesn't matter too much, he was told to halt and didn't. This is a sensitive area. Robbing boats from a foreign nationality, well it is a Federal Offence." Miguel shrugged his shoulders. "We need to find that pistol though."

Sitting in the back of the ambulance, Charlie looked bedraggled, but the colour was returning to her cheeks. She smiled wanly at the two men. "What's the verdict?" Bruce asked.

"It's okay, just a bang on the head and an overindulgence in marina water." Charlie continued. "Can we get back, please? I need to get out of these clothes and get a hot shower." Charlie gave an involuntary shiver. Bruce was pleased with the return of her sense of humour.

The medic did the eye and torch test on Charlie and then spoke to Bruce in Spanish. Miguel translated. "You must watch her for the next twenty-four hours, if she feels sick or dizzy, then you must take her straight to the hospital, this is what she has said."

"Yeah, yeah! Absolutely no problem. Sin problemo!" Bruce's attempt at Spanish was not brilliant, he extended a hand to help Charlie out of the ambulance, effusively saying 'gracias, gracias' to the female ambulance attendant.

"Bruce!" Miguel started. "I will need a statement in the morning 'mi amigo' from both of you, hey. About ten o'clock. I will come with a recorder and then I will get it transcribed and interpreted into Spanish. Is this okay for you?" Both Bruce and Charlie acknowledged the request. Charlie gave a shiver and Bruce put a protective arm around her shoulder. They bade Miguel goodnight and made their way back on board the *Cape*.

Bruce sent Charlie down to her cabin once she had assured him that she was okay and could manage the shower and hair wash on her own. Recovering his reading glasses from the floor of the pilot station, he followed her down but went to his own cabin and threw his wet clothes into the bottom of the shower. They could stay there until he could find a bin bag to put them in pending laundering. He showered briefly, letting the hot water sting his body, after which he dug out a pair of tracksuit bottoms, a T-shirt and a jumper and put them on before returning hastily to the main deck. Bruce noticed that the divers had arrived and that the first pair were just about to enter the water at the stern of the *Cape*. Bruce quickly moved out to the swim deck control station and lowered the deck to make it easier for the divers to access to and from the water. They acknowledged in gratitude as Bruce returned to the salon and poured himself a large glass of Glenmorangie, adding a small amount of water before taking a good mouthful of it in the first swallow. The quantity of the fiery liquid burnt the back of his throat as he swallowed and felt the warmth spreading into the pit of his stomach. Bruce took another swallow in anticipation of a repeat performance but he was disappointed. The first swallow had by far been the best. The dry clothes were also helping him to restore the temperature of his body to some degree of normality however being aware that the alcohol would not be the best method of doing this. Bruce realised that he would have to be careful. Bruce continued to watch the surface party monitor the two divers who were underwater in the marina whilst he sipped his whisky.

He didn't have to wait long, in fact, he hadn't even had a chance to finish his drink when the two divers surfaced in unison, both gave the international signal of okay. Bruce made his way back out on the deck and went aft to the swim deck control. One of the divers was handing the shore party an evidence bag. Although he couldn't make out what was in the bag, it was apparent that the divers had found what they had been looking for. Bruce raised the swim platform to enable the grateful divers to get ashore with ease. They made their way back onto the quay amidst loud talking and the clanking of equipment. Once he had secured the *Cape* for the night, Bruce picked up a second glass and made his way below.

As soon as Bruce entered the small foyer at the bottom of the stairwell, he could hear the sobs coming from Charlie's cabin. Putting the glasses down in his cabin, he went back and knocked gently on Charlie's cabin door. There was no reply, he tried again but the sobbing continued. Bruce cautiously opened the cabin door. No words or actions were restricting his entrance to the cabin. She was sat on the end of her single bunk wrapped in a towel with another towel wrapping her hair up as only a woman can do. "There, there Charlie. It's all over now." He sat down next to her and put an arm around her shoulders, pulling her gently into him.

She responded, turning putting her arms around Bruce. Tearfully she spoke into the nape of his neck. "I thought that I was dead. I swear my life flashed in front of me, I could feel myself sinking through the water, I wanted to save myself, but I couldn't move." She sobbed again. "I just felt so helpless. I knew that I was going to die." Again, she wept. Bruce just squeezed her gently in the reassurance that she was now safe. "Then you were there, in the water with me, we were on the surface, then I knew it would be alright. Bruce, Bruce you saved my life." She squeezed him fiercely. "You saved my life, you saved my life." She repeated. "How do I ever repay you for that?" She pushed herself away from him and looked him in the face. Her tear streamed red eyes looked quizzically at him as she lifted her hands cupping his face. She kissed him very gently on the lips. The kiss lasted two short seconds. Bruce remained absolutely motionless, not responding to the kiss. Charlie then pulled gently and slowly away from him and looked deeply into Bruce's eyes, her hands still cupping Bruce's face in her hands.

Charlie still looked as beautiful as ever despite the red moistened eyes and tear-streaked cheeks. At that moment, Bruce's heart went out to her. Gently and with a slight croak to his voice, he replied. "I have already told you, that as your employer, I have a duty of care for you." He grinned a little sheepishly. "Besides which Charlie Hope, over the past few days, I have grown rather fond of you. Anyway, who else is going to help me find the pirate treasure?" She shivered again. "Come on." He said. "Let's get you out of that wet towel. There is a sensible sized spare bathrobe in my wardrobe, a hairdryer in my bathroom and whisky in my cabin." She perked up at the mention of the whisky. Bruce went back up to the main deck and found a plastic rubbish sack, returning downstairs he went first to Charlie's cabin and picked up her wet clothes from where they had been deposited in the sink and then returning to his cabin he went and recovered his wet clothes from the bottom of the shower and tied a knot in the bag before depositing it in the dirty laundry bag. Charlie was sat at the dressing table, a glass of whisky by her elbow, brushing and blow drying her shimmering black hair. The dressing gown, which was a large size, had fallen open at her knees, half her lovely long thighs were exposed. She smiled in the mirror at Bruce

79

and saw him looking at her thighs, failing at the half-hearted attempt to re-cover her legs.

"How are you feeling?" He asked.

"Still cold." She admitted. "It will take a little time to recover my core temperature and I suppose I am still in some sort of state of shock."

"I can imagine." He looked at her with a degree of concern. "Look, I am really sorry this happened to you. That was some brave move you made, by the way, thank you."

"Just pure gut reaction." She said. "By the way, what happened to the bastard?"

"One of our neighbours put a nine-millimetre bullet in his thigh. There was no exit wound. It looked to me like his femur possibly stopped the round, so the medicos will have to surf for it." He grinned at her.

"But how did he know we had the charts?"

"Speculation and he may have overheard our conversation earlier on." Bruce reached for the whisky bottle and topped himself up and then offered to top up Charlie's glass. She declined. "Miguel asked me about the charts. I denied any knowledge of them. If Van de Niekerk is that determined to get hold of the charts, then he must know what they relate to and…" Bruce paused speculatively. "They must be of some form of value." Charlie had finished brushing and drying her hair. Bruce looked at her. "Right, you, get into bed and get that duvet wrapped around you."

Not removing the robe, Charlie got into the right-hand side of the king-sized double bed, taking the remains of her drink with her and putting it on the bedside cabinet. She turned over onto her left side and looked at Bruce, the duvet pulled up to her chin. "Where are you going to sleep?" She asked.

"Right here." He replied. "I am just going to take a quick look around topside then I'll bring another bottle of water down with me."

"Good!" She replied. "Please don't leave me alone."

"Don't worry." Bruce leant over and very lightly brushed his lips across her exposed forehead. Charlie sighed.

Bruce switched off the main cabin lights and just left the left-hand side reading light on, it gave off a pleasant unobtrusive blue glow to the cabin. Pulling the cabin door to, but not closing it completely, Bruce went out into the passageway and checked that the lights in Charlie's cabin were off before going up to the main deck. His way was lit by the unobtrusive LED lights under the steps on the stairwell. At the top of the stairs, he turned right and went into the pilot station. Looking through the wheelhouse windscreen, he saw that the marina was quiet, there was no movement, even the breeze from earlier had dissipated to nothing. Bruce moved down through the top deck to the stern side of the salon. The quay was quiet. All the fun and excitement from earlier had gone away. He briefly spared a thought for Van de Niekerk and thought of him in the hospital going through either being prepped for or having surgery to remove the bullet. He found himself hoping that the hospital had forgotten to give him any anaesthetic. Then he thought of the wonder woman in his bed below and wondered how he was going to deal with another woman in his life. Certainly, this was something that he had not planned for when he was considering his retirement and the permanent move onto the *Cape*. But then again, he had definitely not bargained on the treasure maps or Van de Niekerk for that matter. All part of life's rich tapestry he thought, picking up the reusable blue plastic water bottle from the fridge.

Bruce made his way back down below and quietly went into his cabin. From the sound of her breathing, he could tell instantly that she was sound asleep. The nightmares would come, he thought to himself. Bruce knew they would come, he also knew that he wanted to be there to hold and comfort her when they did. Had he fallen in love with her? Probably! Yes, definitely, he had fallen in love with her. Bruce went into the bathroom, he stripped his clothes off and showered again, this time languishing in the hot water. He felt the muscles around his shoulders and arms begin to relax. Drying himself off thoroughly, he recovered a fresh pair of underpants from his drawer and slipped them on, just for modesties sake. Usually, he slept as naked as the day he was born. Returning to the bathroom, he sat on the toilet bowl and rubbed bio-oil into the scars on his legs and arm. He would have to forego his amazon's daily massage tonight. He quietly slipped into his side of the bed, visually making sure that Charlie was okay and turning his bedside light down to a minimum, then he turned onto his side facing her and fell soundly asleep.

Charlie stirred and got out of bed, sitting on the edge of the bed. She orientated herself before getting up and going to the bathroom. "Are you okay, Charlie?"

"Shush." She replied. "I just need a wee." The clock projecting the time onto the cabin ceiling indicated that it was 4:36 am. Returning to the bed, she sat on the edge and drank a glass of water, then she shucked off the robe and naked got back into bed. Mentally realising that she was in a wonderfully safe place and feeling inner contentment, she almost instantly fell back to sleep. The sleep was deep and restful until she realised the presence of someone sitting on the edge of the bed and the wonderful aroma of freshly brewed coffee. Slowly she blinked her eyes open to see that the person sat on the edge of the bed was Bruce.

CHAPTER 8

Bruce had woken at his usual time of seven o'clock and had briefly lain awake, in sleep Charlie and Bruce had drifted almost together. He was uncomfortable, he really needed to urinate the case of his swollen and very erect penis was not a situation that he was used to experiencing. This was no doubt caused by the presence of the naked female form that was lying next to him in his bed. From the sound of her breathing, he could tell that she was still very much in a deep sleep. Very quietly and cautiously, he had got out of bed selecting fresh underwear and socks from his drawer, then making his way to the bathroom and relieved himself. Shaving the bits of his face and neck that needed shaving, Bruce had quickly and quietly got himself dressed and did the morning rounds of the *Cape*. Also, checking that the headspace access in the engine room hadn't been disturbed. He had also seen the seamen from the *Rio Jenil* and again thanked them for their assistance during the dramas of the previous night. He noted with interest that there was a slight change of crew from the day before. Miguel had been replaced by a Lieutenant and the young sailor that had shot Van de Niekerk had also been replaced. 'Everyone was going to be donating statements today.' Bruce thought, making his way to the galley, he decided to make coffee for a change. He remembered as a child that in the cold early mornings, in the highlands of Rhodesia, it was a special treat to be allowed to have coffee but it was an extra special treat if he was allowed to have the sweetened condensed milk in it. Thus, giving it a very different smell and taste. Preparing the coffee percolator sufficient for four mugs Bruce again resumed his ponderings about the naked woman below in his bed. She was probably the same age as both his daughters in law, young enough for him to be her father. Come to that, he thought, what about her parents, what would they perceive of this attraction that he had towards their daughter. He felt a pang of guilt as well. Was it too soon after the death of his wife? Were two years enough to mourn? There was something about Charlie Hope that drew him inexorably towards her, it wasn't her beauty aside from that, Charlie was also a very astute, practical woman with a good head on her shoulders. On the other hand, maybe he was just reading too much into the blossoming relationship and that he was just imagining that she felt romantically towards him. He was also confused with regards to the clandestine meeting with the man at the ferry terminal. Bruce was not used to these feelings, so he found his mind reeling. One thing of which he was certain, was that he did not want to lose Charlie. He was sure he was in love with her. Things might just get a bit complicated.

Making his way below with the two mugs of coffee balanced on a small tray, he opened the cabin door. She was still asleep, lying on her left side towards the centre of the bed, her right shoulder poking above the duvet. Placing the two mugs of coffee on the bedside table, Bruce sat down on the edge of the bed. Charlie stirred, turning over onto her back and looked sleepily up at Bruce.

"Morning!" She yawned drowsily. "What time is it?"

Smiling, he replied. "Morning, a little after eight o'clock and all is well with the world."

Charlie smiled back groggily. "My God! This bed is so comfortable I could stay here for the rest of the day. May I move in here permanently, please Captain?"

"Yes, of course, you may. But where will I go?"

"Why Captain, I would want you to stay with me please." Charlie reached up and pulled Bruce's head down to her bosom, most of which was now exposed. "I would want you to stay with me forever." She continued huskily. "Bruce, I have fallen in love with you and this is not just a reaction to last night, I fell in love with you from the first moment I saw you."

Bruce reluctantly pulled himself back up from the place of heaven only because it was twisting his back awkwardly. Straightening himself up, he paused briefly. "Well!" he said, taking her right hand in his. "Charlotte, I love you too. Now drink some coffee before it gets cold."

Charlie smiled and sat up in the bed hooking the duvet up under her armpits just to preserve some of her ample modesty accepting the mug of steaming coffee.

"Mmm!" She purred. "What have you done to this coffee?"

Bruce told her of the treat that the coffee meant to him as a child, then sensing her needs, he said. "Right, I am going to go upstairs and just give the decks a quick swab down. Miguel will be here at about ten this morning. I reckon it will take about an hour to an hour and a half to give our statements. Then there is absolutely no reason why we can't continue with our plans for the day. Providing you are still up for it of course?"

"Wild horses wouldn't stop me now." She replied, reaching for the previously discarded robe on the deck and modestly covered herself as she slipped those long legs out of the bed. Bruce retreated from the cabin and got on with giving the decks a quick clean down with a mop and freshwater with his mind in a euphoric state. Had he imagined the conversation below in the cabin or had it been for real? He was in the process of cleaning the glass with a squeegee when Charlie popped her head around the galley door.

"I am starving." She said. "How about eggs and bacon?" Charlie asked.

The sudden recollection of Charlie emptying the contents of her stomach on the quay the previous night flashed through his mind. "Sounds great." He replied, guiltily looking towards the front of the pontoon and realised that someone else had hosed off the pontoon. Breathing a sigh of relief, he continued with his chores.

Breakfast over, Charlie helped with the window cleaning so that when Miguel came down the quay and onto the pontoon, the *Cape Agulhas* was as always gleaming. The statement taking was over very quickly and within an hour of having greeted Miguel on board the *Cape*, than they were saying goodbyes to him. No sooner had he left than they made ready to get underway. They were like two children on Christmas morning. Deciding that they would go back up the coast to where they had spent the afternoon the day before which was where Bruce had spent his first Saturday.

They devoted the first two hours working with the Williams 435, launching and recovering it as well as operating it. The launch and recovery operations were very simple to carry out. However, the fun and games began with the low-speed manoeuvring of the craft as when it came to positioning it over the quick release cradle on the submerged swim deck. The Williams 435 is 'jet powered'. That is to say, that the engine drives a pump which then 'jets' water out through the drive. This provides the propulsion for the boat. The downside to this is that the only way to have directional control of the boat, was to either have it engaged in either forward or reverse gear. They had a great deal of fun trying to get this right, they also discovered that the tender could just as easily provide a white-knuckle ride.

After a light lunch, they changed into their wetsuits and using the crane they practised the launching and recovery of the Kawasaki jet ski. The Kawasaki jet ski had manufactured eyelets to crane it on and off the deck. Once it was launched it was just a matter of manoeuvring the jet ski back into a position where the crane could then be re-attached. Once the launching and recovery techniques had been mastered. They spent time getting used to it and just generally having fun with the sixty miles per hour plus speed machine. Bruce stood on the foredeck of the *Cape* as he watched Charlie, who was like a child with a new toy getting the jet ski to go airborne as she jumped it over waves, whooping with each jump and tight turn. Surprisingly, Bruce found her antics and enthusiasm heart-warming and rewarding as he continued to watch her get the most out of the Kawasaki jet ski.

Bruce went below and got his camera out, re-launching the 435, he went out and took photographs not only of Charlie performing her tricks on the Kawasaki jet ski but also of the *Cape* lying gracefully at anchor in the bay. Bruce had never felt this happy, the most beautiful woman in the world had confessed her love for him, he had the most beautiful home in the world, the *Cape* and he had all the toys he could wish for.

Charlie brought the jet ski in alongside the tender. "C'mon Bruce. This thing is just some fun. Now I can understand the appeal that they have. Come on, have a go with me. Please?"

"Okay, let me get the tender back to the *Cape* and put my camera away." He put the camera back into its case, stowed it and started the engine for the tender. On the way back, Charlie crisscrossed the wake of the Williams, whooping as she jumped the jet ski. Bruce tied up the 435 alongside the *Cape* and then transferred himself onto the 310LX. Charlie shifted herself back on the pillion seat to allow Bruce access to the front seat, taking the kill switch lanyard and clipping it to his vest. With Charlie clinging onto him, far tighter than she needed to. They spent the next forty minutes playing around and practising picking each other up from the water. Between them, they became proficient with the use of the jet ski. Returning to the *Cape*, they stowed and rinsed everything off, including themselves and their wetsuits with fresh water.

After the day's exercise, they were both exhausted. As Bruce prepared the *Cape* for departure back to the marina for the night, Charlie made them a very welcome cup of tea. On the way back to port, she spent the time in the galley preparing meat and vegetables for a casserole which would be their evening meal. By the time they were making their entry into the marina, the makings were in the pressure cooker, waiting to go onto the stove.

As they came up adjacent to their berth, Bruce noticed the black limousine on the quayside with a fluttering Union flag on it. There was something unusual about how the flag was being flown. Normally, an official car would have the pennant flying from either a mudguard or a bonnet fixture. However, this pennant was being flown from a plastic clip attached to the top of the driver's door. Standing next to the quayside were two men. One was a uniformed driver, the other wore a suit with a lightweight coat loosely draped over his shoulders. Bruce looked at him briefly, picking up the binoculars from in front of him. He quickly focussed on the man. This guy was familiar. Where had he seen that face before, where and when?

Charlie was about to go to her forward station when Bruce said to her, indicating the two men onshore. "I think we have got some company and I would bet that it is all about our evening dip in the marina last night."

The *Rio Jenil* was already alongside, so there was no shortage of helpers to take lines from Charlie and Bruce.

The person wearing the light coat did have the good grace to wait until Bruce and Charlie had finished docking before he first approached Charlie. "Miss Hope?" he inquired.

"Yes." She replied.

"My name is Johnathan Smithers from her Britannic Majesty's Consulate in Gibraltar."

"We're going there tomorrow. We could have saved you the trip." She said cheekily, looking down at Smithers. Smithers was a little shorter than Bruce, so she really did look down at him.

"It's about the incident that you were involved in last night, I am going to need a statement from you I am afraid. Ahh! Williams, isn't it?" Smithers looked at Bruce as he approached him.

"Mr Williams or even Captain to you will do Smithers." Bruce recognised him. Bruce was now certain he knew who he was. Smithers looked sufficiently abashed by the rebuke Bruce had issued.

"Aahh! Yes, my apologies Mr Williams." Bruce could see no signs of recognition from him but then the last time he had seen Bruce, Bruce's face had been masked by desert camouflage.

Questioning Smithers, Bruce asked. "Why would you be needing a statement from one of us? This incident occurred in Spain on the Spanish mainland and nothing was stolen."

"Aaahh! Yes. However, this confrontation involved a firearm, did it not?" Smithers smirked, indicating that he thought that he held the upper hand in this discussion.

Bruce noted, that two of the armed crew from the *Rio Jenil* had moved to the head of the pontoon. Another sailor had moved between the chauffeur and Charlie. The fact that the chauffeur had not remained with the limousine had confirmed Bruce's thoughts. They were going to attempt to kidnap Charlie.

Several things happened at the same time.

Miguel had stepped off the quay onto the pontoon shouting a "Hola Bruce!" The three armed sailors cocked their weapons and levelled them at the two men.

Bruce had stepped sideways, pushing Charlie out of the way, just as Smithers was reaching behind him for a concealed weapon. At the same time as shoving Charlie out of the way, Bruce balled his right fist and straight-arm punched Smithers right into his exposed throat. Smithers went down like a sack of potatoes, followed by Bruce, ready to deliver another punch if it were necessary. It wasn't.

The chauffeur raised his arms and was immediately thrown to the ground and roughly searched. A Sig Sauer pistol was found to have been concealed in the waistband of his trousers. Kneeling on Smithers chest and with the palm of his right hand pushing up on the underside his nose Bruce said. "Your name is not Smithers. Your name is David Hopkiss, formerly of the Royal Engineers, arrested and charged for the possession and smuggling of Class A drugs, also involved in people trafficking and child pornography. The last time I saw you, I was holding your face down in the sands of Iraq just outside the town of Karbala. So, what the fuck are you doing here, you bastard?" Had Bruce chosen to do so and had he exerted sufficient sudden energy on his victims nose, it was possible it could have caused him a great deal of pain.

Already the pressure on Hopkiss's nose was making his eyes water "No, no, please don't hurt me." Hopkiss pleaded with a croaking, nasally voice.

"Who the fuck are you working for arsehole?" Bruce's Rhodesian accent came to the fore. He was about to push harder, when he felt the strong hand on his shoulder, partially restraining his action.

"Leave him be Bruce. Let the authorities interrogate him." Miguel's voice was authoritative.

Bruce flipped Smithers over onto his stomach and removed the Browning 9mm pistol from the waistband of Smithers trousers. Deftly removing the magazine, he slid the slide action back and caught the ejected round in his right hand, handing over the three items to Miguel he then turned to face a grateful and smiling Charlie.

As they were docking, Bruce hadn't had much time to prepare her and didn't even know what to tell her to expect during the brief radio conversation whilst she was at the bow. As Bruce was reversing the *Cape* into position, he had been on the VHF radio that was permanently on guard, the operator on the *Rio Jenil* had been wide awake.

"Miguel, I have to apologise to you unreservedly, these sea maps, charts that Van de Niekerk was looking for last night. I have found them. They were in a constructed space inside the chart locker."

Miguel looked at Bruce with incredulity. "So, who do these charts belong to?" "I guess that technically they are mine, they would have passed into my possession when I bought the *Cape*." Bruce replied.

"Maybe so, but as they are the subject of this much controversy also they may well have been stolen by the previous owner or past crew. I will have to confiscate them." Miguel spoke officiously. "You will go and get them for me now please."

Bruce went back on board the *Cape* and went straight into the engine room, reaching up he undid the access to the void and retrieved the four charts. Returning to the quay, Bruce handed over the rolled-up charts to Miguel, who looked at each one in turn. There were two of islands in the Mediterranean Sea, one of an island in the Adriatic Sea and one of an island in the Aegean Sea. They all had red writing at the top of the charts and little red dots off the coast of the islands. Charlie's jaw dropped.

"God, Bruce, you have just given away our treasure charts, now we will never know."

Bruce stood in front of her "Charlie, I don't give a shit about those bloody charts. Twice in less than twenty-four hours, we have been involved with guns. I care far too much to let anything ever happen to you. I would like us to enjoy our lives and not to have to worry about having to look over our shoulders all the time. I didn't ever think that I could find love again, but now you have come along and you have just turned my world upside down."

Charlie hugged him with all her might and sobbed onto his shoulder. "Oh my God, Bruce! I never thought it possible to love anyone as much as I do you." She pulled away and kissed him passionately on the lips.

Hopkiss and his associate were marched off onto the quay and put into separate Police vans that went off at high speed with their sirens screaming. Miguel placed a friendly hand on Bruce's shoulder. "Bruce, I am sorry that I have to take these away from you." He waved the rolled-up charts. "But maybe it is for your own good and better in the long run. Let's go and have a drink, shall we?"

"That sounds like a very good idea. You go ahead with Charlie, I'll have a large whatever single malt that José has. I am just going to turn off my engines, then I will be right with you." Bruce turned and went back on board, closing down the engines and replaced the roof access to the void.

Two large whiskies later, Bruce and Charlie made their way back to the *Cape* and Charlie put the pressure cooker on the stove. Charlie was about to make her way down to shower before dinner, whilst Bruce kept an eye on the pressure cooker.

"Charlie!" Bruce stopped her. She turned at the top of the stairwell. "About moving cabins?"

"Are you having second thoughts?" She asked with concern in her voice.

"No, no, definitely not." Bruce stood up and moved towards her. "I thought that when I can find the right linen, we move into the Master Cabin. After all, if we are going to live together, we'll need a bit more space than my current cabin. What do you think?"

"I think that you are one hell of a Captain." She came to him and passionately pulled him into her body. "Oh my God! I really must control myself." She turned and went down the stairs.

CHAPTER 9

Bruce retrieved the SD card from his camera and uploaded it onto the laptop. Sitting at the chart table, he was going through the photographs when Charlie came back up onto the main deck wearing a lightweight jogging suit and a T-shirt. Her hair, as usual after a shower, was wrapped in a towel. Coming around behind Bruce, she wrapped her arms around his chest with her head resting on his shoulder watching Bruce going through the photographs. The fresh, clean smell of her body was euphoric and her body contact comfortingly familiar and stimulating. Bruce reacted by pushing gently back against her, marginally increasing the pressure of their bodily contact.

"Oh Bruce! That is gorgeous." She said, pausing him. It was an almost side-on view of the *Cape* at her anchor. The sun had been behind Bruce and was also lighting up the mountains of the Sierras de Tejeda in the background. "Oh, that is lovely." She exclaimed. "Is there any way you could get that printed for me please?"

"Shouldn't be too much of a problem. I'll save it as a jpg file and put it on a stick."

Charlie squeezed Bruce gently as she watched him convert it from the original raw file and develop it. Adding contrast, removing shadows, cutting back on the highlights, adding just a little bit more vibrance and dehazing the mountains in the background so that they really stood out clearly. When he had finished, he clicked to accept the changes, the original image on the screen transformed itself into the completed image that amazingly just jumped off the screen. Charlie squeezed him again and kissed him on the top of his head. "That is just so clever!" Bruce gently pushed his head back into her breasts. She definitely wasn't wearing a bra underneath the T-shirt. "Are we still on for Gibraltar tomorrow?" She asked. "Only I will need to pop out to a shop or chemist for some women's stuff before we go."

Bruce turned around in the seat. "Can I get you anything now?" He pulled her towards him, again she wrapped her arms around him.

"No, no." She replied. "Dinner will be ready soon anyway. I am usually better prepared than this. I think that the combination of last night's swim and you have really wound up my hormones." She hugged him tightly for a moment, emphasising the 'you', before breaking off to check on the meal. Following their dinner, they went below to check on the bedding requirements for the master cabin. They found some fitted sheets a duvet cover and a twelve tog duvet, they decided that the twelve tog duvet would be far too heavy for them to cope with, especially as the nights were getting warmer. Not wishing to be separated, they decided to stay together in the forward VIP until they had everything which was needed for the master cabin.

"Do you know what Charlie?" Bruce said to her once they were back in the salon, with the last of the bottle of wine that they'd had for dinner. "I am beginning to think that one night in Gib isn't going to be enough." Charlie looked up quizzically from her sketch pad. "We could do quite a bit of shopping for the boat instead of having to bring electrical goods out from the UK. Everything in Gibraltar is duty-free, or virtually duty-free, including alcohol and electrical goods."

Charlie put the sketch pad down. "What exactly did you have in mind?"

"Well, it will be about a two and a half to three hours run down to Gib, assuming we get away by nine, that will make it probably twelve to half twelve by the time we have docked. Shopping in the afternoon, then we could spend Saturday seeing the sights, spend Saturday night in Gib and then come back here for Sunday."

"I don't mind at all. Are there any clothes shops in Gib? I could do with a bit of therapy." She smiled.

"Absolutely, they are mostly on Main Street, I think, Dorothy Perkins, Next, Peacocks and there are others as well." He replied.

"And you know this because?" She looked quizzically at him.

"Because I just looked it up on Google." He laughed.

Charlie laughed too. "Actually, on the face of it, that sounds like a brilliant idea, otherwise we are going to be rushing around like lunatics trying to get everything done and not seeing any of the sights."

"Exactly! It is not costing me anything for this berth. Boats.co.uk have paid for it until the end of the month. Unfortunately, we can't venture too far until we have had all the servicing done. So, we might as well make the most of it whilst we can. Even if we have to spend three nights in Gibraltar, I won't mind." Bruce had got up and moved over to where Charlie was sitting. She had a small plain pad and had been sketching. "May I see please?" Charlie turned the pad around and showed it to Bruce. Although the sketch had been done fairly quickly and it was all from memory, the drawing was of the *Cape* cruising at speed, the base image was a copy from the picture that Bruce had taken that afternoon. In the middle distance was the unmistakable image of the lighthouse at Cape Agulhas and the background consisted of a huge breaking wave. "Chaaarlieee! That is absolutely brilliant."

"Thank you." She answered modestly. "Have you thought of having an emblem for the *Cape*?"

"No, I haven't, but if I did, it wouldn't be very far off something like this." Bruce sat down next to her on the sofa, continuing to examine the sketch. "So, were you thinking of having an emblem, something like this on all the bed linen and towels?"

"Yes and the glasses."

Bruce turned and looked at her with renewed interest. "Yes, but something like that costs a small fortune and takes forever. It means that you have to submit the drawings to a professional Graphic Designer, then it has to go to someone who has a special machine and they do all the embroidery. Finally, you have to go to someone else to engrave your glass wear."

"Not necessarily." She shook her head gently. "I have access to an Adobe program that would allow me to do the graphic design and save it to an SD card. One of the first things I was hoping to spend my ill-gotten gains on is a sewing machine. I love sewing and making my own clothes. I seriously do little enough around this boat to earn my keep as it is."

"Oh Really! Well for starters, you are the Chief Officer, you are also the Chief Medical Officer, the Chief Diving Officer, you're the Chief Deck Hand and also the chief cook and bottle washer. As for doing nothing around the boat, you are the instigator of midnight swims and all other decadent things. Apart from that." He hugged her. "Why don't we see if our shopping trip might bring an early Easter present." Charlie responded by kissing him lightly on the cheek and hugged him back.

Friday dawned as another beautiful bright Spanish morning, barely a trace of a cloud in the sky with a gentle warm onshore breeze coming in off the Mediterranean Sea. Charlie had commandeered Ivan and his taxi to go off to the shops, whilst Bruce went to have a word with José. Just to let him know that the boat would be away for a time. Miguel and the *Rio Jenil* had left their berth before Bruce and Charlie had got up but he would try them on the radio later. They slipped their moorings a little after ten o'clock and gently headed out into the harbour. Bruce handed the helm over to Charlie, who had a grin on her from ear to ear. She looked like a kid with a new toy. "Bruce?" She asked. "Why is it that you don't use the flybridge whilst we are in or leaving port?"

There was a short pause before he replied. "I guess it's because I have got so used to helming from here, quite apart from the fact that it is so much easier and quicker to get onto the deck. Rather than having to try to rush down the steep stairs in a hurry." Bruce had already loaded his course for Gibraltar into the navigation system. They would head due south and then follow the Spanish coast down past Torremolinos, Marbella and Estepona, keeping just inside the Spanish twelve-mile limit until they entered the sovereign waters of Gibraltar. He had already got out the courtesy flag for Gibraltar, ready to swap with the Spanish one at the appropriate time. As they cleared the port of Malaga, Bruce coached Charlie through the procedure of bringing the *Cape* up onto the new course and up to that delightful mile eating cruise speed of twenty-two knots. Once they were up on course Bruce phoned the Ocean Village Marina from the sat phone and booked a berth for the next two nights giving his estimated time of arrival of twelve forty-five.

This was going to be a relatively short trip but nonetheless, by far the furthest offshore and the longest that he had done with the *Cape*. The blue waters of the Mediterranean sparkled in the morning sun as she ploughed her way west towards Gibraltar. There was quite a bit of shipping but that was mostly out to their port side and in international waters. Being just twelve miles offshore meant that they were well out of sight of the Spanish coast. There were a couple of sailboats further inshore but apart from that, the *Cape* bounded onwards with the thrumming of the big diesels emanating from the stern of the boat. Looking back over the stern the white, dead straight wake gleamed in the sun. Charlie appeared from the galley with two mugs of steaming coffee, placing one in front of Bruce at the helm, taking hers off to the other side of the pilot station and sat down at the chart table.

"Bruce?" Charlie asked. "What would you like to do for an evening meal tonight?"

Bruce turned and looked at her pensively for a moment. "What about you." He paused for a moment. "Why don't you see if you can book us a table at 'Gauchos' for about eight o'clock this evening?" He smiled at her.

"Okay!" she replied. "So, where is that?" She asked.

"Gibraltar, just outside the marina. The number is on my laptop, give them a call from the sat phone."

She laughed as she got up to pick up the phone. "You had this planned all along, didn't you?" Ending the call, she addressed Bruce. "Well, that was easy." Charlie said as she returned the phone to its cradle at the helm, then wrapped her arms around Bruce.

The remainder of the journey was uneventful as the *Cape* moved from Spanish waters to the territorial waters of Gibraltar, Charlie went up onto the flybridge and changed the courtesy flags over. Approaching Gibraltar from the south, they found themselves having to be more aware of shipping, mostly large cargo ships and tankers transiting the Straights of Gibraltar. As they neared land, the tall red and white lighthouse at the southern tip of the peninsula came into view. Behind that, the King Fahad Bin Abdulaziz Al Saud Mosque with its ornate dome and tower could also be seen.

As they neared the entrance to the Ocean Village Marina, a British Airways Airbus three twenty-one made its short final approach onto the runway at Gibraltar. They were so close to the landing aircraft that they could see passengers waving from the windows. The noise from the landing aircraft was surprisingly quiet until the roar of the reverse thrust being implemented once the aircraft touched the ground. Charlie, wearing her skin-tight leggings, waved back to the aircraft from her position on the bow, as she made the anchor ready for deploying in an emergency. At the marina entrance, Bruce checked his watch, they were two minutes early. Picking up the radio microphone and checking the frequency, he keyed the microphone.

"Ocean Village Marina, Ocean Village Marina, this is the motor yacht *Cape Agulhas*. I am at the entrance to the marina and am awaiting berthing instructions. Over."

The accented male voice replied. "*Cape Agulhas*, stand by. I have a tender coming out to guide you in. Over."

Two minutes later and an inflatable tender with a large outboard engine on it came flying out towards them. It aimed straight at the *Cape* and slewed around under the bows. Then a brief conversation ensued between Charlie and the boatman. Bruce saw Charlie key the microphone on her VHF. "Bruce, he is asking if we would like to go alongside or stern on to a pontoon, over?"

Bruce keyed his mic. "Alongside if there is space, tell him we are twenty-six metres. Over." Charlie continued her conversation with the boatman and then straightened up again.

Keying her mic again. "Bruce, he says that we will be going in alongside on our starboard side. Over." They readied the starboard fenders and then proceeded to follow the boatman into the marina, Charlie came back to Bruce at the helm. Pointing to what appeared to be a moored cruise liner, she said. "I think that is the *Sunborn*, some sort of floating hotel"

"Oh, really and how is it that you know that?" Bruce asked.

"Google is great. Isn't it?" Charlie smirked, getting her own back on him. They arrived in a small basin as the boatman indicated the berth to them.

"Okay, this should be an interesting manoeuvre. What I am going to do is come about one hundred and eighty degrees and reverse her in alongside. This is going to be tight as we come about."

"Would you like me to watch the bow, Bruce?"

"Yes please." He replied. "I'll go to the aft control station, just keep talking to me, please." Charlie kissed him briefly on the lips before going forward as Bruce moved to the aft control station. Teasing the main engines, Bruce rotated the *Cape* and then took her in stern first without using any thrusters he completed the manoeuvre. The marina was very popular and busy. The docking procedures had more than drawn a great deal of interest in the manoeuvring boat, not least of all the gorgeous looking Charlie on the bow. That interest also came from the patrons at the 'Wagamama Asian Restaurant', which was right opposite their berthing point. Bruce smiled to himself as he noticed more than one helpful fellow male sailor volunteering to take a line ashore from Charlie.

Engines shut down, shorelines connected, lunch finished, Charlie had changed into something more appropriate for going ashore in. Then they started their shopping spree. Their first port of call was to Top Choice Appliances Ltd on Waterport Road, not being too far to have to walk and as long as they walked at Bruce's pace, he could manage it quite easily. Strolling hand in hand, they entered the shop as Charlie's eyes lit up. "One thing we could do with is a vacuum cleaner. Unless you know that we have one which I haven't found yet?"

"Do you know, you are right, that is one thing we haven't got." Bruce squeezed her hand. "Clever girl."

"We could do with one of those rechargeable ones that will be ever so easy to move around the boat." Charlie pulled Bruce over to the displays of the rechargeable vacuum cleaners. A sales assistant noticed the couple and came over to them. Once Charlie had decided on the model of vacuum they made their way over to the televisions. Bruce explained that he wanted three televisions and where they were going to be installed. The sales assistant found the manager, who assured Bruce that not only would everything he purchased, be delivered to the quayside but they would also carry out the installations and setting up of all three televisions, removing all the packaging for the goods as well. While they were there, Bruce sent Charlie off to have a look at the sewing machines and a suitable roller iron. Once she had made her decisions on the products that she wanted, she found Bruce in a corner, he had spotted the e-scooters. Two of them were also added to the list. It was agreed that all goods would be delivered at nine o'clock the next morning, which would leave sufficient time for the engineers to fit the equipment by midday. That would leave them enough time to spend some time exploring the sights of Gibraltar in the afternoon. They left an incredibly happy store manager behind as they departed the shop.

Outside the store, they caught a bus which took them down to Main Street, they got out as close as they could to Carlos' Photographic Shop. Main Street and the adjoining roads were all pedestrianised, however, not far from Carlos' was Next. Noticing the direction to which Charlie's eyes had been averted, which was towards the Next shop, Bruce encouraged her to go viewing, agreeing that he would join her there. Once in Carlos's shop, Bruce ordered several prints and some suitable frames as well. They spent a good part of the afternoon visiting various ladies outlets. By the time they had finished, they were loaded down with packages. Charlie had some new clothes as well as another two pairs of the form-fitting leggings that Bruce admired so much. They had also visited a Marks and Spencer and secured a king-sized four tog quilt suitable for the master cabin bed and at the same time, two sets of Egyptian cotton bedding.

Following that, they walked the short distance to Vinapolis, where they ordered a few cases of wine and other alcoholic beverages, sufficient to see them through for the next few weeks. At the same time, Bruce was able to re-stock his dwindling supply of Glenmorangie. Charlie had spotted a couple of decanters, one for the whisky and of course, they had to have one for the port as well. Again, delivery had been negotiated and agreed for ten o'clock the next morning.

They spent a romantic evening dining at Gauchos, both agreed that they had just experienced two of the best rib-eye steaks that they could ever remember. During the meal, they had been sitting on opposite sides of the table to each other. When they had finished eating, Charlie moved around to the other side of the table so that they could sit next to each other. It also made it easier to hold hands. They chatted through coffee and discussed how they were going to spend the next two weeks and the time in the UK. One of the possibilities that they decided to look into, was to go out to the Island of Alboran, where they could spend some time carrying out some underwater photography and snorkelling in the rich marine reserve of the island. They brought that forward to as a maybe for the next week but dependant on the weather forecasts of course. They were contemplating finishing off the bottle of wine and paying the bill when a middle-aged couple approached them from one of the other tables. They were both wearing shorts and T-shirts, as against Bruce and Charlie's more formal wearing of slacks, shirts and jackets. He spoke first. "Excuse me, are you the owners of the big cruiser that came in earlier today?"

Charlie replied. "He is, I am just the crewperson." She squeezed Bruce possessively and they all laughed.

"So?" asked Bruce. "Now our covers have been blown. How can we help you?"

"My name is Mike Dunn, this is my wife Sheila. I thought that I recognised you. You are Ron's Dad. I met you when you came to our Regimental Church parade for the armistice last November, only you were in a wheelchair then."

Bruce concentrated and remembered the day in question. Then, remembering all the faces that he had met at the post-service Officers Mess luncheon. He recalled the man and his charming wife. "I am so sorry." Bruce responded and stood up proffering his right hand in greeting. "Of course, I recognise you now, I didn't recognise you out of uniform and probably because you have now got a bit more facial hair." He added laughingly, referring to Mike's beard. "Let me introduce you to Charlie. She is my partner and friend for life." They all laughed. "Please sit down. Would you like a glass of wine?"

The waiter had caught Bruce's eye and came across to the table. Another bottle of Rioja and an additional two glasses quickly appeared at the table. Glasses charged and once pleasantries had been exchanged, Bruce asked. "So, what are you two guys up to out here?"

"I was given a medical discharge with PTSD. Ron had told me that you were going out to Spain and were in the process of buying a boat. So, with my lump sum, we decided that we would opt for the good life in the sun and use my qualifications to do some diving instruction. I got a job with Dolphin Safari. I start on Monday. We were in the marina looking at a catamaran which we were interested in buying instead of a house or flat when we saw you sail in. Are you based in Gibraltar now?"

"No." Replied Bruce. "At the moment we are based in Malaga but only because the boat is going in to be serviced and anti-fouled at the end of the month. Then the world will be our oyster, so to speak. Registration wise, we are Portsmouth registered. God! I have to take a leak." Bruce excused himself as he went looking for the toilets. When he got back to the table, he found the three of them happily in deep conversation about the merits of diving in the Mediterranean Sea and of course, the best places to go. The evening ended with the Dunn's heading back off to their bed and breakfast accommodation and Charlie issuing them an invitation for dinner the next evening.

As they ambled back to the *Cape* in silence, their arms linked, Charlie stopped them. "Bruce!"

"Yes, Charlie."

"Bruce, thank you for the way you included me during the conversation. It was always 'we' or 'us' and never 'me' or an 'I' and I hope that you didn't mind me inviting them for dinner tomorrow night?"

Turning to face Charlie and taking her face in his hands. "I am absolutely fine about the dinner invite. In fact, I am really looking forward to it." He paused. "Charlie, whether you like it or not, you have never been a crew member to me, despite the verbal contract that we agreed on. I welched on the contract the first time you touched me and sent the most incredible vibes through my body. Now I just want to spend the rest of my life with you. So, now we live on the *Cape* and if you want to entertain people or invite them on to the boat, then that is fine. The *Cape* is as much your home as it is mine." He pulled her face down to him and kissed her very softly on the lips. "Now, I just hope that I haven't said too much and put you off."

Charlie responded by putting one arm around his neck, the other around his waist and pulled their bodies together as she passionately returned his kiss. When they pulled their lips apart, Bruce looked into Charlie's eyes. There was a hint of a tear at the corner of her eyes. Gently he wiped these away with his thumbs then they laughed at each other. "Now, look what you have done. You've got me behaving like a love-struck teenager." Charlie countered as they continued on their way back to the *Cape*.

Saturday morning was pandemonium on the quayside. The Top Choice van appeared spot on nine o'clock and parked next to the *Cape*. The e-scooters were unpacked and put on charge, as was the vacuum cleaner. The sewing machine and iron were also unpacked and set up in the crew quarters. The televisions were installed and set up. At ten past ten, the van bearing the inscription of 'Valapinos' also came onto the quayside and the wines, whiskies, port and gin found their way into various storage areas supervised by Charlie. The decanters were filled and placed on top of the sideboard. The fifty-four-inch television went into the salon and was mounted on the platform which raised it up and down on a plinth. The thirty-two inch was installed in the forward VIP cabin, which Bruce and Charlie were still occupying. Charlie had insisted that she wanted everything perfect in the master cabin before they moved in, which was where the third forty-inch television set ended up. In fairness to the Top Choice lads, they had everything finished, which included removing all the packaging and both Bruce and Charlie suitably instructed in the operation of the televisions by midday.

Bruce and Charlie were sat in the cockpit just finishing lunch in the sunshine, looking out over the marina when a holler from the quayside reached them. "Ahoy the *Cape Agulhas*!" Both Bruce and Charlie stood up to see who it was that was calling them. A gentleman, possibly quite a lot older than Bruce, was on the quayside. He was wearing grey flannel trousers and a navy blue blazer with some sort of badge on the left breast pocket, his head adorned by a white straw hat.

"How can I help?" Bruce asked, wiping his mouth with a piece of tissue.

"I am looking for the bounder that owns this boat?" Came the extremely well-spoken response from the quayside.

"You are looking at him." Bruce replied, not suppressing his annoyance at the question.

"Ahh! Has the boat recently changed hands, Sir?"

"Yes!" Replied Bruce. "And you are?"

"I do beg your pardon, Sir, I am George Lucas, Vice Commodore at the Royal Gibraltar Yacht Club. The previous owner of this boat was a member of the club, it appears that he has skipped town leaving a rather hefty bar bill. Of course, when you entered harbour yesterday, you were seen by a couple of members who subsequently informed me."

"I am sorry to hear that. How do I address you? Commodore? Would you like to step aboard?"

"Thank you, just George will do. We don't stand on formalities you know." George stepped onto the deck of the *Cape*, removing his shoes as he did.

Bruce extended his right hand in greeting. "I am Bruce Williams, this is Charlie…"

George had interrupted Bruce. "Lovely to meet you Mr Williams, Mrs Williams."

"No, no!" Bruce smiled. "It is just Bruce and Charlie and we …." Again, Bruce was interrupted.

"It's lovely to meet you, Charlie." George enthused.

"Would you like some refreshment George? We have some ready-made squash or perhaps something a little bit stronger?" Charlie asked, being the perfect hostess.

"Ooohh! Is it ever too early for a G and T?" George asked.

"No, I don't suppose so." Charlie smiled charmingly. "I am afraid that we don't have any bitters. But ice and a slice?"

"That will do nicely." George replied, parking his backside on the chair that Bruce had been occupying. "Ahhh! This is wonderfully comfortable indeed. She really is a beauty." Bruce wasn't sure if the comment was directed at Charlie or the *Cape*.

Excusing herself, Charlie cleared away the lunch plates and went to fix George's G and T.

"So, what are your plans for the *Cape Agulhas*? Are you planning to base yourself out here in Gib?"

Bruce started to explain that he was retired and that they were planning to cruise the Mediterranean when Charlie re-appeared with George's G and T and sat down next to Bruce on the sofa drawing her feet up under her.

"Yes, very strange chap, the previous owner was." George continued. "I believe that he used to run charters, she was Maltese registered, the *Cape* was as I recall, however, rumour had it that he was very heavily involved with some of the Russian underworld. Still, I see that you now have her registered in Portsmouth. Good move old chap."

"What nationality was the previous owner then?" Bruce asked.

"Oh! He was English, I think, frightfully well-spoken chap if you know what I mean. Claimed he had been up to Cambridge and all that." George took a pull at his drink and a third of it disappeared. "Come to think of it I thought that he had some property here in Gib because otherwise, he wouldn't have been eligible to join the club, if you see what I mean."

"What was his name, do you recall?" Bruce asked.

"Yes!" George extended the word in thought. "Donaldson, I seem to recall."

Bruce shook his head in thought. Strange, that hadn't been the name he had seen on the transfer papers for the *Cape*. Bruce decided to keep this information to himself.

Bruce nodded his head. "Surely you can trace him through his property here in Gibraltar in that case. Do you recall what he looked like?"

"Ahhh! Yes of course, why didn't I think of that before. He was quite a tall chap, had wavy blond hair. Anyway, must be getting on, can't keep the memsahib waiting you know." George picked up his glass and drained the liquid from it in a single swallow. "Look, if you are down this way again, we would love to extend you temporary membership of the club. Do look me up, won't you."

Bruce picked up George's glass as he watched him disappear down the quay.

Bruce and Charlie spent the afternoon going to visit some of the sights. They managed the Governor's Residence, the Trafalgar Memorial and the Cable car trip up to the summit of the rock. Then they walked across to the Skye Walk Station. On their way back to the *Cape*, they discussed the evening meal. Charlie was planning a Chicken Fajita mix served on a bed of rice with sour cream and guacamole.

Getting back to the *Cape* just after five o'clock, Charlie started to prepare the evening meal, as their guests were not due until seven for half-past seven, Bruce decided to give his eldest son Ron a call. After all, he hadn't spoken to anyone from his family since he had left for Spain. The evening was wonderful. Charlie was a natural-born hostess, wearing a red dress with white spots which accentuated her figure with the hem of the dress coming to well above her knees. After their guests had left, they had curled up on the sofa with a nightcap of recently resupplied Glenmorangie. The dishwasher was whirring away in the galley and they could hear the night sounds of the marina in the background. Charlie changed her position by stretching out on the sofa and placed her head in Bruce's lap, sighing, she said. "I really enjoyed this evening Bruce, thank you for letting me do it."

"Charlie, entertaining is very obviously something you love doing, so you just carry on because I love you doing it. And by the way, you look absolutely gorgeous." He said pulling her head into his stomach. She lifted her left knee and the edge of the dress fell away exposing her left thigh to her flimsy French knicker line.

The *Cape Agulhas* cleared the Port of Gibraltar at eleven o'clock the next morning, informing the port authorities that she was bound for Malaga. This time they stayed close to the coastline remaining for the most part no more than a half-mile out. It made the relatively short journey back to Malaga more interesting as they could make out the beaches of Estepona, Marbella, Fuengirola and Torremolinos. They took turns at driving the *Cape*, delighting in the handling of the sixty-ton boat cruising effortlessly at twenty-two knots. As they were passing Fuengirola, they closed to within four hundred yards of the coast, that was when they were joined by three jet ski riders who made the most of jumping the wake of the *Cape* until they passed out of range. The jet skiers all rode sensibly, staying safely away from the stern of the boat. The riders waved their hands in friendly acknowledgement and farewell as the *Cape* passed on up the coast towards Malaga. The trip up along the coast was enlightening as both Bruce and Charlie, visually and from confirmation of the chart plotter, found several interesting areas which were definitely worthy of further investigation for snorkelling and diving as well as underwater photography. As they came up past Torremolinos, Bruce spotted them first, about two hundred yards off their starboard quarter, a small pod of Common Dolphins. Charlie had been on the computer and was researching the local area for diving opportunities when Bruce said. "Charlie, come and have a look at our escort." He brought the throttles down and slowed the boat down to five knots, keeping pace with the pod. Charlie was thrilled and brought the binoculars over to get an enhanced view of the dolphins. Before long, the dolphins headed further out to sea, Bruce pushed the throttles open, bringing the *Cape* back up to her comfortable cruise speed, Charlie returned to her local research on the computer.

As the *Cape* came up into the Malaga marina, preparing to berth, they were greeted by waves and hola's from José and his family, which made Bruce feel all deep and warm inside. It was almost like coming home after a long trip. The two sentries from the *Rio Jenil* that were on duty, joined in the greetings as well. Both of them slinging their machine carbines on their backs as they readied themselves to take the lines from the *Cape* as she came alongside the pontoon. It was just after half-past three in the afternoon when Bruce and Charlie had completed berthing and coupling up shorelines for power and freshwater. Clouds had bubbled up from the southwest, promising to put a damp ending to the sunny weekend. Bruce had got the freshwater hose out and was engaged in spraying off the saltwater from the tender and swim platform, which would always get wet whilst underway. Charlie was at the bow carrying out a similar exercise with fresh water, just to get rid of any other salt deposits from the spray. That was when Miguel came over to where Bruce was on the swim platform.

From the quayside, he asked. "Bruce, this man, Hopkiss, how is it that you recognised him?"

Bruce looked over to Miguel. "Is this official or unofficial?"

"Very unofficial."

"Hopkiss, he was a sergeant, cook, with the British Army. Various organisations, including the Military Police, were interested in him for people and drug smuggling. My organisation, with its special skills were asked to keep an eye on him. The British Military Police in Iraq gained intelligence that he was about to send out a large consignment of drugs. These were going to be flown out by a floatplane, from a lake near the town of Karbala. This is sort of southwest of Baghdad. So, we got the drop on him and we captured him. Basically, that is all I know about the bastard. The only reason that I recognised him, was that my team and I had spent quite a lot of time watching him. He obviously didn't have a clue as to who I was though." Bruce concluded just as Charlie came down to the stern.

"Yes, I see. Hello Charlie. How are you?" Miguel greeted her, then addressing both of them. "Look, why don't you come and join us for a coffee?" He asked.

Charlie nodded her greeting to Miguel and said. "Lovely idea, I'll just slip a pair of jeans on." She was wearing a new pair of skin-tight leggings. Bruce was beginning to consider that this was Charlie's standard sailing gear.

They joined Miguel and Clarissa at an inside table as José came bustling over to take their order for coffee. Clarissa, whose English was nowhere as good as Miguel's, was chatting to Charlie in Spanish.

"So, Bruce. What else can you tell me about this man Hopkiss?" Miguel asked.

"Not a lot. I think that he had strong links with an eastern bloc underworld of one form or another. I am afraid that at that time, I had considerably more on my mind. I just lost track after the day we got our hands on him." Bruce shook his head apologetically. "Is he not talking to you?"

"We have handed him over to the Policia Nationale but now no one will tell me anything. I think that he is, how do you say, slippery." Miguel looked disappointed.

"So, what about my charts?" Bruce asked.

"They too were handed over to the Policia Nationale. They insisted I am afraid, Bruce."

Charlie had stopped her conversation with Clarissa and was listening to the conversation that Bruce and Miguel were involved in. Bruce leaned back in his chair, stirring his coffee with care. "So, I suppose those charts will have disappeared off the face of the earth as well." Bruce said dejectedly.

"What was on those charts, Bruce? Did you work out what the coordinates were?" Miguel asked.

Bruce explained about the charts omitting to mention the pinpricks that they had discovered. Charlie watched Bruce apprehensively and brought Clarissa up to speed as to what the conversation had been about.

"To be perfectly honest." Bruce continued. "I am really glad that I have got rid of those charts at least we won't be having any more midnight visits. I mean I am supposing that Van de Niekerk and Hopkiss are working for the same organisation?"

"I don't know. As far as I know, he is still in hospital being guarded by the Policia Nationale. I will try to make some more enquiries during the week."

The topic of conversation changed as Bruce and Charlie gave accounts of their weekend in Gibraltar with the story of George raising a laugh all around. Both Miguel and Clarissa had noted how close Bruce and Charlie had become in such a short space of time.

CHAPTER 10

Bruce and Charlie returned to the *Cape* just in time to avoid the rain as it started to pour down. Dinner was a beautiful Bolognese accompanied by a bottle of The Guv'nor, after which they both cleared the dishes and tidied up. The topic of conversation was the program for the next two weeks leading up to the *Cape* being removed from the water and their subsequent departure back to England. They both concluded that it was preferential for them to explore the coast local to the nearby area rather than being trapped five hours out to sea off the Island of Alboran, especially as storms could blow up off the African coast very quickly at this time of the year. Bruce wanted the *Cape's* engines serviced before pushing them too far, although the big nineteen hundred horsepower engines would probably be able to push the *Cape* all day and every day at her full power if he asked them to.

They spent the rest of the evening curled up on the sofa watching some catch-up television on the big new screen, then came the news with Brexit and the Coronavirus being the main topics. Not realising how much the Coronavirus or Covid nineteen would affect them in the future. They both groaned, turned off the TV and made their way down to their cabin. They still hadn't moved into the Master cabin. Charlie had wanted to launder the new bedding before she put it on the bed. They showered separately, retaining a degree of modesty although the bathroom door had been left open through which they continued to chat. Bruce had raised the topic of diving and was surprised to learn how things like decompression tables had changed. They were very much more stringent in this modern world. Charlie was in absolute disbelief when Bruce had described and explained his first Draeger triple tank set, which had a negative buoyancy. Equally, Bruce was in awe with regards to modern setups and dive computers and how they worked.

Bruce came out of the bathroom following his shower Charlie was sat with her legs crossed at the dressing table, putting the finishing touches to her hair. She was wearing an almost sheer negligee with a pair of matching knickers.

Bruce gulped. "Wow! You look gorgeous."

She smiled at the compliment. "Right, you. On that bed, let's have a look at that leg, especially as we missed it last night." She went into the bathroom and got the towel that she had reserved for the leg treatment and the oils, sitting herself down on the edge of the bed. When she had finished with the leg, she moved further up the bed and started to work on his left arm. Bruce had had his eyes closed but opened them again when Charlie moved. Bruce could feel the warmth from her body as their hips touched. Delighting in the sensuous feeling and the gentle fragrance that issued from her body.

"Do you know Charlie Hope that you are the most beautiful woman I have ever seen."

She stopped massaging briefly as she looked at him with a wry smile. "Not so beautiful in one place, but you can keep passing me those compliments all day and every day."

Her face was close to Bruce's and he could smell the natural freshness of her breath. Bruce came up slowly on his left elbow. "Really! I think that I have just about seen all of you that there is to see, you are pretty well uninhibited, I mean that in the nicest possible way. I will just say that I am not complaining."

Charlie smiled. "Oh good, so I got your attention then."

"No, not really. I am afraid that you are going to have to try a little harder. So where are you not beautiful then? We haven't showered together yet." He smiled at her.

Charlie had a serious look on her face and said. "Do you remember I told you that I had been wounded in the lower abdomen?" She stood up slowly.

"Yes!" Bruce replied as he swung his feet over the edge of the bed.

Charlie faced Bruce. Her navel was at his eye level two feet from his nose, as she slowly lifted the short negligee to just above the level of the top of her knickers, which in turn she slowly pulled down, exposing the top of her pubic hair. The puckered wound glared at Bruce. It weaved a diagonal course, from a level just below and to the right of her navel to a point just above the top of her pubic bush.

"Oh my God! Charlie!" Bruce stammered. He gently pulled her towards him and kissed the scar across her abdomen several times. Charlie's instinct was to pull away from him, but then she realised that his actions depicted a genuine tenderness for her. "You are still the most beautiful woman in the world. Everywhere!" Bruce started to stand up. Charlie took his face in her hands and kissed him on his lips with such passion that she felt the incredible desire for sex well up inside her. This was a desire that had not been aroused in her for a long time as she felt the warmth deep down inside her. Bruce's penis felt massive as he pushed gently against her as she felt the throbbing hardness of the flesh. It wasn't an act of desire, only that of natural arousal that was pure and a cause of the circumstance. The situation having been brought about because there wasn't an awful lot of space between the edge of the bed and the bulkhead. Still standing to the edge of the bed, she gently parted his lips and delicately inserted her tongue in his mouth. Every contour of their bodies touched, for the most part, separated only by the negligee that she was wearing. Bruce's robe had fallen open exposing the front of his body, save for the underpants he was wearing. Bruce put his arms around her and slowly ran his hands down her back till he reached the top of her buttocks. His left hand came back around the side of her body and moved up to her right breast, gently caressing it, his thumb finding the erect nipple. His right hand remained on her back, slowly moving up and down teasing the top of the crack of her buttocks.

He had found her sweet spot as she moaned, thrusting her pelvis forward gently gyrating. Charlie felt the heat and dampness that ensued from her vagina, her clitoris had extended as she became further aroused. Had she taken him too far? If she tried to stop him now, how would he react? Questions went through her mind, could she stop if she wanted to? No!

"My God! Charlie, what are you doing to me?" He groaned. His penis felt that it was going to explode. It was years since he'd had sex, let alone a hard-on like this.

"Bruce, do you trust me?" Her voice was husky with her arousal.

"Yes! Of course." He nuzzled her neck.

Pushing him gently back onto the bed, she bent, removing his underwear with one swift move, simultaneously removing her knickers. Then removing her negligee, she straddled his hips.

Her breasts were beautiful, taught and creamy, nipples enlarged and looking like ripe cherries. Bruce reached up and gently cupped a breast in each hand as she bent down, offering them to his mouth. Gently, in turn he sucked on each nipple, stirring emotions in what was left of her uterus that she had never ever felt before. She could feel the fluids escaping around the sides of the tampon. Charlie groaned in ecstasy. 'This was going to be messy'. As she gently gyrated her hips over his penis. Straightening her knees, she lay across the top of Bruce. Then she reached down and took hold of his swollen penis and placing it between her buttock cheeks and moved her hips in an up and down movement. It didn't take long. Bruce moaned as he ejaculated. That was enough to finish Charlie as she felt the hot fluid explode from Bruce's penis. Charlie climaxed as never before. Sobbing, she collapsed onto Bruce burying her head in his neck as she pulsed with the sobs as her climaxes continued. Clenching her buttocks together with each pulse. Bruce could feel the warmth of her tears on his neck and that of her fluids as she climaxed again and again. He reached up with his right hand and put it on the back of her head, shushing her at the same time. Her climaxes passed whilst Bruce continued to hold her head into his shoulder.

She sniffed. "Oh my God! Oh my God! Bruce Williams, what have you done to me? Oh, God! What a mess!" She felt the congealing fluids around their crotches. "Tell you what, you stay still, whilst I get you something to clean up with but just give me a few moments in the bathroom. If you don't mind?"

"Charlie, I am as much to blame. Hell! I have never experienced anything like this before either. Get yourself sorted darling, then I'll grab a shower when you are ready. Okay?"

Charlie got off Bruce, grabbing her discarded negligee. She stuffed it between her legs, heading for the bathroom. "Charlie." Bruce called. She stopped and turned to face him. "You are truly the most beautiful person in the whole wide world." Charlie grinned at him before gently closing the bathroom door, leaving Bruce to reflect on the last ten minutes. He had never felt so elated, somehow, he and Charlie had some form of fantastic ability to satisfy each other so completely. Replaying the last ten minutes in his mind, Bruce found himself in a state of semi arousal. Saved by the door of the bathroom opening and a naked Charlie towelling herself off.

"Your turn." She said.

They went to sleep in each other's arms and awoke with Charlie spooning herself into Bruce's back in the middle of the bed. Charlie stretched and Bruce turned over. As he did so, she enfolded him in her arms and kissed him lightly on the lips and pulled his head gently to her breasts. He snuggled gratefully into the warmth and softness of her flesh and nearly went back to sleep, save for the fact that he had a full bladder making it an urgent necessity for him to have to urinate. His penis was rigid and a little sore from the activities of the previous night.

The day had dawned grey and misty with drizzling rain. By the time Bruce and Charlie had gone up to the main deck to get breakfast, it was nine o'clock. The *Rio Jenil* was not on her berth on the other side of the pontoon, the drizzle had increased to heavy rain. They opened the blinds to the rain pouring down the windows and very few people on the quayside, other than those dashing about their business. During breakfast, Charlie turned to Bruce. "You are very quiet this morning. Is everything okay?"

"Yes! Oh yes!" He replied. "I just feel guilty about having taken advantage of you last night. I really hadn't meant for that to happen."

"What, no way." She replied softly, coming around the table and perched herself gently on his lap. "I am the one that led you on. I just can't get over what we achieved together. In truth, words fail me, my darling. You are the only man to have made me orgasm. Ever!" She hugged him around the neck. "I was thinking just yesterday afternoon that it has been just over a week since we came into each other's lives, for most of that time we have hardly been separated. Now we have been lovers and I am not regretting a single second of it." She looked tenderly at him as she caressed the long hair at the back of his neck and looked deeply into the blue eyes. He reached up and kissed her affectionately on the lips.

"Do you mind if I ask you a personal question?"

Getting up off his lap, conscious of the degree of discomfort it must have been causing his leg, she replied. "No, of course not."

"There must have been a lot of damage to the area around your womb however you still menstruate. Does that mean you are still able to bear children?"

She sat down at the chair next to him and held his hand as he asked the question, concern on his face and in his voice. "No, I can't have children. When I was injured, I was menstruating at the time and there is still a small part of my uterus left in my body. So, a combination of the two means that I still have a period, but not all the time. When I went for a swim the other evening, I wasn't kidding you. I thought that I was never going to see the light of day again. That plus the shock and near hypothermia, has given me the granddaddy of all periods. Mentally, maybe I went back to the time when I thought that I was going to die in Afghan." She smiled at him and concluded. "Of course, a lot of this is all your fault.

"Oh! How so?"

!Because I fell in love with you and all sorts of strange things start to happen down there to a woman when she falls in love. Not to mention you have literally been my saviour."

Bruce smiled back at her. "Come here you." Taking her gently in his arms and squeezing her.

As they weren't going to go anywhere outside, Charlie wanted to finish getting the master cabin ready for them to move into and at the same time, she also wanted to play with the sewing machine as well. Bruce decided that he would go down to the crew quarters and tidy everything up and store everything in a better fashion so that Charlie could set up the sewing machine. He finished just before lunch. The rain had eased off and the sun was threatening to come out as he felt a lightness in his step when he re-entered the main salon. Charlie appeared at the head of the stairs and beckoned him below, leading him to their new cabin. She had moved everything in from the forward cabin and had then stored all their clothing and goods in their rightful places in the master cabin.

"So now I'll never be able to find anything." He joked.

"That's right. So, now you'll have to ask me for everything. Now I will be invaluable to you and you will never be able to afford to get rid of me." They hugged each other. "Come on sailor, let's get you some lunch."

Once lunch was over, they had cleared away and washed up. Bruce and Charlie went aft down into the crew area and discussed the best place to set up Charlie's sewing machine. Once that was set up, Charlie gave it a quick test on some cotton fabric that she had magicked up from somewhere. Her skill with the machine was impressive as she sewed the letters B and C freehand onto the cotton fabric. Returning to the pilot station, Charlie settled herself in front of Bruce's computer and set about playing with the design of a logo that she had in mind.

The rain had stopped and suspiciously Bruce looked up to the sky, finally deciding that it was safe to do so, he started to do a quick window clean. He was still on deck when the *Rio Jenil* appeared and was about to start her manoeuvre onto her berth. Bruce stepped off the deck onto the pontoon and stood by, ready to take the forward line as she came alongside. The young Lieutenant leaned out of the bridge access and rudely waved Bruce away from the side of the pontoon. Bruce shrugged his shoulders in resignation and stepped back onto the *Cape*. The Lieutenant was giving the boat far too much throttle and was constantly shouting orders at his crew. The *Rio Jenil* was heading backwards far too fast. 'This could be a rough landing'. Bruce thought. Realising his mistake, the Lieutenant gave the *Rio Jenil* full throttle ahead, which unfortunately didn't stop the boat in time before she ran back into the quay with some force. Bouncing off the quay, with her engines set at full ahead, the *Rio Jenil* leapt forward, knocking the crew to the deck. The Lieutenant, whose head had been stuck out of the bridge access, banged into the metal mullion knocking his cap flying into the marina. The Lieutenant fell to the deck like a sack of spuds. Another of the bridge officers managed to take over the controls, succeeding in subduing the forward charge of the boat before any further damage could be caused. Charlie had heard the ensuing over-revving of the engine, she had looked up from the chart table, taking in the event. Bruce turned to Charlie and was about to warn her of the event when he saw her back disappearing down to where the first aid kit was stored. The *Rio Jenil* came back onto the pontoon at a far more sedate pace. This time Bruce's offer to take the mooring line was gratefully received. The boat was still sliding back when Charlie vaulted the rail and went straight to the fallen Lieutenant. 'This will cost someone some report writing.' Bruce thought. 'And this time it isn't going to be me'. Charlie had the injured Lieutenant on his back. He was conscious, and one of the sailors was holding his officers head straight whilst Charlie wound a dressing around his head. Staunching the bleeding and speaking reassuringly to him in Spanish whilst insisting that he remain where he was and very still.

It wasn't long before the ambulance arrived. With care, the medics got the Lieutenant onto a gurney stretcher and assisted by a couple of the crew, got him onto the quayside where the ambulance was parked. Miguel arrived just as the ambulance was departing and after having had a quick briefing from the crew, he thanked Charlie for her help. Returning on board the *Cape*, Bruce couldn't help thinking, that was the third time that blues and two's had been at the pontoon in the space of a week. Charlie returned to the computer just as the sat phone rang, answering it she discovered that it was Mike Dunn. They had been doing some internet surfing and thought that they had found a suitable boat for themselves to live in. Having seen the *Cape,* they had decided to look for a motor cruiser instead of a sailboat and had booked a viewing of a fifty-four foot, fifteen-year-old Prestige with twin Penta engines. Nowhere as refined as the *Cape*, however, they thought that it would be more practical for them than the sailing catamaran that they had been looking at. The Prestige was lying at the small port of Puerto Banus just west of Marbella. They were going to drive up to see it the following Saturday and asked if they could borrow Bruce and Charlie's expertise in looking over the cruiser. When Charlie told Bruce, he agreed to it willingly. Then Bruce had an idea. "Charlie? How would you feel if we were to take the *Cape* down to Puerto Banus, check out the Prestige with them and then all four of us can do some snorkelling, then they could spend Saturday night with us?"

"Brilliant idea." She smiled. "I get to practise my entertaining skills again."

Charlie went off to phone Sheila to update her on the arrangements and then disappeared back to her sewing machine. Forty-five minutes later, Charlie found Bruce sat at the chart table reading the owner's manual for the quad. Which he still hadn't tried out. This wasn't going to be possible until he had the registration documents and plates made for it. Unfortunately, that was going have to be something that he would have to wait for until he got back to the UK.

"I have got something to show you." Charlie exclaimed excitedly. She was almost jumping up and down with excitement.

"What?" He queried, smiling at her excitement.

From behind her back, she produced a navy blue baseball-style cap, presenting it to Bruce, with the peak facing him. It read CAPE AGULHAS the printing was arched, beneath it was the word CAPTAIN. On the peak of the cap, she had printed ornate gold leaf in keeping with the decoration expected with the status of a Captains headwear. Then she put it on his head. Bruce laughed, Charlie produced a second cap which again had the arched inscription CAPE AGULHAS and underneath it, was printed the word MATE. Just in front of the word, MATE, in small letters was the word Captains. Bruce hugged her "Time for a beer, methinks mate."

Having arranged to meet the Dunn's at Puerto Banus on the following Saturday, Bruce and Charlie spent the next five days taking the *Cape* out to various locations on the Costa del Sol and snorkelling in the clear inland, sheltered coves. They combined this with giving the Seabob plenty of exercise. The machine operated as well on the surface as underwater. It was possible to tow a passenger at up to fourteen knots. On the surface, it was exhilarating. Underwater the speed became face distorting and exciting as the rider guided the scooter amongst the rocks and seaweed on the seafloor. The sensation was simply amazing. The gentle hum that the motor and impeller emitted didn't seem to frighten the fish, it was possible to get closer to them than while just swimming. They took turns riding it solo and then allowing the machine to tow them as a pair, the forward and rear-mounted cameras providing some hilarious footage along with some excellent footage of the marine wildlife. Charlie was impressed with Bruce when she discovered that he could manage an easy forty five-second free dive. The highlight came on Friday afternoon when Bruce and Charlie were, for want of a better term, cavorting, in the water with the Seabob, which was now referred to as *Bobbi*, when they were suddenly aware of a small pod of Common Dolphins watching their antics. Although the dolphins appeared quite shy and wouldn't allow themselves to be touched, it was an incredible experience swimming slowly, hand in hand, so close and alongside the mammals, nor did they seem to mind the Seabob. The dolphin's visit lasted just over a half-hour, so making their total time in the water just one and a half hours, exhausting both the Seabob battery and Bruce.

Bruce pulled himself up onto the swim platform. His left leg ached with the exertion of having worn swim fins whilst swimming with the dolphins and the added resistance of the fins in the water. He supposed that the exercise must be doing the leg some good and strengthening it up. Although the sea was a relatively cool fifteen degrees, the sun was warm, Bruce was elated with the intimacy that they had shared with dolphins, but the leg ached and started to go into cramp. Charlie followed him up onto the swim platform, which they had partially submerged for the very purpose of making it easier to access the water and for that matter, to return to the boat. She shook her head as cascades of water flew from her hair and caught the early afternoon sun in a glittering array of the colours of the spectrum. "Oh wow! That was an awesome experience." She gushed, glancing over to Bruce and noting the pain on his face. The smile vanished. She had already removed her fins and tethered the Seabob before leaving the water, she moved straight over to Bruce. "Oh, honey, sweetheart, come on, let's get those fins off." Together they swung his legs over and got the fins off and in no time, she went straight to the root of the pain. Bruce grimaced as Charlie gently applied pressure to ease the cramp. Three minutes of gentle ministrations by Charlie and the pain had subsided sufficiently for Bruce to stand up and start to remove his wet suit. Slowly between them, they got his legs out of the neoprene as he sat on the edge of the deck, letting the warmth of the sun work its magic on his body. He could feel the warmth going deep into his leg. It just felt so good.

Charlie started to remove her wet suit, under which she was wearing a red one-piece costume that did everything to accentuate her firm bosom, cleavage and hips. She stood in front of him, hands on hips, a vision of loveliness. The 'V' at the crutch of the bathing costume, very much highlighting the shape of her labia. "How's the leg now?" She inquired. Doctor Hope was very much back in business again.

"Yeah, it has eased off a lot now, thanks, hun." Bruce replied with a grin. Charlie moved over and sat next to him on the edge of the deck, their shoulders intimately touching each other. Five minutes passed by then Charlie decided that she would go and make some tea. Bruce feeling considerably better for having had the massage and the rest got up, rinsed off and hung up the two wetsuits. Charlie returned with the tea, only to find that Bruce had gone into the crew area and was in the shower, naked, rinsing off his bathing costume and himself. Putting the two mugs of tea on the table next to the washing machine, she stepped into the shower.

"Room for a little one?" She asked as she stepped into the shower stall, still wearing her swimsuit. Bruce smiled and moved over to allow her to get in under the water. Bruce had set the shower to rainfall and in the proximity of the stall, their bodies touched, separated only by the thin material of Charlie's swimsuit. Slowly their heads came together, their lips met. Bruce reached his hands up, gently brushing Charlie's breasts. There was a hint of a faint gasp as tongues explored each other's mouths. They were about to embark on only their second bout of lovemaking. Bruce hooked his thumbs into the shoulder straps of the swimsuit and gently pulled the straps down, freeing her breasts from the constraints of the costume. The feeling of delight was felt by both of them as naked nipple touched naked chest. Charlie could feel the warmth spreading down inside her as she felt Bruce's erect penis pushing against her labia. Bruce gently disengaged from the mouth to mouth contact and moved his hands down to encompass both her buttocks, at the same time, he nuzzled into her neck, then gradually moved his mouth down to her breasts and her hardened nipples. Charlie fondled the back of his neck and gently pulled his head into her breasts, enjoying the sensation that it brought to her deep down. Bruce moved his hands inside her costume, fondling her buttocks and pulling her body into

119

his torso. Disengaging from Charlie's breasts, Bruce moved his head down to Charlie's waist and gently pulled the swimsuit down past her buttocks to a point just above her knees. Charlie obliged by lifting her right leg up and out of the costume, allowing it to slip to the floor, draping itself around her left foot on the floor of the cubicle. Going down on one knee, Bruce was at eye level with her womanhood. He knew that she took care of her intimate bits, but this was the first time he had seen her this close. Charlie was not totally devoid of pubic hair, the area was neatly trimmed and lined in a 'V' shape, which would allow her to wear a thong bikini, should she ever choose to do so. Bruce leant forward, tilting his head slightly to one side, he kissed the top of her labia, inserting his tongue in as deep as he could. As he did so, Charlie gently pushed her hips forward, the better to encourage his actions. Charlie moaned with ecstasy but knowing how uncomfortable it was for him kneeling on the cubicle floor, she very reluctantly and gently pulled him up. Charlie turned within the encirclement of his arms to turn the shower off and felt his hands slide up her wet torso and encompass a breast in each hand. At the same time, she felt his rigid penis between her buttocks. The feeling was one of pure ecstasy as she gyrated her buttocks, gently pushing back into his manhood. Slowly, she turned to face him again.

"Oh my God, I really want you inside me. Now!" Her voice was urgently husky. Being nearest the door Bruce opened the cubicle door and stepped out, grabbing the two draped towels, that had been left next to the shower. Passing one to Charlie, he went into one of the crew's cabins and got a foredeck sunbathing cushion out, which he put on the floor. Nowhere near dry, he gently pulled Charlie down beside him. She didn't need any encouragement at all and propped herself up one elbow.

"Brucie?" Her voice was still husky with sensual desire. She had never felt like this before. "Do you still trust me?" She started to roll on top of him. Bruce shifted under her to help on the narrow cushion, in the equally narrow passageway.

"You know I do, with my life."

"I need you to know that my hole, you know down here." She emphasised the hole with a gentle thrust of her pelvis. "Is very small and I need to be very careful how you go in there. I need you to let me do everything.

Please. Trust me!" She kissed his mouth and put her tongue between his lips. Charlie's legs were apart as she moved to a kneeling position. Taking Bruce's erect penis in her hand, she gently rubbed his glans in the folds of her labia. Bruce groaned with euphoria from the sensation that it brought. The urge not to thrust up into her was overwhelming, then it happened. Charlie, herself moaning with the pleasurable elation that her actions were giving her. Then it was as if by magic, she felt his penis slip up into her vagina. No pain, pausing momentarily at the sensation of having the throbbing penis inside her, Charlie gradually sat down further onto his hips until Bruce's penis was fully inserted into her body. They remained still not daring to move, they both could feel each other's sexual muscles throbbing. Gently, Charlie started to move her body, as she felt the orgasm coming from somewhere low in her stomach. Bruce had been fighting for self-control and writhed under her as she pushed her body harder onto Bruce's pelvis in a wanton act to impale herself further on his penis. Bruce could feel his orgasm welling up inside of him and finally, it exploded deep from somewhere low on his back. Charlie felt Bruce's hot fluid deep inside her and moaned as her climax caused her to cry out in ecstatic delight. A short time after their mutual ejaculation, Charlie pushed her feet backwards, lying on top of Bruce, Charlie brought her legs together, trapping Bruce's penis inside her and trying to stop the combination of their fluids from escaping from between her legs.

They lay together until Bruce's penis had more or less lost its erection and their combined fluids were beginning to dry. Charlie kissed Bruce, longingly and lovingly on the mouth, parting her lips from his. She spoke for the first time. "I have never experienced anything like that before." Her voice was still hoarse but more from dryness. "God, how I truly, truly love you my darling. Please, please promise me that you won't ever leave me."

Bruce turned them over so that they were on their sides, gently allowing his penis to slip out of her. "Trust me, I won't!"

CHAPTER 11

Saturday morning dawned bright and sunny. The sunshine was beginning to have more strength in it now, even at nine o'clock in the morning, Bruce could feel the warmth through his hooded top when he was on deck. There was a gentle three-knot breeze blowing, causing some gentle rattles among the rigging lines of some of the adjacent sailboats. Charlie had returned from stowing mooring ropes, fenders and securing the anchor. As she returned to the helm station, Bruce, with his 'captains cap' on, smiled at her, memories of the previous afternoons lovemaking still fresh in his mind as he looked at the beautiful woman. "You okay, hun?" He asked.

"Oh yes, thank you." She smiled back at him and hugged him, then started to remove her Crewsaver. "Are we going to go right into the marina at Banus?"

"No, I don't think so. I think that it might be easier to anchor outside the marina and then take *Willie* into the marina and bring them back with us." *Willie* was the name that Charlie had decided on for the Williams 435 tender.

"Please, can I drive *Willie*?" Charlie asked excitedly.

"I thought you drove him hard enough yesterday." Bruce looked at her with a sideways grin.

She moved over to where he was at the helm and slowly placed her hand on his crotch, gently squeezing his genitalia. "And I am going to drive him again very soon." Her voice had taken on that deep husky tone again.

As they cleared the harbour, Bruce opened up the throttles and took the sixty-ton boat up to twenty-five knots. The *Cape Agulhas* flew down the coast, past Fuengirola and towards the shores of Marbella. Puerto Banus was just beyond Marbella and the beach at Puerto Banus was just outside the entrance to the marina. The beach area consists of five horseshoe-shaped, manmade stone breakwaters. Bruce had seen this when he researched the trip. The second sheltered area from the marina entrance looked like it would suit their purposes best and that was where he directed the *Cape*. Arriving at Puerto Banus, Bruce manoeuvred the *Cape* into position and Charlie removed the safety pin for the anchors. Once they were in a suitable spot, Bruce let go of the anchor from the lower helm control. Charlie remained at the bow and called out the length of chain that had gone over, allowing the *Cape* to snub upon her anchor chain with her bows into the gentle breeze. Satisfied that she wouldn't drift anywhere, they went about their now well-practised launching of *Willie* and with Charlie at the helm, made their way up into the marina.

They found the Dunn's at the far end of the marina close to the Prestige, making *Willie* fast, they scrambled up a short ladder onto the quayside and greeted the couple. The girls hugged each other whilst Bruce and Mike shook hands.

A man was standing at the stern of the Prestige looking somewhat perplexed at the additional people coming to inspect the boat. As the vendor spoke very little English, Charlie was nominated as the interpreter for the day. Wasting no time at all she introduced herself and Bruce saying that they were only there to offer advice and for translating. A slightly more relaxed vendor invited the group on board. Bruce opted to stay in the cockpit to avoid creating too much of a crowd inside the boat. After all, he had looked at a couple of Prestige boats in the quest for his own boat. The Prestige 420 was called *Annabella* and was registered in Puerto Banus. Bruce knew that she would have her master cabin around the midships with access to the accommodation from the main deck salon. Alternative accommodation was available in the form of a forward VIP with access to this from the left front of the main deck, the lower helm being on the right of the main deck. She had what was termed as a sports flybridge with a biminy cover to provide sun protection to people on the flybridge.

Sheila came back out of the forward VIP on her own and sat down at the stern with Bruce. "I don't like this boat, there is a strange smell, like a musty oily smell." she wrinkled her nose.

"Probably needs a good airing out, especially if she has been closed down all winter." Bruce observed.

"Yes, I know but everything feels cramped and especially when you compare her to your *Cape.*"

Bruce pondered his reply. "Sheila, the *Cape* is almost twice the size of this boat so, it is difficult to make comparisons. I agree that this boat feels cramped, despite the size. However, you do have a far more spacious salon than there would have been on the catamaran that you had been looking at. The cabins are bigger and don't forget you have an outside area above us." He indicated the flybridge. Mike and Charlie joined them as he continued. "Quite apart from that, you haven't got a bloody great big stick coming up out of your salon." They all laughed at the remark.

"Well, I have seen enough." Mike remarked. "I think he is asking way too much for it anyway and I think that he has something wallowing around in the bilge that shouldn't be there."

"Okay then." Bruce and Sheila stood up. "Let's get out to the *Cape* and enjoy the rest of the day."

They thanked the vendor for his time and wished him luck with selling the Prestige. Mike and Sheila recovered their overnight bags and were given two spare Crewsavers before joining Bruce and Charlie in *Willie*. Getting back to the *Cape*, they decided on a brew before getting underway and were sat in the main salon, enjoying their tea.

"Mike?" Bruce asked. "Forgive me for being personal, but how much were you planning on spending on a boat?"

Mike pondered the question. 'Maybe Bruce knew something he didn't, after all, he had been around boats a lot longer than he had'. "About £750,000." He looked over to confirm the figure with Sheila. "Once we get the money from the house in the UK." Both Charlie and Bruce were aware of the sale of the Dunn's house in Amesbury, they were only days off exchanging.

"Okay!" Replied Bruce. "I happened to see a Sunseeker when we were at the Chandlers last week. Would you like me to give Sergio a call and find out what the situation is regarding that?"

"Oh, yes, please." both Mike and Sheila responded at the same time. Charlie just beamed at her clever man.

Bruce went forward to the helm station and picked up the sat phone, now renamed the 'batphone' by Charlie. She had a penchant for giving inanimate objects nicknames. A short conversation followed and Bruce returned to the other three in the salon. "Well, if you want to see a Sunseeker today, we had better get this boat underway." He continued aft to check that *Willie* was secure on the swim deck and that the deck was fully raised.

Main engines started, Bruce took the *Cape* forward as Charlie wound in the chain until she told him via the VHF that they were directly over the anchor. Bruce held the boat steady whilst Charlie operated the windlass and brought the anchor up, hosing down the chain and anchor with fresh water.

"You are a very lucky guy Bruce." Mike observed, looking forward to where the two women were engaged in the anchor recovery.

"Yes, Mike, I know I am. And very right now a very happy man as well." Bruce turned his head towards Mike and winked. The girls returned to the helm station as Bruce started the *Cape* forward and edged her off and away from the beach towards the open sea, setting her on a course back to Malaga at twenty-five knots. An hour and a half later, they were preparing to go alongside the quay at Boats.co.uk. Charlie was instructing Mike and Sheila on setting up the fenders and preparing the ropes for going alongside on the port side. A beaming Sergio was on the quayside to greet them. Pumping Bruce's hand and exchanging cheek kisses with Charlie. Bruce introduced Mike and Sheila to Sergio, who was offering coffee or boat viewing. Mike and Sheila opted for the boat viewing so, they made their way over to the Sunseeker Manhattan Sixty. She was out of the water and it seemed that work was being carried out on her hull. Sergio had already had a set of gantry steps set up on the stern and a shoreline connected to provide power to the boat. Bruce and Charlie opted to leave Sheila and Mike in the more than capable hands of Sergio, whilst they took the *Cape* around to the marina service point. There they refuelled the *Cape* with diesel, bringing her up to half tanks and then both the Williams, the Sea-Doo and the two Jerri cans with petrol, at the same time, they emptied their waste tanks.

Returning to the Boats.co.uk quay, they were just in time to see a beaming Sheila and Mike leaving the Sunseeker, heading towards the chandlery and Sergio's office. All three of them beckoned for Bruce and Charlie to join them, which they did.

A beaming Mike greeted them. "Well, we have only gone and done it, mate."

"We've bought a Sunseeker." Gushed Sheila. "It is just what we wanted." She continued. "Thank you so much for bringing us here today." She promptly kissed him on the cheek, then hugged Charlie.

By the time that the initial necessary paperwork had been completed and deposits paid, the time had gone four o'clock. Charlie cornered Bruce. "Honey, it has gone four. What if we go back to our berth on the marina and take them across the road to José's for a meal tonight?"

"I think that you should be the captain." He replied, hugging her at the same time. They informed the other two of the change of arrangements. "We can get a reasonably early start in the morning and go down to our favourite cove where we saw the dolphins. Then we'll get you back to your car in the afternoon." Bruce concluded. "How does that sound?" They were both in agreement so, Charlie picked up the phone to book their table.

Mike and Sheila had been given the forward cabin with the double bed, previously occupied by Bruce and Charlie and were given a quick tutoring on the operation of the TV and bathroom facilities. They had an early evening drink before retiring to their respective cabins for showers. Charlie wanted to wash her hair, so she got first dibs on the shower. Bruce was sat watching the end of the rugby on the new TV in the cabin when Charlie emerged from the bathroom. She was stark naked, save for the traditional towel wrapped around her hair. The contrasting tan line of her bikini very clear on her beautiful skin. Memories of the previous afternoon's lovemaking still firmly rooted in his mind, Bruce felt the stirring in his loin as she brushed past him to get to the dressing table.

"Hey, gorgeous lady." Charlie turned towards him as she sat and crossed those magnificent long legs. Smiling, knowing the effect she was having on him. "I really love you." Bruce got up from the chair, moved across to where she was sitting and kissed her delicately on her lips. The smell of her freshness was adorable. Stripping off his clothes so that he too was naked, he stood unabashedly in front of her. His penis wasn't erect but mildly swollen.

Charlie looked at this man, my man she thought. He gave off an unfathomable aura. As yet, she hadn't been able to define it. He was quietly confident, polite, mentally very strong, his personal hygiene was second to none. He was more than twenty years older, mature with a fantastic sense of humour. Charlie looked at his body, the scarred leg and arm weren't pretty, but the flat stomach and well developed pectoral muscles were gorgeous. Despite the scarring to his left arm, the biceps and forearms were very well developed. The full head of hair and neatly trimmed beard, despite the streaks of grey, gave him an almost film star look. The creases around his eyes seemed to bear testament to the hardships he had born in the past and those beautiful blue eyes, well, they were something else. The penis wasn't huge, certainly nowhere near the size of her former fiancé, but this one really worked fine. The faint feeling of ever so slight bruising in her vaginal passage was a testament to that. Although Charlie had been through some frustrating and painful experiences, this was the first penis ever to fully penetrate her vagina. She smiled at him. "I love you too Brucie." Charlie stood up and wrapped her arms around his neck, her fingers entwined in the hair at the back of his head as she kissed him gently on the lips. "I really, really love you Brucie. Promise me that you will never, ever leave me, please my darling."

Arriving at the restaurant, they were greeted by Senata, who insisted on kissing everyone on the cheek, then taking Bruce and Charlie's arms in a conspiratorial manner leading them to the family table. José came over and shook hands with the men and treated the ladies to cheeky kisses. The food as always was delicious and towards the end of the evening José, Senata and Maria joined them as did Miguel and Clarissa. The evening was wonderful, with far too much wine having been consumed. By the end of the evening, Mike and Sheila were as much a part of the family as were Bruce and Charlie. Bidding their goodnights, the two couples returned to the *Cape*. While Bruce and Charlie each had their glasses of Glenmorangie, Mike and Sheila opted to sample a glass of the twenty-year-old Sandymans Port from the decanter. It had gone eleven-thirty, when Mike and Sheila made their way down to their cabin, Charlie left Bruce to do the last rounds, turn the outside lights off and do the final night checks. She could hear Bruce having a chat about the weather for the next day with the *Rio Jenil's* sentries, having finished in the galley she had made her way down to their cabin.

Whilst sitting at the dressing table preparing to remove what little makeup she wore. Charlie distinctly heard two loud solid clunks against the rear of the starboard hull. Barefoot and as quietly as she could, she rushed up the stairs and onto the deck, Bruce was just saying good night to the sentries.

"Bruce, quickly, something has just banged into the starboard side of the hull below the waterline. It sounded like a metal object and it was loud." Bruce reacted instantly diving into the pilot station, he switched on the underwater lights. There shouldn't have been anything near them. The nearest boat to them now was five berths up and it was unoccupied. One of the *Rio Jenil's* sentries had accompanied Charlie and all three of them were looking to see what it was that had knocked into the *Cape's* hull.

Charlie was the first to spot the problem, bubbles came to the surface near the stern. "Diver below us, near the stern!" She exclaimed.

Bruce saw the two shadowy shapes, one behind the other emerge from under the boat. They started to swim away from the bright illumination under the hull, the first one was a good five yards in front of the other. Flashing through Bruce's mind was the thought that there was no reason why anyone should be involved in underwater activities other than for a malicious reason. There was no hesitation from Bruce, a red rage passed in front of him as he launched himself at the diver closest to the *Cape* and practically landed on top of him. Surprise very much to his advantage. Leaning forward, he locked his left arm around the neck of the diver at the same time, Bruce reached around with his right hand and literally ripped the mouthpiece out of the diver's mouth tearing teeth out in the process. This caused the diver to scream. The action of forcefully removing the mouthpiece also caused the divers facemask to be knocked off.

The shock of the cold water and instant action brought Bruce's fighting instincts to the fore. Realising two things, firstly, that the diver would very probably be carrying a knife, usually somewhere around the knee or lower leg. Secondly, there was no doubt in his mind that the leading diver would have heard the splash of Bruce entering the water and may well turn around to assist his colleague. Bruce needed to keep his man's thoughts occupied in surviving pain. Trying to see past the squirming diver to see if his buddy was going to come back to help him. Bruce stuck the index and forefinger of his right hand into the man's nostrils and pulled up forcefully, making every attempt to rip his nose off, twisting and pulling as hard as he could. This caused the diver to take in a lungful of water, at the same time he had put both his hands on Bruce's forearm in an attempt to save his nose from literally being torn off his face. The shock of the aggressive assault and the lungful of water caused the diver to kick for the surface as hard as he could. This action suited Bruce completely who had by now got his legs locked around the diver giving him a better purchase on the diver as he attempted to inflict as much damage and pain to his victim as he possibly could.

As Bruce's head broke the surface, he gasped a breath, removing his fingers from the diver's nostrils, he moved his right hand to the back of the diver's head and pushed it forward onto his left arm trying to put additional pressure onto the man's neck and keeping the head underwater. In the back of his mind, Bruce had every intention of trying to kill him. The diver realised this and feeling his life ebbing away from him, thrashed under Bruce trying to relieve the pressure on his neck and draw a much-needed breath. The Spanish sentry that had come on to the *Cape* with Bruce handed his weapon to Charlie and jumped in to assist Bruce.

"Cuidado, tiene un cuchillo!" (Careful he has a knife!) Bruce warned the sentry. "Charlie, drop the swim platform for me please hun." Bruce gasped with the exertion from the short fight. Charlie obliged and between the two sentries, they got the diver coughing and bleeding badly from his nose and mouth onto the submerged swim platform. He was very quickly relieved of the knife that Bruce had suspected he would be carrying and then none too gently his hands were manacled behind him. Charlie was still raising the swim platform when the questions started with a kick to the diver's thigh from the sentry who had assisted Bruce in the water. Rapid Spanish ensued and with a couple more kicks for emphasis. As yet the blues and twos hadn't arrived, so the interrogation continued. Whilst the grilling had been ongoing, Bruce had collected his face mask and a torch from amongst the snorkelling equipment, shivering from the cold and reaction of the fight during his first plunge into the marina, he went in again, still fully clothed.

The underwater lights in the hull of the *Cape* did a wonderful job of illumination around the hull but it was only with the assistance of the torch that he saw the package suspended from the starboard propeller shaft. From the object on the propellor shaft, another cable was looped to one of the propeller blades. Having seen enough, Bruce kicked for the surface, climbing back onto the swim platform. By this time, the goings-on had got Mike and Sheila up and onto the cockpit where they were stood with Charlie, still holding a machine carbine.

As Bruce clambered back up onto the swim platform, he spoke to Charlie. "Okay, so I think we have got what possibly looks like an explosive device attached to the prop shaft. It might be set to be detonated as soon as we engage the drive and the screws start to turn. Just to be on the safe side, let's get everybody off the boat. Clear the pontoon and the quay. I am now, really seriously fucking pissed off."

Space blankets had materialised from the *Rio Jenil*. Ernesto, the guard who had helped Bruce in the water, spoke good English and handed a blanket to Bruce, who put it down on the deck. In the distance, the sound of blues and twos reached Bruce's ears.

"Ernesto, gracias mi amigo. Does this rat speak any English?"

"I don't know Capitain." Ernesto shook his head.

"Well! I am just going to find out." Bruce shaking with a combination of rage and cold turned to the hapless prisoner. "Even if I have to rip the rest of his fuckin' nose off his face. Who do you work for mother fucker? Speak English?" Bruce positioned himself behind the manacled, kneeling prisoner, placing his right knee in the small of his back and seizing a handful of lank wet hair. Bruce yanked the prisoners head backwards and with his right index and forefinger again ready to resume his purchase on the diver's nasal cavity. "Now, who sent you? Who do you work for, names?"

Charlie was rooted to the spot, in the relatively short space of time she had known Bruce and fallen in love with him, she had been totally unaware that the man she had come to love so much, was capable of extorting so much violence in such a short space of time. From the time that he had plunged into the water, till the time that he had surfaced with the diver, had been no more than seven seconds. Even when he had surfaced with the diver, it had seemed to her that he was trying to kill the man. Now his fury seemed to know no bounds. Even the two Spanish sentries were so bewildered at the Englishman's violence that they just stood and maintained their distance.

Bruce reached the forefinger and index finger back into the diver's nostril when the diver screamed. "Tockalov, Dimitri Tockalov!"

"Who was your dive buddy?" Bruce removed his fingers now that they had an understanding.

"Donaldson, an Englishman called Donaldson." He blubbered. "Don't hurt me anymore."

"So, what is your fuckin' name and is that a bomb under my boat?" Bruce yanked back further on the man's hair to add a bit more emphasis on the urgency of the question.

"Yes, it's a bomb, you're right." He snuffled spitting blood from his mouth. There was a shout from the quay. Bruce looked up, a uniformed man was standing on the quay waving a sidearm in the air.

"Name? Your name?". Bruce threatened him with the fingers in front of his nose.

"Botha, Janus Botha!" Snivelled the diver.

Bruce looked around, the uniformed man who had been waving the sidearm around was now pointing it at Bruce and yelling in Spanish. Bruce recognised him. It was the Guardia Civil Lieutenant that had crashed the *Rio Jenil*. Bruce started to raise his hands. Charlie yelled at the Spanish Officer in Spanish. Ernesto joined in, but not heeding a word that was shouted at him, the Lieutenant pulled the trigger on the weapon. Because of where Bruce was standing in relation to the Lieutenant and Botha, his body was almost between them, it seemed that the Lieutenant was trying to shoot Bruce. Bruce saw the muzzle flash from the weapon as it was fired and mentally waited for the impact of the bullet to hit him. Nothing happened. The sound of the report crashed out around the marina and Botha screamed as the nine-millimetre bullet tore down through his chest into his stomach. Ernesto's colleague reacted with lightning speed. He had his weapon cocked and aimed at the Lieutenant as he got between Bruce and the Lieutenant, advancing on the Lieutenant as he did so. Cops were arriving at the quay as the sentry disarmed the Lieutenant, keeping him covered whilst the situation was explained to the new arrivals as to just what had happened. Ernesto bent down to see how badly hit Botha was. The swim deck was now awash with blood. By now the crew of the *Rio Jenil* who were on constant standby at the nearby barracks had been scrambled back to their boat and a call had gone out to their commander, Miguel.

Bruce had gone into the crew area shower and got his wet clothes off and was doing his best to get warmed up. As soon as he had got naked into the shower with the hot water cascading over his body, the reaction and realisation set in and he found himself sobbing uncontrollably, as much with frustration as with reaction from the recent event. Charlie had gone down to the master cabin to retrieve dry clothes for Bruce. When she got back, she found him still in the shower, the sobbing had stopped. Reaching into the shower she turned the water off and wrapping one of the swimming towels around him hugged him close to her and gently rocked him till he pulled away from her.

Taking his face gently in her hands, she lifted the crestfallen head and looked into the two tear moistened eyes and said. "My darling, you are a real hero, god only knows how many lives you have just saved. When I saw you on the swim deck and I saw you lose it with that guy you caught, I thought that I had lost my kind, considerate lover that I had found. Now I know that you are not just an ordinary human being but someone very special. I know this because otherwise, you would not be reacting the way you are." She pulled his head into her shoulder. "There is no shame in reacting to what you have just gone through. Oh my God, I am so proud of you. I just love you so very much."

Bruce pulled away from her and then kissed her on the lips, just briefly, he sniffed and wiped his eyes on the towel and then found a tissue and blew his nose. He finished drying himself and got dressed without a word, Charlie handing him articles of clothing as he required them. Feeling better about himself once he was dressed, he hugged Charlie and said. "I am sorry I lost it, but all I could think of was that someone was trying to take away all the things that I love."

"I know!" Charlie hugged him back.

José and his family, having been disturbed by the goings-on and the shooting, had opened the restaurant and were providing hot coffee for all.

It was back at the family table that Bruce and Charlie found Mike, Sheila, Miguel and two other men in plain clothes. They were introduced to them as Spanish CNI (*Centro Nacional de Inteligencia*). Their English was passable and Bruce recounted to them all of the facts since he had bought the *Cape Agulhas* including the discovery of the secreted nineteen forty-seven charts and the subsequent handing over of those charts to Miguel. They made notes and comments about two of the charts not even applying to Spanish waters. Bruce told them about his conversation with Botha and the fact that he had been hired by Tockalov. In the interim period, the divers had arrived and set up. The *Rio Jenil* had been started and she was moved off the pontoon, remaining at the entrance to the marina. Not that anyone was entering or leaving the marina as it was now one o'clock in the morning. The CNI agents left assuring Bruce that they were going to have a little chat with Mr Tockalov. They were also going to interview both Botha if he survived the shooting and the Lieutenant. It seemed possible that somehow Van de Niekerk may also be involved with them. So, he was another person of interest that they would be having a chat with. Miguel commented on the involvement of the Lieutenant, adding that none of the men liked him anyway. They were also going to contact both the Police in Gibraltar and the Spanish Border Police in La Línea de la Concepción to keep a lookout for Donaldson. They all shook hands and went their separate ways. Bruce offered to pick up the tab for the coffees and other beverages that had been consumed during the early morning soiree, an act for which José was extremely grateful. Senata and Maria had taken a flask of coffee over to the divers who had made their cutter fast alongside the pontoon opposite the *Cape*, where the *Rio Jenil* had been moored. Mike and Sheila had taken another flask of coffee for the Police and Guardia Civil who were manning the taped off, 'no go area' during the disarming of the bomb.

The divers made short work of removing the bomb from the *Cape*, making it safe they then passed it over to the bomb disposal group that was on the side of the pontoon. Throughout the recovery of the bomb, Bruce and Charlie sat together holding hands. He wasn't even sure if the insurance would cover the cost of the boat if it were to blow up, inwardly it wasn't the cost that mattered to him. It was the fact that most of his world was on the *Cape* and that would be difficult to replace. The rest of it was sitting next to him.

It was just after four am when they were finally allowed back on board. Bruce apologised profusely for the inconvenience and the disrupted night as well as the danger that they had been placed in, only to be reassured that it definitely wasn't his fault. Bruce's mind was a whirlwind of thoughts. There had been four separate incidents now and they had all occurred in the marina at Malaga. The Lieutenants involvement was apparent as he was in a position to give his co-conspirators the heads up as to when the *Cape* was in the marina. It appeared to Bruce that the Lieutenants last act was to try to shut Botha up. To stop him from speaking to the authorities, he was certain that his interrogators would be asking him some awkward questions very soon. Bruce was clear of some other things as well. He would very much like to have a word with Tockalov and Donaldson regarding his and their futures.

Unbeknown to Bruce, but it was at the same time that the two CNI officers, were at that moment in time, outside an address on the Calle Los Olivios in Marbella. They were escorted by armed tactical officers of the Policia Nationale and were in the process of giving Mr Tockalov an early morning call, incidentally, not accompanied by tea or coffee. At the same time, the Lieutenant was being harshly interviewed by two senior officers. At some stage, he must have run into a door along the way, because his left eye was very red and his nose and mouth were both oozing blood.

Mike and Sheila made their way back down to their cabin, with promises that no one would be disturbed before ten o'clock. Charlie was left to shut down the *Cape* for what was left of the night. Bruce had gone below to take another shower and treated himself to a small whisky. He was in the process of drying himself off when Charlie came into the bathroom and squatted on the pedestal and relieved her bladder. Having washed her hands, she dried them on Bruce's towel, putting her arms around his naked torso. "What are you thinking about my hero?"

Bruce dropped the towel, wrapped her in his arms and said. "Well, all the problems that we have had, have occurred while we have been here in Malaga. I am thinking that we have just over a week to go before we depart for the UK and as much as I have loved being here, I think that it is time for us to make it a little more difficult for people to find us."

"What are you planning honey?"

"Well, my thoughts at this moment in time are that we get underway when we can in the morning, spend a little time with Sheila and Mike snorkelling then drop them off at Puerto Banus. After that, we know of enough safe anchorages along this coast to sort of hide out for a few days and then just take each day as it comes. What do you say to that?"

Smiling at him she replied. "I still think that not only are you my hero but you are also a brilliant captain."

CHAPTER 12

Bruce had woken up at ten o'clock and when he turned over Charlie's side of the bed, it was empty. Stumbling naked and still half-asleep into the bathroom, he squatted on the toilet and urinated copiously. Finishing off, he washed his hands and the sleep out of his eyes, quickly getting dressed then made the bed. Closing the cabin door behind him, Bruce smelt the whiff of fresh coffee wafting its way down from the galley. He knocked briefly on the forward cabin door and got a response from inside. Then made his way up to the galley. Charlie's skills in the galley were second to none. There was coffee in the percolator, mushroom, tomato and Mediterranean herb omelettes, toast and marmalade ready and waiting to be cooked for the late-morning brunch.

"Good morning, my Captain." Charlie greeted him. "Welcome back to the land of the living. You were so deeply asleep I didn't have the heart to wake you." She hugged him.

Returning the hug and kissing her at the same time. "Morning, I do seem to remember going for a swim in the early hours of this morning."

Charlie poured Bruce a mug of coffee and added some sweetened condensed milk as a treat. Taking it up to the chart table he got out the chart that covered Marbella down to Gibraltar, pondering the chart and Google earth when Charlie joined him. "Looking for an anchorage for tonight?" She asked.

"Yep!" Bruce replied, turning to her. "That cove where we saw the dolphins, we'll go there this afternoon again and check it out, it's got a relatively narrow entrance, although there is an 'urbanisation' it is a good three hundred feet above us and set well back from the top of the cliffs. Once we are in there, we would be invisible unless someone was standing right on the edge of the cliff. How would you feel about that?"

At that moment, Sheila, followed by Mike, appeared at the top of the companionway. Charlie started on the omelettes cooking the first one for

Mike and Sheila, the second one for herself and Bruce. There was plenty of toast and marmalade to be washed down by freshly brewed coffee from the percolator. By eleven o'clock, breakfast had been finished, plus the dishwasher was stacked and running. The *Rio Jenil* hadn't returned to her berth on the pontoon. Bruce assumed that she had gone back to her normal berth outside the headquarters building further down the quay.

Bruce had started the twin Cats and as they burbled away gently, he went ashore to speak to José. He handed him a slip of paper with the sat phone number on it, telling him that they were leaving to go off-grid for the next week until they were due to bring the *Cape* into Boats.co.uk for service. José fully understood and promised to relay the information to Miguel and Sergio. Returning to the *Cape*, he slipped his Crewsaver on and gave his crew the thumbs up to cast off. Once out of the marina, he let Mike have a go at helming the big cruiser down to the harbour entrance. Then he let Sheila take the helm as he coached her to push up the throttles until they were cruising at twenty-two knots and both engines were at one thousand seven hundred revolutions. Instead of following the coast as they usually did, he took them further out to sea before turning west and running parallel with the coast. The cove that they were heading for was located between Fuengirola and Marbella. After a half-hour, he swapped Sheila over with Mike on the helm. The two girls thought that they would go up to the flybridge to see how cold it was at twenty-two knots. Whilst he had Mike to himself for a few minutes, Bruce asked him. "Mike, I know that you are a bit of a whizz kid when it comes to electronics. What can you tell me about tracking devices and how can I check that I don't have any surveillance devices on the boat?"

Looking puzzled by the question, Mike replied. "Firstly, when it comes to surveillance or tracking devices, they would have to be above the waterline. The best place to put a tracking device on this boat would be somewhere like the flybridge. If someone wanted to listen to your conversation as in an audiovisual recording, it would be in some sort of innocuous place and well away from any electronics. Possibly motion or audio sensitive to conserve power but it would also have to be easily retrievable as well. They could also just use something like a bug that would transmit directly to somewhere close by where the audio would either be recorded or listened to directly. Do you think you have been bugged?"

"There is a possibility. We have told you the story of the charts and although they have been handed over to the authorities. The other side may think that we have made a note of any coordinates, which we have but they don't mean anything at all. Possibly they don't know that and are interested in disposing of us anyway." Bruce replied, pausing for a moment. "Maybe I am just overreacting and being paranoid after the events of last night. After all, this guy Tockalov will have probably been picked up and questioned by now."

"Probably!" Mike replied. "Tell you what, I'll have a quick look up on the flybridge for you when we stop. Later I'll phone my Dad. I have got a couple of bug sweeping devices at home. I'll ask him to put them in the post to me. I should get them in a couple of days."

"That would be great, thanks, Mike, but look it really is no biggy. I should be able to pick one up in the UK when we go back next week." Turning around, Bruce heard the girls coming back into the salon, they both looked cold.

Arriving at what Bruce and Charlie now referred to as Dolphin Cove at a little after one o'clock, Mike and the two girls got ready to do some snorkelling and got *Bobbi* out onto the swim deck, ready to put in the water. Bruce opted to stay out of the water for the day but went below to put on his shorts.

As soon as Bruce was out of earshot, Charlie got hold of Mike and Sheila. "Look guys, Bruce has got some really bad scarring on his legs and arm, unfortunately, he is really self-conscious about it, so please don't react when he comes back up in his shorts."

Mike nodded as Sheila said. "Yes, we couldn't help noticing his arm yesterday. What happened?"

"Car accident!" Charlie replied, not caring to elaborate.

They spent a couple of hours snorkelling in the clear waters of the cove, taking it in turns to play with *Bobbi*. Unfortunately, there was no sign of the dolphins that afternoon, but there were plenty of fish. Good to his word, Mike had a quick look up on the flybridge to see if his trained eye could spot anything untoward. To be fair, there were so many places that a tracker could be hidden. What he needed was a detector.

Bruce and Charlie took Mike and Sheila back up to Puerto Banus to pick up their car, this time, Bruce took the *Cape* right up into the marina, going alongside a pontoon close to the car park. They bade them farewell without tying up. Returning to Dolphin Cove, they put out both anchors and a stern line as well. There was plenty of daylight left, but not enough to sunbathe with. Deciding to try out his new fishing rod, Bruce went onto the swim deck and cast the lure out, slowly reeling it in. Charlie was sat on the main deck cockpit watching him and was about to ask him what he would like for dinner. Bruce had just started to reel the lure back in when it was taken. Charlie whooped with glee and scrambled down to the swim deck to get a better view. It took Bruce two minutes to land the seven-pound wrasse. Once he had it hooked on his fingers through its gills, he held the wriggling fish up proudly to show Charlie. "Dinner!" Hastily, Bruce dispatched the wriggling fish with a blow to the back of its head.

Peering over Bruce's shoulder at the twitching wrasse, Charlie commented. "Hmmm! A bit more than one meal there sweetheart. Tell you what, you deal with it, I'll fillet it then we can have half tonight. How's that for a thought?"

"Okay! But how's this for a thought. What about I'll deal with it, you fillet it, then we take it ashore, build a fire on the beach and braai this sucker with some spuds accompanied by a bottle of Chardonnay?" Bruce finished with a grin.

Charlie looked at him, her face taking on a serious look. "I think that you are an even better Captain than you were before." They both burst out laughing. Where the water met the shore at the base of the cliffs was a narrow beach with a lot of driftwood on it. Whilst Charlie prepared the food, Bruce launched *Willie* and went ashore gathering driftwood. He got the fire started and once it was lit, he gathered more firewood before returning to the *Cape* to pick up Charlie. Charlie had prepared the single fillet into two portions wrapping them together in foil with butter, salt, pepper and lemon. She had also wrapped two large potatoes in foil and packed everything, including condiments, glasses and wine, into one of her shopping bags. Charlie included a blanket from one of the wardrobes of her original cabin.

It was almost last light as they finished their meal and lay back on the blanket. Bruce had built up the fire again from the embers once the food had been cooked and inner peace had been restored. Charlie rolled over onto her side and put her head on Bruce's shoulder and kissed his cheek. "This is just such bliss." She murmured. Bruce could smell the combination of fish and wine on her breath when she spoke. He breathed it in deeply, replying by pulling her into him. They lay there for nearly an hour. They had both nearly fallen asleep twice. The fire had died down and the night was bright with stars as they looked in awe at the heavenly vista. A three-quarter new moon had poked above the horizon and the riding lights on the *Cape* had come on automatically with the light sensor. Stiffly they got up, making sure that the fire was well and truly out and clambered back into *Willie* to return to the *Cape*.

A small swell was coming in through the cove entrance but it certainly wasn't anything to be worried about. They both cleared up in the galley and because Charlie wanted to wash her hair, Bruce decided to find something to watch on TV. He poured himself a large whisky and found a film on Amazon that he started to watch, making himself comfortable with a cushion on the sofa. The combination of the gentle swell which was working its way from the bow to the shore facing stern, lack of sleep from the previous night and the wine from the evening were more than enough to cause Bruce to fall asleep. Charlie, in her shorty pink gown, hair wrapped in a towel, returned to the salon to find Bruce sound asleep on the sofa. His untouched drink on the coffee table. Charlie went around closing down the blinds in the salon and poured herself a drink, then hating herself for having to do so, she gently woke Bruce before he went into too deep a sleep. Sitting up, he yawned, stretched and wiped the sleep from his eyes.

"Gosh, I hadn't meant for that to happen." Bruce yawned, swinging his feet back to the deck, cocking an eye at his untouched drink. Charlie sat down on the sofa next to him. "God, you smell nice enough to eat." Whereupon, he turned and making animal noises, pretended he was going to devour her. Charlie, in fits of laughter, giggles and yells, fell back on the sofa away from him, exposing her buttocks. Bruce immediately pretended to bite her right buttock. Muffled by the buttock he was pretending to devour, he continued to make the noises of a scoffing animal. In an attempt to avoid him, Charlie turned on her back, her lower abdomen and crotch were exposed. Trying gently to push Bruce, away with her feet on his shoulders still issuing fits of giggles, Bruce twisted, her feet fell away allowing Bruce to fall forwards between her legs, his face coming to rest at Charlie's crotch. There was a sharp intake of breath from Charlie as she realised the sensation of Bruce's proximity to her womanhood. Neither of them moved for some three seconds. Then, slowly Bruce turned his head and started to kiss her labia. Charlie groaned with ecstasy and changed the position she was lying in as Bruce, now silent, placed his head between her legs and ministered his lips and tongue between her labia, inserting and withdrawing his tongue from her vagina. Holding his head gently, Charlie guided his head between her legs and directed his tongue and lips to different points, including her extended clitoris. When her orgasm came, it was just one huge one that started in her stomach and ended as a rush that soaked Bruce's face. Charlie screamed as the orgasm went down through her vagina. They lay almost motionless, Bruce's wet face resting on her lower abdomen. Charlie lay, sobbing gently, as she stroked his head and face on her stomach. Bruce sat up and took off his jumper and T-shirt. Using his T-shirt, he wiped his face and neck, then gently placed the shirt between Charlie's legs, then kneeling, he tenderly kissed Charlie on the lips.

"Please don't cry Charlie, I didn't mean to hurt you or do anything to embarrass you."

Charlie looked at him in almost disbelief, wiping her eyes with the sleeves of the gown. "Brucie, Brucie, my darling Bruce, you don't understand, do you? I don't know how you do it but you have just turned my legs into jelly and my heart for you to something I have never, ever experienced." She reached up and pulled his still damp head into her bosom. It was only for a few seconds, for as much as Bruce loved where his head was and the soft touch of her hands stroking his head and face, he was bending over in a very awkward manner. Bruce slowly pulled away from the most heavenly place in the world, again gently kissing her on the lips. Bruce handed Charlie her drink and retrieved his, emptying it quickly, he refilled it and sat down next to her. "What next?" Bruce asked.

"Another shower for me, I think." Charlie replied, she was wearing a smile that said, 'I am the happiest woman in the world.' "So, let's close up here and go below my super lover."

Bruce had only had to get up once in the early hours at a point just after four am to relieve himself. Charlie was sound asleep, lying on her side facing away from Bruce when he got back into bed. He cuddled up into her back. Charlie turned over in her sleep and pulled Bruce's head down to her breasts. Seventh heaven, Bruce was almost instantly asleep again. By the time he awoke fully, it had gone nine am as Charlie was just getting dressed. The sun was shining brightly in from behind the cabin blinds.

They spent what was left of the morning catching up on laundry and housework. Bruce rigged a drying line across the stern of the cockpit, not something they could do on a marina. Due to the lateness of them having got out of bed, they had decided to skip breakfast and have an earlier lunch. This would free them up to go for a swim in the afternoon. Having completed the chores, Charlie went below to her sewing machine, whilst Bruce prepped the Sony RX100 camera for the afternoon. After which he recovered the SD card from *Bobbi* and went through the film that had been captured the previous afternoon. He selected several stills and was in the process of saving them to a portable hard drive. As he was working at the chart station, Bruce decided to check the weather for the next few days, just to see what was happening. After all, it was still winter in Spain. The forecast was excellent, with wall-to-wall sunshine for the next five days but with temperatures dropping off during the evening. Glancing at his watch, he realised that it had gone one o'clock and it was later than they had planned for lunch. Going aft to the crew area, he heard the sound of the sewing machine going hammer and tongs. As he walked in, Charlie carried away in her work, had also lost track of the time.

She looked up at him in surprise. "Hey, honey!" She greeted him with a warm smile.

"Hey! How are you doing? Would you like me to make you a sandwich or something?" Bruce asked.

Charlie looked at her wrist, realising that she hadn't put her watch on and asked. "Oh my God, Bruce! What time is it?" Charlie started to stand up. She had been doing something with a piece of cloth that she had acquired during their visit to Gibraltar. Charlie started to stand up, straightening her back as she stood.

"Charlie, it's only a little after one, I can get lunch for us both if you like. I am more than capable."

Charlie started to move to the crew area access. Turning back towards Bruce she said with a smile. "Don't you dare go into my galley without written consent from me." Charlie had dressed very casually that morning. She wore the shortest of denim shorts possible that exposed every inch of her lovely legs, although the shorts did go up to her waist, they really accentuated the contours of her buttocks. Her top, if it could be considered that, was a pink blouse that was tied in a knot just below her breasts accentuating her ample cleavage. Bruce was starting to think 'To hell with lunch, I think that I know what I would rather be doing'. Once at the top of the stairs, Charlie turned around and put her left hand in his right hand. It was almost as though she had read his mind as she pulled him into her, pushing as much of her body into his and kissed him full on the mouth. It wasn't a wanton act of sexuality, but it was done in a warm and gentle loving manner.

Charlie had moved her hands up behind Bruce's head as he put his arms around her waist, as the kiss continued for the next ten seconds before they gently parted. "Wow! I had better get some lunch for you, sailor. I need to keep your strength up." Charlie said, unwinding herself from the embrace.

Bruce got the condiments, glasses, juice, knives and forks out and set the table on the aft of the cockpit. Charlie brought out the plates. They had half an avocado each with some smoked mackerel, tomato and bread. They had half an apple each afterwards. The meal was just so simple it was beautiful. They discussed the program for the rest of the week, deciding to spend the next two nights where they were for the moment. The weather forecast was good and they had sufficient food on board, especially as Charlie was trying to minimise the contents in the fridge to allow it to be switched off for the time that they would be away.

After lunch, Bruce cleared away the plates and washed up whilst Charlie returned to her sewing machine in the crew area. Bruce was just about to settle down for an afternoon nap when the sat phone rang. It was Miguel. It seemed that Botha had died due to the gunshot wound to his stomach, the Lieutenant had now been charged with his murder. Tockalov was assisting the CNI with their enquiries whilst Donaldson had apparently not surfaced anywhere but was still wanted for questioning. Van de Niekerk was of great interest to the CNI and when it was possible, he would be transferred to custody in Madrid along with Tockalov. There was still that mystery regarding Donaldson, saying that he had been the previous owner of the *Cape* but the name on the papers saying that the previous owner was a man called Singleton. The conversation had gone on for some thirty-five minutes.

Charlie had finished what she was doing on her sewing machine and had found Bruce in deep conversation with Miguel on the sat phone. When Bruce had finished his chat with Miguel, he brought Charlie up to speed with what was happening it seemed that apart from finding Donaldson, everything else had been taken care of. Noticing the piece of material that Charlie had in her hand, he asked. "So, what is that you have got there, my lovely?"

"Just a little something to show you and see what you think." Charlie replied, handing Bruce the piece of cloth. Taking it, he turned it around and gasped in amazement.

"You have just created a crest for the *Cape*." He exclaimed, examining it with care. The crest depicted the boat at full speed, broadside on in the foreground with the distinctive lighthouse of the Cape Agulhas behind the boat, whilst the background consisted of a big green wave breaking at the top. The wave was rounded at the top with the inscription. 'CAPE AGULHAS'. It was amazing.

"Charlie!" Bruce stammered. "This is absolutely fabulous, I don't know how you have done it, but this is just too fantastic for words. So, what are you planning on doing with this now?"

"Well!" She said, pushing herself up against him. "With this design, I can embroider it onto anything that the heavy-duty needle can penetrate, including your cap but I'll wait until I have some new ones. So, in short, I can embroider, T-shirts, towels, sheets. I can even make a flag but as yet I am not sure of the background colour that I would use for something like that. With my program, I can send this to have T-shirts printed as well."

"Seriously!" Bruce squeezed her. "You are an absolute star." Then they heard them and went out on deck to see the dolphins circling the boat. It appeared that there were only nine of them and it was probably the same pod that they had swum with before. Moving down to the swim platform, they lay on their stomachs, patting the water to attract them. Charlie jumped up and disappeared into the galley, returning some three minutes later with the remains of the wrasse cut into small strips. She handed one to Bruce, who wiggled it in the water at arm's length. This certainly drew some attention from the dolphins but still being very wary of the strangers, they were not quite up to being hand-fed. Withdrawing his hand from the water, he flicked the piece of fish towards the nearest dolphin, who took the fish and swallowed it. Taking it in turns, Bruce and Charlie flicked the pieces of wrasse out to the dolphins who were now swimming considerably closer to the swim deck.

Bruce stood up and went into the crew area, he retrieved both his and Charlie's face mask and snorkels, as well as the Sony camera. Taking off his shirt, he lowered the steps on the side of the swim platform and let himself down into the water, inwardly gasping at the chill. As he got into the water, Bruce looked up to see Charlie removing her shirt and the skimpy bra that she had been wearing. With his face in the water, Bruce hovered in the vicinity of the steps until Charlie had joined him then together, they swam slowly nearer to the dolphins, At one point, they assumed that it was the bull dolphin that came up and hovered in the water, presenting himself almost as a pose, by standing on his tail. Bruce had him in the viewfinder, the autofocus was on and Bruce got a stunning picture. A little later, he was following Charlie as she dived down into the clear water she was swimming casually, not trying to chase the dolphins. Bruce dived after her and to the side of her, Charlie's naked breasts were hanging down. Bruce framed the picture and captured it, just as a dolphin swam very close to her and passed her on the opposite side to Bruce. 'Photo of the day!'

Bruce thought to himself. Charlie turned towards Bruce and motioned to go up. The shutter on the camera opened and closed several times, capturing the 'mermaid', dark hair flowing gracefully behind her, as she kicked for the surface. Surfacing, they both decided that it was too cold to continue, so they decided to quit while they were ahead. Shivering, they got out onto the swim deck, Charlie being the first one out, took the camera from Bruce. "Get any good shots?" She asked.

"The proof is always going to be in the pudding." Bruce retorted, shivering as he climbed the steps. Charlie had gone to get a couple of swim towels from the utility room. Returning, she wrapped one around Bruce, pressing her naked breasts against his chest. They made love there and then on the swim deck in the sun. It wasn't urgent like their lovemaking had been in the past, but the slow, languid lovemaking of a couple with all the time in the world. Which was exactly what they had that afternoon.

With the weather forecast set for fine for the remainder of the week, Bruce and Charlie decided to remain at anchor in Dolphin Cove for the remainder of the week. They snorkelled, photographed, sunbathed, had the occasional naked swim during the day, on two occasions going back to the beach for a braaivleis. After lunch, on Saturday they lifted the *Cape's* anchors and with a feeling of regret, having decided that they would have to return to the marina at Malaga to prepare for the *Cape* to be lifted out of the water. Of course, they also had to get their things ready for the trip back to the UK. Their tans had turned them almost coffee coloured and the week of activity had improved the strength in Bruce's leg and arm considerably.

Charlie had the helm when she spoke to Bruce. "Brucie! How do you feel about on Sunday lunchtime we have José and family and Miguel and Clarissa, essentially, all the people that have been nice to us, onboard for a sort of drinks and tapas type party? Just to say a 'thank you' for all the help we have had."

Bruce pondered the answer before replying. "You do realise that we will have to wear clothes. don't you?" He looked sideways at her, a wicked little smile turning the corners of his mouth up. Pausing, he continued. "I think that maybe you should be the Captain."

Switching the helm over to the autopilot, Charlie left the wheel and went over to Bruce, who was sitting at the chart position and placed her arms around his neck, pressing her body up against him. "We haven't made love here yet."

An hour and a half later, they arrived back on their berth in the marina. They were greeted by José, Senata and Maria almost as long lost friends. The *Rio Jenil* was back on her normal berth further down the marina outside the barracks. The rest of the weekend flew past, Charlie's Sunday lunchtime soiree was a huge hit with their guests. Splitting up their guests into two groups, they gave everyone a tour of the *Cape*. All the men opted for Charlie's tour, probably because of what she was wearing. It was a lovely low cut, navy blue with white polka dot dress which ended well above her knees. So that left all the ladies to have to go on Bruce's tour. Bruce was certain that it was Charlie's dress that had tempted the men to go on her tour.

Monday was spent moving equipment out of the crew area in preparation for the conversion, bedding was stripped from the other cabins, washed and put away into storage cupboards. They packed the overnight bags that they would need for their stay at Burgos and during the ferry crossing, deciding what gifts of alcohol that they were going to take back to the UK. Not to mention what they would require for themselves for the short time that they planned to be in the UK.

CHAPTER 13

It was just after nine o'clock on the morning of Tuesday when Bruce brought the *Cape* alongside the chandlery dock. Sergio was there to greet them and once they had finished tying off, Bruce spoke to Sergio. "Sergio, if there are any parts that need to have to be replaced, then please just go ahead and do it, don't wait for me to authorise it. I will need to have the boat back in the water for the afternoon of the seventeenth of March. The other thing is this." Bruce explained his idea to Sergio about the fitting and installing of as many solar panels as possible onto the roof of the flybridge, then installing a bank of batteries in the forward section of the engine room with an inverter. The batteries could then be used to provide power for the fridges and freezers and essential lighting. This would relieve the necessity, to continuously run a generator whilst they were anchored off-grid.

"That is very easy to do Bruce. I can also fit an automatic switch to start/stop the small generator so, that when the voltage in the batteries has dropped, then the generator will start then stop again when a full charge has been reached. This is no problem at all, my friend."

By the time that Bruce and Charlie had carried their small amount of luggage from the moored *Cape* and stowed the cases into the rear of the minibus, it was nearly ten o'clock. Bruce felt a pang of regret and almost a sense of loss, leaving the *Cape* in the hands of strangers, but he knew they would be in good hands. All their personal goods had been locked into the master cabin. That was the one cabin that wouldn't be required for access during the servicing and conversion of the crew quarters. Bruce now felt that the *Cape* was the only existence that he knew of and he had certainly had the most wonderful three weeks imaginable. As he got into the unfamiliar driving seat, Sergio came over to bid them a safe journey and reassured Bruce that the *Cape* would be in good hands and promised to stay in touch.

Making their way out of Malaga, they followed the A45 to Granada, then the A44 towards Madrid, stopping for a light lunch at some services just off the motorway. Changing drivers, they passed Madrid and found the A1 motorway which got them to Burgos for just after six o'clock that evening. Finding their pre-booked hotel on the Calle de la Merced, they checked in with their overnight bags. Bruce made certain that he had at least one bottle of The Guv'nor and a bottle of Glenmorangie in his bag. The room was gorgeous, very spacious and airy, with a view out over the Rio Alarnzon. They dined in the restaurant with an accompanying bottle of Rioja and then, following their meal, took a gentle stroll around the area of their hotel before making their way back up to the room for an early shower.

As the ferry wasn't due to sail until three o'clock the next afternoon, there was no hurry to have to get up too early. Charlie ordered room service coffee for nine o'clock then they made their way down to breakfast for a quarter to ten. In the dining room, they enjoyed a continental breakfast before going back up to their room to complete their daily routines. Although they had only been together for a relatively short time, they both respected each other's privacy when performing the one smelly function a day otherwise, they were perfectly open with each other. They finally left the confines of the hotel at eleven forty-five and with Charlie at the wheel, they made their way to the Port at Bilbao. On arrival at the docks, they cleared the booking in process and picked up their cabin passes. Finally, they were directed into a lane pending the last customs checks and boarding procedures. The lane they were put in contained a few commercial vehicles and some small motorhomes. Deciding that it would be some time before they were called forward they locked up the minibus and went down to the small quayside coffee shop where they got sandwiches and coffee. Then returning with the refreshments to the minibus. Following that they didn't have long to wait until they were summoned forward. It was fun explaining to the customs people that they had British Passports and a Spanish registered vehicle and that neither of them had been to Morocco recently. Charlie's fluent Spanish was a great help. The vehicle was swiftly searched, presumably to make sure that they weren't carrying any illegal passengers, then they were called forward to board the ferry. Finding their way up to the eighth deck and their cabin was easy and they were soon settled in.

The *Cap Finistere* was an amazingly comfortable ferry with dining and bar facilities, a duty-free shop and even a swimming pool on the open tenth deck but being winter, it was now closed. They decided to go and explore the ship and found the chart plot repeater on the starboard side on their way to investigate the menu in the restaurant. Having made their restaurant reservations for seven-thirty, they went back to the bar and settled down watching the dockside activities whilst they sipped their beers. Not something they would normally do at three o'clock in the afternoon. An elderly couple asked if they could share the table with them, remarking on their tans and asking if they had been on holiday. So, it was with great delight that they told the couple that they lived on a boat, which was currently in the south of Spain. The couple were returning to the UK after spending some time with their motorhome in Portugal and gave apt and enthusiastic accounts of their tour. Finally excusing themselves, Bruce and Charlie withdrew to their cabin and sitting together on a bunk leaning up against the partition, they chatted about their plans for the next week. Charlie was going to stay with Bruce, as her parents had rented her room out to a young trainee nurse at the NHS Hospital, Portsmouth. Save for the two days that she needed to go up to Ripon to collect her belongings from her ex-flatmate. Bruce was wondering how he was going to fill in his days whilst in the UK. On the *Cape*, there was always something to do. There was family to have to visit or be visited and discussing how they would accomplish it. What he had not foreseen was just how busy they were both going to be.

"Do you know, I have got an idea as to how I think it would be best for you to meet my children." Bruce had felt that this was going to be quite difficult. He had no idea as to how his sons and daughters in law would react to the introduction of someone new in Bruce's life.

"Go on then." Charlie turned to face him. This was a subject that Charlie had been dreading.

"Well, if we were on the *Cape*, that would be on our turf so to speak. So, that automatically gives you the advantage." Bruce squirmed around on the narrow bunk to face Charlie.

"Yes." She said pensively. "But the *Cape* is a thousand miles away and we are going to be in England."

"Ah, but we are going to be staying in my, our, bungalow and we invite them to us, therefore giving us the psychological advantage over the kids." Bruce placed a heavy emphasis on the word ours.

"Brilliant idea!" Charlie beamed at him.

When Charlie had left the Army, she and a fellow former officer from the QARANC had bought a flat together in Ripon. They were both working at the Ripon and District Hospital so, the flat had formed an ideal base. Before Charlie had gone off on her travels, she had sold her half of the flat to her friend. Her friend had agreed to look after some of her clothes and personal items until Charlie had been able to find somewhere permanent to move to. Bruce had long agreed to let Charlie take the minibus up to Ripon to pick up her belongings and not wanting to interfere or get too involved with Charlie's past, he hadn't involved himself in her plans to go to Ripon.

"Okay, so when do you want to go up to Ripon?" Bruce asked.

"So, maybe Tuesday or Wednesday next week." She paused. "Brucie, will you come up with me, please. I don't want to be away from you, even for two days. We could find a nice hotel for the evening." Swivelling up onto her knees, she pushed him back on the bunk and started to get on top of him. "And it might mean that we could even christen another bed." She concluded with her voice getting a little huskier and kissing him deeply on the mouth.

"Well, how could I possibly refuse an invitation like that." He mumbled when his mouth became free. They lay on the narrow bunk facing each other, Charlie had her left arm under Bruce's neck with his head comfortably on Charlie's shoulder whilst they continued chatting about plans for the next week. Bruce described the three bedroomed, two bathrooms, one study bungalow to Charlie, with the kitchen and separate dining room that was on the seafront at the corner of Hound Lane of Hayling Island.

"Just you remember one thing though." Charlie's breath was on Bruce's cheek and smelt so sweet as he breathed in deeply and squeezed her gently with the arm that was around her waist. "I am still your Catering Officer, so the galley, I mean the kitchen, is still mine. Comprendo!" She smiled and kissed him on the forehead. "Oh, God! My arm has gone to sleep."

Groaning, they both separated, Bruce virtually falling off the bunk because it was so narrow and he had been right on the edge. It raised a chuckle from Charlie. It was just after seven o'clock so they readied themselves to go up to the dining room for their evening meal. They both opted for the soup of the day, followed by the roast chicken accompanied by a couple of glasses of a beautifully chilled Chablis.

The rest of the crossing to Portsmouth was uneventful. As they came into Portsmouth, passing the Isle of White off to their port side, Bruce got a signal on his mobile phone. He decided to phone his eldest son. He had hardly spoken to his children at all over the past three weeks, other than to say that he was enjoying the sun and had made friends with someone called Charlie. Charlie was helping him crew the boat. They were both sat in the lounge at the time, having vacated their cabin and with their overnight bags between them on the floor.

Speaking to Ron, his eldest son, he let him know that he was now back in English waters. "So, it would be lovely for you and Mel to come down for the weekend, come down Saturday, we can take Jasmine to the Southsea Fun Park, stay have a meal and we can have a catch-up chat. What do you say?" Bruce paused after the question and listened to Ron for a short time, the smile on his face increasing all the time before replying. "That is fantastic, thank you, yes, of course, I'll be there." The call ended shortly afterwards. Bruce's face beamed. "Well! That is this weekend and next weekend taken care of my lover."

"Bruce! What exactly have you told your family about me?" Charlie asked.

"Well, I think that they think you are possibly a bloke." Bruce sniggered.

"What!" Charlie burst out laughing.

"Well, the few short phone calls that I have had with them, have been along the lines that I have met a person called Charlie and that Charlie is helping me crew the boat and that Charlie is a brilliant chef." Bruce continued to chuckle. "It hasn't been until now that I have realised, I have sort of kept you under wraps, so to speak. Oh! And by the way, I have had an invitation to Ron's mess ball next weekend."

"Oh my God!" Charlie chortled. "Saturday is going to be immensely hilarious."

Bruce repeated the phone call to his youngest son, Luke and extending a similar invitation for the following Sunday. The option of the following weekend was out of the question. However, a day's visit on the coming Sunday was agreed as Bruce's eldest granddaughter, Angela, had a birthday party to go to on the Saturday following and both girls had some dance rehearsals the following Sunday. Apart from which Luke was tied up with work that had been previously agreed on. They continued sitting in the lounge chatting, passengers were called forward to go down to the car decks and a mad crush ensued at the stairwells and lift access. Bruce and Charlie opted to remain seated until the crush dissipated. They were sitting almost opposite each other. Bruce was leaning forward towards Charlie and was wordlessly staring into her hazel eyes. Charlie looked quizzically at him. "Bruce, what is it?"

"Charlotte Hope!" Bruce paused and took a deep breath. "Charlie, would you be my partner forever and ever, as my wife or as however you feel is right for you?"

Charlie reached forward and took his hands in hers, sitting up she opened her mouth smiling, shaking her head in total surprise. "Oh, Brucie! God! Where did that come from sweetheart?" She stood up, pulling him with her. "I want to be your wife now and forever, my darling." She flung her arms around him and hugged him so tightly. Tears cascaded down her cheeks as she kissed him again and again with joy.

One of the bar staff had been clearing tables nearby and had overheard the proposal. He put one hand on each of their shoulders and said. "Congratulations, Madame et Monsieur. Bon chance!" In rapid French, he conveyed to his colleagues as to what had just happened. There were shouts of congratulations whistling and a good round of applause from his co-workers. Bruce wiped tears of joy and emotion away from his eyes and kissed the tears of happiness from Charlie's face, who then managed to find a couple of tissues for them both. Bidding the staff farewell and thanking them for their good wishes, Bruce and Charlie headed down to the car deck. They didn't have long to wait until they drove off the ferry and emerged into the weak English sunshine. At least it wasn't raining, they both joked. Bruce drove them through customs and then onto the A27 heading down towards Hayling Island.

The drive down to the island only took twenty-five minutes. They stopped at the local Sainsbury's shop and got bread milk, eggs and ingredients that Charlie chose for their evening meal, which included a couple of nice-looking steaks. From there, it was a very short drive down to the bungalow. Bruce parked the minibus on the driveway and to one side of the accompanying double garage. They entered the bungalow, holding hands. Bruce made for the thermostat on the lounge wall and then proceeded to show Charlie around, still holding hands. The whole bungalow seemed very spacious. Ostensibly because although it was fully furnished, it lacked any pictures or homely features and was very much a bleak bachelor's pad. They went into the guest double bedroom and opened the blinds, similarly those in the small single bedroom. There was also a small office that housed a desk on which there was a large television screen, which obviously substituted as a screen for a laptop. A noticeboard with a list of telephone numbers and countless pictures of boats, most of which she recognised as being of the *Cape* and various aspects of her. There were other pictures on the wall, one of a leopard lying across a branch, another one of a young man with a German Sheppard and a leopard on either side of him, another of a young boy and a German Sheppard in deep sleep with the boy cuddled into the dog. In the whole of the bungalow, this was the only room that looked as if it was lived in. In front of the desk was a very comfortable looking leather swivel chair. The three shelves on one of the walls contained several framed pictures depicting children and grandchildren during various stages of growing up and a three-quarter bottle of Glenmorangie a glass and a small glass water jug on a silver platter. Above the window, a series of military memorabilia plaques were mounted. To the side of the desk was a comfortable looking reclining chair with a footstool in front of it facing another television screen mounted on the wall opposite.

The main bedroom housed an unmade double bed the wardrobe, however, had a couple of suits, slacks, shirts and ties, obviously Bruce's clothes. The ensuite bathroom was bare and devoid of any personal articles at all. That would change soon, Charlie thought, as would the rest of the bungalow. She smiled to herself, she was going to make her future husband very happy.

Charlie had found the bedding for the master bedroom stored in the top of one of the wardrobes. Bruce had apparently not used this bedroom or bathroom since he had bought the bungalow. She had found some articles of Bruce's in the family bathroom and the single bed was made up. He must have rattled around here, poor soul, she thought. Going into the kitchen she found the kettle and filled the filter jug, locating the tea bags and sugar, she prepared two mugs for tea.

Having brought all the goods in from the minibus, Bruce had gone around to speak to his neighbours. They had been keeping an eye on the bungalow for him during his absence. He left them with three bottles of a 2014 Rioja in gratitude. Returning to the bungalow, he sifted through the mail separating it accordingly. The vast majority was destined for the recycle bin. There were four pieces of correspondence that he was interested in. The first one was from a solicitor which he opened immediately. Skimming through it, he smiled to himself as he refolded it and put it to one side. The second was the new registration documents for the quad. Opening the third letter, he discovered it was from the NHS. He groaned.

"What is it, honey?" Charlie asked.

"Letter from the NHS, it appears that I have an appointment with my surgeon." He checked the calendar on his phone, did a quick mental calculation, and said. "Next Tuesday, nine o'clock at Frimley Park Hospital. Aargh!"

"No worries." She replied calmly. "Probably a final check over before he gives you a clean bill of health. Then we can go and live it up in the sunshine." Charlie smiled, cupping the tea mug in both her hands. The temperature still hadn't gone past nineteen degrees but had improved on the fifteen degrees it had been when they had first arrived.

Bruce opened the fourth letter. It bore the official crest of Ron's Regiment at Tidworth, addressed to Bruce it was a formal invitation to attend the Spring Ball at the Regimental Officers Mess at Tidworth Garrison on the evening of Saturday the 14th of March, 2020. The invitation included a plus one. Bruce issued a low whistle and an exclamation of "Wow!"

"Now what?" Charlie asked quizzically.

Handing Charlie, the letter to see for herself, he replied. "We are going to the ball, Cinders."

Taking the letter Charlie skimmed through it and then handed it back to Bruce. "Well then, I had better not lose my slipper then." They both laughed.

After tea, Bruce and Charlie went into the master bedroom. They both made the bed and stuffed the duvet into its cover, Charlie plumped up the pillows and sat down on the edge of the bed, watching Bruce unpack his bathroom gear and then the few clothes that he had brought back with him, which mostly amounted to socks and underwear.

"Bruce?" She asked. "Has anyone apart from you stayed here since you bought this place?"

Bruce shook his head. "No, just me. Why do you ask?"

"Because we are going to have to do some shopping if we are going to have people over to stay for the weekend."

"Yep. I see what you mean." There were only two sets of towels and no sheets or duvet cover bedding for the other double bed "I had planned on taking you shopping tomorrow anyway." He continued. "There is the small matter of a traditional ring." Charlie's mobile phone rang before she could reply. He left her in private to have the conversation and went into the office in search of a pad and pen to start the shopping list. He couldn't find his pad, so he took a sheet of A4 out of the printer and started scribbling on that, the list to include soaps and shower gels.

Charlie came into the office with the phone held close to her chest. "My Mum and Dad would like us to come over for dinner tomorrow evening?" She sat down in the recliner. Bruce nodded his head in agreement. Charlie continued her conversation with what sounded like her mother, crossing her legs as she leaned back comfortably into the recliner as she smiled at Bruce.

Bruce picked up the small water jug and went into the kitchen, returning almost immediately with the water jug filled and a second matching glass. He poured two generous measures of Glenmorangie into the glasses and spilt a small amount of water into each one, then returned to his desk chair. He placed one of the glasses on the corner of the desk next to where Charlie was sitting just as she was saying her goodbyes.

"Bit early for this?" She smiled.

"Well! Here is to you, the future Mrs Williams, that is only if you want to change your name, of course?" Bruce raised his glass.

Charlie got out of the recliner picking up the whisky and clinked her glass with Bruce, parking her bottom on the edge of the desk to the side of his leg. "There is nothing that would make me happier than to be able to take your family name." Charlie replied.

That evening Charlie cooked a gorgeous Steak Chasseur, accompanied by asparagus and new potatoes. After which they settled comfortably together on the sofa, with their wine in balloon glasses and a selection of music coming from the office where Bruce had activated 'Alexa'.

"Charlie, there are a lot of things we don't know about each other, some we will find out in due course as time goes by, but there are things that you will need to know about me and certainly before you meet them, my children. However, I do have one statement to make before we do anything else this evening."

Charlie nodded her head in acceptance. "Okay!" she said. "Statement away then."

Bruce laughed. "This afternoon you accepted my proposal, I gave you the choice of being my wife, partner or whatever. You accepted to be my wife." Charlie nodded in agreement. Bruce continued. "It must have come as a bit of a shock to you and I realise that getting married is generally considered to be a girl's biggest day of her life." Again, Charlie nodded in agreement. "Well, I would like you to take your time and consider how, where and when you would like us to get married and who you would like to involve."

"When do you want to know by?"

Bruce got up to refill their glasses from the bottle on the sideboard. "Honey, I will know when you know. Now then, you'll need to know about my financial situation. Just so that you know, that within reason, we have very little constraints when it comes to money."

For the first time since they had met, Bruce revealed the truth about his fortune courtesy of the National Lottery. He had told his children that the windfall was a very modest amount. The truth was that the donation from

Camelot had been more than eighty-five million pounds. As far as Bruce was concerned, apart from his bank manager and Camelot, Charlie was the only other person who knew the truth about Bruce's fortune. He had given his sons a million pounds each and set up trust funds for his grandchildren as well. The confirmation letter for this he had received from his solicitor that afternoon, the transfers were due to take place a week on Monday.

Pausing, Charlie looked at Bruce quizzically. "But I don't understand." Charlie stammered. "You could have bought a brand new superyacht and paid people to crew it for you. This bungalow, you could have bought a mansion with its own marina and a private airfield."

Bruce thought for a moment before replying. "Yes, I know. However, I have a beautiful bungalow here with no one to share it with, until now I have lived in my office. In hindsight, I should have bought a one-bedroom flat. What was the point in buying a mansion when I am only going to be able to use one room? As for the *Cape*, what is the fun of having to pay other people to have the enjoyment of driving your boat? The *Cape* or a boat of her size, is probably going to be the biggest boat that I, now us are safely going to be able to handle on our own, possibly with certain modifications in place. When I moved into the *Cape* I went to the forward cabin, not too small and not too big. I had no idea that I was going to meet you and find happiness again. Before you came along, I was bloody lonely. I couldn't even stand the depressive winters and the attitude of the people, to be blunt even, the attitude of some of my own family at times. That is why I searched for a place in the sun. Ron and Mel, mostly Mel wanted me to move in with them, but probably only so that they could have a live-in childminder. Melissa can get very overbearing and bossy if you understand my meaning. Don't get me wrong, I love my grandchildren, but now I have done my share of parenting, not to mention that I need my own space to share with you."

"I think I know where you are coming from." Charlie smiled in understanding and hugged Bruce. "You won't be lonely again, my darling."

CHAPTER 14

Friday morning dawned and by eight-thirty they were both up, dressed and breakfasted with scrambled eggs, toast and marmalade which set them up for the day. "Are we taking the minibus into Portsmouth?" Charlie inquired.

"No." Bruce replied with a smile, pressing a button on the key fob he was carrying. "I fancy a bit of classic." The double door of the garage swung up and open. There was one vehicle in the double garage covered with a dust sheet. Removing the dust sheet with a 'Ta Da', Bruce revealed the gleaming British Racing Green 1973, Triumph TR6.

Charlie exclaimed. "Oh! Crikey! that is stunning." Walking around the car, she said. "I just hope that the heater works." Bruce disconnected the float charger and closed down the bonnet. Pulling on the hand brake and taking the gearbox out of gear, he again checked that the vehicle was in neutral before putting the key into the ignition and turning it on. The fuel pump hummed, allowing the pump to run for about three seconds before turning the key further and engaging the starter motor. The engine turned over briefly before catching, one gentle blip on the throttle and Bruce let the engine idle. The burble of the straight-six two-point five-litre engine came as music to Bruce's ears. Charlie poured herself into the passenger seat. 'Just as well I am wearing jeans'. She thought to herself, whilst Bruce folded the dust sheet and put it on the workbench. There were cases of tools stacked on the workbench but apart from that, the garage was bare and as clinically clean as Bruce kept the engine room on the *Cape*. Pristine.

The short drive into Portsmouth didn't take long. They found a parking spot in the main car park and made their way to Ernest Jones on Commercial Street. Almost at once, Charlie fell in love with the ring, it was beautiful and only set Bruce back twelve hundred pounds. Putting the diamond ring in his pocket, he explained to Charlie. "Sweetheart, I know I asked you yesterday but I would like to ask you again after I have sort of asked your father for his consent this evening."

"What a lovely idea Brucie. You are such a lovely romantic." Charlie linked her arm into Bruce's arm and hugged his arm into her. "And I am going to say yes again. I have decided I would really like to get married as soon as possible while we are in the UK so that our families can be there as well. If that's possible?"

Bruce leaned over and kissed her lightly on the cheek. The rest of the morning was a whirlwind of activity, as was the afternoon. The last call of the day was to the local Registrar, explaining their circumstances, they were granted a special permission to get married. The time and date were set for eleven am on Friday, the thirteenth of March. Lucky for some and in the past, Friday the thirteenth had always been a lucky day for Bruce. 'Whirlwind romance, whirlwind wedding'. Bruce thought.

Bruce had ordered an Uber car to collect them for seven pm that evening and to collect them again at eleven pm from Gosport. Charlie looked absolutely spectacular that evening. She was smiling from ear to ear. "When are you going to do the deed?" She asked.

"Probably after the meal and by the way, you look utterly stunning." Bruce walked across the room and took her in his arms hugging her.

"You don't look too bad yourself, Brucie baby." Charlie responded by hugging him back. Bruce was wearing a pair of light brown slacks, a royal blue shirt and the navy blue and maroon tie of the Guards Division over which he had a navy-blue blazer.

Suddenly, realising as well that he had no clue as to what it was that Mr and Mrs Hope did or their names for that matter. All he knew was that they lived in Gosport. "So, what is it that your Mum and Dad do for a living, Charlie?" He asked.

"Well, Dad is now a retired Surgeon Commander, his name is James and he specialised in orthopaedics, so he was quite interested in you when I told him about your past medical history. I think that the two of you will get on famously. He has a Triumph Stag which he restored, nurtures and fusses over it like it was a new born child. So, I reckon when he finds out about your TR6, he'll be wanting to see it." She smiled at Bruce.

"Our TR6." Bruce corrected her, holding her at arm's length. Bruce looked deeply into those beautiful hazel eyes. "Our bungalow, our boat. What's mine is yours from now on." Charlie saw the blue eyes staring into her eyes with every ounce of passion and meaningfulness. Her heart melted.

Shaking her head, Charlie pulled him back into her arms, squeezing him tightly. "No, no Bruce, I can't do that, please can we discuss this later?" At that moment, the Uber driver rang the doorbell.

"Sweetheart, of course, we can. Let's get in the car."

Once they were ensconced comfortably in the back of the Mercedes, Charlie continued to tell him about her family. "Mum is also a retired surgeon, her name is Mary, she used to specialise with pandemics and tropical diseases. Mum did a lot of work with the Ebola crisis in Africa. You will love her she has got a really wicked sense of humour. Oh! By the way, they both love sailing, they have a Hans Christian 48T."

Arriving at the Hope's family home in Onassis Way, Gosport, they were greeted at the door by Mary. Mother and daughter embraced and kissed. There was an obvious really strong bond between them.

"So, and who do we have here?" Mary turned her attention to Bruce.

"Mummy, this is Bruce." Charlie introduced them. Mary stood back and looked at Bruce with a faint smile on her face. Like Charlie, she was a tall woman, but not as tall as Charlie. Bruce formally offered his right hand, which Mary brushed away and embraced him warmly, kissing him on each cheek. Charlie laughed. Moving through into the lounge, a tall man got up from what was very obviously 'a his' chair. Charlie and James embraced, but not with the same feeling as she had embraced her mother.

Standing aside after the embrace, Charlie introduced Bruce. "Daddy, this is Bruce."

Still clutching the bunch of flowers in his left hand and with the bottle of Sandymans in the crook of the same arm, Bruce extended his right hand. "James, lovely to meet you."

"Welcome to our home Bruce. We have heard so much about you over the last few weeks."

Glancing at Charlie, Bruce replied. "Oh! I hope that there was some good in there. Anyway, these are for you from us." Bruce handed the flowers to Mary and the bottle of port to James.

The roast beef was simply exquisite. There was no doubt in Bruce's mind as to who had taught Charlie some of her cooking skills. The accompanying Bordeaux complemented the meal beautifully, which was completed with cheese and grapes. James opted to open the bottle of Sandymans, Mary produced the port glasses and once these had been charged, Charlie glanced across the table at Bruce and nodded quizzically.

Bruce got to his feet. "Aah! If I may be so bold." Bruce paused, Charlie grinned. "Aah! Sir, James, Mary. Aah! I have asked Charlie for her hand in marriage. She has agreed. And I aah! Would like your consent to formally, propose to your daughter?"

A beaming James replied. "My dear man. Please do!"

Bruce was already moving around the table behind Mary, removing the ring from his pocket and approached Charlie, who swivelled expectantly in her seat towards Bruce. Bruce knelt on his right knee. "Charlie, I fell in love with you the first moment we met, now I want to love you forever. I would like to ask you now, my love, if you will marry me and take me to be your husband?" Bruce took Charlie's left hand and placed the ring on her finger.

Tears of happiness streamed down Charlie's cheeks. "Brucie, I fell in love with you when we first met." Charlie sniffed. "And yes! I will marry you but only if you will take me to be your wife?" She stood up from her chair, pulling him from the floor at the same time. "Come here you." She kissed him hard on the lips.

The rest of the evening flew by. There was so much to discuss and so many plans to make, it was like a short-lived tornado. Before they knew it there was a gentle tap on the door by the Uber driver.

The next morning Bruce and Charlie were up and dressed by eight o'clock, not expecting Ron and family until about eleven o'clock. This would give them sufficient time to get everything ready. Bruce ran the vacuum cleaner around the bungalow whilst Charlie busied herself in the kitchen getting the Bolognese sauce ready to go into the slow cooker. Then together, they put the new freshly laundered bedding onto the guest beds. They had already decided that lunch the following day, when they had the whole family together, was not going to be easy in the bungalow. So, Bruce had already booked a family table at the Maypole Inn, which was just up the road from the bungalow. Charlie was in the kitchen, preparing the percolator for Ron and family's imminent arrival when Bruce heard the unmistakable sound of a Range Rover's V8 engine pulling up on the driveway in front of the garage.

"I think we have company, sweetheart." Bruce said to Charlie as he went to the front door.

First out of the Range Rover was Jasmine, his youngest granddaughter, who came rushing over to him. "Grandad, grandad." She flung her arms around Bruce's midriff. "It's great to see you again. Are you staying here forever now? Please don't go back."

"Sorry, sweetheart." Bruce replied. "But I am afraid that I am going back out to Spain to live on my boat, then you can come out and visit me in the sun."

Ron had got out of the vehicle, he and Bruce embraced each other with genuine affection, accompanied by the big manly pats on the back that some fathers and sons do. "Great to see you, Dad. How's the boat?"

"Great to see you too, boy." Bruce responded. "She is great, I have got loads of pictures to show you the weather has been brilliant!"

"Your tan looks fantastic. God! You look so much better than you did. What was it three weeks ago?"

Before Bruce could respond, his daughter in law, Melissa, put her arms around him. "Hello, Dad." She kissed him on each cheek with the emphasised sound of 'mwhah' that the 'hollywoodies' do.

"Go on through." Bruce said to his family. "I'll help Jasie with her shoes."

Whilst at Dolphin Cove, on the Sunday following the bombing attempt. Sheila had picked up Bruce's camera and amongst other photographs, had taken a beautiful picture of Bruce and Charlie.

They were on the foredeck with their arms around each other and their heads together smiling into the lens. It was only the day before that Bruce had taken in several images on a USB stick and had had them printed and framed. These, Charlie had distributed around the lounge and dining room the previous evening.

Ron and Melissa had gone on ahead into the bungalow whilst Bruce helped Jasmine with her shoes. Holding his granddaughter by the hand, he led her into the lounge.

Ron had picked up the photograph of Bruce and Charlie. "Err Dad?" He asked. "Who is this?"

At that precise moment, Charlie made her entrance into the lounge. "Hi, all!" Charlie, as always, looked stunning, but now she looked even more spectacular. Ron and Melissa's mouths dropped open with surprise.

"That, and this is Charlie." Bruce introduced her moving over and putting a possessive arm around her waist, still holding Jasmine's hand.

The first to react was Melissa. "What the hell! No! Sorry, I didn't mean that. You have got a girlfriend?"

"No!" Bruce replied. "I have got a fiancé and we are getting married in six days' time." Bruce finished. Mouth gaping in shock and surprise, Melissa sat down in what was normally Bruce's recliner which Charlie had moved out of the study for additional seating.

Recovering quickly, Ron made his way over to Bruce and Charlie. Kissing Charlie on the cheek, he hugged his father. "Well! I just can't believe it." He said. "Congratulations! Both of you. I hope that you will both be very, very happy."

Charlie replied for both of them. "Thank you, Ron, we already are."

"Are you going to get married, Grandad? Are you going to get married?" Jasmine burst in.

It was seemingly reluctantly that Melissa made her way over and congratulated them both. Plans to take Jasmine out to the park at Southsea were put on hold for the time being. Bruce offered Ron the job of best man, which he readily accepted. As they weren't going out, Charlie decided that she needed to pop out for a moment to get some supplies for lunch.

"Ron. Would you move your car so that Charlie can get ours out, please mate?" Bruce asked.

"What? Are you going to let her drive your TR6?" Melissa burst out.

"It's okay, Dad. I'll run her down." Ron replied, reaching for his keys.

Melissa jumped up. "No! I'll take her."

Realising Melissa's intention of giving Charlie a grilling, Bruce intervened. "Thanks, Ron. I would appreciate it if you wouldn't mind."

Charlie came over to Bruce and took his hands in hers. "I am so sorry, Brucie. I didn't want to come between you and your family." In the meantime, he had seen Ron go over to Melissa who was whispering a one-sided, terse conversation in her ear. Having seen the look on his face, he was unimpressed with his wife's performance.

"Sweetheart, there is only one person who is not being very nice to you and I am not going to let it happen. You will be fine with Ron."

After Ron and Charlie had left, Melissa continued to sulk in Bruce's recliner. Jasmine had gone out the front to play with her skipping rope whilst Bruce cleared up the coffee mugs in the kitchen.

"I just don't get it?" Melissa stormed into the kitchen. "You have met this girl, who is no older than me, then you say you have fallen in love and now you are going to marry her. She is only after you for your money and your things. Worse still, no one is allowed to drive your bloody precious car but oh, fuck me, yeah, she can."

Unfortunately for Melissa, she took Bruce's silence to indicate that she could continue her tirade against her father-in-law, nor had she noticed the expression on Bruce's face.

"I don't understand why you can't just be sensible. We have got a perfectly good room for you where you can spend quality time with your granddaughter. Anyway, what can she give you that I can't?"

Bruce slammed his fist on the work surface top. "Well for starters, she gives a really good fuck!" Realising that she had overstepped the mark, Melissa's face paled. She had never seen Bruce so angry. "As for a room, that is it. I have two homes, my primary one is in the sun, where I am going to live with Charlie as my wife, whether you fuckin' like it or not. A word of advice Mel. Never, ever cross me again or try to control me in any way, shape or form." Pointing his finger at her chest and leaning threateningly towards her he continued. "If ever you are tempted in any way to threaten or try to hurt Charlie in any conceivable way, I don't know how or what, but trust me, there will be dire consequences because I will also consider it as a personal attack against me. Now, do you fuckin' understand me?" Bruce hadn't raised his voice, he hadn't needed to, the firmness and annunciation of his words were more than sufficient. Melissa had burst into tears and was about to escape her father-in-law. Bruce continued but his tone was softer. "I had hoped that you and Charlie would have hit it off as good friends. I had wanted that to happen, and God only knows you can't get enough of those these days. You haven't burnt your bridges yet there is still time to make it up to Charlie and Ron for that matter."

Bruce changed his shoes and went outside to play with Jasmine. "C'mon Jasie! Let's see if you can beat me at skipping then?"

Bruce and Jasmine were still playing outside at the front of the house when Ron and Charlie pulled up on the driveway. Ron looked at his father through the windscreen before turning to Charlie and saying. "Do you know Charlie, I haven't seen Dad look so happy for a long time. Thank you!"

Charlie put a hand on his arm and replied. "It works both ways, Ron."

Jasmine, holding her grandfather's hand, dragged him towards her father. "Daddy, Daddy, I won the skipping against Grandad."

Bruce took the shopping bag from Charlie and putting an arm around his son's shoulder he very quietly spoke. "I am afraid that I was pushed into a situation where I had to have words with Mel." Ron stopped and looked at his father. Charlie guessing what was going on, took Jasmine's hand and skipping together they went to the front door. Very quickly and concisely, Bruce recounted the incident to Ron.

Ron's response was with a wry smile. "Well, she more than deserves that Dad, she has forever nagged me to get you to stay with us. Mel doesn't get it that you have your own life to lead. And Dad, what an absolute corker Charlie is. She is just so lovely, I am jealous as hell." He hugged his father with genuine love and affection.

Bruce put the shopping on the kitchen table. "Well, so what can I do to help with the lunch?"

Charlie hugged him and then kissed him on the lips. "I just love you Bruce Williams. You have a wonderful son. Jasmine?" She called through to the lounge. "Would you like to come and tell me what you would like for your lunch, darling?" Charlie was in control of their bungalow and that suited Bruce down to the ground. After having been put back in her place, Mel had gone through to the spare double room and had been left to reflect on her actions. That was where Ron had found her.

CHAPTER 15

There was a choice of beef, ham, salami, cheese, prawns, olives, sausage rolls and baguettes. Bruce had set the dining room table with the new silver candlestick holder as the centrepiece that Charlie had chosen. He then set out four wine glasses and opened a bottle of Chablis from the fridge. Jasmine didn't need any encouragement to get to the table, she was there before Bruce announced that lunch was ready. Except for Melissa, they all sat down at the table. "Will Mel be joining us?" Charlie enquired of Ron.

"I thought that she was on her way." Ron replied, annoyed, starting to get up. "I'll go and get her."

"No, no!" Charlie replied. "I will, excuse me." She got up and left the table.

"What's wrong with Mummy?" Jasmine enquired.

"Mummy's not feeling very well, so Aunty Charlie has gone to see if she can help make Mummy feel better." Ron explained. "Did you know that Aunty Charlie used to be a very special nurse and she has also helped to make Grandad better as well?"

"I love Aunty Charlie Daddy." The child replied, stuffing a second sausage roll into her mouth.

It was five minutes later when Charlie led an apologetic and contrite Melissa into the dining room after which the afternoon passed very pleasantly. They decided to take a stroll on the seafront and allow Jasmine to burn off some of the calories that she had accumulated during lunch. During the stroll, they discussed the upcoming wedding and the increasing worry of the Coronavirus spreading through the world.

"What will you guys do if it gets to Spain?" Mel asked Bruce.

"I haven't discussed it with Charlie yet." He looked at Charlie. "But my thoughts are probably to load the *Cape* with as much food and fuel and provisions as possible and sit it out somewhere. I am going to phone the yard in Malaga on Monday anyway."

"What about you?" Mel asked, addressing Charlie.

"I'll go with whatever my Captain decides for us." Charlie laughed, linking her arm into Bruce's.

The rest of the afternoon and evening passed agreeably, with Auntie Charlie having to read a bedtime story for Jasmine. They did make time to phone Luke and Lucy, Bruce's youngest son and daughter in law, to let them know about the engagement, so at least it wasn't going to be a massive surprise when they arrived the next morning. With Jasmine getting up at seven o'clock, no one had any peace at all after that. Fortunately, Charlie had put on a negligee and Bruce a pair of pants before going to bed. Because Jasmine's first port of call that morning was jumping into bed between Grandad and Auntie Charlie, who had to read her another story. They were rescued by Mel, who was about to admonish her daughter when Jasmine pointed at Bruce's arm and said how much better Grandads scars were and had said how good a nurse Aunty Charlie was because she was fixing Grandad after the fight with the crocodile.

Charlie did scramble eggs and smoked salmon for breakfast, followed by toast and marmalade. Preparations were made for the imminent arrival of Bruce's youngest son Luke, his wife Lucy and their two daughters, Angela and Tracey. The relatively short drive from Swindon shouldn't take any more than an hour and a half. However, well known for usually arriving up to an hour late in the past and often with an excuse like 'the girls weren't ready' or 'Tracey wasn't well'. Causing Bruce and Ron to jokingly estimate their arrival time at being at least midday, which was fine as the table at the Maypole had been booked for one o'clock. A two-hour leeway. From Bruce's point of view, there was only one downside to having the whole family together, that was that his daughters in law didn't get on with each other. An aspect that he mentioned to Charlie when they had a private moment. Bruce and Ron decided that they would take Jasmine across the road to the seafront with a kite that Bruce had found in a cupboard in the garage. It was an absolute joy for Bruce to be able to share the time with his youngest granddaughter. Ron stood back and took some photographs on his phone. "Let me have copies of those, won't you!" Bruce shouted over to Ron.

"I think we have company, Dad." Ron indicated behind Bruce. Bruce turned around to see Luke walking over towards them. Father and son hugged, brother and brother, hugged, niece and uncle, hugged. Bruce checked his watch it was five past eleven. Ron took over kite flying duties with Jasmine, this gave Bruce and Luke a chance to catch up. They got ten minutes together before they were joined by Charlie, Melissa, Lucy, Angela and Tracey. The two girls raced on ahead and flung arms around their grandfather. Lucy advanced at a more sedate pace and hugged Bruce, kissing him on the lips.

"You are really looking so much better, it looks like Charlie has done a great job looking after you. Your tan is wonderful." Lucy beamed. "When can we come out to see you?"

"Just speak to my Chief Officer and book your time with us." Bruce laughed, putting a conspiratorial arm around both Lucy and Charlie.

"Now then, Lucy." Bruce continued. "Charlie and I would like to have all three granddaughters as brides' maids. Would that be alright with you and Luke?"

Lucy stepped around in front of Bruce and gently took hold of the lapels of his jacket. It brought Charlie and Bruce to a standstill, releasing her left hand from Bruce's lapel, she placed it on Charlie's right shoulder and drew the little group in together. "Dad, I think that is an utterly wonderful idea. But before we ask them." Luke joined in the group hug as Lucy continued. "Luke and I think you two getting married is fantastic. We sincerely wish you every happiness for the future." Then she did a series of little up and down jumps of joy. "And we just can't wait to get out to Spain to see you and the boat. Well, the boat, really."

They all laughed at the comment as Bruce turned to Luke. "Luke, I have asked Ron to be my best man. But we, that is Charlie and I would like you to be our master of ceremonies at the ceremony and the reception?"

"Oh, Dad! That is wonderful. Of course, I would be honoured to do that for you." Luke kissed Charlie and then hugged them both.

They spent a further half-hour on the seafront letting the children expend a bit of energy, then it started to rain, so they all made their way back to the bungalow. Back in the bungalow with everyone crowded into the lounge, the children were relegated to the floor, Bruce and Charlie were able to regale stories of their brief adventures and swimming with the dolphins. Photographs were passed around, not those of Charlie swimming topless. Also, accounts of having braaivleis on the beach and eating freshly caught Wrasse and Lobsters, friends they had made and the trip down to Gibraltar. They left out the story of the treasure charts and the ensuing problems that they had caused. Both families were seriously considering going out to join Bruce and Charlie. Luke and Lucy needed to check their calendars but said they would like to come out during the upcoming school Easter holidays. They would have to check dates first. Ron was keen to get out as well, but Mel said she would probably end up being seasick for the whole time and didn't think that it was such a good idea after all.

Charlie and Ron had started a conversation regarding some of Bruce's escapades as a young man. Charlie was also very curious about some of the photographs that were on the wall in the study. "The leopard Ron, it intrigues me?" Charlie asked.

"That is Saba. Dad rescued her when he was growing up in Rhodesia." Pointing to the German Shepherd. "And this is Sheba, she was a sort of a rescue dog that Dad took a shine to as a child. They became inseparable. This picture is of the original Williams family. So, that is my Grandma and Granddad with Natalie and her husband and their son. Apart from Dad and his eldest sister Sarah, the rest of the family were massacred during the Bush War in Rhodesia in the 1970's. This picture is of Sarah and her husband. They were killed in a car bomb also in Rhodesia, Saba was in the car with them, she died at the same time. All this happened whilst Dad was out on operations, again, in the Rhodesian Bush War. Dad lost everything, everyone he loved and his inheritance in 18 months."

"Good grief!" Charlie exclaimed. "I hadn't realised that it was that bad out there. Do you know which regiment he was with?"

"Yes, he was with C Squadron Special Air Service. When he came to England after Rhodesia became Zimbabwe, he joined the Para's and then D Squadron, Special Air Service. He is pretty tight-lipped about his time in the Army. I remember some of it, being brought up as a 'squaddie brat' with Dad being away for months at a time. Sometimes he would come back with a fantastic suntan, other times not. He got the Military Cross you know. I remember we all went up to Buck House for that."

"What did he do for that Ron?"

"He saved some guys in Northern Ireland and then I think he did something in Africa. As I said, Dad doesn't talk very much about his service life."

"Ron, I would love to know more about his early life."

"I think Dad still has a container somewhere in South Africa that has some of his families belongings in it. He could never afford to have it shipped over, or the space to store it but I am sure that he still pays an amount every year for the continued storage of it."

Then they were joined by Jasmine. "Aunty Charlie, I am hungry, can I have some cheesy bicks, please?"

"Jasmine, don't be so rude, please." Ron admonished his daughter. "I was talking to Aunty Charlie." Ron picked up the girl. "I'll be more than happy to let you know as much as I know, sometime when we have got more time."

They decided to leave for the pub at just after twelve-thirty. The landlord welcomed Bruce readily as Bruce used to take at least four meals a week there when he was staying in the bungalow. The family sat around the huge, reserved family table, with Jasmine insisting that she had to sit next to Aunty Charlie. More questions followed about the *Cape* and where they were planning to sail to. Where were they going to explore and when would they be coming back to the UK again. The meal was excellent with menu choices of Lasagne, Roast Beef or Roast Pork and the crazy calorific sweets and a cheese board as well. The mealtime subject hinged around the forthcoming wedding and what their plans were for returning to Spain.

Monday morning dawned, cold cloudy and drizzly. Spain was an hour ahead of the UK and Bruce was impatient to try to get a hold of Sergio to enquire about the progress with the *Cape*. In the interim time, Bruce and Charlie discussed the types of stores and that they may require to survive for up to six weeks without re-provisioning. Charlie decided that she would prefer to order fresh meat and vegetables and that although it would mean considerably more work for both of them. It did mean that they could both prepare and freeze the goods in portions suitable for their requirements. They also decided that they would take out items like tea bags and tinned goods that weren't as readily available in Spain like tinned pilchards, potatoes, as well as certain soups from a specific brand.

Although they were departing Portsmouth at eleven-thirty on the night of Sunday the fifteenth, they wouldn't get back to the *Cape* until late on the evening of Tuesday the seventeenth. Charlie wanted the supplies delivered to the quay by eleven o'clock on the morning of the eighteenth, the morning after their return, that was a confirmed stipulation that she had made with the victuallers in Malaga.

When Bruce spoke to Sergio, he discovered that it was all good news, the conversion of the crew area was just about completed, the fuel bladder and compressor had arrived that morning and would be installed today. The antifouling was due to be completed within the next two days, the only problem that had occurred was that one of the drive shaft bearings was suspect. So, Sergio had asked for all the shaft bearings to be replaced regardless, which would be completed in three days. Sergio assured Bruce that the *Cape* would be back in the water by the end of the day on Monday the sixteenth as the engineers from Caterpillar wanted to do sea trials. This was to ensure that the engines were balanced and there were no more problems with the propeller shafts. Everything seemed positive and on schedule. Bruce was relieved. Charlie's phone rang, so she got up and went into the lounge to chat with her mother.

"Sergio, one other thing, please, my friend, would you source me another Seabob F5 SR, blue if that is possible. It's for Charlie so that she will have her own."

"This is no problem, Bruce. I will have it here in three days from Cayago, four days maximum." Sergio concluded.

They spent the afternoon surfing Amazon for items they needed and some that maybe they didn't, including a new printer and loads of spare ink, sheets, material, cotton, sewing pins, drawing equipment. The list seemed endless.

"Charlie?" Bruce asked. "I couldn't help feeling that our first aid kit on the *Cape* is grossly inadequate, given your qualifications, what sort of equipment would you recommend we have onboard for us to facilitate a first-class, first aid kit?"

"Now I know why you are the Captain." Charlie grinned at Bruce. "I was going to talk to you about that. I have given it some thought. How about I phone my Mum and Dad to see what they think and get some advice from them."

"That would be fantastic, cost is no problem with this. I am a firm believer in the saying that if you haven't got it, you will need it and if you have got it, then you won't need it."

Charlie moved from the easy chair that she had been sitting in and moved next to Bruce tucking her legs up under her at the same time, she started the call to her parents.

Tuesday morning arrived, another drizzly damp morning with a distinct chill in the wind from the northeast. They started their drive up to the north with the stop at Frimley Park Hospital for Bruce to see his surgeon at nine o'clock. Parking was surprisingly easy as usually there was a queue to get into the parking area. It was just a final check and his surgeon was impressed with Bruce's rate of improvement. They continued their journey up to Ripon, stopping for a sandwich and coffee at the services outside Wetherby and then continued to Ripon to collect Charlie's possessions, including her guitar. They returned to Hayling Island in the early evening and just after last light. They decided that fish and chips from the local chippy would be more than adequate for their evening meal.

Wednesday morning, they were again up and breakfasted early. By eight-thirty, Bruce was getting the Triumph out from the garage to run Charlie to meet her mother at Portsmouth Harbour railway station. They had planned to take a train up to London for some serious shopping. They were also planning to get Charlie's wedding dress for Friday. Before kissing Charlie goodbye, Bruce handed her his spare debit card with the strict instructions that she was to use it for absolutely anything and everything that they bought, including the train tickets. Following that, he made an appointment with his bank to discuss investments. Bruce was also considering opening an offshore account, having previously opened a bank account in Spain and was using an online third-person transfer system between the two banks, saving him a small fortune in transfer charges.

Following Bruce's meeting with one of the Branch Managers and an advisor of his high street bank, he met with Ron for an early lunch and then kept their appointment with Moss Bros to arrange for their suits for Friday. They decided on the formal grey morning dress for the wedding. Bruce had volunteered to take care of the flowers and buttonholes, which was where they headed after their Moss Bros meeting. Parting from Ron, Bruce phoned Charlie to see how she was doing. It sounded as though they were having fun. This was the longest period of time that they had been apart from each other since the day they had met. However, assuring Bruce that she was fine and that she would get a taxi back to Hayling Island because she doubted that she would be able to get everything into the back of the TR6.

14 Intelligence Company also referred to as The Det was a special operations unit formed during the Northern Ireland troubles in the late 20th Century. Their task, as the name implies, was to gather information on terrorist activities. These troops were recruited from all factions of the services and trained by a special training unit from 22 SAS, who also supported The Det on the ground. As a sergeant then rising to a commissioned officer with D Squadron, 22 SAS, Bruce had been very much involved with The Det in Northern Ireland and then subsequently in the Balkans. A few ex-members of The Det had formed their own organisation, operating clandestinely and running their own intelligence gathering. In some cases, illegally seeing that justice and retribution was carried out against those who placed themselves above and beyond the reaches of the law. So it was that Bruce filled in the remainder of the afternoon with many phone calls to various past associates and friends, resulting in several new and very interesting discoveries.

Charlie arrived back at the bungalow at six-thirty. Bruce went out to help her with the packages, it was raining again. Scampering back indoors laden with bags, Charlie dumped an armful of shopping on the floor and flung her arms around Bruce. "Oh my God! I really missed you Brucie baby." Charlie smothered Bruce with kisses.

"Missed you too, sweetheart." Bruce hugged her and returned the kisses. "By the way, your Dad phoned. He has managed to book the Royal Naval and Royal Albert Yacht Club for our reception on Friday. We need to go there first thing tomorrow to discuss menus etc."

"Oh, fabulous! And by the way, I have bought you a present, well you have bought yourself one but you'll have to wait until after we are married." She laughed, backing away from him and picking up her abandoned shopping from the floor.

"Well, I have bought you a present as well, but you'll have to wait to get it until we get back to the *Cape* next week." Bruce said, following her through to the bedroom.

Charlie made them a Spanish omelette for their evening meal, during which they discussed ideas for their wedding breakfast and their plans for the next day. Thursday morning dawned wet, cold and drizzly, again. It was the sort of cold that just went straight through and gnawed at the bones. The drizzly rain just soaked through everything. After toast and coffee, they decided to leave the Triumph in the garage and used Uber instead. The first thing they did was to go to the reception venue on Pembroke Road and discussed the menu with the Chef and General Manager, Louise Morley. Then to pick up Ron and Bruce's morning suits from Moss Bros. After that it was then off to Ernest Jones to collect the wedding rings for the next day, it seemed to both of them, that like their romance, the whole week had been a flurry of activity and the time had flown by. Returning to the bungalow for a brief lunch and to gather an overnight bag, Bruce couldn't help feeling a sense of dread and foreboding. The news about the impending Coronavirus was spreading, already several cruise ships had been affected, one of which was in isolation in Singapore, another cruise ship was seeking assistance off the west coast of America. The province of Wuhan in China was already in lockdown with many deaths.

Bruce broached the subject with Charlie. "Hey, hun, what do you think we should do with regards to this spreading Coronavirus?"

"If possible, I would prefer to sit it out on the *Cape* in some warm sheltered cove, to be honest. I can't see that this isn't going to spread like wildfire, also I think that this is going to hit everyone very hard. Are you worried Bruce?"

There was the sound of a car outside and Bruce went to the front door, it was James and Mary. It had been arranged that in keeping with tradition, Bruce and Charlie would spend the night apart but to keep Charlie company, James and Mary would stay with Charlie at the bungalow. Bruce would spend the night with Ron and Melissa. James had opened the rear of Mary's BMW estate car and had removed a large white coloured soft bag with red crosses on it. 'Probably our new first aid bag'. Bruce thought to himself. It was easily the size of a suitcase. Bruce went out to help with the rest of the luggage, closely followed by Charlie. Bruce relieved James of the heavy first aid pack and also took in Mary's overnight bag. Then there followed the suits for the morning. Once inside, they completed the greetings. "Right, Charlie, I will need to go through everything in there with you." James indicated the first aid pack. "Bruce, how are you?" He slapped Bruce on the shoulder and gave Charlie a peck on the cheek.

"Yes, fine, thank you!" Bruce responded to the greeting. "What on earth is in there?" Bruce pointed at the first aid pack.

Smiling, James replied. "Well, apart from sticky plasters and bandages, there are Paracetamol, Aspirin, Ibuprofen, suture kits, scalpels, saline drips, stethoscope and a selection of syringes, local anaesthetic, clamps and more."

"Some of the drugs like penicillin have to be kept refrigerated, we have got a special cool box for those, so pick them up on Sunday before you leave." Mary finished, giving Bruce a hug and a peck on the cheek.

"Wow!" Bruce exclaimed. "I seriously hope that you don't have to use any of that gear, Charlie."

Grinning Charlie replied. "I was hoping to get some practice on you."

The afternoon went well with James and Mary passing opinions on the prevailing Coronavirus and regaling their expectations of sailing their yacht down to the Mediterranean during the spring of 2021. In fact, the time passed too quickly. It was five past five in the afternoon when the distinctive sound of Ron's Range Rover arriving outside the bungalow, signalling the imminent departure of the groom to be.

Ron came in to meet James and Mary, whilst Bruce and Charlie went into their bedroom. Hugging each other, neither of them wanted to be away from the other.

"Look!" Bruce said. "The next time we see each other, your Dad will be walking you down the aisle to me. Then in a very short space of time, we will be wife and husband, then tomorrow night, we can make up for having been apart tonight. Maybe just for once, we can have a bit of peace and quiet to ourselves. This week has just been so manic."

Charlie sniffed and smiled. "Tomorrow can't come soon enough." There was the hint of a tear in the corner of her eye. Bruce softly wiped it away with his thumb and kissed her gently on the lips.

CHAPTER 16

Melissa had prepared a shepherd's pie for their evening meal which they sat down to eat at half-past six Bruce, however, preferred his meals a little later, but for one night, he didn't mind. Dinner over, Bruce supervised Jasmine with her bath and saw her into bed whilst Ron and Mel cleared the dinner table. Two stories later, Bruce went back downstairs and addressing Ron and Mel said. "You had better say goodnight to your daughter before she falls asleep." Melissa was lounging on the sofa with her feet tucked up under her and a magazine in her hand.

"Oh! Okay." She groaned.

Ron looked quizzically at her as he stood up. "I am going to take Dad down to the Dog and Gun for a drink once I have said good night to Jasie." He informed her.

"Well, you had better not get him pissed, or you will be in trouble." She retorted off-handedly.

During the short walk down to the pub, Bruce spoke to Ron. "Ron, are you guys alright. I am sort of picking up on some strange vibes from you and Mel?"

"As far as I know, we are okay. I think that since you came back with Charlie, she has sort of had her nose put out of joint. Ever since Mum died, she has always considered herself as being the senior woman in the Williams household and now she isn't." Ron smiled. "I also think that she is still smarting from the dressing down you gave her on Saturday." Ron chuckled.

"Is she going to be upset about us staying with you on Saturday after the ball?" Bruce inquired.

"No, absolutely not Dad. Mind you, when we first heard that you would be back in the country, the first thing she said was that she was going to get you to mind Jasie whilst we were at the mess until I told her that you had already been invited. The look on her face was priceless." Ron chuckled as he held the door open for Bruce to step into the piano bar. "She couldn't understand how you could get an invitation to an Officer's Mess when you weren't a serving officer."

Bruce recognised the landlady, Pauline, and exchanged greetings with her, she in turn, remarked on how well he looked. After having had two pints of lager, Bruce felt bloated. Examining the shelf behind the bar, his eyes locked on to the bottle of Glenlivet, it was nearly full. There were a few couples in the bar but everyone was talking quietly within their little groups. Picking up his whisky Bruce, sauntered down to the piano and opened the keyboard cover, casually fingering a few of the keys and assuring himself that the piano was still in tune. Putting the glass of whisky on the top of the piano, he sat himself down on the piano stool and played the first verse of 'There Is A Tavern in The Town', before launching himself lustily into the song.

Pauline was leaning over the bar and said to Ron. "He's very good. Isn't he, do you think I could hire him in the future?"

Ron smiled. "I am afraid not Pauline he is getting married in the morning, then they are off back to Spain to live on their boat. Tell you what, may I borrow your guitar and then I'll join him and make sure he keeps it civil and behaves himself."

Ron joined Bruce just in time for the last chorus as some of the other occupants of the bar were beginning to join in. Bruce turned around on his stool. "Any requests folks?"

"Whisky in the Jar." Came one reply. "Wild Rover." Was another.

Bruce swivelled back to the piano and launched into 'Whisky in The Jar', by the time the 'Wild Rover' had started the lounge bar was emptied and everyone was crowded around Bruce and Ron at the piano. There was a slight lull in song choices from the audience and honorary choir members, Bruce swivelled on his stool to face his audience.

"Okay, next song." He said. "Is I Love a Lassie, but here is the variation, the girl's name is 'Charlie and she is my Hants Blue Bell'." Bruce sang that part of the song so that everyone got the idea before turning back to the piano. Ron's phone rang, moving away from the crowd, back to the bar so that he could hear. It was Charlie phoning to make sure everything was alright and to say goodnight to Bruce. Bruce had left his phone in the guest room, Mel had answered the phone and given Charlie Ron's number. In answer to Charlie's question, Ron held up his phone just in time so that Charlie heard the personalised chorus.

"Please, Ron, look after him, I am going to go to bed now, so would you just tell him I love him and I'll see him in the morning." Charlie had never heard Bruce sing other than the odd ditty or whistle while he was in the shower, let alone leading a sing-song and playing the piano. She choked back an emotional sob of happiness.

Mary was with Charlie when she had made the call to Ron's phone and picked up on her daughter's emotions. "Is everything alright darling?" She put a hand on Charlies' shoulder.

"Oh, God! Yes Mum, he's banging away on a pub piano leading a sing-along. I didn't even know that he could play a bloody piano, let alone lead a sing-along." Charlie choked back a sob of happiness and hugged her Mother.

Father and son got back to the house just after eleven o'clock, they weren't drunk but they were in a more than mellow mood. Bruce drank a large glass of water, cleaned his teeth and emptied his bladder before quietly rolling into bed. His last thought before the combination of alcohol and exhaustion, wrapped him in the gentle arms of Morpheus was that of being hugged into Charlie's bosom.

The morning of Friday the thirteenth of March dawned, a beautiful early English Spring morning, with a light breeze blowing in from the northeast, it would keep the threatening low pressure at bay to the south-west of the United Kingdom for the rest of the day. Ron and Bruce looked resplendent in their pale grey morning suits with their crimson carnation buttonholes as they stepped out of the Range Rover outside the civic hall on Charles Dickens Street. Having dropped off Ron, Bruce and Jasmine, Melissa then took the car back around the one way and into the Podium Car Park. Jasmine, insisting on holding Grandad's hand so that he wouldn't go away. It was only ten forty-five as Bruce, Ron and Jasmine made their way towards the room allocated for the service. As they entered, Bruce was greeted by Angela and Tracey dressed in precisely the same dresses that Jasmine was wearing. Lucy had certainly done a terrific job in the task of coordinating the dresses for the three girls. Luke had sourced a morning suit in pale blue and both he and Lucy looked resplendent in their finery. They continued greeting other members of their friends and guests, shook hands and exchanged hugs.

Bruce spotted Mary, excusing himself, he went and greeted her, exchanging kisses he asked. "How's Charlie this morning?"

"She is fine, she was a bit worried about how you would be today following your outing to the pub last night." Mary grinned, standing back a little she held him at arm's length and looked into his eyes. "Not too bad. I expected worse."

Ron caught up with Bruce. "Five minutes Dad. Nervous?"

"In all honesty, Ron. Yes!" Bruce replied with a wan smile.

On the stroke of eleven o'clock, the hastily recruited organist started to play 'Here Comes the Bride' as a beautifully resplendent Charlie on her father's left arm entered the ceremonial room, behind them were the three girls. Charlie's dress was a full-length white chiffon and lace combination, hanging off her shoulders the full length lightly laced sleeves accentuated Charlies deep tan. The slightly plunging neckline emphasised her breasts whilst the full length, figure-hugging, down to the floor-length dress highlighted her waist, hips and buttocks. Charlie's eyes were fixed on Bruce who in turn fixed his eyes on Charlie. With his heart pounding and a knot in the pit of his stomach, the march up the aisle seemed to take ages for Bruce but eventually, James and Charlie arrived. James handed Charlie's hands over to Bruce before standing back with a paternal smile and joined Mary.

"You look so beautiful, I could eat you." Bruce whispered to Charlie. Remembering the last time Bruce had mentioned that subject, Charlie smiled a knowing smile and blushed mildly. The registrar coughed loudly and commenced the short formal ceremony.

The rest of the day including, the elegant reception at the Royal Naval and Royal Albert Yacht Club, seemed to pass in a whirl. The speeches and toasts were both sincere and humorous, with a tribute to family and friends past and present. Bruce and Charlie had chosen their Wedding Dance to waltz to the music of Andre Rieu playing Abba's 'The Way Old Friends Do'. It was quite a complicated dance and fortunately, not only had they been blessed with not having two left feet, but they had managed to practice it a few times as well and performed it brilliantly. Tears of emotion welled in Charlie's eyes at the end of the beautifully haunting melody as their friends, family and guests joined in rapturous applause. Bruce and Charlie exchanged wedding gifts. Charlie had bought Bruce an Omega Seamaster to replace the Casio that had been drowned during the second-night swim in the marina, a beautifully thought of gift. Turning to Luke he took an A4 picture from a tube and showed her the picture of the blue Seabob F5 SR. Charlie was ecstatic, her very own top of the range Seabob.

Bruce accompanied by Charlie, got Ron and Luke into a quiet adjoining room away from the main reception. Gently closing the door behind him and with Charlie linking her arm into Bruce's, Bruce commenced his little and well-prepared speech.

"Believe it or not, I had originally planned to do this via email. However, circumstances have now allowed us to do this together and because Charlie is now my wife and also your stepmother. I thought that it would be appropriate for us to do this jointly." Bruce coughed, looked at Charlie and they both smiled at each other. Bruce withdrew from his inside breast pocket two envelopes. "As you are well aware, I was fortunate to have a sizeable win on the National Lottery. So now I, we have arranged for you both to receive one million pounds each." The boy's jaws dropped, both utterly speechless. Quickly Bruce continued. "The transfers will take place at one minute past midnight on Monday morning. The next thing is that I, we have set up trust funds for the three girls, the sums of five hundred thousand pounds each have been put into interest-earning accounts to which they will have access upon reaching the age of eighteen."

"Dad!" Luke's eyes moistened. "Mum!" Luke sobbed. Charlie opened her arms and hugged him and then did the same with a speechless and tear-streaked face of Ron. Bruce and Charlie hugged the boys until they managed to overcome their emotions when the door of the room gently opened and framed in the entrance was Lucy.

"Is everything alright in here? You guys have been in here for ages." Lucy sounded genuinely concerned.

"Hell, yeah!" Luke announced. "We are millionaires, or we will be on Monday morning." He walked over and took Lucy in his arms and kissed her. "Even the girls have been given trust funds for when they are eighteen." He declared.

"God! I could do with a drink after all that emotion." Bruce proclaimed.

Charlie replied saying. "I will be with you in a moment sweetheart. I would just like to have a quick word with the boys. If I may?"

"No problem hun, come on Lucy." Bruce put an arm around her shoulders as they left the room.

Charlie addressed the two boys. "Give me your right hands, please." They complied and she put them between her hands. "I love your father very, very much and my promise to you is that I will do everything I can to be a loyal, loving and trustworthy wife. I thank you both from the bottom of my heart for having welcomed me into your family, as I welcome you into mine. I am not here to try to step into your mother's shoes. No person could ever fulfil that, however, if there is ever anything you need, you have only to ask. As for names, I am very comfortable being referred to as Charlie or as Auntie Charlie by the girls or however you feel appropriate. Thank you for this moment."

The Chef and all the staff at the Royal Naval and Royal Albert Yacht Club surpassed themselves. Bruce made sure that they were well tipped for their efforts and left this duty to Ron. As was customary, Bruce and Charlie were the first to leave. Initially, saying their goodbyes to their friends and guests, then came the turn of the family including James and Mary. James, it seemed, had picked up on the William's method of greetings and farewells and surprised Bruce by encompassing him in his arms giving him a manly hug. The waiting Uber whisked them back to the bungalow on Hayling Island.

Exhausted from the events of the week, they both settled on the sofa after relieving themselves of the formal clothing they had put on robes for comfort. Together they discussed the events of the day, remarking on various people and the reactions of others during the ceremony and subsequent reception. Charlie moved closer to Bruce and put her head on his right shoulder. "Oh, baby! Our dance, I can't believe it, we just nailed it." She squirmed closer to him. "I am so proud of you, I think my heart is going to burst with my love for you."

Bruce squeezed her hand. "Thank you, sweetheart, I just followed you. I thought that your Dad's speech was brilliant, short, sweet and absolutely to the point."

Charlie laughed. "Well, if you had heard the original one. Mum made him change it last night. I loved Ron's speech. It was really funny when he referred to toasting his daughter and nieces at his father's wedding." She giggled.

"Charlie? There was a middle-aged guy, he was sat at the back of the ceremony room on your family side on his own. He was wearing a dark suit and some sort of regimental or organisational tie. Any idea as to who he is?"

"No, no idea. Was he at the reception?" Charlie started to sit up.

"I later saw him on and off at the reception but I didn't see him seated at any of the tables, which was what I found strange." Bruce seemed to lose interest in the subject. "I feel sticky. I think I am going to have a shower before I do anything else."

"And I am coming with you." Charlie added.

Their lovemaking lasted over an hour and a half of the most tenderest moments. Starting in the shower, they bathed each other taking it in turn to do the washing and was finalised by Charlie taking control and straddling Bruce's hips. Their climaxes exploded together as their vocal constraints knew no bounds. It was the first time they had made love since having left Spain and they lay wrapped in each other's arms, never wanting to be parted. Bruce was the first to stir.

"I am sorry hun." Bruce whispered. "But I am afraid I need a wee." Untangling himself, he kissed Charlie on her lips. Making his way into the bathroom, he returned almost immediately with a hand full of tissue, which he tenderly placed between Charlie's legs in a vain attempt to absorb some of the moisture that had evolved from their lovemaking. Having emptied his bladder, he started the shower as Charlie brushed past him and squatted on the toilet. As her urine tinkled in the toilet, she blew him a kiss. "Yes, I love you too." Bruce said as he stepped into the shower.

Saturday was once again a whirlwind of events. The morning was spent shopping for their supplies that were difficult to get in Spain. In the afternoon they travelled up to Netheravon from where they attended the Early Spring Ball at Ron's mess in Tidworth. The next morning, they said their 'goodbyes' to Ron and a very tearful Jasmine. Mel hadn't been well during the night and had opted to remain in bed.

Once back at the bungalow, Bruce started to unload their formal wear of the evening before from the minibus and began the strategic loading of all the other purchased and acquired goods. These would be transferred out to the *Cape*, which included many tools and materials. Charlie had made sure that all laundry had been washed, was dried and put away in preparation for their next visit to the UK. This was a process that she had started the day before. Charlie rustled up a sort of breakfast using up as much out the fridge and pantry as she could and by half-past four, the minibus had been fully loaded, the bungalow was ready for them to leave. The TR6 had been cleaned and put up on blocks with the float charger connected and the dust sheet over it. They sat down on the sofa with a final cup of tea. "God!" said Bruce. "I feel completely exhausted, this week has just flown by."

Charlie wiggled closer to Bruce and put her hand in his. "I have to say that when we left the *Cape*, I never could have envisaged such a week and with a wedding to boot." She kissed Bruce on the cheek. "I am just hoping that we can get back to the *Cape* before they start banging in travel restrictions."

"You and me both." Bruce echoed her sentiments.

CHAPTER 17

It was a quarter to six in the evening when they arrived in Gosport at the home of James and Mary, Mary greeted them at the door. "You two look exhausted. Did you have a good time last night?"

Bending slightly to kiss her mother, Charlie replied. "Yes, thank you, Mum, it was a wonderful evening. I think that we will probably sleep for the whole of the trip to Bilbao."

"Bruce!" Mary inquired. "You are limping a bit today. Are you okay?"

"I'll be fine." Bruce replied with a smile. "I'll have my private nurse see to me later." As they went through to the lounge, there was a very butch young woman sitting in one of the easy chairs near the fire. Mary introduced her as Mitch, the live-in trainee nurse. Mary and Charlie went through to the kitchen to finish preparing the evening meal. Bruce went out to the garage in search of James, who he found with his head inside the engine compartment of an immaculate, yellow Triumph Stag.

Hearing Bruce enter the garage, James lifted his head out from the engine compartment to greet Bruce. "Ah, there you are. How was the ball last night?"

"Exhausting." Bruce replied. James chuckled. "Actually, James, on Friday at the ceremony, would you have noticed a man in a dark suit. He was sat at the rear of the ceremony room on your family side, sitting on his own. His hair was swept straight back and he was wearing some sort of organisational tie, I think it was blue and white." James looked quizzically at Bruce as he continued. "I later saw him at the reception, however, I didn't see him sat at any of the tables."

"I am afraid that I have no idea as to who you are referring to." James looked puzzled. "Look, I'll tell you what I'll do." James was cleaning his hands on a clean piece of lint. "First thing in the morning, I'll get hold of the chaps that did the photography and see what light they can shed on this fellow." Moving towards the door and the light switch, James continued. "What is it about this guy that has aroused your interest in him?"

"I really can't put my finger on it." Bruce turned to face James. "We had one or two problems in Spain regarding the boat and somehow, this guy just didn't seem right, it was almost as if he was being evasive. He certainly didn't approach Charlie or me. I don't know, there was just something strange about him and his demeanour."

Facing Bruce, James placed both his hands on Bruce's shoulders, holding him firmly at arm's length he asked. "Would one of these instances be when you saved my daughter's life after she had been thrown in the marina? This was following some sort of altercation with a Dutchman. We do talk." James finished.

"Yes, except I thought that it was the other way around, which was the cause of her ending up in the marina." Bruce looked James directly in the eyes.

"Bruce, whatever." James pulled Bruce to him in a paternal manner. "I have only got one daughter and now I have only got one son, so please, please look after both of you." Releasing Bruce with a smile, he turned towards the door. "Right, now let's go and see about a drink shall we."

Making their way back to the lounge, Father and son-in-law bantered as only service or ex-service people could do. Returning to the lounge, they made themselves comfortable. James in his worn leather armchair and Bruce on the sofa as Mitch had commandeered the other easy chair and was watching TV. The evening news had just finished and the weather forecast was on. The programme presenter was issuing warnings about storm Ellen gathering strength to the southwest. She was due to hit mainland UK in the next twenty-four hours with widespread disruption due.

"I think we will be in for a very rough crossing over the next two days." Bruce commented to no one in particular but was overheard by Charlie who stuck her head out of the kitchen.

"What was that hun?" Charlie asked.

"I think that we will be in for a very rough crossing over the next two days." Bruce repeated. Mitch gave Bruce a disgusted look of annoyance for having spoken over the television.

Noticing Mitch's disgusted look, Bruce became quite intrigued by her and studied her out of the corner of his eye. She was a good five foot ten inches tall, possibly mid-thirties, with large breasts and almost masculine facial features. She had a short-cropped mannish hairstyle, portly but with a build that would have suited a middleweight wrestler. She was wearing a man's shirt with a tank top jumper and with her shirt sleeves rolled up. Her trousers were brown slacks and she had light brown lace-up boots on her feet. This was strange, as normally, Mary and James would remove their outdoor shoes before entering the house from the porch. When she was spoken to by either James or Mary, she responded in a very casual and indifferent manner.

"So, Mitch?" Bruce asked. "How far are you along in your training now?"

Looking at Bruce in a manner that said, 'what the hell has it got to do with you' she replied. "Nearly at the end of my third year."

"Oh! I see. Do you have aspirations of specialising in any specific area, maternity, surgery?" Bruce asked.

Obviously peeved at the questions, Mitch replied. "I would like to concentrate on male geriatrics." She shot Bruce another disdainful glance.

Bruce was beginning to enjoy himself. "Oh, really, I had no idea that speciality was available. Will you stay with the NHS, go private or maybe join a branch of the armed services?"

Mitch gave Bruce a filthy look as she got up from the chair. "Look! Why all the questions Mister, fuckin' busybody?" Bruce was out of the sofa and on his feet like a cat and facing the threateningly advancing Mitch. That was enough to stop her in her tracks. Her face paled, here was somebody she couldn't bully.

That was sufficient for James. "Right Mitch! You can get away with a certain amount of rudeness to Mary and me but not to our guests. As far as threatening Bruce is concerned, I would say that you have just picked on the wrong person."

Mary and Charlie witnessed the incident. Mary gasped at the speed at which Bruce had moved and the unfolding incident. Mitch flashed a furious look at James, maliciously saying. "Careful old man or I will be reporting you for sexual molestation and assault. And as for you, you old goat." Mitch turned on Mary. "Bring my dinner to my room when it's ready."

Together Charlie and Bruce exclaimed. "What!" Not believing what they had just heard.

Charlie turned towards Mary. "What on earth is going on here, Mum? You are not taking anyone's dinner to any room."

Mitch turned on Charlie advancing on her threateningly. "You mind your own fuckin' business bitch." Turning to Mary and pointing her right forefinger at her. "If you know what's good for you, you'll get rid of these fuckers right now, or else."

"Or else what?" Charlie demanded.

"Or else I make it public that he has been involved in a gay affair with a certain Admiral." Mitch made the mistake of continuing to point her index finger at Charlie, who had not forgotten her Aikido lessons from the Army. She took the offending index finger, twisted and bent it against the joint, dislocating it.

Mitch screamed and withdrew her hand, nursing it into her body and continued to emit what could only be described as gurgling grunts.

Bruce shook his head in disbelief. "You!" Bruce pointed his right index finger at Mitch. "Sit down before I make you fall down. Charlie! Lovely move babe." Addressing James, Bruce asked. "What is all this about James?"

Both James and Mary responded. "It's not true." James continued. "She has been blackmailing us saying that she will go to the papers and the Police with evidence that I have been involved in a gay affair." James sat down dejectedly and put his head in his hands. "I haven't, she has set the whole thing up. She has even got doctored pictures."

Taking his mobile phone from the inside pocket of his jacket, Bruce started to look in his contacts. Turning to the other three, he said. "Do you remember Brian Stone? I introduced him to you on Friday at the reception." Charlie nodded briefly. "Well, he only lives a few hundred yards from here." Bruce selected the number and put the phone to his ear. "Brian, I am sorry to trouble you on a Sunday night but I am with Charlie and her parents here in Gosport. I have a situation which I think you may be interested in." Bruce passed on the address and hung up. Mary was sat on the arm of James's chair with her arm around James. Mitch had gone a deathly pale shade of white with Bruce standing over her whilst she nursed her finger.

Brian was at the front door in less than five minutes. Charlie answered it and let Brian in. "So, what do we have here then Bruce? Ahh! I see it's Mitch the Bitch, so, what is it this time then, demanding money and accommodation by saying that she will expose you as paedophiles That's her usual trick." Bruce and Brian shook hands.

"Mary, James this is Brian Stone. On Friday, I introduced him as a friend of mine, he is in fact, Detective Superintendent Brian Stone from the Hampshire Constabulary's Serious Crimes Unit and it seems that your lodger has previous." Bruce looked smugly at a pale and trembling Mitch the Bitch, addressing her he said. "So, not so demanding and bossy now are you? I have a passionate hate for people like you. You are a nasty little bully and I really despise people like you." The approach of two-tone sirens could be heard fast approaching the house. Charlie again went to the front door to allow the uniformed officers access.

Dinner was a little later than had been anticipated. However, two very relieved people were very grateful to Bruce for having initiated the spark in Mitch to cause her to lose her temper. Whilst serving dinner, Mary passed behind Bruce's chair, putting her arms around him and hugging him, she kissed the top of his head. "Charlie you are a very lucky girl to have found this wonderful man. Look after him."

Charlie smiled. "I have every intention of doing exactly that, Mum." It was wonderful to see her mother happy. She hadn't realised just how tense they had been with the threat of Mitch hanging over them.

Changing the subject, Bruce enquired about their Hans Christian and their hopes to sail to the Mediterranean for a winter. "Charlie and I can always fly back and crew for you some time, we'll even bring our own gear over. What do you reckon, Charlie?"

"That would be amazing fun. Yesss!" Charlie replied between mouthfuls. The meal continued with the conversation about sailing the Hans Christian.

"There is a couple who have sailed their Hans Christian down to the Med last year. I have been following them on YouTube and I think that they are now somewhere around Cartagena at the moment. They did the Biscay crossing with some sort of flotilla organisation going from Plymouth, as I recall."

"That sounds like a great idea." James replied. "Would you and Charlie really come to crew for us down to say Gibraltar?"

"Oh, yes!" Charlie and Bruce answered together. "We could leave the *Cape* in the very safe moorings of a certain club we know in Gibraltar." Bruce added. Then both he and Charlie started to laugh with the memory of the incident with George Lucas, commodore of the Royal Gibraltar Yacht Club. It fell to Charlie to regale the incident to her parents.

After dessert and whilst the girls cleared the table, Bruce privately said to James. "I am going to let you have Brian's contact details, I am sure he won't mind. But if anything at all comes up and you need any help, please give Brian a call." Reaching in his pocket, he removed the spare key for the bungalow on Hayling Island. "This is our spare. I would be happy for you to look after it for us." Bruce finished pressing the key into James's hand.

They decided that they would leave James and Mary at about ten o'clock for the short drive around to the Brittany ferry terminal. Hopefully, that would give them plenty of time to get settled in before the scheduled sailing at eleven-thirty. After fond farewells and tears from the two women, Bruce drove them to the ferry terminal. At the check-in, they picked up their tickets and cabin passes. Then joined the short queue for customs and the obligatory security search before boarding the *Cap Finistere*. Ironically, they had been allocated the same cabin as they had been assigned on their inward trip to the UK. Stowing the small amount of luggage, Bruce opened a bottle of Famous Grouse and using the supplied plastic mugs from the bathroom, poured two generous glasses of the whisky whilst Charlie showered. Bruce had just got into the shower when his phone rang. Charlie answered it for him. He briefly heard her explain to the caller that he, Bruce, was in the shower and that they were about to leave the UK and would not have any cell coverage. Assuring the caller that she would get Bruce to call when they arrived in Spain on Tuesday morning. Bruce dried his feet and legs before stepping into the cabin where he unabashedly completed his drying in front of Charlie, taking an occasional sip from his whisky.

"So, who was that on the phone?" Bruce asked as he dried his back.

"That was Brian. They haven't charged Mitch yet because they think that there is someone else involved. But I said you would give him a call sometime on Tuesday once we are back in Spain." Getting up off the bunk she had been sitting on wearing the wrapped around towel, Charlie crossed to Bruce. Taking his towel from him, she continued to dry him, including his genitals. They kissed and Charlie's towel fell to the floor.

They woke together, still entwined in each other on the narrow cot. At first, Bruce hadn't worked out what had woken him until some moments later when the ship again plunged into the Atlantic trough with the sound of an express train hitting the side of the mountain. The *Cap Finistere* shook with the impact, the vibrations going right through her hull, as she again started up the wall of the next wave.

Bruce looked at Charlie. Her eyes were wide open. "Are you alright sweetheart?" Charlie nodded her head, indicating she was okay. She looked a little shocked. "I think that we have hit some rough seas. I must have a wee." Bruce awkwardly and stiffly got off the bunk, then steadying himself against the ship's motion, he made his way into the bathroom. Sitting on the pedestal, as much for convenience and safety, he relieved himself with a sigh, managing to wash his hands whilst remaining on the pedestal. Bruce made his way back into the cabin, allowing Charlie the opportunity of the bathroom. Again, the ship plunged into a trough with a bang before making her way up the next wave. Fortunately, the plastic beakers they had drunk from were empty because they were rolling around on the deck. Bruce picked them up and placed them in the cup holders, finding the bottle of water, he filled the cups up offering one to Charlie.

"Is it going to be like this all the way to Bilbao?" Charlie asked.

"No hun. It will probably ease off as we get closer to Roscoff or they may change their minds and go to Brest for the crew change. Either way, it will get easier as we approach and depart the port. I am hoping that they will go for Brest because then we will be able to get some lunch." Bruce took Charlie's hand as she sat next to him, naked on the edge of the bunk as the *Cap Finistere* continued through the heavy seas. This was the edge of storm Ellen.

"Brucie, do you always think of food darling?" She smiled at him.

Bruce grinned back at her. "No, I was just considering the practical aspects."

"We wouldn't sail the *Cape* in this sort of weather, would we?" Charlie asked with a look of concern on her face.

"It would have to be a matter of life or death and that is our lives or deaths that I am referring to, no one else's. If there is more than a two-foot wave, we are staying in port or a very safe anchorage." Bruce emphasised. They drank their water and rolled into their respective bunks for the rest of the night. Neither of them slept very much and by nine o'clock, the crazy bucking of the ship had eased a bit. Bruce got up and poured some more water for them and then went back to sleep for three hours. When he awoke, Charlie was just coming out of the shower, standing naked she towelled herself down then sitting on the edge of the bunk, she leant forward and kissed Bruce tenderly on the lips.

Her breath smelt beautifully fresh and minty. "Morning sleepy head." She smiled at him and briefly kissed him again before standing up and pulling on a pair of lace knickers. Then reaching for the matching bra turned towards him as she did it up behind her, the 'V' of her crotch was brilliantly highlighted in a beautiful 'camel toe' effect.

Groaning, Bruce got up and made for the shower. The *Cap Finistere* had almost stopped her bucking antics and the rolling motion was contained by the stabilisers on her hull. Fifteen minutes later and Bruce and Charlie were headed up to the restaurant on the deck above them. Looking out of a window they could see the storm-battered French coast going past on their port side as they made their approach to the port of Brest. They both ordered an all-day breakfast and coffee. They decided to take their last coffee and finish it whilst watching the French coast sail past in the lounge bar area. It was necessary to share a table and they did so with an elderly couple returning to their home just outside of Valencia. Naturally, the subject of the Coronavirus took precedent, as they speculated as to whether they were going to be allowed home to El Perello, which was to the south of Valencia. Equally, Bruce and Charlie didn't know as to whether or not they would be allowed back to Malaga and the *Cape*. It went without saying that the other couple were intrigued by the *Cape* and Charlie entertained them with pictures and stories about the dolphins and their aspiration to explore the various regions available to them.

Retiring back to their cabin, Bruce and Charlie took time to catch up on their reading with their Kindles.

The afternoon passed quickly enough and after the brief stop at Brest to change her crew, the *Cap Finistere* left in a south-westerly direction keeping the French coast on the port side. By seven-thirty and two glasses of wine later, they decided that they did not want a three-course meal in the restaurant. Opting instead to venture up to the Sun Deck on deck ten, where the bar offered single course meals. The choice was either pizza or beef bourguignon, they both opted for the beef bourguignon accompanied with chips instead of rice, which they hastily ate at one of the many vacant tables. It was cold up on the exposed deck. Going back below to deck nine they had a wander around the duty-free shop, Bruce secured two bottles of Laphroaig, this was a particularly 'peaty' whisky and two bottles of their favourite, Glenmorangie, one of which they opened as soon as they got back to their cabin. "Slainte Mhath." (Pronounced Slanj-a-va) They toasted each other with the malt whisky sitting on a bunk and talked about their options. If the Spanish locked down their borders and wouldn't let them sail from Malaga or worse still kicked them out of Spanish territorial waters, then they would have to sail to Gibraltar, where at least they could seek shelter as a British registered boat in a British port. If there was a lockdown, then they mutually agreed that they would prefer Dolphin Cove and their own company with the freedom and security from the outside world. But there was only so much speculation that they could carry out at this time until the international understanding of the Coronavirus. But at least at the moment, they had options that they could explore.

CHAPTER 18

Tuesday morning dawned with a partly cloudy sky, but remarkably warmer than the England they had left on Sunday evening. Bruce decided that it would be easier for Charlie with her fluent Spanish to take the first stint of the driving whilst getting through the customs and security at Bilbao. This was something that Charlie was amenable to as she loved driving anyway. They needn't have worried as the Spanish Guardia Civil took one look at the Spanish registered minibus and just waved them through, their passports weren't even required. During the long drive down to Malaga, Bruce made several phone calls. The first was to Sergio to let him know that they were on their way and hoped to arrive sometime between five and six o'clock that evening. In turn, Sergio assured Bruce that the *Cape* was back in the water that they had carried out engine trials and concluded that there were some adjustments needed, after which a second trial was due to be carried out during that afternoon. Sergio would wait at the chandlery until they arrived that evening and then he would lock them in allowing them to remain alongside for the night. There was also a lot of talk about a lockdown being implemented although sea borders would remain open. The second phone call was to Brian Stone to enquire about the progress regarding Mitch. Brian had said that owing to the time constraints, he had had to charge her and had applied to have Mitch retained in custody. However, this had been refused and she was bailed to appear in two weeks at Portsmouth Magistrates Court. Brian and his colleagues were convinced that Mitch had been put up to this crime by someone else. One other thing was that he had received a visit from an officer claiming to be from Special Branch. He had asked questions regarding Mitch but later when Brian had contacted Special Branch, it seemed that no one had heard of this person. He had said that his name was Donaldson. Bruce's heart nearly stopped at the mention of the name, pointing out that there was an Interpol warrant out for Donaldson. He suggested that they check their CCTV footage to see if they could lift a facial image, after which Bruce explained the reason why. The third phone call was to James, to let him and Mary know that they had arrived safely in Spain and were on their way down to Malaga and that one of them would phone again once they had arrived at the boat.

The ten-hour long journey seemed to pass very quickly helped by 'spot the bull' on various hillsides. Anyone who has travelled through Spain in the central area will have seen the huge cut-outs of bulls placed strategically on the sides of hills. Charlie drove from the ferry at Bilbao up to an approximate halfway point between Burgos and Madrid. Stopping for fuel and coffee, they swapped drivers with Bruce driving down to a point, one hundred and fifty kilometres short of Granada, where they stopped again for the toilet and to grab a snack and a coffee. Swapping over again, Charlie took on the final leg down to Malaga, where they arrived at the Boats.co.uk chandlery at a quarter to five in the afternoon. They were met by a welcoming Sergio and parked the loaded minibus as close to the *Cape* as possible. Then they were assisted by Sergio and two other staff with the unloading of the contents of the minibus onto the *Cape*. Leaving everything on the aft cockpit, Bruce and Charlie assured them that they would put everything away at their leisure. Sergio gave Bruce a quick tour of the crew space conversion now to be termed as the workshop come dive station pointing out the features that had been installed. Agreeing that they would do a full handover in the morning and leaving Bruce with a key for the main gate, Sergio bade them a 'good evening' and departed the secured marina.

It certainly felt good to be back home on the *Cape*, the gentle rise and fall of the deck as she moved gently in time with the swell coming in from the harbour. Bruce made a quick external tour checking the mooring lines and fenders. Charlie found him prowling the foredeck and examining the anchor winches and chains.

She had two mugs of coffee in her hand. "Hey hun, what are you doing?"

"Just checking the anchor winches. Thank you." Bruce took the offered mug of coffee.

"You do realise, my Captain, that we don't have any milk, eggs or ingredients for dinner, tonight don't you?" Charlie was standing in a provocative feet apart stance, nursing her mug in both hands.

"Simples." Replied Bruce. "We take our little electric scooters out for a spin around the harbour to the Coviran shop, get some supplies to see us through until the victuallers get here, then we pop round and have dinner at José's and give them the news."

"You are truly a great Captain." Charlie leant forward and pecked Bruce on the lips. They both went back to the aft cockpit and started stowing the goods in appropriate places on the boat. The tools that Bruce had brought back were neatly stowed in the workshop area. They decided that probably the best place for the first aid kit would be under the bunk that Charlie had first used, Bruce also moved her sewing machine into there. The dry and tinned goods were stowed in the huge empty walk-in cupboard under the access stairs to the main deck. There was still a great deal of space left in the cupboard. They re-stowed the external cushions for the forward sun loungers by standing them up in the workshop area and used bungees to keep them standing up against the wall. In the dive station area, Bruce looked at the three sets of scuba equipment with the combined harnesses and dive computers. Also, in the dive area was the new compressor. Above which were stowed the two Sea-Doos on bulkhead mounted brackets. The new blue F5 SR was labelled 'Charlie's Blue'. Charlie was thrilled she checked out the massive upright two hundred and twenty-litre freezer. The door of which had been left slightly ajar. Knowing that it would be required the next day, Charlie switched it on, closed and latched the door. They both went into the almost silent engine room, only the gentle hum of the air conditioning system could be heard. Whilst there, they checked the huge bank of batteries and inverter that had been installed.

Rummaging around amongst the goods that he had brought from the UK Bruce found what he was looking for. He got the Micronic ACE frequency detector out of its box and connected the antennae to the detector and made his way up to the flybridge then switched the device on. Almost immediately two of the LED's lit up, indicating a signal. As he moved towards the front of the bridge, the signal got weaker then turning back towards the stern of the flybridge, the signal got stronger. As Bruce pointed the antennae at the quad, four LED's lit up then as he approached the quad all five LED's lit up. Bruce removed the quad cover, switched off the frequency detector, then rummaged around the quad looking for the bug. Opening a storage container at the back of the quad he found the tracking device. It had been attached with a magnet to the top of the compartment where part of the metal frame was exposed. Removing it and putting the cover back on the quad, Bruce moved the tracking device and attached it to the underside of the minibus. This was still parked alongside the quay from where it had been offloaded earlier.

Illuminated by the surrounding security lights, Bruce and Charlie let themselves out of the chandlers yard and by sticking to the dockside for most of the way, embarked on their maiden voyage with the scooters. By the time that they had got around to the Coviran shop some five minutes later, they had become quite proficient with the scooters. Collecting fresh milk, butter, eggs and other essentials pending the arrival of the victuallers the next morning and packing them into a rucksack that Bruce then put around the handlebars of his scooter. Then they scooted around to José's, where they were greeted like lifelong friends. Charlie showed them the rings on her finger and even more hugs and kisses followed. The restaurant was quiet for a Tuesday night and then the subject came around to the Coronavirus. Italy was already on lockdown and it was thought that France, Portugal and Spain would follow shortly, possibly as early as the next day. They spent the evening sat at the family table catching up and speculating before they got back on their scooters and cautiously made their way back to the chandlery and the *Cape*. Bruce stowed the scooters in the racks above the two Seabobs and put them back on charge.

The morning dawned bright and sunny with a gentle onshore wind they were both dressed and breakfasted by eight forty-five, it was almost warm enough for shorts Bruce thought. At five to nine, Bruce made his way down to the main gate and unlocked it, faces that were familiar to him greeted him. They all knew him as Capitain Bruce. Once Sergio had arrived he greeted him warmly, he was aware of the victuallers coming to re-supply the *Cape* during the morning. Taking Bruce to one side, Sergio said. "I have heard from Miguel. He has said that with effect from twelve o'clock today, he has been instructed to close the port of Malaga. Bruce, you and Charlie should maybe go to Gibraltar, there it is British, you will be able to stay there."

"Only as a last resort, Sergio. We know a cove down the coast where there is a very safe anchorage and nowhere near people where we should be able to sit it out for a few weeks." Bruce replied.

"Will you tell Miguel?" Sergio asked.

"Yes, I must. If anything happened to us, I would want him to know where he could find us." Bruce added. "Can you supply me with these items please Sergio?" Bruce asked, handing him the list which included a step ladder, marine ply, wood stain, nylon rope, flares and a tarpaulin.

Sergio looked at the list. "This is no problem, Bruce." Sergio went into his office to organise Bruce's shopping list. At half-past nine the victuallers van arrived at the chandlery and the goods were transferred from the van onto the *Cape* with Charlie meticulously checking that the quality and quantities agreed with her list.

"Charlie, sweetheart." Bruce said to her. "They are going to close the port at midday the sooner we get out of here, the better. As soon as we are out of the harbour, I'll give you a hand with the stowing. Okay?" he kissed her briefly.

"Bruce, I am scared" Charlie looked worried.

He hugged her and kissed her gently on the lips. "Don't be, we're together." Bruce went to organise the storage of his recent shopping list acquisitions. They said their goodbyes to Sergio and his crew of workers and then slipped their moorings.

They had got as far as the outer harbour where the *Rio Jenil* was already on station. Bruce slipped the gearboxes into neutral and waited for the *Rio Jenil* to come alongside, Bruce and Charlie re-deploying the recently stowed fenders. As the two boats touched gently, the *Rio Jenil* crew made fast to the *Cape*. "Permission to come aboard Capitain?" Miguel formerly requested.

"Of course, welcome aboard Capitain." Bruce replied formally. Bruce ushered Miguel inside the pilot station.

Once inside the privacy of the *Cape*, Miguel removed his cap and extended his right hand. "I understand that congratulations are in order.

Well done." He said, taking firm hold of Bruce's hand and kissing Charlie on the cheek. "So, now where will you go? I cannot let you back into port once you leave." Miguel added.

"I know." Bruce replied. "And thank you for the heads up." Bruce moved over to the chart table and indicated Dolphin Cove on the chart to Miguel. Miguel nodded. "The plan is to hole up there until all this blows over and the pandemic passes, which I think it will. It is a good, sheltered cove with protection from all sides, plus we have a lot of supplies." Bruce indicated the pile of stores in the salon. "Also, with full fuel and water tanks, we should be alright for a while." Bruce finished.

"I know this cove well, it is a good choice. My instructions are to close the port and nothing else." Handing Bruce a slip of paper with a telephone number on it, he continued. "This is my cell number, if you need anything, give me a call and I will see if I can help you in any way. All my crew like you guys as well, so don't be afraid of us. If we can help you, we will."

"Thank you." Bruce and Charlie echoed.

Charlie pulled Miguel's uniform jacket sleeve. "Miguel, please give our love to Clarissa and tell her we hope to all be back together again soon. Please be safe." Charlie kissed his cheek.

Lost for words and not wishing to show his emotions, Miguel pulled his cap back on and left the pilot station re-boarding his own boat. Regaining the bridge of the *Rio Jenil*, Miguel issued a crisp order in Spanish "Desechar" (cast off) He turned to the port of his bridge and stood to attention, the crew followed his example, as the two boats parted, Miguel threw a formal salute to the *Cape Agulhas*. "Adios mi amigo."

Hastily, Bruce and Charlie recovered the fenders and stowed them inboard. Bruce went back to the helm and headed the *Cape* out to sea. As the boat came up to twenty-two knots, he couldn't help feeling that she was handling differently. She was far more responsive, the slight hint of vibration was gone as she surged forward. The bright blue of the Mediterranean and the white caps of the three-foot windswept swells passed beneath the hull of the *Cape Agulhas* as she flew across the ocean. Turning back to Charlie, who would normally have been on the pilot station with him, she was ensconced with selecting various cuts of meat and doing the final butchering into generous portions for two people. Then, putting the portions into bags for the freezer. An hour and three quarters later and Bruce was single handily operating the anchors. Dropping first the starboard anchor and then using the two thrusters moved the boat some fifty yards to port before dropping the port anchor. He let the *Cape* drift backwards before remotely engaging the capstan locks and allowing the boat to snub up on her anchors. Launching Willie, Bruce then took out a stern line and made that secure to a large boulder ashore. Dolphin Cove was almost shaped like a fat, shortened quarter note (♩). Whereas on previous visits, Bruce had anchored in such a fashion that they could see straight out to sea which also meant that they could be seen by any vessel passing close to the cove. On this occasion, Bruce had positioned the *Cape* further over to the left of the cove so that they could only be seen by another vessel if it entered the cove. This also allowed the shape of the cove to provide more shelter in the event of a storm.

They spent the next two and a half hours preparing and freezing meat and vegetables, at the same time storing the other essentials that had been delivered that morning. Amongst which was an indecent amount of alcohol. Bruce was checking the news feed on his computer, not that the news feed was a particularly accurate source of information. It did, however, give him some idea as to what was happening in the outside world. Spain had gone into total lockdown, a term with which the world was as yet unfamiliar with, however, it would become part of the global language associated with the Pandemic of Coronavirus, which was now termed Covid 19. The Spanish government were anticipating that the lockdown would remain in place for the following three weeks. Charlie had joined Bruce at the chart table and he passed on the information. "So, effectively, my darling, we are stuck here in our own little bubble of isolation for the next three weeks. Think you can handle it?"

Hugging his arm into her breast, Charlie replied. "Finally, we get to have our honeymoon. If we have to be in isolation for the next three weeks, I can't think of a nicer place to be, or person to be with. What shall we do now?"

"How about we check out the dive gear, the weather is set for good for the next couple of days, so you can get to teach me some diving." Bruce kissed Charlie on the cheek as they then made their way out to the stern of the boat.

Charlie took out the first cylinder from the rack and inspected it. Handing it over to Bruce, she showed him how to switch it on and test the demand valve was operating, also how to reset the dive computer. Then of course there were the BCD's (buoyancy control devices) to which the cylinders would be attached. These provided superb comfort and security and served as a trim facility for the diver. Very clever stuff nothing like what he had used for his previous diving experiences.

It was nearly five o'clock in the afternoon. Charlie had prepared a big beef stew which she was going to cook in the pressure cooker. They would have half for their evening meal and the other half would be frozen and would serve as a meal for another time. Since they had stopped, the *Cape* had been silent without any generators running since they had arrived in the cove. The main engines had been switched off once Bruce had finished his anchoring manoeuvres, so this was a testament to the effectiveness of the new battery pack. Indicating that they were working a treat. They made phone calls home to let everyone know that they were safe. James had asked to speak to Bruce to let him know that unfortunately, the mystery man at the wedding had done a very good job of not having had his photograph taken. Bruce told himself that no one was going anywhere, so really it didn't matter anyway. Once the phone calls were finished, Bruce motioned Charlie to silence, whispering in her ear. "I am just going to run a 'bug check' in here."

Charlie stepped away mouthing the word. "What?"

Bruce motioned for Charlie to follow him with his index finger held to his lips, motioning silence. Leading Charlie down to the workshop area, he retrieved the Micronic frequency indicator and switched it on. He carried out a sweep of the whole of the aft section of the boat, no lights were illuminated on the indicator. So, he explained. "Last night I found a tracking device, attached to the quad."

"Oh my God! Where is it now?" Charlie looked genuinely nervous. "How long has it been there?"

"It is now attached to the underside of the minibus, back at the chandlery." Bruce grinned. "Now, I have an idea how long it has been there, but not who put it there. But I think it is safe to say, that down here we are free to speak freely as it appears to be free from bugs. What I would like to do is to carry out a sweep of the main deck area to see if there are any audio devices."

Charlie took Bruce by the shoulders. "What if there are any listening devices. Do we throw them in the sea?"

Pausing for a moment, Bruce replied. "No, not yet. We play them at their own game and act naturally. If we are clever, we can feed them information, for instance, false data about a destination, not that we are going anywhere anyway."

"Bruce, do you think they have listened to us making love?" Charlie was genuinely troubled at the thought of that probability. Her face had gone very pale.

Bruce wrapped his arms around her. "No, my love, I think that the bug on the quad was put there whilst we were in the UK. If and only if we have got any audio bugs upstairs, again they will only have been put there whilst the boat was in the chandlery and while we were away."

Seemingly reassured, Charlie took Bruce's hand in hers as they started back towards the main salon. Bruce switched on the main salon TV to see if they were going to be able to pick up the early evening news. Charlie got them beers. Switching the Micronic frequency finder on, it immediately showed three lights, as Bruce pointed it towards the TV, four lights came on and as he approached the TV, he got five lights. Going up towards the bridge area he again got a signal response and when he got to the chart table, he got five LED's illuminated. Going below, Bruce swept first the master cabin and the double and single cabins, those three were clear but he got a positive reading from behind the mirror in the forward VIP cabin. Bruce closed and locked that door. Returning upstairs to the main deck, he picked up his beer from the sideboard where Charlie had left it for him and went out to the cockpit overlooking the swim platform. Speaking quietly to Charlie, Bruce said. "So, there is one in the TV housing, one somewhere inside the chart table and one in the forward VIP behind the mirror. I am not anticipating any visits, but in the morning, we can start taking some precautions just in case."

Looking sideways at Bruce, she asked. "How will you do that Bruce?"

"With the help of some fishing line and a couple of flares, my darling." Bruce winked at her.

CHAPTER 19

Thursday dawned, a cloudless sky, but because of being in the cove and protected by the mass of land around the cove, the sun didn't get to them until nine o'clock. Bruce's plan involved the construction of three devices to which he could insert and secure a flare in each device. The idea is that when attached to a tripwire, the flares would fire into the sky and as such provide an early warning system to Bruce and Charlie indicating that their privacy had been compromised. Launching *Willie*, they found two suitable positions where they could set a length of fishing line across the entrance to the cove. Anchored on one side of the entrance and then placing a flare and container on the opposite side of the entrance. Then attaching the free end of the line to the trigger of the flare, meant that anything entering the cove over two feet above the surface of the water would trigger the flare. Returning to the narrow beach, they surveyed the possibilities of anyone accessing it from above. The curved beach was some one hundred and fifty yards long, with a width of approximately twenty-five yards. The cliff above them rose for over three hundred feet. Having studied an image of Google Earth, Bruce thought that the nearest house was set back over 300 yards from the side of the cliff. It also appeared that the urbanisation was positioned from the centre of the cove, extending to the east. So, that there were no dwellings on the western side of the cove. Anyone wanting to access the beach from the top of the cliff would probably do so from the western side of the cliff, thereby minimising any interference from any residents. Once more, utilising some fishing line, Bruce rigged up two trip lines again connected to flares. Standing back and admiring his handiwork, Bruce said to Charlie. "Well, that should give us a bit of a heads up should anyone try to get into our cove." Bruce smiled at Charlie and was admiring the profile of 'Mrs Crusoe' in her skimpy shorts and T-shirt, the protrusion of her nipples confirming that Charlie wasn't wearing a bra that morning.

"What will they do?" Charlie inquired, pointing to one of the flares.

"When one of these babies goes off, it shoots a red skyrocket type projectile up to about 350 feet and then it goes off with a huge bang, which will really draw someone's attention. Surprisingly, if you point one at something it makes a wonderful weapon and there are another twenty-one of these on board."

Charlie moved around in front of Bruce and placed her arms around his neck. "Do you know what, Brucie baby?"

"No, know what?" Bruce replied, their faces a mere inch from each other.

"I am really glad that I am on your side." Charlie drew his face into hers and they kissed with gentle passion.

Returning to the *Cape*, they had an early lunch and started to get their wet suits readied and the cylinders secured to the BCD's in preparation for the afternoon's dive. After allowing a good hour for their lunch to digest, they kitted up, with spare weights being available on the partially submerged swim platform. The first task was to get their buoyancy adjusted, once that was done and holding hands, they swam off towards the deeper water of the cove. Taking the time to check to see how the two Manson anchors had set perfectly on the sandy sea bed. On this first outing, they had decided not to complicate matters with the addition of cameras or the Seabobs. Bruce concentrated on regulating his breathing and getting used to the bulky equipment around him. The clear waters of the cove revealed abundant and versatile marine life. Still holding hands, Bruce took them up to the hull of the *Cape* where they were able to inspect the new antifouling and the clean lines of the hull.

Then they heard them before they saw them, the little clicks and short, high-pitched whistles. Bruce and Charlie squeezed their hands simultaneously and looked at each other through their masks. Then they saw the pod of dolphins come into sight from the direction of the cove entrance. The humans suspended in the water beneath the hull of the *Cape* emitting bubbles as they vented air from their lungs must have looked a strange sight to the dolphins. Slowly Bruce and Charlie started to swim towards the dolphins. The dolphins calmly circled the two divers who were still holding hands. It was the same pod, Bruce recognised the bull, the same one that he had captured on camera swimming past a topless Charlie. This time one of the young cows came in very close to Bruce. Very slowly, Bruce extended his arm towards the cow's dorsal fin and then he saw it. The hook and the fishing line entangling the cow's dorsal fin, Charlie saw it too, for the first time since they had entered the water, they let go of their hands. The large game fishhook and the barb had passed right through her dorsal fin. The only way Bruce was going to be able to remove the big, needle-sharp hook was to cut the vicious barbs off.

Signalling to Charlie that he needed to get to the surface he made a scissor action with his fingers and pointed at the barb. They rose slowly to the surface, the cow rising with them. Surfacing very close to the stern and the swim platform of the *Cape*, Bruce spat out his mouthpiece, shrugged off his BCD, then rotated himself up onto the partially submerged deck. Bruce slipped off his fins and made straight for the workshop, he was back in less than sixty seconds armed with a pair of heavy-duty cutters. Charlie was still in the water, with her face mask on her forehead and her mouth free, she was gentling the dolphin with murmurs and stroked her gently on the forehead. Bruce slipped back into the water with the cutters and slowly approached Charlie and the dolphin. As gently as he could, Bruce cut the barbed end of the hook off with a loud snap, using his left hand with which he had been steadying the hook, he removed the remainder of the hook and tangled line from the cow's dorsal fin. The dolphin sensing her freedom swam away slowly then came back and nuzzled Bruce. He stroked her forehead above her eyes, then she turned over on her back to let Bruce tickle her tummy, laughing Charlie joined in as well. Disposing of the side cutters, the remainder of the hook and nylon onto the deck of the *Cape*, Bruce replaced his fins and BCD and they spent the next thirty minutes leisurely swimming with the dolphins. The cow now minus the hook and nylon never leaving Bruce's side, other than to surface for air, which on this occasion the humans didn't need to. Eventually, their air supply did come close to running out and Bruce and Charlie needed to return to the *Cape* as the dolphins went out to sea to hunt for their dinner.

Bruce and Charlie hauled themselves and their equipment out of the water and sat on the swim deck. They were sitting together, Bruce was leaning forward, Charlie realising that something was wrong, put her arm around him. "Bruce, Bruce darling what's wrong?"

"Oh my God!" Bruce stifled back his emotions. "It has been a long, long time since I have encountered that sort of a relationship with a wild creature. She just knew we would try to help her." He sniffed again and wiped his eyes with the back of his hands.

Charlie rubbing his back in empathy said. "And then she wouldn't leave you alone. I think I am going to call her 'Daphne'. What do you think Bruce?" She recalled Ron telling her of his father's ability, to not only communicate with animals but also his understanding of the creatures. It had started with Sheba, a German Shepherd and continued with Saba, a rescued leopard and didn't end with Rusty, a Roe fawn.

Lying backwards in the shallow water on the partially submerged swim platform, Bruce looked up at Charlie, his lower legs and fins still dangling over the edge of the platform. "That is a really appropriate name for her." Bruce smiled, recollecting the dolphin swimming next to him and nuzzling him. "So, my Chief Diving Officer, what did you think of that little adventure?"

Lying down next to Bruce in the shallow water but then turned so that she was on her stomach and resting up on her elbows, Charlie replied. "You are really a natural. If I hadn't known better other than getting used to the BCD, I would say that you haven't missed a days diving since you completed your diving course. I was very impressed, sweetheart."

"I would like to try the Seabobs on our next dive tomorrow, but I would like to go out of the cove and get a feel for what is outside the cove and under the surface. If you know what I mean?" Bruce stated. The gentle lapping of the water against the hull of the *Cape*, the slight movement of the deck with the swell and the warmth from the sun, was making Bruce drowsy, Charlie lying on her side, had her head resting on Bruce's shoulder in an equally drowsy state. They remained there for a further ten minutes enjoying the indulgence of not having to rush to do anything or go anywhere. The rush and anxieties of the previous ten days seemed to wash away as they luxuriated in the warm Spanish sunshine. After ten minutes, the warmth of the sun through their wet suits began to become uncomfortable. Stretching lavishly, Bruce and Charlie got out of their wet suits and rinsed them, as well as the diving equipment and themselves with fresh water. Charlie, only wearing a pair of bikini bottoms, was obviously enjoying the newfound advantage of the freedom that self-isolation provided with the ability to be able to go topless. Bruce wasn't complaining. "What about we take *Willie* out of the cove and see what we can fish for?" Bruce suggested.

"Great idea!" Charlie beamed. "Can I drive, please? I have really missed driving *Willie*."

Bruce looked sideways at her with a sardonic grin. "What?"

"The boat, I mean, silly." Charlie stood in front of him, just allowing her nipples to brush Bruce's chest as she kissed him lightly on the lips.

"Any more of this and we won't be doing any fishing today." Bruce responded by returning the light kiss.

They collected their fishing gear, buckets and had cast off from the *Cape* in less than five minutes. Charlie had driven them out of the cove, by-passing the trip line, as they headed for a point about five hundred yards off the coast, Charlie turned off the engine. Bruce set up Charlie to do some spinning with the same lure with which he had caught the Wrasse on, just over two weeks earlier. In the meantime, he decided to do some 'jigging' for sardines, using the very same technique as used for catching mackerel in the UK waters. Swapping places with Charlie, who went up to the bow, Bruce then opened a tin of fish meal, scattering a small quantity on the surface of the water. Amazingly, almost immediately the water in the vicinity of where the fish meal had been scattered was boiling. Drawn by the fish meal, the sardines had risen to the surface and were feeding on the bait. Realising what had happened, Bruce picked up the landing net, scooping it in the water he hauled in twelve sardines and dumped them into one of the buckets. Charlie watched in astonishment as Bruce repeatedly scooped in the sardines and very quickly, he had a half bucket of wriggling, flapping fish. Taking the second bucket, Bruce filled it with seawater and poured it into the first bucket. Instinct made Bruce look up and he saw them coming in from the open sea. "Charlie, quick reel in. We don't want to catch a dolphin." Charlie responded instantly and reeled in her lure. "Well, we won't be catching anything else hereabouts this afternoon." Bruce remarked as the dolphins tore into the shoal of sardines, joined by many gannets and other sea birds. The feeding frenzy was taking part literally just yards from the boat, giving them a fantastic view of the natural spectacle and leaving Bruce wishing he had brought a camera with him.

"I guess we are going to be having grilled sardines tonight." Charlie said looking into the bucket. "What was that you put in the water to attract them?" She quizzed.

"Just some fish meal, which we brought back from the UK." Bruce replied, holding up the tin. "We must have been sitting right on top of that shoal to have brought them to the surface that quickly." Leaving the gannets and dolphins to finish their meal, Bruce took *Willie* back into the cove, firstly replacing the trip line and then mooring alongside the *Cape*. Sitting on the swim deck, they sifted through the sardines. Bruce dispatched and prepared sixteen of the largest fish and returned the remainder into the water. Then he took them up to the galley where Charlie was preparing foil and freezing material.

"You have done a great job with those." Charlie looked at the sardines. "There are some whoppers there. If I butterfly the four big fish, we could brai them on the beach." Charlie suggested.

"Great idea! It will give us a chance to try out the new bucket barbeque." Bruce replied. "If you get stuff sorted here, I'll go ashore and get the fire going and then give me a holler and I'll come back for you." Bruce finished.

Bruce disappeared into the workshop where he recovered another of his purchases from the UK, a large bucket barbeque and placing that into the tender made his way to the beach. Having gathered some wood, he got the fire lit in the bucket. In the meantime, Charlie selecting four of the largest fish, butterflied them and rubbed them with olive oil, paprika and wrapped them in foil. Then constructing a separate foil package, she cut up some small salad potatoes, placing them in the foil package with seasoning and mixed herbs, then closed the end temporarily. Placing everything in a cool bag, including four tins of Alhambra and a cold bottle of Chardonnay, Charlie made her way back to the stern to await collection by Bruce.

Well before the flames of the fire had died down, Charlie got the package containing the potatoes, taking a can of Alhambra, she opened it and poured in half the contents of the liquid. Finally, sealing the aluminium foil package before putting it on the barbeque. This method of cooking the potatoes gave them a unique flavour with the combination of herbs infused with the beer. Twenty minutes later, she put the sardines on in their foil packages and set about preparing the plates. Six minutes later, Bruce and Charlie were enjoying a spectacular meal. Lying back on the blanket afterwards, Bruce belched quietly. "Sorry, that was appreciation." Charlie turned around and smiled, then lay down next to him and put her head on his shoulder, her breasts pushing up against his chest. "Charlie, do you enjoy not wearing a bra?"

Turning her head marginally up towards his chin she answered. "Yes, do you mind?"

Hugging her in towards him Bruce replied. "Good grief, no hun. Please wear as little as you like. I love it."

Charlie turned over, leaning on her elbows, she reached across and kissed Bruce gently and lovingly on his lips.

The first inkling that Bruce had that the storm was imminent was the flash across the sky to the south and east of them and then the marginal increase in the sound of the wind. It was their fifth night in the cove and they had just been preparing to go below and shower before going to bed. Bruce switched on the computer and checked the AEMET weather forecast. Sure enough, there it was, high winds and rain forecasted for overnight and into the next day. One of the things that Bruce did every night before settling in was to ensure that all the weather covers were on and that all the sun lounger cushions were stowed and 'Willie' was secured. So that in the event of an emergency they would be able to put straight out to sea. Charlie had already gone ahead and was in the shower when Bruce got down to the cabin. He was stripped off by the time Charlie vacated the shower and had started to dry herself off when the cabin blind rattled ominously. Bruce's shower was very brief as much as to conserve space in the waste tank, but also he was impatient to get back to the pilot station. There were several things that concerned him, not least of all was the amount of protection the cove would afford them and the fact that it would be dark and visibility would be severely hampered. Admittedly they had the big searchlight that they could use and of course, there was always the drift alarm as well. Bruce wanted to be wide awake and at the helm should anything go wrong. The shelter of the cove was as yet untested.

Bruce was towelling himself off in the shower and again there was a marginal increase in the sound of the wind. He finished drying himself and went back into the cabin, Charlie with her mini pink towelling robe on was sat at the dressing table making her final preparations for the night. "We have got our first storm coming up." Bruce said. "I am going to get back up to the helm and spend the night there to keep an eye on things." Bruce started by pulling on a pair of underpants and then a pair of cargo pants followed by a clean T-shirt.

"Bruce." Charlie was getting up from the dressing table. "I don't want to be down here on my own. Please, can I be with you?"

"Of course, you can." He smiled at her and reached across to kiss her. "Before you come up, would you please just make sure that all is secure down here!" Charlie was already closing the slightly open window on the port side.

On reaching the pilot station, Bruce switched on the main generator enabling him to have immediate power for the hydraulics and main engines should they be required. Just as Charlie reached the head of the stairs so they felt the first slight increase in the swell. It was pitch black outside and as the night progressed so the state of the weather worsened with the rain invisibly lashing the hull. By one o'clock in the morning, the sound of the wind was really loud, however, the anemometer on the pilot station was only indicating a wind speed of twelve knots. The shape of the cove was giving the *Cape* maximum protection as the wind speeds had been predicted at thirty-five, gusting to forty knots. Every ten to fifteen seconds, the night sky and the cove were illuminated with flashes of lightning in a surreal manner. The rain continued torrentially.

During the early part of the night, lulled by the gentle hum of the generator, Charlie had dozed off. At the first clap of thunder almost overhead, she awoke wide-eyed, looking startled like a gazelle caught in the headlights of a car at night. Moving from his seat across the bridge to where she had been sitting at the chart table, Bruce put his arm around her and comforted her. After Charlie had dozed off, Bruce had switched off the main lights and had lit the bridge with the dim red night lights, which gave everything an ethereal look and that probably contributed to her surprise as much as the clap of thunder. Although the size of the waves in the cove had increased quite considerably, the motion of the boat hadn't, this was a testament to her size, weight and stabilisers. The cove was doing a great job at protecting the *Cape*.

Charlie offered to make coffee for them both. It was at about four pm that Bruce noticed a slight depreciation of the severity of the storm, the wind eased slightly, as did the rain. It was becoming harder for Bruce to stay awake. After the coffee, Bruce had encouraged Charlie to stretch out on the double seat on the other side of the pilot station opposite the chart table, which she did after retrieving a spare blanket from a vacant cabin.

During the course of the previous day, they had completed two thirty five minute dives. On the first dive, they had been going through deep water rescues, on the second dive, they had spent the time picking up four lobsters. The dolphins were nowhere to be seen, presumably, anticipating the storm coming in, they had probably been out at sea feeding. One big discovery of the day was that Charlie thought that they had possibly found a bed of scallops at about a depth of sixty feet just to the west of the cove entrance. They had also spent part of the day doing housework chores and laundry, changing linen and had effectively had a pretty active day so that they had been left naturally tired at the end of the it.

To help stay awake, Bruce had settled in front of his computer at the dining room table. Some things troubled him and there were answers to questions that he needed to find. Who and where was Donaldson? Singleton the previous owner of the *Cape Agulhas* had apparently drowned in some form of accident. Who was the person with the swept-back hair that kept coming to light?

Bruce decided on a Google search of Singleton and discovered an image of him at some social bash in Palermo. The image looked familiar to him. Bruce had seen a picture of him somewhere before but he couldn't place it at the time. The image also met with the description that George Lucas had provided for 'Donaldson', saying that he was the owner of the *Cape* in Gibraltar. Why would Singleton impersonate Donaldson? Suddenly, it dawned on Bruce where he had seen the image before. Hastily he searched

Salisbury poisonings on the internet and two minutes later he had found the image. But it was a picture of two men and Singletons name wasn't Singleton. The second man in the photograph had swept back straight hair, but he wasn't called Donaldson either. They were called Boshirov and Seltskin and were identified as being associated with the Russian GRU.

Returning to the helm station, Bruce resumed his seat in front of the controls. The chart plotter was live on the left-hand side of the two screens, turning on the right-hand screen to see if he could get the radar plotter to indicate the weather for him. Unfortunately, the edge of the cove was too high for the radar to detect anything beyond, but turning down the brightness of the screen he decided to leave it on anyway. The storm resumed its full ferocity at about five o'clock. By six o'clock, Bruce could just about make out the beach behind them and the glistening wet steep walls of the cove as the first glimmers of daylight appeared. The angry swells coming into the cove were about six feet high but swiftly lost their magnitude and ferocity, reducing down to about two feet in height by the time they passed under the hull of the *Cape*. Bruce was pleased with his choice of anchorage. The *Cape* hadn't moved an inch.

Charlie yawned and stretched at about half-past six. Looking out through the windscreen she exclaimed. "Good grief! Is it still going on?" On her way to the day head, she kissed Bruce on the forehead and gave him a brief hug. The lightning and thunder that accompanied it had long since dissipated, the ferocity of the wind had also dispelled somewhat, but the rain seemed relentless.

The galley of the *Cape* was equipped with amongst other things, a four-burner induction hob, which would only work if the main generator were running or if they were hooked up to a shoreline. To minimise diesel consumption, Bruce had decided that when they could, they would use a little twin burner portable gas cooker for preparing hot meals, or they would barbecue on the beach. "Bruce?" Charlie asked. "Whilst we have still got the main generator running, would you like a full English breakfast, my love?"

"Oh, what a fantastic idea." Bruce swivelled himself around in the helm seat to face Charlie. Breakfast finished and the dishwasher run, Bruce was feeling a bit more human and relaxed. The rain had diminished considerably, as had the wind, but the waves coming onto the *Cape's* bow remained at the height of two feet. However, Bruce thought that they may well increase in size as the day wore on. The twin anchors were certainly doing their job as the *Cape* rode the waves. By nine-thirty, the wind had almost totally died down. "Charlie?" Bruce asked. "Do you have any plans for today?"

"Nothing specific. Why? What do you have in mind?" Charlie replied.

"Well, I was wondering if you wouldn't mind doing a bridge watch for a couple of hours, while I get some shut-eye?" Bruce inquired.

"No hun. Of course not. Where will you be?" Charlie came over and hugged Bruce.

"Right over there where you were." Bruce indicated the double seat. Picking up the discarded blanket, he lay down on the seat and smelling Charlie's scent on the blanket, Bruce was almost instantly asleep.

It was almost one o'clock in the afternoon when Charlie gently stroked Bruce's forehead. He surfaced to that delicious smell of fresh coffee mixed with sweetened condensed milk. "Wakey, wakey my Captain. It is just coming up to thirteen hundred and I am thinking that we are through our first storm." Bruce stretched, rubbing the sleep out of his eyes, he looked out through the windshield then took in the beauty of Charlie's smiling features. "Besides which, if I let you sleep on, I won't get you to bed tonight."

Sleepily Bruce said. "I'll get into bed with you anytime, my lovely. I don't need to be tired." He grinned at her.

"That, my darling, you will have to wait for another week or so." Charlie smiled sadly.

Bruce got up and hugged her fiercely to him. "That doesn't matter, we have got each other and in the meantime, we can look forward to being able to make up for the lost time when we can."

The rain had stopped, the wind had dropped to almost nothing and the size of the waves in the cove hadn't increased. There was even the hint of a weak sun trying to get through the diminishing clouds. Sipping at his coffee, Bruce checked the instruments and shut down the chart plotter and radar. After which, he shut down the main generator so that they were now back on battery power with the smaller generator kicking in when it was required. They passed the rest of the day doing odd jobs around the boat. Bruce had decided that he had had enough of the eves dropping bugs, so decided to remove them and put them in the engine room, which was pretty well soundproofed anyway. Charlie had been below with her sewing machine going hammer and tongs, triumphantly emerging with the flag that not only had she designed but had made as well. The flag measuring some three feet long by two feet wide was on a white background depicting the crest of the *Cape Agulhas* in the centre. The flag of the union in the top left corner. Charlie found Bruce at the chart table, open on the top was the chart that covered the south of Ibiza, puzzled she watched him silently for a while as he referred to notes that he had made on his phone and referring to both Google maps on his laptop and the chart plotter. He hadn't heard her come up the companionway as he had music playing through the AV system in the salon area when he surprised her by saying. "I suppose you are wondering what I am up to?" Bruce hadn't looked up.

Stammering, Charlie asked. "How did you know I was here? You couldn't have heard me?" She walked towards him.

Turning around, Bruce replied. "At first, I sensed you, I loved it that you just watched me. It felt nice and then I could smell you." Bruce met her halfway from the pilot station and put his arms around her. "Whether you like it or not, you emit a very special scent. It isn't a perfume that you wear, it is just a very special smell that you give off. From the very first time we met, I could smell it and I loved it." Charlie looked bewildered. Continuing, Bruce said. "You see that blanket over there?" Bruce indicated the now-folded blanket on the seat next to the chart table. "When you used it last night, you left some of your special smell on it and when I went to use it, I could smell you and then I knew I was in a safe place where you had been, then I slept."

Charlie looked confused. She knew that she hadn't worn any perfume for many days. "I hope that I don't smell that bad." Charlie wrinkled her nose.

"No, don't get me wrong, it is always a lovely fresh smell that you emit." Bruce nuzzled his nose under her neck. "Anyway, what is it that you have there?" Bruce inquired.

CHAPTER 20

Triumphantly with a 'Tah Dah!' Charlie held up the flag for Bruce to see.

"Wow! That is magnificent, we can fly that from the bow when we are next in a civilised harbour." Bruce exclaimed, the smile beaming across his face. "Wow, I am just so proud of you." He hugged her.

"Okay so, what are you up to then my Captain?" Charlie inquired.

"Take a pew. Because this is going to take a bit of time." Bruce indicated the helm seat to Charlie. "I need you to consider this. Charts made in nineteen forty-seven are going to be far less accurate than charts made today or more recently. Simply because of the methodology used back in those days. Today, we can use satellite imagery and GPS coordinates to get accurate fixes and shapes and just to throw another angle of probability into the equation is this. What about magnetic variation or magnetic declination for that matter? If a grid reference is taken using two fixed points and the lines drawn on a chart to provide a location in nineteen forty-seven. How accurate is that position going to be by today's standards? And here comes the kicker." Bruce continued. "If all the variables I have just mentioned have already been put there, just to throw someone off a plot. What then?"

Charlie, with the flag draped across her knees, looked at Bruce quizzically. "Are you referring to the positions that we took from the 'treasure charts'?"

"Yes, I am." Bruce smiled ruefully. "If those charts were genuinely made in 1947, then the shapes and positions of those islands would be quite different from today's charts, but they aren't. They are exactly the same, indicating that the 'treasure charts' are current with today's charts. Charts manufactured in 1947 were Admiralty charts and depths were marked in fathoms, our 'treasure chart' depths, are marked in metres."

"But one small little problem, my Captain." Charlie smiled at Bruce. "We don't have those charts anymore because my Captain gave them to the authorities to protect us from the nasty villains."

"Ah, yes, your Captain did give some charts to the authorities, my lover. But not 'the' charts. The charts that got handed over were copies but with no pinpricks in them." Bruce reached to the back of the chart table and opened a tube and from it, he removed the four charts. Charlie jumped from her seat and wrapped her arms around Bruce.

"I just knew it. Bruce, you sneaky bugger. When and where did you get the copies made?"

"I got Sergio to do them. He has a chart printer remember. When you were ordering up the diving equipment, I got him to copy them then." Bruce grimaced. "This now leads us onto a whole load more problems."

"How do you mean?" Charlie asked, looking concerned.

"Well, in the first instance, Sergio will have recognised those charts from which he made copies. He has possibly told Miguel that I had copies made but he wouldn't have known about the significance of the pinholes, which was why I made certain that I retained the originals. I think that it was Sergio or someone from Ellis Marine that put the listening devices in here and there." Bruce indicated the chart locker and the TV in the salon. "He also thought that we or I were still occupying the forward cabin. That is why he put another device in behind the mirror, not realising that we were now occupying the master cabin. I forgot to ask him not to put the safe in the forward cabin, yet another reason why he would have thought that I or we were occupying the forward cabin."

Bruce stood up and slowly rotated himself around through three hundred and sixty degrees. He paused and looked at Charlie pensively with his right hand on his chin. Charlie paled visibly, almost as though she knew what was coming. "No matter what I am going to say to you now, my feelings for you have not and will not change. This I need to be clear on. Okay?"

Charlie nodded her head, remaining seated at the helm, a tear escaping the corner of her left eye.

"The only way that I can put this to you is frankly and I apologise for my bluntness." Bruce's voice had taken on a serious and matter of fact tone. "I have known about you since you returned to the *Cape* on day one with your luggage. I had a brief conversation with Ivan when I went to pay him.

He told me about this person with the swept-back hair." Bruce continued. "To be honest, the only innocent person in this whole sorry mess is me. I have just bought a boat, that's all. Donaldson has had you on the ropes, so to speak and he has been able to do that through your Mum and Dad. As you now know, I have some friends in high places and some in some very low places as well and the rest has just fallen into place as we have gone along. Let us talk about you first. Not wishing to go into too many details. But essentially, before your former fiancée died in Iraq, you were having a lesbian affair with a married, very senior ranking member of the government. You were about to call off your wedding plans when Gerry, your fiancée and his mates died in that accident. At some point later, James, your father, was also supposedly having an affair. This was purported to be a homosexual affair and involved a very senior Admiralty Officer, except it wasn't true. This was borne out when we discovered what it was that Mitch was up to. Brian Stone and his colleagues were convinced that she was working with someone else." Bruce paused to gather his thoughts. "Back to you. The evidence was made up and planted by an officer from the Russian GRU. The woman you were having an affair with lost her government place and ended the affair. The KGB or GRU apparently had some irrefutably convincing pictures. Enter Donaldson. He is a former KGB officer and is now working for the Russian mafia. Not only did he have the dirt on you over your indiscretion with a married politician. But he also had the dirt on James because it was planted there some time ago by the KGB. Just for the record, I am not being judgemental here. These things happen."

"But how did you find this out?" Charlie looked incredulously at Bruce.

"My friends in the low places who I still remain in touch with known as 'The Det' or Fourteen Field Intelligence Unit from the days of Northern Ireland. A couple of them were given the nod by Brian Stone, who by the way is also ex Det. They picked Mitch up from just outside the Police Station after her release from custody, then they spent a few hours having a friendly chat with her and kept her safe until her hearing." Bruce ended the statement.

Charlie was sobbing, tears running down her cheeks. "Oh, Brucie, I am so sorry. I really didn't mean to deceive you. I truly fell in love with you and still love you more than anything in the world. How will you ever begin to forgive me?"

Bruce pulled Charlie's head onto his shoulder. "Sweetheart, there is nothing to forgive. What happened is in the past now and what matters most is that we continue to love each other. The recent new Russian owner of the *Octopus* is Dimitri Tockalov and his very close number two is Donaldson. When getting rid of the English-speaking crew, including you, Donaldson and Tockalov saw the opportunity of trying to get you onto the *Cape*. Now you probably didn't and don't give a shit about the world finding out about your affair but you do care about your Mum and Dad and their reputations. So, enter Mitch, she was put there just to keep an eye on things in Gosport, whilst Donaldson and Tockalov got you on to the *Cape*. But the mistake they made was that they hadn't counted on true love, then they made the mistake of trying to kill you, not me. How does that sound?"

Charlie pushed herself away from Bruce's shoulder and looked at him. "How and when did you find out all this information?"

Bruce took the flag that Charlie was still clinging onto and gently wiped the tears from her cheeks. "Some of it initially was suspicion given that you had a conversation with a strange man when you picked up your luggage. The attempt to kidnap you was potentially to put pressure on me to give up the charts and probably to get rid of you at the same time. Then the night they tried to blow us up actually did it. Although Mike Dunn was from the same regiment as Ron, he transferred to Military Intelligence and he never had PTSD. He has just been based out in Gibraltar with MI and has used his discharge with PTSD as a cover. He may well have been an inconsequential target as well. By the way, Mike doesn't know that I know that he is MI. Some of it I got whilst you were in London with your Mum, the rest of it I got last night and this morning."

"Bruce!" Charlie took Bruce's face in her hands. "So, you knew all about me beforehand but knowing that you still went ahead and married me. Why did you do that?"

"Charlie, how many more times do I need to tell you. I don't give a shit what you have done in the past, or the circumstances that we came to meet or the reason you came on board. I loved you then and I love you now.

Nothing is going to change that. We don't have to give these charts up to anybody now. Together, my love, we can beat them. Don't you see? We are the only ones who know where they are."

"Oh my God, Bruce, I am just so lucky." Charlie pulled Bruce to her and kissed him warmly on the lips. "How are we going to do that?"

Bruce pulled away and took Charlie's hand in his. "There are two, possibly three factions involved here, the first one is the Russian mafia and I think that the other is possibly the Russian GRU along with western intelligence units. The third is Van de Niekerk and his band of cut throats. I also now know that what we are all looking for is not pirate treasure but something more terrifying than that. If it were to fall into the wrong hands it could be used in an act of terrorism. Let's have some tea and then we can continue." Bruce kissed Charlie's lips.

Moving to the galley, Bruce put the kettle on whilst Charlie prepared the mugs and got the milk out of the fridge. Sitting on the sofa, mugs of tea in their hands Bruce resumed. "Do you remember back in, I think it was about March of twenty eighteen, two Russians were poisoned in Salisbury?"

"Yes." Charlie nodded.

"The poison used, was stuff called Novichok. It was manufactured somewhere around nineteen ninety-three by the Russians, at that time there was a guy called Boris Yeltsin who was in charge. The west came to find out about the Novichok and under some agreement or other, it was agreed by the west and Yeltsin that the Russians would destroy the Novichok. Around about the same time, there was a guy called Putin, Vladamir Putin who was at that time serving as a KGB Foreign Intelligence Officer. The KGB later became the FSB, however as a former FIO, Putin knew about the Novichok and I think he was encouraged to ensure that some of it had to be saved. This was handed to the GRU and specifically to Unit 29155 to be retained should a 'just in case scenario' ever evolve."

"I have heard of the GRU, but what is this Unit 29155?" Charlie asked.

"Unit 29155 is a Unit within the GRU that is specifically designated for foreign assassinations. Very nasty people." Bruce emphasised. Charlie nodded in understanding and Bruce continued. "To cut a long story short, apparently around about 2017, a quantity of Novichok disappeared as did a quantity of Sarin gas. Around October of 2017, the Assad regime in Syria dropped a quantity of Sarin gas on a civilian habitation somewhere north of Damascus, this caused widespread condemnation. The Russians and Putin categorically denied supplying it to the Syrians. I think it was supplied by people called Boshirov and or Seltskin."

"I know about Sarin gas, but where did it come from?" Charlie asked.

"Sarin gas, my lovely was invented by the Germans in the 1930's, it is colourless and odourless and can be deployed from the air, as in the case of Syria or from the ground or just sprayed from an aerosol can. As you well know, essentially it attacks the body's nervous system and eventually you die because you can no longer breathe or your heart stops."

"I know, horrible stuff." Charlie grimaced.

"Oh yes, it is definitely nasty and that is why we are not going to go hunting for it ourselves either. I would rather that people who are trained to deal with these things find it themselves. They will know how best to sort it out." Bruce finished.

"Question is who do you trust?" Charlie asked.

"I don't know." Bruce shook his head. "But now I think I know what the significance of the charts are, or at least I think so anyway." Making his way back to the chart table, Bruce found a large-scale map of the Mediterranean, Aegean and Adriatic seas and getting Charlie to read the coordinates for the eastern and western bearings of the pin hole location. He drew a line between them. Repeating the process for the southern and northern positions in the Adriatic, Bruce again drew a line. The line intersected at or close to the village of Sedilo in the centre of Sardinia. It was unfortunate that they didn't have access to better equipment to provide a more accurate position on the island. However, this idea seemed more plausible rather than their previous theories of four separate locations. The thought of hiding something like Novichok on the ocean floor where the container would be susceptible to deterioration in saltwater didn't bear thinking about. "If we are talking about Novichok?" Bruce echoed his thoughts to Charlie who agreed.

"Just one other thing that has just fallen into place is that Singleton purchased the *Cape* from a yacht broker in Cagliari, Sardinia."

"Bruce?" Charlie questioned him. "How do you know or think that what we are looking for is Novichok or Sarin?"

Bruce looked Charlie in the eye. "Because I think that I know who Donaldson is, I have found a photograph of him taken in Salisbury in 2018. I think that Donaldson is or was a Russian called Alexander Boshirov and he was photographed in Salisbury at the time of the attempted assassination of two Russians. Boshirov was accompanied by a second GRU Officer called Seltskin and they had stupidly been caught on candid camera and identified by MI6 and other western agencies. Ironically, they were named and shamed internationally, which wasn't very good for their careers with the GRU."

"Oh my God! Yes, I remember that." Charlie exclaimed. "But I thought that they had found the Novichok that they had used. Didn't a woman find a perfume bottle or something like that. She died I think."

"Absolutely right." Bruce agreed. "But unknown to other than a few, there were two other containers that the Novichok was in. One was an aerosol canister and the other one was a seal safe type bottle from which the liquid could be withdrawn by a syringe. Anyway." Bruce continued. "Following that, they rapidly found themselves without a job, so took up on the side of the mafia, taking the Novichok with them. Seltskin had another name, Singleton, the registered previous owner of the *Cape Agulhas* who died last year and subsequently, the *Cape* was put up for sale by the creditors. I also think that it was Singleton that posed as Donaldson in Gibraltar."

"But Bruce?" Charlie looked puzzled. "How have you come to this conclusion in such a short space of time?"

"When you have very little to do during a long stormy night, a little online perseverance and it is amazing what is available." Bruce took Charlie to the laptop and opening the browser, showed her the Wikipedia page surrounding the circumstances of the Novichok attack. The second one was the Mirror, with the image of Boshirov and Seltskin having been named by SIS and MI6.

"That's Donaldson!" Charlie exclaimed, pointing at the image of Boshirov.

"Correct." Bruce agreed.

The third page was an article by Bellingcat supporting Bruce's theory.

"Who is this Bellingcat, Bruce?" Charlie asked.

"These are investigative journalists, scientists and investigators who put together a lot of stuff that governments and organisations don't want the likes of you and me to know about."

"So, what can you do about it?" Charlie asked.

"Right now, I don't know. It is knowing who I can trust. There was a day when it was just a matter of calling Bradbury or Stirling Lines but even now that has all changed and anyway, we are all on lockdown and in isolation, so I don't suppose that anyone is going anywhere soon." Bruce concluded in frustration.

"Never mind, hun." Charlie circled Bruce in her arms and pulled his body in close to her. "I feel such a fool. I should have trusted you from the outset."

Bruce put his hands behind her, just above her buttocks. "Don't feel like that, please. I wanted to tell you that I knew sooner but then I had sort of hoped that you would tell me. From past experience, it is very difficult to keep a secret, one just hopes that one can keep their secret safe." Bruce felt the warmth of her body and breathed her scent in deeply.

"What happened?" Charlie asked, not raising her voice.

"I once cheated on my previous wife. Eventually, she found out and it nearly cost us our marriage." Bruce spoke quietly into her shoulder.

Charlie just moved her hand up behind Bruce's head and gently fondled the long hair on the back of his neck. Kissing Bruce on the forehead, she asked him. "How would you like me to do the Rib Eyes that I got out of the freezer earlier?"

Without moving from where he was hugging Charlie, Bruce thought for about thirty seconds. "Pepper sauce, rice and sweetcorn, please." He rocked Charlie in a gentle side to side motion.

Laughing Charlie replied. "Well, in that case, I had better get on with it then." She gently pushed Bruce away, kissed him and started towards the galley. "Would you like to get some wine then please?"

"On it." Making his way past the galley, Bruce saw Charlie bending over near the bottom of the fridge, gently he tapped the exposed flesh of her left buttock. "You should have a hazard sign for those shorts." He teased her, drawing a bit of a pout before she broke into a wide-mouthed grin. Bruce winked in return.

The weather over the next week continued to improve and warmed up even more. They were getting daytime temperatures of between twenty-four and twenty-six degrees and had windows and cabin doors open for a through draft. Of course, the *Cape* had a full thermostatically controlled air conditioning system but that required power and the running of a generator. Following the storm, the water in the cove and off the coast cleared and even started to warm up by a couple of degrees.

Two days after the storm passed, the United Kingdom announced that it was going into lockdown. Spain announced that they would continue on the lockdown for a further three weeks following the planned period. This would take the lockdown period for up to six weeks. At this point, there had been over fifteen thousand deaths in Spain alone. Italy had suffered considerably more deaths and positively more infections than anywhere else in Europe. This caused Bruce and Charlie to reassess their situation and supplies.

They had prepared and frozen most of the vegetables that could be frozen, including runner beans and corn on the cob, they had some potatoes but these were in the form of being in tins or frozen as chips. They had plenty and a good variety of pasta, rice, frozen beef, pork, lamb and sausages. Bruce had also ensured that they had brought with them from the UK an adequate supply of cured and dried meat called biltong and a quantity of sudsa, which was ground maize. Plus, currently quite a lot of their food was coming from the sea in the form of fresh fish, lobsters and of course scallops. They had plenty of freshwater, especially as they had a water maker on board. The 'black' sewage tank was only half full, the grey water tank was over three-quarters full, but their biggest problem was rubbish. Having realised that this may pose a problem over time, Bruce had taken all cardboard and paper and incinerated it on the beach. All other plastics and recyclable material that they had, was stored in double wrapped green plastic sacks and stored in the workshop area. As well as the general rubbish which was also placed in double wrapped black plastic sacks. There were now a total of five plastic sacks of rubbish in the workshop area, which was now beginning to smell a bit like a garbage truck. Soon, there would be another black double plastic sack.

One of the problems that they were going to face was the disposal of rubbish and of course waste from the grey and black water tanks. Bruce knew that one and a half nautical miles down the coast was a small beach with a now closed restaurant. Outside the restaurant were three large dumpsters that would serve for Bruce to dump their rubbish. There was also a small Coviran shop a very short distance from the dumpsters, which meant that they could get fresh eggs, milk and bread. Provided of course that they wore facemasks which they didn't have. However, Bruce knew that he had two snoods that would do the trick until they could get proper face masks.

Having made his decision, he found Charlie at her sewing machine and settling himself on the spare bunk he announced. "In light of the extended lockdown, I have come to a conclusion."

Charlie looked up with interest. "And what would that be then?" Bruce explained the problem regarding the rubbish and the filling waste tanks.

"So, tomorrow morning, with the weather seemingly in our favour, we'll load the rubbish sacks into *Willie* and whip them down the coast to that beach where we did some snorkelling before we went to the UK." Charlie looked puzzled. "Do you remember the one where there was a little beach café where we had coffee and cake in the afternoon?"

"Oh yes." Charlie replied with interest.

"Well, just next to it there were three dumpsters, as I recall. I reckon that they should still be there and that is where we will get rid of our rubbish."

"That sounds like a great idea, honey. But what happens if the dumpsters aren't there any longer?"

"Think positively my lover, plus there is a little Coviran shop about five hundred yards from the restaurant where we should be able to get fresh eggs, milk and so forth."

"Truly, you are a great Captain." Charlie laughed. "But what about our now nearly full grey tank. Surely you are not considering pumping out into the cove?"

"Absolutely not." Bruce recoiled in mock horror. Smiling, he continued. "We take our big baby out to sea for about ten miles and drop our tanks at sea. The engines could do with a good run anyway."

"That sounds like a great idea." Charlie got up from behind her sewing machine and stood in front of him. She reached down and around behind his head and pulled it into her abdomen. "I can make our face masks complete with pleats and elastic bands to hook over our ears." Charlie continued as Bruce reached around her with his arms and pulled himself tighter into her belly.

The following morning, they were up at seven-thirty and were breakfasted and ready to load *Willie* by eight o'clock. Fishing around in the workshop, Bruce found one of the plastic tarpaulins. Taking it, he spread it out across the bow of *Willie* and then loaded the rubbish sacks into the boat, completing the loading by folding the tarpaulin over the sacks and then lashed the tarpaulin down. The trip down the coast took no more than ten minutes travelling at twenty-five knots. Beaching the boat, they ferried the rubbish sacks up to the dumpsters in less than five minutes. Then they found the Coviran shop, which was virtually devoid of customers but extremely well stocked.

Returning to the *Cape*, they took her out top a point just outside Spanish territorial waters and dumped both the black and grey water tanks. An hour and a half later saw them anchored back in the cove, almost as they had never been away.

The following four days passed without incident. The weather, apart from two days when they had rain, continued to improve. The dolphins became regular playmates when they were in the water, Daphne never being far from Bruce and Charlie, who had now decided to call the large bull Dougie. Bruce's leg continued to get stronger and the cramps less frequent. The Seabobs continued to be as much fun as they had been on day one, Bruce and Charlie could now hold their breaths for up to ninety seconds, which meant that they could travel a considerable distance underwater when they were towed by the Seabobs. Charlie now had only a slight tan line around her breasts, both she and Bruce had distinct deep, coffee coloured Mediterranean sun tans which only served to highlight the scars on Bruce's leg and arm. They had continued their phone calls and contacts with the families and of course, Mike and Sheila Dunn in Gibraltar. The Dunn's were now happily living in their Sunseeker but were frustrated because they couldn't take it out for a cruise. In fact, Sheila and Charlie were becoming very close friends, swapping recipes, sewing tips and jokes, courtesy of Zoom. If it were possible Bruce and Charlie had become even closer as a couple. It soon became apparent that the one thing that Charlie regretted was that she could never experience motherhood.

CHAPTER 21

The 27th of March, 2020 dawned a beautiful day with the sun and low wind speed making this the warmest day of the year thus far in Andalusia, Spain. In Hampshire, England, the weather couldn't have been much worse. The predicted high for the day was for 4° C with low clouds scudding across the sky and depositing a constant drizzle that seemed to penetrate whatever clothing one wore.

Georgina Taylor was a beautiful child with one of those oval-shaped angelic faces and bright blue eyes. Her blond hair came halfway down her back. She was an exceptionally intelligent seven-year-old who attended the local primary school and was popular amongst her classmates. Her father, an immigrant from Albania, worked in the local transport industry, her mother was Polish but as far as Georgie was concerned, she was English through and through, even to the point where she had a rather posh, albeit slight Hampshire accent. Her mother had left her when she was five for a Polish man who owned his own transport business and was considerably wealthier than her husband. Georgie's father was bordering close on being an alcoholic, spending every spare pound on his favourite Raki, which unfortunately wasn't cheap in the UK. When Raki wasn't available, cheap Russian Vodka used to suffice.

Ardy Taylor (Ardrian Hoxa) had changed his surname for convenience. He was actually an illegal immigrant with a false passport. This had been very easy to do once he had got into the United Kingdom and had started work for the Albanian owned transport company based in Reading. In the UK, it was easy to get false papers and credentials. Especially, if you knew who to approach in the first instance. The English people were truly ignorant, tolerant and open to people from other non-civilised European and Eastern European countries. He hadn't even passed a legitimate UK driving test, although he held a full driving licence.

Life without his demanding and lazy Polish bitch of a wife, she wasn't even legally his wife, was difficult at first. However, he soon got used to it making his daughter, Georgina, do the housework and some of the chores in the two-bedroom rented apartment. Because he had satisfied the authorities that he was a single parent and that he was on a low income, Georgina would get free school meals whilst he got a subsidy for his income. He wasn't even sure that Georgina was his daughter. For fun, he used a local sex worker to satisfy his needs either once or maybe sometimes twice a month, depending on how much he'd had to drink, which would always make a difference to his sexual ability and appetite.

The mistake happened when he was drunk, but not too drunk and his sex worker friend wasn't available. He had got home to find Georgina in bed, she was partially uncovered and her nightdress had ridden up over her naked buttocks. The opportunity for Ardy was just too much and he didn't consider the consequences. He tried to rape his daughter but couldn't insert his penis into her. Georgina had screamed and in a vain attempt to shut her up, he pushed his penis into her mouth. That was the next mistake. Georgie had bitten down hard on the object that was suffocating her. Her sharp little teeth drew blood from the offending penis. Sadly, it cost her several severe slaps around her head, which drew blood from her nose and ear.

The next morning Ardy had threatened her with everything he could think of that would terrify a seven-year-old girl. There had also recently been a lot of focus on rapes and child abuse. The one thing he couldn't afford to do was to become a known sex offender. So, he put his plan into action. Through his contacts and a bit of research he got in touch with a man called Abadi in Lebanon and arranged for the sale of his daughter. The date and time for the exchange was set for the 27th of March at a layby, to the south of Basingstoke, at seven o'clock in the evening. He told Georgina that she was to go with these people, a Polish man and woman, who wouldn't hurt her and that she was to do exactly what they said. The United Kingdom was into its fifth day of lockdown and the fact that everyone was expected to stay at home and that schools were closed was a bonus. No one would miss her or him for the foreseeable future.

After getting rid of his daughter, who could have cost him a lengthy jail sentence, he made his way to the eastbound motorway services of the M4, where he met with the next part of his arrangements. Having arranged to meet a Lithuanian driver of a heavy goods vehicle, who was on his way to Dover and subsequently to Poznan in Poland. From there, he would meet with an Albanian driver to return to Albania, where he could then disappear. Of course, the European Coronavirus lockdown excluded the transport of goods and the movement of trucks.

Georgie was put into the front of the small truck between the driver and the woman who stank of body odour, albeit she seemed kind enough and it was warm in the cab. The truck was a Polish registered extended chassis transit that had a canvas tilt body on the back and an overhead cab bunk. Before they arrived at Dover, they stopped at the services at the Channel Truck Stop services on the M20. Georgie had dozed off against the shoulder of the woman, she was woken, forced to use the bucket in the rear of the truck and given a drink of warm milk, after which she almost immediately fell asleep. The sleep was deep and she was bundled up into the overhead sleeping area, followed by the woman. As they drove through the customs at Folkstone, disgustingly foul smells were emitted by the woman. An inquisitive customs officer carrying out a cab check was told by the driver, that his wife had stomach problems. That and the ensuing foul smell emanating from the bunk area prevented an overzealous search of the cab.

Georgie and the truck continued through France and into northern Spain. They avoided overnight stops at services and motorways, they also abstained from using any routes that were known to have cameras on them. After a painfully long and tiring thirteen days of avoiding any major roads, towns, camera's and some days remaining static in well-concealed places, the truck arrived at the Spanish village of Vados de Torralba, located about one hundred miles north of Granada. The house at which they had arrived was surrounded by a high wall and an electronic gate. From the truck, Georgie was transferred to a small outhouse, where she was bathed, fed, her clothes were burnt and she was given a dress to wear. The toothless old Spanish woman that tended to her, spoke no English and seemed very much to be of Eastern origin, not that Georgie realised this. By this time, she had become almost indifferent as to her outcome. She had lost weight, not that she had had much to lose in the first place and from the continuous drugging that she had received, almost wanted to do nothing but to sleep the whole time, which suited her guardians.

In the middle of the afternoon of the 11th of April and fifteen days after Georgie had been sold into slavery, three men entered the outhouse in which Georgie was kept captive, they ushered her unceremoniously into the rear of a Seat panel van. It was hot in the back of the van. She was accompanied by one man in the back of the van, the other two were sat in the front all three of them were carrying pistols. The drive down to Puerto Banus was accomplished by using all the back roads, save for the final part and the approach to the marina, arriving there just as darkness was falling. Instructing the driver to park in the car park, the man in charge got out of the van and made his way down the marina in search of Van de Niekerk and the *Esmeralda*, all to no avail. A man was tending to a boat that had a 'For Sale' sign displayed on it seemingly he had finished what he was doing and was about to depart the marina. The man looking for the *Esmeralda* spoke to the owner of the boat which was for sale and enquired of him if he had any knowledge regarding the boat he was seeking. He was informed that he had seen the boat depart two days before with two men on it, as there were crab pots on it, he presumed that they were going to set the pots. But as yet, the boat hadn't returned.

The owner was asked if he would like to earn €2,000 for a night's work which he readily accepted. Returning briefly to the van, an inert Georgie was bundled into a large hessian sack and was carried aboard the *Annabella*. The nervous-looking owner was handed the two thousand Euro's in cash and was told to cast off and to make for the open sea to the south of them. They were well out to sea when a drugged Georgie soiled herself and started to come around. That was when the owner realised what was in the sack and decided that he was not prepared to have anything to do with human trafficking. Unfortunately, it cost him a fatal knife wound to his chest. His attacker took him out of the wheel station and placed him dying in the rope locker to the front of the wheel station.

This had been a mistake, neither of the three had the faintest idea of how to use the Garmin navigational equipment, let alone sail a boat. Arguing between themselves for nearly two hours and trying to get the equipment working, they decided that the best thing they could do was to return towards the shore, but this was now a long way out of sight.

Having stripped Georgie of her soiled knickers and ditching the sack overboard, she was made to sit just outside the open door of the salon because of the smell from her. Then she started to be sick and retching up what little bile was left in her stomach. The leader of Georgie's custodians decided that they should return to shore until alternative arrangements could be made. The only instrument open to them that they could follow was the compass rose in front of the pilot station. Turning the boat north, they started to make their way towards the shore. Eventually, they could see the lights of the distant shore and continued in towards the coast, but decided they needed to wait until daylight so that they could go ashore somewhere where they would be less conspicuous. Then the storm broke with lightning, thunder and torrential rain. It was just in time that the helmsman saw the looming cliff face ahead of him and turned the boat to the left, deciding to follow the coast. It was shortly after seven-thirty when the shoaling wave hit them.

Unbeknown to Bruce and Charlie who were languishing in Dolphin Cove and enjoying the freedom that isolation had benefited them, other factors in the world were going on that would have a direct effect on their lives in the future.

The first to note was that the *Star* had sailed from Freetown in Sierra Leone on the 4th of April, this was some nine days before the last storm that had hit the south of Spain. The *Star* was a Dutch constructed general merchant cargo ship. She was just over seventy-five metres in length with a displacement of 7,500 metric tons and a crew of eight that included a person loosely termed as the captain. She had been constructed in the early nineteen nineties and was common to literally thousands of similar coastal traders that ploughed the coasts of the world. In twenty seventeen, she became the property of one Ben Yousif Abadi who was a well-known figure amongst the less popular of people of Beirut and indeed Lebanon.

There was no other way to describe Abadi, he was a slaver and an illegal trader who did very well in the trade of children, both male and female of all ethnicities, as well as the smuggling and trading of the most sought-after species of animals. All of which were endangered varieties, not to mention ivory and anything else that turned a Lebanese pound or preferably a US Dollar. Abadi had acquired the *Star* as he discovered that he could sail the Atlantic and Mediterranean oceans with almost impunity around his favourite coasts of trade, which included West Africa, Morocco, Tunisia and of course Libya. He controlled his business and his finances by satellite and computer from his seventh-floor apartment in Saifi Village, not far from the centre of Beirut.

Having departed Freetown and taken on her legitimate cargo of groundnuts and bananas, the *Star* headed north up the coast of Sierra Leone and anchored off Kortimaw Island in the mouth of the Greater and Lesser Scarcies rivers. The crew and the boat had been here before, they were familiar with the stink of the land and mud around the estuary. It wasn't long until the two skiffs came alongside the *Star* and the four men transferred their goods which were hastily placed in secreted positions in the hull and some hidden amongst the other cargo. The live cargo consisted of six girls and two boys, between the ages of eight and ten. Also, a cage of an assortment of wild birds, two female mountain gorilla's, they were approximately six months old, three female chimpanzees, again about six months old. There was a quantity of elephant and hippo ivory and dried Nile crocodile skins.

Mustapha Ben Azil, the master of the *Star*, made his way below decks to inspect the children. It was very important that none of them had been interfered with and skilfully he examined each of them in turn without a care for their feelings. To assist him he had taken two of his crew with him, both eunuchs and chosen as such because they would be the only crew members to have contact with the cargo, as they were referred to. It was very important that he delivered only undamaged goods, otherwise, the discerning clientele of Abadi would not be happy because the goods would then be worthless. Should that occur, then Captain Mustapha Ben Azil would be out of a job. At best.

The last child to be examined was a nine-year-old boy, he was brutally bent over, his legs spread apart and his buttocks were spread. The anus indicated relatively recent penetration and there was a faint trace of blood, not uncommon in this essentially Muslim country. Speaking in Arabic, Azil instructed one of his eunuchs. "Take this worthless piece of stock topside." On his way to the deck, he went via his cabin. Azil opened a safe and removed four hundred US dollars in twenty-dollar notes. Securing the safe, he returned to the cargo deck where he addressed the four men in the local language of Krio. "Which of you sons of dogs have got shit on the end of your cocks?" Reaching around behind him, he withdrew the hooked traditional knife called a khanjar. "I ask you again, you sons of whores, who was it that messed with this merchandise?" None of the men would look at Azil. "Look at me!" He commanded. Azil was standing behind the terrified boy and as the four men turned to look at Azil, he reached around the front of the boy with the khanjar and without a second's hesitation, slit the boy's throat from ear to ear. An action that he was well practised in. Bleeding copiously and pumping blood from the fatal wound to his neck, but still alive, the boy was unceremoniously thrown from the deck into the estuary. The corpse would be disposed of by the many Bull and Mako sharks that frequented those waters.

Without giving the boy a second glance, he held up the bundle of notes, he removed two notes and continuing in Krio, he addressed the four men. "Here was four hundred dollars US. I have taken twenty dollars because you have delivered me with damaged goods. I have now taken a further twenty dollars because I have had to remedy your mistake and I will now have to pray to Allah for forgiveness because I cannot deliver unto my master, goods that should be his." Turning, he handed the three hundred and sixty dollars to the eunuch. "Pay them when they are in their boats and off my ship." Turning again to the four men, he continued. "If in the future you sons of pestilence, wish to continue to trade with me, you will ensure that this does not happen again." Upon which Azil turned and headed for the bridge feeling very pleased with himself as he pocketed the forty dollars. As soon as the skiffs cleared the side of the *Star*, Azil gave the order to raise the anchor.

Once underway the *Star* continued north-easterly to clear the Guinea island of Uite, calling on the Gambian port of Banjul for fuel and two eleven-year-old Mauritanian girls. Continuing north and then northeast until they entered the straights of Gibraltar. From there, the *Star* headed into the tiny Algerian port of Marsa Ben M'hidi where they again took on fuel and freshwater.

Just before sunset, they were preparing to slip their moorings when a Toyota Landcruiser pulled up on the quayside, a tall blond-haired man got out of the passenger side and walking with a pronounced limp, he approached the gangplank. The hair was unkempt and a pair of sunglasses were tipped back on top of his lank, blond hair.

CHAPTER 22

On Saturday the 4th of April and at the same time as Azil was raising the anchor of the *Star*. Van de Niekerk learned that he was shortly to be transferred from his comfortable isolated, albeit guarded, hospital bed to the hospital prison wing in Madrid's Valdemar Prison. This establishment was well known for its overcrowding, generous beatings and non-exemplary cuisine. Whilst languishing in his hospital bed in the Hospital de Santa Maria off the Calle Blas de Lezo, he had given serious consideration to making good his escape. Van de Niekerk knew that if he got into Valdemar prison, there was every likelihood of him never seeing the light of day again. Certainly not for a very, very long time.

The Police had taken DNA samples from him that were going to link him to at least one murder/rape in his own country, a murder in France and at least two rapes in Spain. One was a fourteen-year-old girl. The Spanish didn't like children being raped, nor does anyone for that matter. He had already been interviewed by two men in civilian clothes who had questioned him about his association with people called Tockalov and Donaldson, of which he genuinely knew nothing about. Then they had wanted to know what the significance of the charts were that he had been trying to steal from the *Cape Agulhas*. This he agreeably told them, that at some time previously, the boat had docked at the Malaga Marina to pick up a charter and to have some repair work done to her. The owner had gone ashore, got very, very drunk and had boasted to a prostitute about a fantastic weapon that he had secreted somewhere in the Mediterranean. But he was the only person that could ever find it.

Pedro, who used the sex worker as well, was accordingly informed by her. Occasionally, Pedro assisted the Dutchman with some of his clandestine operations and had duly informed him too. The illegal aspects

237

of their operations had been, needless to say, left out of the conversation with the Police.

There were usually two armed Police Officers guarding Van de Niekerk, who was cuffed to the rail of the bed, with one on the door outside and one sat opposite him. They rotated every half hour on eight-hour shifts. This team were now in the seventh hour of their shift, the one outside his door had stuck his head in to say that he was just going to take a leak. One minute later a nurse with his medication came into the single ward, she was slightly built and as such the ideal candidate for his plan. During his stay in the hospital, he had made every effort to conceal the fact that he was indeed healing very well and could walk exceptionally well. This was something he got to practice daily when he was taken to the toilets in a wheelchair. The guards would ensure that there were no other people in the toilets, allowing him the full use of the whole toilet block. He had on one occasion considered getting out through the roof voids, but upon examination, found that the plan wasn't practical.

Things happened very quickly. Van de Niekerk had been feigning sleep when the nurse entered the ward when she came around to the side of the bed which he was facing. The nurse wearing full anti pandemic protection of mask, visor, gown and gloves had in her top left breast pocket amongst other items a pair of scissors. As the nurse placed the medication on the locker beside the bed, Van de Niekerk moved in one swift turn. He was out of the bed and pulling the nurse in front of him, he had her turned around so that her back was to him, removing the scissors and had the improvised weapon held to her throat. The guard hadn't even realised what had happened until it was over.

Van de Niekerk motioned the guard over towards him. "Come here maldito culo! Pistole aqui." He indicated the bed. "Dos dedos." He held up his thumb and forefinger with his manacled left hand. "Rapido!" The young cop was probably in his first year of the job and was clearly nervous and obliged Van de Niekerk by doing precisely what he was instructed to do. The nurse being held against the big Dutchman was trembling with fear. As he pushed her forward, she started to cry, this was just what Van de Niekerk wanted. Terror! Addressing the nurse, he said. "Silencio!" Then to the cop, he said. "Llaves!" (Keys.) Then. "Vuelta." Obligingly, the cop turned around. In one move, Van de Niekerk reached forward with his right hand, dropping the scissors on the bed, he picked up the Sig Sauer pistol and with a terrifying crack, hitting the young police officer on the side of the head, just above and behind the ear. The cop knocked sideways by the blow, crashed to the floor. The nurse wet herself as the Dutchman threw her away into the wall where she collapsed in a heap with blood trickling from her neck where he had viciously pressed the scissors into her throat. Taking the keys, he undid the manacle from his wrist, checking the pistol he noted that the chamber was empty, so pulling the slide all the way back and releasing it, causing a round to be chambered into the breach. Van de Niekerk took up a position, standing behind the door to await the other cops' return. He didn't have long to wait. Pushing open the door to announce his return, he saw his colleague on the floor, eyes wide open and a pool of blood forming from the right ear. The cop made the biggest and last mistake of his life by rushing to his colleague's assistance. The raised Sig Sauer came down with the speed of an express train and hit the cop at the base of his skull. He crashed to the floor, not having heard or seen a thing, lifeless.

Moving as fast as he could and ignoring the sobs of the nurse, Van de Niekerk dragged the two bodies into a position where they would not be easily seen from the doorway. At the same time relieving his second victim of the service Sig Sauer pistol. Putting on the hospital issue terry-towelling robe, he grabbed a towel and sat in the wheelchair, which had been left there for convenience. Motioning to the nurse to start pushing the wheelchair. "Salida, salida pronto!" Indicating the pistols. "Silencio!" He secreted the pistols under the bath towel. "Te mataré primero, perra." (I will kill you first, bitch.) "Ir salida! Pronto!"

The exit was right next to the emergency ambulance bay and there just by chance, was an unmanned ambulance with the back doors open, the engine running and the strobes still flashing. Getting out of the wheelchair, Van de Niekerk took the nurse by her arm and very casually walked around the back of the ambulance. He quietly shut the doors and then pushed her into the front of the vehicle, motioning her to the cab floor and then getting in behind the steering wheel. Selecting 'D' on the auto transmission, he let the brake off, switched off the strobe lights and casually drove out of the hospital onto the Calle Blas de Lezo. Approximately two minutes later, Van de Niekerk pulled the ambulance into the large car park of a SuperSol supermarket. Once parked, not far from the entrance/exit, he dragged the nurse into the rear of the vehicle and bending her forwards tied her hands behind her back. As he was doing so, his crotch pressed up against her buttocks, feeling the arousal in his groin as the carnal desire for sex rose up in him. Thinking better of it, he turned her around and stuffed a dressing in her mouth and secured that with another bandage. Then taking a third bandage, he tied her neck to the handrail for the stretcher, making it impossible for her to move. Van de Niekerk then settled at a point from where he could watch the comings and goings in the car park. He spotted his mark as he drove into the parking area and left the Mercedes Benz saloon car very close to the hi-jacked ambulance. He was a big man almost the same size as Van de Niekerk. Slipping out of the rear of the ambulance, he ambushed the man as he walked past the back of the vehicle. Then stuffing the barrel of the pistol in his face and taking the keys in his free hand he marched his victim back to his own vehicle. Unlocking the luggage compartment with the key fob, he persuaded his hapless victim into the trunk with a casual swipe across the face using the barrel of the pistol. His prey didn't need any more encouragement. Van de Niekerk got into the driver's seat and casually drove out of the car park. He knew that he had to get out of Malaga and the surrounding area as quickly as possible after all, he had just killed two cops and very soon Malaga would be closed down like a sardine can. The problem was that there were cameras everywhere, but it would take the authorities a little while to work out that he had hijacked the Mercedes. Then they would be tracking its progress with the CCTV and number plate recognition.

Van de Niekerk had concluded his planning for this eventuality whilst lying in his hospital bed. He had also physically planned for this contingency. Just to the east of Malaga, Van de Niekerk had at some time previously purchased what amounted to a one-room dwelling in what was, to all intents and purposes, a very run-down area. The outside of the building suited the surroundings in which it was located, which mostly housed guest workers and the other less salubrious contributors to Spanish society. The approach road had no CCTV cameras, however, the Spanish Police regularly used helicopters to patrol these areas. To the side of the dwelling, Van de Niekerk had constructed a lean-to, large enough to house a vehicle. The first thing he needed to do, was to get out of the hospital dressing gown that he was wearing.

So, within one minute of leaving the SuperSol car park, Van de Niekerk had driven the Mercedes down a very narrow and seldom used alley during the day. Stopping at a point where he would be relatively inconspicuous, he got out of the driving seat, opened the trunk and told his captive to remove his clothes. Swiftly replacing the hospital attire that he had been wearing with the clothes taken from his hostage. From there, he continued out of the city for a short distance on the M74 autovia heading east. Then he left the autovia continuing east but on an un-made road used for servicing the many fruit and vegetable growing areas under polythene that were prevalent in that area.

As he drove, Van de Niekerk considered his situation, he was tempted to hide the Mercedes and lie low for a couple of days, allowing the hue and cry to die down. On the other hand, the Mercedes would be bound to be discovered in a matter of time, one of the locals would sure to be over-inquisitive and either try to steal it or worse, go to the cops. His best plan, he thought was to get a change of clothes and to get out of Spain. Pronto! Arriving at the shack, he rummaged under a tin at the back of the lean-to and retrieved the spare key for the padlock that secured the chain of the front door. He then drove the Mercedes into the lean-to, switched off the engine, leaving the keys in the ignition. Ten minutes later, having recovered a fake passport, a quantity of cash and wearing fresh clothing, he wheeled the Spanish registered Yamaha 125 motorcycle out of the dwelling. Re-locking the front door he pocketed the key, put on the crash helmet and departed bound for the small marina at Puerto Banus. That was where Pedro should have his boat moored. From there, a quick trip to North Africa where he had numerous contacts that he could use to his own ends. Using the coastal route as far as was possible, it took Van de Niekerk just over two hours to get to the marina and then to discover that there was no Pedro and worse still, no *Esmeralda*.

Keeping a cool head and knowing that he would be easily recognised in the marina area of Puerto Banus, he re-mounted the motorcycle and headed towards the larger marina at Marbella. This was where he would be unknown and it would also be easier to steal a boat from there to get him to North Africa. One thing was certain and that was that he would now be a very much wanted man anywhere in Europe. He knew of a few people who would give him a fair price for a stolen motor yacht, after all that was where he had acquired the Benateau, *Esmeralda*. He also knew of the *Star* and her comings and goings and her favoured port in Algeria, Marsa Bin M'hidi.

Van de Niekerk and the Captain of the *Star*, Azil had had plenty of dealings in the past and although he hadn't met with Abadi they had both communicated in a business-friendly manner. It was Van de Niekerk who was the tall, blonde-haired man that had got out of the passenger side of the Toyota Landcruiser.

"Oi! Azil, you son of a dog." Van de Niekerk shouted at the bridge in English.

Azil heard the shout and moved out onto the bridge wing, immediately recognizing Van de Niekerk, he smiled. "What do you want? Dutch eater of filth." Azil's English was quite good and he was the only person on board that had any clue to the understanding of that language.

"Your father copulated with a pig so your mother was a sow." Van de Niekerk shouted back, laughing at the insult he had delivered. "I need some help my friend and I need to get to Lebanon."

"Then you had better get your sorry, sick Dutch arse on board." Azil shouted back as he started to make his way down from the bridge wing.

Van de Niekerk limped his way up the gangplank and met with Azil on the deck. As old friends do, they embraced each other warmly. "What happened to you, my friend?" Azil asked, taking in the discomfort that Van de Niekerk was displaying and the obvious favouring of his right leg.

"I took a bullet from a fuckin' Spanish cop." He spat over the side of the ship. "And that dog Pedro has disappeared off the face of the earth with my boat."

"Come, my friend, let us toast your good fortune of freedom." Azil put his arm around the big Dutchman. "Besides, we have much to discuss and

I do not doubt that we may even come across that thieving Spanish infidel, Pedro."

Taken aback by Azil's remark Van de Niekerk allowed himself to be led towards what passed as the Captain's cabin, reassured by the Police issue Sig Sauer tucked into the back of the waistband of his trousers.

The *Star* slipped her moorings and hugging the coast for the short distance, anchored off the beach known as Moscarda Two. It was a quarter to midnight when the three trucks loaded with one hundred and twenty-one refugees pulled up on the road at the top of the beach. The pre-inflated boats had been lashed down on top of the canvas roofs of the lorries, with the outboards attached to the tailgates. As silently as one hundred and twenty-one refugees could, they unloaded the six inflatables and one per boat laid the six outboards down in the well of the boats. As evenly as possible the guards, armed with semi-automatic rifles, supervised and allocated people to the boats, finally equipping the refugees with paddles. The *Star* lying just seven hundred and fifty yards offshore was the temporary destination for the refugees in their inflatable boats.

These refugees had paid the equivalent of twenty thousand US dollars per person to be smuggled into Europe. What they couldn't pay, they would then have to work off as a debt once they got to their destination. Abadi's cut in this deal was one thousand dollars per head. All he had to do was get Azil to transport the refugees from the coast of Algeria to the fringes of the twelve mile Spanish territorial waters, launch them in their inflatables with outboards and point them in a northerly direction. The journey would take twenty-four hours and funds were paid in advance. Once the refugees were on board the *Star*, it became a different story.

The passengers were all examined, the little luggage that they had was carefully inspected. The lucrative business of people smuggling was obviously very profitable, however, one of the problems that had recently reared its ugly head, was where the westernised governments had become so inundated with illegal immigrants, that they had started to infiltrate or recruit refugees equipping them with sophisticated tracking devices. The various Navies of Spain, France, Italy and the United Kingdom would then be on the lookout for the tracking devices and could now stop and board ships like the *Star* in international waters. Under Article 22(1) of International Maritime Law, if they were believed to be creating an act of piracy or engaged in the slave trade, which they most certainly were, they could then be expected to be boarded legally.

Once all the luggage had been searched, they were all then subjected to a full body and cavity search, this included men, women and children. They were searched one at a time by experts and any valuables that were discovered, which usually included diamonds or high value paper bills, were confiscated. Those that Azil thought that may be of a profit to Abadi and of course to himself, were separated and moved to a cabin below decks. These only included women and children. He found two girls, one aged eight and the other eleven, which he added to the collection of nine that he already had.

Van de Niekerk, having watched the proceedings with interest, seized a young black woman and took her before Azil. "Do you mind if I borrow this one for the night? It has been a long time since I last had a woman." The vivid recollection of the Spanish nurses' buttocks coming into contact with his skimpily clad genitals during his escape back in Malaga, had set his desires in motion.

Azil smiled at Van de Niekerk. "She looks clean my friend, she even smells clean, maybe I will join you later."

Van de Niekerk dragged the squirming Ghanaian woman to the cabin that he had been allocated. The moment that his naked penis touched her vagina, was the moment he signed his death warrant. It was as well that Azil's duties kept him busy and that he didn't join Van de Niekerk as originally planned.

The next morning, Van de Niekerk and Azil managed time over breakfast to catch up. Azil admitted to knowing of Van de Niekerk's arrest in Spain and his remark about coming across Pedro was signified by the information that he was due to pick up a blond English girl at a rendezvous during the course of Sunday night, early Monday morning. The rendezvous was supposed to have been with him, Van de Niekerk, the confirmation emails had been received over a week ago. The only other person that would have had access to the information would have been Pedro. Van de Niekerk was looking forward to seeing Pedro again, not that Pedro had done anything wrong as such, but it would be nice to have him continue his business with the boat.

The long hot day in the mid-Mediterranean Sea continued into Sunday, with the *Star* continuing to make her way North, steering away from the sight of any other ships. In the late afternoon of Sunday, 12th of April, Azil arranged for the launch of the inflatables and the fitting of the outboards. The inflatables were loaded with the refugees that then continued on their journey by being towed behind the *Star*. The occupants were told that they would be towed to a point just inside the twelve mile limit, where they would then be cast adrift. It was then the time for them to start the outboards and then continue in a northerly direction until they came across the coast of Southern Spain. The fact that there was barely sufficient fuel to get them to the coast, was not the concern of Azil, besides which they did have paddles as well. It was a little after eleven fifteen that night that Azil gave the order to cast the inflatables adrift. He then increased his speed to twelve knots and turned west, south-west staying parallel to the Spanish coast.

Both Azil and Van de Niekerk were on the bridge of the *Star* closely monitoring the radar and VHF radio. The engine was stopped at the appointed meeting point and then it was just a matter of waiting for Pedro to appear. At five o'clock in the morning, the storm broke with vicious rain and a strong wind blowing up from the south-east, lightning lit up the barely dawning sky, still the radar plot remained empty and the radio was silent. They had been on station since two minutes past midnight, the appointed meeting time had been for one o'clock in the morning. By half-past five, with the storm increasing in ferocity, Azil decided that he could not delay any further. So, he set a course back out to sea and headed the *Star* away in a south easterly direction taking the storm on her bow.

CHAPTER 23

It was late afternoon on Thursday 9th of April, this was the day after Bruce and Charlie had completed their first rubbish disposal and the day before the *Star* departed the port of Marsa Ben M'Hidi. Rupert Donaldson Esquire, late of the GRU and otherwise known as Alexai Boshirov was securely ensconced in a safe house on the waterfront of Puerto Banus. The safe house had no connection with the GRU, who just as a bye the bye, would have liked to have had Boshirov disposed of. For no other reason than because of the cock-up for the Salisbury poisonings in 2018. Having been assigned the Salisbury assassinations, Seltskin had been the senior officer and Boshirov was forced to work according to Seltskin's instructions. It was as a result of the man's incompetence that the Salisbury mission had failed so miserably and had cost the Russian government and his former boss, Putin, so much embarrassment. It had been Seltskin that had deposited the used container with the Novichok into a dumpster and had then fled with the other two containers of Novichok. Seltskin or Singleton as he was also known, had been an idiot and had maintained a highly visible high life purchasing a boat and seemingly conducting charters, living well beyond his means. In 2017, it had been Seltskin and another former GRU officer that had engineered the sale of Sarin Gas to the Syrians. Bashar-al-Assad had paid over ten million dollars US for that delivery. Of course, this was something of which the Russian government knew nothing about and genuinely refuted any connection to the sarin gas affair. Suffice to say that Seltskin's accomplice didn't live very long after that transaction. He died from organ failure. Possibly through having ingested a quantity of sarin gas himself, needless to say, that a post-mortem examination was never carried out, only because there was no body to examine.

As a result of the 2018 Salisbury fiasco, Boshirov knew that his career with the GRU was over, but he had known Dimitri Tockalov for some time and it was to Tockalov that he went, offering his services. Tockalov with his black-market contacts had often furnished the GRU with items that they would use for their clandestine operations. Tockalov had readily agreed to Boshirov's terms of service. One of his attributes was that he could manufacture evidence to indicate that a person was complicit in anything that suited him and then blackmail his victim. One of his recent victims had been a young Lieutenant in the Guardia Civil. The one thing that most law enforcement agencies hate, for instance, is child sex abuse. Boshirov had constructed fantastically brilliant photographic evidence that the young Lieutenant was guilty of precisely that. Boshirov would have liked to have added that no young children had been hurt in the production of this evidence but of course, he couldn't.

Tockalov had found himself indebted to Boshirov when he took on the security for his sixty-metre yacht *Octopus*. With his experience as a Foreign Intelligence Officer, he had gone into the background of all the staff and had discovered that three of the staff were ex British service personnel, the other four spoke and or understood Russian. The attractive woman that worked in the galley also had prominent parents within the medical world. Tockalov had only taken her on for her looks and had been unsuccessful in trying to bed her. It wasn't until Boshirov, with his ability to access information, had informed his boss that she was a lesbian and had previously had an affair with the then minister for defence procurement. This then accounted for her lack of response to his advances. It was Boshirov's suggestion that the whole crew be dispensed with. This would then enable them to take on a new crew that had no understanding of the Russian language. Subsequently, enabling Tockalov to conduct his business safely and openly in Russian.

Boshirov had also informed Tockalov about the missing containers of Novichok. He suspected that Seltskin had secreted the Novichok somewhere and had pointed out the advantage of having such a powerful weapon. It was worth millions of dollars to the right person and Assad had lots of money to start with. The Chinese would also probably be very interested in it as well. After all, they had been messing around with pandemics for some time. Now they were suspected of unleashing the Covid 19 virus on the world.

So, it was with the blessing of his new employer that Bosirov intercepted Seltskin in Mallorca and it was off a lonely, out of the way beach where he had a one-sided conversation with his former colleague. The conversation was interrupted on several occasions when Seltskin involuntarily took in quantities of the Mediterranean Sea. Unfortunately, it seemed that at one stage, Seltskin took on too much of the ocean and that was when his mortal soul passed from this planet. Disappointedly, Boshirov searched the *Cape Agulhas* for some indication as to where his former colleague had secreted the Novichok or some indication as to where it had been hidden. All to no avail.

Boshirov remained adamant that there was bound to be some form of a clue hidden on the motor yacht which related to where the Novichok had been secreted. After all, Seltskin had no other property owned or leased anywhere in the world. Seltskin had boasted that the boat was his world. So, Boshirov became very concerned when the blond-haired Dutchman and his crony from Ellis Marine started to take an interest in the boat. He had them followed, their conversations listened to and that was how he came to discover that there was some sort of chart or charts that existed, supposedly hidden somewhere on the boat. When he had learned of the sale of the boat to this man Williams, a cripple from England. He arranged for the blackmail of the Hope woman's father, a prominent surgeon and at the same time, he recruited Mitch to keep an eye on the family. Using this as a lever to persuade the Hope woman to get herself hired by Williams and gain his trust.

Hopkiss, a disgraced former British Army Sergeant, had been in collaboration with Tockalov for a considerable time. They had been involved with drugs, the trafficking of women and children for the sex trade. When the attempted robbery on the *Cape Agulhas* had gone wrong and the fair-haired Dutchman had got himself shot by the Guardia Civil. It appeared that Williams and the Hope woman were possibly involved with each other or certainly getting that way. Boshirov got Hopkiss to instigate the kidnapping of the Hope woman, initially to dispose of her as she could identify him and also link him to Tockalov. But it might also put pressure on Williams to surrender anything that he may have discovered. Watching from the sidelines, so to speak, Boshirov had not anticipated that Williams had unfathomably recognised Hopkiss and had the Guardia Civil primed when Williams and Hope had come ashore. He had not believed the speed at which the cripple, Williams, had moved and had floored Hopkiss with one blow to his throat. Williams was certainly not the person he appeared to be. It was after this that the cripple had surrendered the charts to the authorities. This was confirmed by the Hope woman when he had followed and spoken to her in the shop.

Using his new friend, the Lieutenant from the Guardia civil, to keep him informed of the *Cape's* comings and goings. He then arranged for one of his employees, a South African expert in underwater demolition, to make ready a bomb to be planted on the stern of the Williams boat. The idea would be to serve two purposes. One was to kill the Hope woman, one of her crew duties were, that as the boat left the pontoon, she worked her way from bow to stern recovering the fenders. The bomb had to be triggered when the propellers were engaged, but there had to be sufficient delay to allow for her to get to the stern. The explosion was to be sufficient also to disable the boat beyond economical repair but not to sink it. This would allow for Tockalov to pay for the salvage of the *Cape* and then they could search the boat piece by piece at their leisure, just in case the Hope woman was lying. Boshirov had insisted on accompanying Botha on this mission but he was not as an accomplished diver as Botha. It had been his cylinder that had noisily made contact in the dark with the hull of the *Cape Agulhas*. This had alarmed the occupants, again the speed of reaction and viciousness of the attack on Botha reminded Boshirov not to underestimate the Englishman's ability and aggression. He was a very dangerous person.

When Boshirov had been looking into the activities of the blond Dutchman and his associate at the former Ellis Marine, he had installed one of Tockalov's men as a worker. The man had weaknesses that Tockalov facilitated. The man known as Manuel was an excellent carpenter and was an absolute expert with fibreglass and gel coat, very quickly making a name for himself as a quality worker. Exactly the sort of person that Boats.co.uk needed, so the comings and goings of the *Cape* were made knowledgeable to Boshirov. He had instigated the installation of the listening devices and tracking devices on the boat while Williams and Hope were in the UK. Flying to the UK himself and attending the wedding had been a very bold and a huge risk, he had been hoping to unsettle the Hope woman. It had also been unfortunate that Mitch had been discovered because of her temper. Following her arrest and then subsequent release, she seemed to have vanished into thin air, which was very worrying for Boshirov.

Boshirov's appearance had changed considerably. His hair and now with a beard was a blond grade four cut all over, he wore baggy jeans and a crew neck jumper, fitting in perfectly with the local fishermen and townspeople in appearance. The one single problem that he had was that he didn't speak any Spanish or very little. From the apartment and in keeping with Spanish law, he maintained isolation, this fitted in well with his requirements. From the front window of the apartment, he had an excellent view over the marina and constantly watched the comings and goings, making copious handwritten notes that included times and numbers of people visiting the marina. He had also seen the fifty-foot Benateau Swift Trawler, *Isabella*, he had noted with interest that it appeared to be owned or operated by a swarthy looking Spaniard who appeared to live onboard the boat in a full-time capacity. Boshirov had recognised the Spaniard as the former employee of Ellis Marine and who was also Van de Niekerk's sidekick. They had both been sharing an unhealthy interest in his former partner's boat, the *Cape Agulhas*, whilst it had been moored, in the marina at Malaga.

Boshirov was no fool and knew that he was very probably being looked for by the authorities. This would undoubtedly include the British Government and his own past co-workers. As such all electronic devices that he had with him were turned off and this included his mobile phone.

Upon Tockalov's rude awakening and arrest following the foiled bombing attempt of the *Cape Agulhas*, the Captain of the *Octopus* had been instructed to sail from her homeport of Marbella into international waters and to remain there until further notice. If and when they did require re-supplying and re-fuelling, they should carry this out at the little-known port of Nadar in Morocco. Apart from the four crew, that included the Captain, was also Tockalov's beautiful Lebanese wife, Adeline, a four-year-old daughter and six-year-old son. They had fled from their casa on the Calle los Olivios in the classy area of Marbella as soon as her husband had been arrested by the Spanish Police.

Five days before Van de Niekerk had made his murderous escape from his guarded hospital bed. Boshirov, continuing with his observations, had seen Pedro with the Benateau re-fuelling at the marina fuelling point and then returned to the berth where the boat was normally moored. He made his decision, taking one or two essentials which included the Russian made PS 22 silenced pistol. He locked the apartment and secreted the key under one of the large unkempt flowerpots that adorned the entrance to the residence. With a duffle bag over his left shoulder and the PS 22 tucked into the waistband of his trousers, he very casually made his way down to the dock and onto the pontoon which led to the Benateau. Quickly and calmly, he made his way in through the open rear access salon doors and was able to surprise Pedro just as he was making his way back into the salon from the cabin spaces below. Producing the PS 22, Boshirov waved it threateningly in Pedro's face. In perfectly accented English, he asked. "Do you want to die?" He spoke in an offhand manner.

Completely caught off guard, Pedro stammered. "No, no!"

"Good!" Boshirov continued. "Because I could just kill you and sail this boat to where I want to get to on my own. Now get this piece of floating garbage underway."

Pedro reacted with alacrity and within five minutes they had slipped their moorings and were heading out of the marina. Truthfully, Boshirov knew very little about boats and even less about sailing one. Instructing Pedro to take a southerly heading straight out into international waters, he set about exploring the Benateau. This man lives like a pig, he thought to himself, there was nothing dirt-free, there must have been at least three days of washing up in the galley sink. The whole of the boat stank of stale smoke, unwashed body and stale urine. God only knew what he would find should he go below to the heads and accommodation space. After one hour of cruising at twelve knots, the Benateau was well into international waters and Boshirov called for a course change.

"I now want you to make your course in the direction of the North of the Island of Alboran, but you must remain outside of Spanish territorial waters. Is this understood?" Boshirov instructed.

"Si signor." Pedro nodded and brought the boat around to a south, south-east course and then fed the destination into the Raymarine navigation system.

"Now tune your VHF radio to a frequency of 122.2 MHz." Boshirov commanded. Pedro complied and handed the microphone to Boshirov, who took it and keyed the mic.

"Octopus, Octopus this is Diva. How copy?" The reply was one little hiss of squelch.

Boshirov waited sixty seconds and repeated the call, the response was the same. He checked his watch. It was two minutes to eight in the evening. He cursed himself for being so stupid as he recalled the emergency system he had set up with the new Argentinian Captain. On every hour at the hour, one of the two VHF receivers on the *Octopus* would be tuned to 122.2 and monitored for five minutes. If a caller were to say 'time' that would indicate a frequency change to exactly two hours in advance of the current time. So, in other words if the call for 'time' came at three minutes past eight in the evening the frequency change would be to 122.03. If the call came at three minutes past eight in the morning, the frequency would change to 110.03.

At four minutes past eight, he tried the radio a third time. "Octopus, Octopus, this is Diva. How copy over?" Boshirov waited.

Then the accented response came. "Diva. Diva this is Octopus, I read you strength two by five. It is good to hear you again. Over."

Breathing a sigh of relief, Boshirov continued. "Octopus, Octopus, I require Time. I say again Time. Out." Boshirov checked his watch and the chronometer on the bulkhead. It was five past eight. Addressing Pedro, he said. "Reset the frequency to 122.05." Pedro complied.

Pressing the mic switch again, Boshirov called the *Octopus*. "Octopus, Octopus this is Diva. How copy over?"

The reply came immediately. "Strength two by five, how may we be of assistance? Over." The same accented voice of the Captain.

"I require a rendezvous as soon as possible. I am currently heading on a course for the north of Alboran from a point fifteen miles due south of home. I will call you again at Time plus two slots. Out." Two slots meant two hours ahead of the current slot so that the frequency would be 124.00, two hours to have to kill, Boshirov thought.

Matias Gonzalez, the skipper on the *Octopus*, was a retired Argentinian Naval Officer. He had lost some good friends on ARA General Belgrano when it was torpedoed on the 2nd of May, 1982 by HMS Conqueror during the Falklands conflict. This had resulted in the loss of over three hundred lives and had sent the entire Argentinian Navy scuttling for port with their tails between their legs. He was no lover of the British and very much still believed that Los Malvinas very much belonged to the Argentinians, as did many. Spanish was his native language and like many Argentinians, he spoke both French and English but had no understanding of the Russian language. He was given a somewhat free hand to choose the remainder of his crew but the requirement was that Boshirov got the last word in as to who was hired. The Captain had hired a young stewardess from Chile on the understanding that she would favour his sexual requirements, he had a penchant for anal sex and young boys. A lifetime in the Argentine Navy had seen to his demands for this in the past. The third crew member was a middle-aged Frenchman who spoke excellent Arabic, an absolute necessity if you are going to do any off-grid southern Mediterranean sailing. The fourth member of the crew was a young Italian, responsible mainly for the cooking, although he was also required to carry out deck and watch duties. So it was, that Gonzalez who had been carrying out a racetrack course in the international waters to the east of the Island of Alboran, took out a chart of the western Mediterranean Sea. He then plotted an approximate course to intercept and meet with Boshirov. Immediately Gonzalez changed the course of the *Octopus* and brought her new heading onto a north-westerly heading, enabling them to pass to the north of the island of Alboran.

Noting the change of course and the increase in speed of the big Azimut yacht, Adeline went forward into the wheel station, speaking to the Captain. "Why have we changed course?" She demanded.

Turning sideways and addressing her. "Madam, I have been instructed to meet with Mr Boshirov. I have changed course to meet with him." Gonzalez answered her civilly.

"What! Where? Is my husband with him?" Adeline questioned him.

"Madam, I am sorry, he did not say whether your husband was with him. The radio conversation was very brief and of poor quality. I will be contacting him in just under two hours." Gonzalez retained his civility. He didn't like the woman, she was too full of herself.

"You will notify me when you do Captain, if my husband is not with Boshirov, then Boshirov does not come aboard this vessel. Is that clear?" Adeline had a fear of Boshirov. She had once seen him callously drown a former employee with a hosepipe in the family garden. Fortunately, the children had not been there to witness the cruel and heartlessly barbaric act.

"Yes, of course, Madam. Where will you be?" Gonzalez bowed slightly in acknowledgement of the command.

"In my stateroom." Adeline turned and strutted from the pilot station, not allowing Gonzalez to respond.

One hundred feet beneath the surface of the Mediterranean Sea and just over 2,000 yards from the Octopus, the sonar operator onboard *HMS Astound*, turned to the Officer of the Watch. "Sir, she has just changed course and increased speed, new course of two, zero five, speed eighteen knots."

"Thank you, Pings." The Lieutenant of the watch responded. "Make our course two, zero five and increase speed to eighteen knots." He picked up the telephone and informed the Captain of the update. Then turning back to the sonar operator, he said. "Pings, keep a special ear open for that Kilo, just in case she has doubled back."

"Aye, aye, Sir." Pings replied.

HMS Astound had been on a routine patrol and chanced across the *Octopus* sailing a very slow racecourse pattern. Once they had identified her and reported the unusual behaviour, the fact that the craft was owned by Dimitri Tockalov and the Intelligence Services now knew that Boshirov/ Donaldson was an associate of Tockalov, suddenly made the *Octopus* a vessel of interest. There were certain people back in the UK who wanted to have an extended chat with Boshirov or Donaldson who had seemingly not been seen for many weeks. Come to that, certain people in Moscow would have also liked to have had a lengthy dialogue with him as well. One week earlier the *Astound* had chanced upon a Russian Kilo class submarine sneaking around in the Mediterranean Sea, they had followed it for a week until they had come across the *Octopus* doing her racetrack pattern. The Kilo had just gone on past and had either ignored the *Octopus* or hadn't had the intelligence information relating to Boshirov and his link to the *Octopus*.

Boshirov had spent some of the previous two hours considering his options. He knew that Adeline and her children would be aboard the *Octopus* and he also knew that she didn't like him. If he were to announce that he was on his own, Adeline would most likely not allow him to board the *Octopus*. He also knew that the Captain was one of his men and that he despised the Lebanese woman. So, it would probably be to his advantage to control the situation by bluffing that he had Tockalov with him until he got on board. It had just gone ten o'clock in the evening when he again moved to the pilot station on the Benateau, instructing Pedro to retune the VHF to the required frequency.

"Octopus, Octopus, this is Diva. How copy, over?" Boshirov released the mic and there was a brief sound of squelch before the reply came.

"Diva this is Octopus. I copy you, strength three by five. Do you have Gold with you? Over." Gold was the codename assigned to Tockalov.

Just as Boshirov had anticipated, Adeline was suspicious. "Yes, do you have the RV coordinates, if so, send immediately. We may be being monitored. Over."

"Roger, I understand. Coordinates as follows. North three six, zero two, nine, eight, three. West two, five, seven, six, nine, eight (N36°02.983′ W2°57.698′). Out." Apart from a little burst of squelch, the radio was silent.

Boshirov instructed Pedro on the new course to take and to call him twenty minutes before they arrived at the RV point. According to the marine chart plotter, their arrival time was eleven fifty-five, in just under two hours.

Onboard the *Octopus*, Adeline was furious at Gonzalez for not having pursued her wish to speak to her husband and ascertain his safety. Defending himself, Gonzalez said. "Madam, we are in international waters, there are those that would seek to have this boat impounded and searched.

The less time that we spend on the radio means that there is far less chance of someone being able to listen to what we are saying or for that matter to be able to triangulate our position. There are also those that would incarcerate you and your children and sell them to the highest bidder for their entertainment."

The latter statement was a figment of his imagination, but Gonzalez smiled inwardly at the reaction it gained. Suddenly Adeline's beautiful brown face turned a deathly paler shade as she swiftly departed the pilot station with god knows what going through her mind.

It was a quarter to midnight when the Raymarine plotter on the *Octopus* indicated that they were five hundred metres from the RV point. Gonzalez slowed the engines and put the gearboxes into neutral, allowing the boat to come up on herself and start a sickening roll, which he knew that the Lebanese woman hated. The second Raymarine screen was selected for radar and that was indicating a small blip which was about five nautical miles from them and on a converging course. That surely must have been Boshirov, Gonzalez thought as he summoned the other two male members of his crew to the deck to prepare the fenders.

One hundred feet beneath the Mediterranean Sea *HMS Astound* had kept track of the motor yacht as it progressed. The sonar operator was a figure of astute concentration as he made minute adjustments to his instruments. "Captain, Sir, I have another boat on a converging course. Twin engines making fifteen knots. The boat we are following, she has stopped dead in the water."

"Thank you, 'Pings'. All ahead slow and bring us up to periscope depth if you would please Number One. I want to be as close as possible to her so that we can have a good look to see what's going on."

"Aye, aye, Sir." The First Lieutenant replied.

Turning back to an officer who was in combat uniform, the Captain continued. "Okay, Mac, I think that your guys should get ready to deploy should they be needed."

Lieutenant McIntyre of 'X' Squadron Special Boat Service replied. "Aye, aye, Captain. On it." He turned and moved forward towards the bows of the submarine and his team of twelve highly trained operatives.

The *Octopus* was lit up like a Christmas tree. Every single deck light was on, making it very easy for both Pedro and Boshirov to see her. "Make for that boat and go alongside her." Boshirov instructed.

Pedro slowed the Benateau down as he approached the stern and made to go along the starboard side of the *Octopus*. "No funny stuff. Comprende old man?" Boshirov stated in his best Cambridge English, as he went out onto the deck, retrieving a line and throwing it to the waiting crew on the deck of the *Octopus*. The decks at this point were almost level with each other. "Hold the boat." He instructed the French crewman. Boshirov went back into the Benateau and instructed Pedro to start making his way below. Pedro had got halfway down the stairs when there were two little 'phut' sounds, simultaneously two holes opened in the back of Pedro's head. The Spaniard was stone dead before his legs crumpled and he fell the remainder of the way down the stairs.

Exiting the cabin of the Benateau, Boshirov vaulted across the railings and onto the deck of the *Octopus* where he was greeted by Gonzalez. "Welcome on board, Sir. Will it just be you tonight?"

"Yes, Gonzalez. Thank you. The Spaniard is deadbeat. Can we arrange for that boat to sink please?" Boshirov enquired of Gonzalez.

"Yes, absolutely, Sir. By the way, you may expect some harsh questions from Mrs Tockolov. She gave me instructions not to allow you onboard without her husband." Gonzalez spoke politely.

Boshirov grunted. "Fuck her!" And went straight into the salon where Adeline was sitting.

Gonzalez spoke to the French member of the crew who immediately sprang across to the deck of the Benateau and let himself into the engine room. He was gone less than two minutes before he reappeared back above deck and then returned to the *Octopus*, watched by Gonzalez.

"Okay, let it go." He said to his two crewmen, allowing the *Esmeralda* to drift off, rapidly taking on water from the open seacocks in the engine room.

Petty Officer Nadine Hayward of X Squadron, SBS, had been the first-ever woman to qualify for the British Special Forces. She spoke fluent French, German and Spanish. She had already, as had the other ten members of the team, had a pow-wow with the boss who was normally referred to as Mac or boss. They had decided that they would let the French take the blame for tonight's raid. There was nothing on them to identify their nationality, apart from the French Tricolour badge on the shoulder of their tunics. Nadine was the only person who would give any vocal instructions.

As the Benateau had gone alongside the larger *Octopus*, the two silenced RIB's left the safety of *Astound* and made their way swiftly across the short expanse of water to the opposite side of the *Octopus*. Silently they boarded the boat, Nadine with one Lance Corporal and two Marines made their way into the salon through the rear doors, following Gonzalez in. Mac hung back as four more troopers seized the two crewmen on the starboard deck, bundling them to the deck, plasti-cuffing and placing hoods over their heads.

At the same time, Nadine entering the salon with her silenced MP5 pointing at Boshirov speaking in French said. "On the deck. Now! Hands where I can see them. Now!" Two of her colleagues happily but none too gently helped Boshirov down to the deck and disarmed him. Within five seconds of having entered the salon, the occupants were plasti-cuffed and had hoods over their heads. All the deck lights were switched off and the inboard lighting was also minimised.

Adeline, Gonzalez, the two-deck crew and the rounded-up Chilean stewardess come bed warmer were locked up somewhat unceremoniously in one of the guest cabins. The two children, still asleep and oblivious to the drama, were locked in their cabin but were not plasti-cuffed. Boshirov was rudely placed in a seat, had the hood briefly removed, whereupon Mac using a portable device took a photograph of him and then the hood was replaced. Two minutes later, Mac holding his hand to his right ear looked at Nadine and nodded his head. Boshirov had been positively identified. Wordlessly, he was picked up by two marines who made their way to the aft salon door and stood on the swim deck. One of the RIB's quietly made its way to the stern where Boshirov was helped in and then forced face down into the bottom of the boat. Another two marines climbed aboard as well. Both RIBs made their way straight back to *Astound*, dropped off their passengers and then both RIBs were re-stowed on board the *Astound*, leaving the eight remaining members of the squad on board *Octopus*.

Mac took the helm of *Octopus*, engaged the gearboxes and headed her north in the general direction of Adra on the southern Spanish coast. Dawn was breaking as the pirated *Octopus* and her occupants crossed into the twelve-mile Spanish territorial waters. Looking behind them they couldn't see anything, but they knew that *Astound* would be very close. They passed the ten-mile offshore point, when Nadine made the Mayday call, identifying the boat, with their position and stating that they had engine problems and were drifting. As the reply came, Mac shut off the engines and the eight-person SBS crew jumped off the swim platform into the dawn chill of the Mediterranean Sea. The *Octopus* carried on drifting towards the nearing Spanish shore, leaving the SBS team treading water. One minute later, *Astound* surfaced as far as the top of her conning tower, twenty yards from the group of sea soldiers. One minute later and she was completely lost to sight and heading back out towards international waters.

CHAPTER 24

It was a bleak Monday, 13th of April, when the second storm broke at four am in the morning and announced its arrival with a huge clap of thunder almost over the top of the *Cape*. This was accompanied by an instant deluge of rain. With that, Bruce and Charlie were out of bed relatively rapidly. This storm had escaped the forecast and with the sound of the wind increasing as well as claps of thunder, Bruce went up to the pilot station carrying his shorts and T-shirt, immediately getting the main generator running. The sea hadn't yet built up, so there was only a swell of about one foot however, Bruce knew that it would rise. Going through to the salon, he opened the blinds, checking to make sure that all the windows were secured, he was shortly joined by Charlie, pulling on a pair of her short shorts. As before it was just a matter of staying awake and monitoring the *Cape* for as long as the storm lasted.

Unusually, the beginning of a gloomy morning reached them at about six o'clock, Bruce could see that the level of the waves in the cove were now running at about two feet, with the *Cape* hardly responding to them at all. To pass the time, Bruce and Charlie had been discussing the merits of sailing the *Cape* to the Aegean to winter there for the forthcoming winter, Covid allowing, of course. Charlie, who was sitting at the chart table, was on the computer getting comparative differences on the weather as well as the prices of fuel, availability of the foods that they liked. Of course, another consideration was that neither of them spoke Greek.

It was just after eight o'clock and Charlie had just mentioned seeing what she could do in respect of breakfast, fresh eggs were very much still on the menu. Charlie had just got up to go to the galley when she glanced out of the rain-soaked side screen. "Bruce, you need to see this, the dolphins are acting kind of weirdly."

Looking out of the starboard helm window to see where Charlie was looking, he could see the dolphins seemingly trying to attract their attention by standing up in the water and executing tail slaps. "There is something wrong. I hope one of them isn't in trouble again." Grabbing a slicker jacket and his Crewsaver from the locker at the back of the helm station, Bruce went out onto the deck through the pilot station access, making his way aft to the swim platform. Surprisingly, the dolphins then all swam off towards the cove entrance and repeated their performance there. They were over one hundred and fifty yards from the *Cape* and visibility wasn't good at all. In fact, he could hardly see anything at all. Then he saw her but only because either she moved or a scrap of her clothing blew in the wind. Clinging onto the rocks was a small person or a child.

Bruce needed to get out to the cove entrance and instantly his mind went into overdrive considering the options that were available to him. Swimming wasn't going to be an option as the two-foot waves would tire him far too quickly. Launching *Willie* would take a little time in these waters and the wind at the entrance of the cove would blow *Willie* straight up onto the rocks. Launching the STX jet ski in this weather wasn't an option either. Poking his head back into the pilot station he told Charlie what he had seen. Making his way back to the workshop, Bruce divested himself of the slicker but retaining his Crewsaver he picked up *Bobbi* the Seabob, as well as his swimming goggles.

Bruce launched himself from the swim deck just as Charlie came out on deck herself wearing a slicker and Crewsaver. Bruce had decided that it would be easier to complete as much of the outbound journey underwater and so that he would not have to contend with the waves on the surface. Bruce covered the first seventy metres underwater before surfacing for a breath and to orientate himself with his target and the dolphins before again disappearing beneath the surface. Glancing to his left he could see Daphne swimming alongside him with her fixed grin. Looking ahead, Bruce eventually came up on the rising wall of the cove entrance only about five yards in front of him. He slowed and started to surface with *Bobbi*. Looking up towards the side of the cove entrance, he spotted her and saw the bewildered look on her face as the human surfaced amongst the dolphins.

"Help me! Please help me!" The small stricken English voice pleaded. "Please help me." She sobbed. Long blond hair partially stuck to her and partly blowing in the wind, the girl looked so forlorn and terrified. "Please, please help me." She wept.

Spitting out saltwater and managing to stand on a shallow rock, Bruce consoled her. "It's okay. It's okay. You are safe now." Bruce shook water from his mane of hair. "I am going to take you back to our boat." Bruce pointed to the dim outline of the *Cape*. "What I need you to do is come down here and get on my back, then I will give you a piggyback. Okay?"

"What about those big fish?" Terrified, she pointed at the dolphins.

"These are dolphins and they are our friends. I promise they won't hurt you." Bruce explained. "Honestly, they won't hurt you. They have probably saved your life. Look that is Daphne and that is Dougie." Bruce had probably pointed to the wrong dolphins in his haste but all he wanted to do right now was to get himself and the hypothermic child back to the safety of the *Cape*. The child was wearing a loose dress and the absence of anything else was born out as a gust of wind just about blew the dress off her. "C'mon!" Bruce encouraged her, extending his hand. "We really need to get going before this storm gets worse."

Trembling with a combination of fear and cold she crawled down to where Bruce was. Getting on his back, she wrapped her legs around Bruce's waist and her arms in a stranglehold around his neck. Bruce lowered them both to the water and he started the journey back to the *Cape* being towed by the sea-bob and accompanied by the pod of dolphins as an escort. At times Daphne almost touching Bruce and the terrified child. Through mouthfuls of saltwater, Bruce continued re-assuring the child on his back as *Bobbi* towed them both back to the *Cape*. The journey back took considerably more time, with the child riding high on his back, it cost Bruce a few more mouthfuls of water. Charlie, in anticipation, had lowered the swim platform and was standing on it knee-deep in the water waiting for the two of them to get back. Reaching down, she lifted the child off Bruce's back and whilst clutching the girl into her, Charlie looked to see what she could do to help Bruce.

"You see to the child. I am alright." Bruce said, stumbling on the deck and reaching out to give Daphne a quick pat on her head. "Thank you, Daphne, and all of you." Bruce spoke to the dolphins.

Charlie was operating the swim platform back up. "I am going to get her straight into the shower in the dive station why don't you get yourself in there as well with her whilst I'll get towels and dry clothing." Charlie said as she headed down the access companionway with the girl still held in her arms. Putting the Seabob back in the rack, still fully clothed and wearing the Crewsaver, Bruce stepped into the shower, testing the water at the same time to make sure it wasn't too hot.

"Come on, let's start to get you warmed up." Bruce said, gently pulling the terrified child into the cascading warm water. Bruce sat on the shower floor and gently started to rub the child's arms and legs, chest and back, Bruce made rub, rub, rub sounds in time to his movements by this means, half-heartedly making a game of it. "So, and what is your name, young lady?" Bruce spoke just loudly enough to make himself heard over the sound of the running water. To the child, the voice was even, clear and calming. The slightly accented English voice to her ears was nothing but warm, friendly and gently reassuring.

"Georgina." The child stammered. "But everyone calls me Georgie." She continued quietly and wide-eyed, half expecting to be warned to silence.

Not stopping the gentle massage and rubbing. "That is a really lovely name Georgie." Bruce continued in a gentle, matter of fact tone. "Well." He paused and looked up at her face. "I am called Bruce and the lady who carried you down here is called Charlie and we live on this boat."

"Thank you." Georgie stammered, still shivering but basking in the comfort of the warm water flowing over her body.

"Would you like the water a little hotter now?" Bruce gently asked as he tenderly continued to massage her arms, attempting to get her circulation going again. Georgie wasn't sure what was happening to her. Extraordinarily, and for the first time in her life this, elderly adult person was speaking to her as an equal and he seemed kind. Because she was standing and he was sitting with his clothes on, well shorts, T-shirt and a strange thing that looked like it might have been a lifejacket of sorts. She actually looked down at him. He smiled up at her. The smile was genuinely warm and friendly, the handsome face with long brown hair and grey streaks, the neatly trimmed beard. He blinked his eyes from the water. Those beautiful warm blue eyes, there was something special about those eyes. Then slowly reaching towards her face with his right hand, he gently cupped the side of her face and said. "You know it is okay now. Right now you are safe. No more worries now. Okay." She noticed his deep blue, intense eyes and knew then that he was right. She was safe now. Not sure how to react, she continued to look at his eyes. Georgie tried to smile but tears came to her eyes instead. Then she sobbed. Bruce reached up and put both his arms around her and gently pulled her down into his chest, she didn't resist as he tenderly comforted her. To Georgie, this unfamiliar act of kindness and sincerity was just so overwhelming. The feeling of having those powerful arms around her made her feel overwhelmingly safe for the first time in her life. This was the moment when a very special, unwritten bond of trust and love was formed, between the man and the little girl. It was a feeling that neither of them wanted to end or would ever forget.

Charlie came back into the dive station, her arms loaded with towels and clothing to witness the act of tenderness between the man and the girl and felt a very short-lived pang of jealously. In her heart, she realised then, that she would have to share Bruce's love with someone else. But a different type of love.

Placing her burden on a convenient chair, she opened the shower door and said. "Honey I need to get that rag of a dress off her and then get her hair washed."

Bruce stiffly got up from the shower floor. "Georgie, this my wife Charlie, Charlie this here is Georgina, but I think she prefers Georgie" Bruce removed the Crewsaver and his T-shirt before taking the offered towel from Charlie and stepped out of the shower. Taking the towel and dabbing himself with it he moved around the corner into the workshop area, out of sight from the shower.

Oblivious to the water from the shower, Charlie was on her knees and reached into the cubicle and had started to remove the soil stained dress from Georgie's body by cutting it straight down the back with a pair of scissors. Once that was done and deposited in a rubbish bin, she again reached into the shower picking up the shampoo and hair conditioner that she kept in there. "Shall we wash your hair now as well?" the blonde hair came halfway down her back and seemed horribly matted.

"Yes, please." Georgie replied hesitantly. She couldn't remember when someone else had offered to help her with her hair. Her long, naturally blond hair was Georgie's pride and joy. It took two shampooing's and a good dose of conditioner before Charlie was satisfied with the results. It also gave Charlie an excuse to visually examine the skinny body noticing the past evidence of physical abuse. Charlie refrained from asking any questions while drying her down. There was a sudden clap of thunder immediately overhead the *Cape*. Georgie jumped with fright and turned around flinging her arms around Charlie's neck.

"It's okay! It's okay, it was only some thunder, we are really very safe here." Charlie gentled the child by pulling her into her chest and held her head whilst rocking her gently.

Wrapping Georgie up into two towels, Charlie announced. "Bruce, I am going to take the young lady up to the main salon." From around the corner, Bruce acknowledged and Charlie continued. "Come on then Georgie, let's get you upstairs and into the warm shall we." Charlie stood up easily with Georgie double wrapped up in the towels and made for the companionway.

Bruce finished drying and dressing, then tidied up by putting the wet clothes into the washing machine and pushed a mop-up and down to get rid of the puddles of water. Replacing his slicker and Crewsaver, Bruce made his way back to the pilot station. It was pointless to check on the radios unless there was another boat very close. Because of potential lightning strikes, Bruce had folded down the tall VHF antennas for safety.

It was shortly afterwards that Charlie brought Georgie up to the pilot station. "Bruce, I need to go below and get some things together as well as a hot water bottle so, would you mind if I pinch a couple of your T-shirts, please. You know the ones that are too short for you now?"

"No, help yourself, Georgie can stay up here with me." Bending down he lifted the still shivering Georgie onto the pilot seat. Charlie had cocooned her up in a soft fleece blanket. Before she left, she whispered in Bruce's ear a caution not to let her fall asleep.

Charlie was gone for less than five minutes, when she returned, she had amongst other things a stethoscope, hot water bottle in a fluffy pink cover, Calpol, hairbrush and a hairdryer. Whilst the kettle was boiling Charlie, got the hairdryer plugged into the socket and moderated the heat to a gentle warm blow. Whilst Bruce started on her hair, Charlie saw to the filling of the hot water bottle. Every time the warm air from the drier passed the nape of her neck, Georgie gave an additional involuntary shiver, but this was one of pleasure of feeling the warmth blowing down her back. Undoing the blanket parcel of Georgie, Charlie pushed the hot water bottle against her as she started to warm up the business end of the stethoscope.

Bruce explained. "Don't be afraid Georgie, Charlie is like a very, very special Doctor. All she is going to do is to check you out and make sure that you are not sick. Is that okay?"

Georgie's response was an affirmative nod of the head. Charlie talking gently to the child listened to her chest, back and front, checked her eyes for reaction to light, took her pulse and her temperature. There were a large number of questions beginning to well up in Bruce's mind, however, they would have to wait. The most important thing was to get her core temperature back up with some food in her stomach and let her have some sleep. For the moment, the questions would have to wait.

Georgie managed a small portion of scrambled eggs and bacon and a solution of warmed diluted sweetened condensed milk. As her eyes started to close, Charlie lifted her down from the table and lay down on the salon sofa with the child wrapped in the blanket and cuddled tightly into her. Bruce cleared and washed up the breakfast goods and checked the weather. The rain had decreased somewhat as had the wind, visibility, however had improved. Two hours later after he had scoured the news feed for missing children or boats missing in the Mediterranean, Bruce went aft to the salon to check on Charlie and Georgie. Charlie stirred as he kissed her on her exposed cheek. Gently he put the back of his hand on Georgie's forehead, she had stopped shivering and had stretched out, removing some of the covers from her as well as the hot water bottle. That was a good sign that she had overcome the hypothermia. But she wasn't out of the woods yet, not by a long chalk. Charlie quietly got up from the sofa, yawning. She made certain that Georgie was still covered and rubbing the sleep out of her eyes, smiled at Bruce and got up. Bruce made tea, Charlie excused herself and went below, leaving Bruce with the sleeping child in the salon. To pass the time he sat with the laptop and spent some time playing chess against the computer, when he got bored with that, he switched to casually searching the internet for nothing in particular. An hour and a half passed then Georgie started to stir. She seemed to be suffering some minor mental turmoil. Bruce went over to her and gently stroked a mildly damp forehead.

"Georgie, it's alright, you are safe now." He gentled the child. "It's okay sweetheart. It's okay. It's alright honey, you are safe now."

Georgie opened her eyes and looked wide-eyed at Bruce. A few moments passed before she realised the reality of her situation, then she hesitantly raised her little arms up to Bruce and wrapped them around his mildly bruised neck. "Can I go to toilet please?" Her voice was very subdued with sleep and uncertainty.

"Of course you can." Bruce picked her up in the blanket and got up from the sofa just as Charlie appeared at the head of the companionway. "We are off to the heads." He announced to Charlie as they moved forward towards the day head. Opening the door, Bruce sat Georgie on the toilet, which was shortly followed by the sound of 'tinkling'. "Right! I think that at this point, I can safely leave you girls to get on with things." Bruce declared.

Charlie grinned and for the first time, Georgie smiled feebly as Bruce left them to it. 'She has had a rough time of it'. Bruce thought to himself. Some two minutes later, the two of them disappeared down the stairs to the accommodation deck, only to reappear about forty minutes later. Charlie, leading a shy Georgie by the hand, approached Bruce who was sat on the seat at the chart station. Georgie was wearing something familiar to Bruce. It was the colour that did it. He recognised one of his older T-shirts which had been cleverly refashioned into a matching top and knickers, the bruises on Georgie's arms and legs were apparent.

"Well, now, look at you. I never knew that my T-shirt could look so good on someone else. What a clever Charlie." Bruce extended his arms towards the child, there was a slight hesitation as she slowly got up next to Bruce and wrapped her arms around his chest. With a natural parental hug, Bruce pulled her into his chest.

"Can I say something, please?" Georgie asked, her voice muffled by Bruce's chest.

"What is it, Georgie?" Bruce looked down at her as she looked up at him.

"You saved my life today." Georgie looked up into the tanned, handsome bearded face. It was that same strong, kind, wet face that had looked up at her in the shower, again it was that powerful arm gently enfolding her that she again felt that feeling of protection and belonging.

Pausing awkwardly, Bruce replied. "Well, I don't know about that."

Sitting down, so that Georgie was sandwiched between Bruce and Charlie and putting her arm around Bruce's shoulder, Charlie quietly intervened. "He does make a habit of saving people's lives. He saved mine not so very long ago." The not too distant memory of Bruce rescuing her semi-conscious from the dark marina waters of the Malaga marina flashed through her mind.

Intrigued by Charlie's statement, she looked up into the beautiful hazel eyes in the kind tanned face framed by the jet black hair. Somehow, Georgie realised that the face looked somewhat familiar, but couldn't place where she had seen it before. Sandwiched between these two relative strangers and for the first time in her short life, she felt as though she belonged. At first, she thought she was dreaming all this as she momentarily closed her eyes and then opened them again. No, she wasn't dreaming she could feel the warmth from the man and the woman and knew then that she was in a very special place.

After two minutes of silence, Georgie again looked at Charlie and said. "I am glad that he saved our lives, otherwise we wouldn't be here now." The statement was so matter of fact that Bruce and Charlie exchanged glances and smiled at each other.

Gently Charlie asked. "Are you going to come and help me fix us some lunch?"

"Oh, okay, I guess so." Disentangling herself from Bruce, she engaged her hand in Charlie's and walked up to the galley with her.

Bruce couldn't help again noting how pale and skinny she was, he would have to get some information out of her after lunch. Someone, somewhere, must be worried sick about her. Bruce continued to watch her as Charlie showed her how to set the table for lunch, where the cutlery was and the table mats. The storm gradually continued to dissipate as Bruce took up the binoculars, he cast around the beach and the shore of the cove to see if there was any evidence of a shipwreck. There was nothing obvious to be seen at the time other than a re-supply of his driftwood collection on the beach.

It was after lunch, Bruce was sitting on the sofa watching Sky News when Georgie came over to him. "Can I sit with you, please?"

"Of course you can, sweetheart. You can come and sit with me anytime you like." Bruce lifted an arm up for her to snuggle into him. Charlie was finishing up in the galley and was making hot drinks all round. Surreptitiously, Bruce switched the recording device on his iPhone to record.

"Georgie, do you mind if I ask you a few questions, like how old you are and how you came to be here?" Bruce turned the TV off.

"No, that's alright. I know that you are going to try to help me. But this is the nicest place I have ever been and you are the nicest people I know." Georgie rested her head on Bruce's chest.

"Georgie, do you know your surname, darling?" Bruce asked.

"Yes, it is Taylor." Came the slightly muffled answer against his T-shirt.

"And do you know how old you are and when your birthday is?" Bruce asked.

"I am seven years old and my birthday will be on the fourth of July and then I am going to be eight. I was called Georgina because George Washington was the first American President." Georgie volunteered.

"Okay!" Bruce exclaimed. "That is really very special Georgie. Do you know where your Mum and Dad are now?"

Charlie joined them on the sofa, putting the drinks down on the table.

"Georgie, I have made you some hot milk like you asked, but give it a minute or two because it is very hot. Okay?"

"Okay." Georgie nodded against Bruce's chest. "I think that my Mum went to live with another man and my father gave me to a nasty man and a woman who stank. I think that they gave him some money and I was in a truck forever. I don't remember much because I was asleep most of the time." Georgie spoke almost as though she was bored with the subject and wanted to move on.

"Do you remember what happened then?" Charlie asked gently.

"Then I was put in a room, sometimes it was hot and sometimes it was cold and this old woman looked after me. She was quite kind and gave me some strange food to eat." Georgie paused and looked at Charlie then twisted to see Bruce's reaction.

"What happened then?" Bruce encouraged her with a gentle squeeze.

"They put me in the back of a van and I don't know where we went. We seemed to drive for ages. I had to do toilet in a bucket in the back of the van. Urghh! And then they put me in a boat and then I was in there for a long time as well. It got very stormy and then I saw a big wave and I think that the boat sank and then you found me on the rocks this morning. Were those really dolphins that you were with this morning?"

"Oh, okay! Uh yes, they were dolphins and they have now got quite friendly with us, sometimes we have games in the water with them. Do you know how to swim, because then you can come and play with us too?" Bruce added.

"Yes, a bit. Will you teach me more?"

Bruce replied almost noncommittedly. "Well, yes of course I will, I don't see why not. So, do you know whereabouts in England you live?"

Georgie thought for a moment before replying. "Yes, it is number forty-five, Browning Close in Popley at Basingstoke and I go to Purnell School." Georgie twisted her head up to look at Bruce for approval.

"Do you know what, young lady?" Bruce looked down at her. "I think that you are one very brave girl. And we only have one question left to ask you, it is a difficult question for us to ask, but we really need to ask you and we also need you to answer it truthfully, no matter how difficult you may find it. Okay?"

"Okay!" Georgie responded almost brightly.

"Georgie, do you trust us?" Charlie asked.

"Oh yes!" Georgie replied.

"Georgie?" Charlie began. "Did those people or has any man or woman done anything to hurt you or touched you where they shouldn't have at any time?" Charlie asked the question speaking very slowly and quietly.

Almost, immediately Bruce felt the tension in her little body and the first sob came as she buried her head in Bruce's chest. Charlie moved right up next to Georgie putting her arm around both Georgie and Bruce.

"You are safe now sweetheart. No one is ever going to hurt you again if we can help it." Charlie gently stroked her arm.

Bruce softly stroked her temple and felt the heat of the liquid as the tears flowed through his shirt. Inwardly, Bruce felt the hate for the person who had done whatever they had done, it took all his strength not to let his feelings go through to his body or his words and actions.

Looking at Charlie, Bruce could see the tears trickling down her cheeks as well. "Shush, shush, just take your time." He gentled her. "No matter what anyone has done or said to you it was not your fault." Continuing to stroke her temple. "I will protect you, no one is ever going to hurt you again. I promise you."

"Bruce?" It was the first time she had used his name, Georgie sobbed. "Will you promise not to send me home? Please." She pleaded.

Continuing to stroke her temple, Bruce spoke quietly. "Georgie, if you need me to promise not to send you home, then I promise that I will never send you home. Will we Charlie?"

Charlie was finding it very difficult to control her emotions, but she replied to the question. "No never, we are very much together on this. We will never send you home and trust me, you need to know that the man who is holding you now, does not give up on anything. Ever!"

Georgie turned her head to look at Charlie and then looked up at Bruce again. "He said I would be in very, very big trouble and that he would make me sick for the rest of my life." Georgie sniffed.

Unemotionally Charlie asked. "Who said that to you, sweetheart? Who told you that?"

"It was my father, at first he tried to put his willy in my hole and it hurt so much that I screamed very loudly so then he tried to put his willy in my mouth. It was horrible." Georgie was racked in sobs again.

It was almost too much for Bruce. Gently he squeezed Georgie into him and checked back on his emotions, managing to control his body and his immediate instincts to swim to England and cut the balls off the man who had done this to his own daughter. Slowly the sobs eased. Charlie rescued some tissues from the sideboard and handed a couple to Bruce. Holding a tissue to Georgie's nose, he commanded. "Blow!" Gently Bruce and Charlie explained where they were and also the problems surrounding the Coronavirus and that was why they couldn't go anywhere because they were in isolation. Charlie, more than aware that Bruce was going to need to make some phone calls, took Georgie back down to the cabin on the pretext of making her some more clothes out of Bruce's T-shirts.

Reflecting on the emotional roller coaster day the child had endured had helped to make Bruce's first choice of a phone call an easier matter. He switched his iPhone recorder off. Brian Stone answered his phone on the fourth ring. Clear in his mind as to what he was going to say, he told Brian about the circumstances surrounding Georgie and her father. Bruce confirmed that he could provide proof and sent him a picture that he had surreptitiously obtained of Georgie. His next phone call was to Miguel, again explaining the rescue of the little girl. Miguel appeared annoyed that Bruce hadn't called him sooner but after Bruce had fully explained his reasons for not calling immediately, he understood. He also agreed that Georgie should remain on the *Cape* for the foreseeable future and certainly until the situation became clearer. As it was beginning to get late, Miguel said that they would look around for any sign of a wreck in the morning, as yet there had not been any information of missing boats or mayday calls reported.

Bruce's third phone call was to Mike Dunn. After the usual exchange of pleasantries, Bruce gave Mike the chapter and verse in respect of Georgie and his recent conversation with Miguel and what had been agreed. Bruce also indicated that he could do with a package of necessities to be prepared for Georgie. How they would be able to get it to the *Cape* was something that they would work out shortly. Possibly a controversial Covid19 restriction breaking rendezvous at sea. In the end, it was agreed that Bruce and Charlie would prepare a list of requirements for Georgie and email it to Mike. He, in turn, would call back at about 1:00 pm the next day, once he had received the list. In the interim period, they would try and work out a legally safe way of getting the completed list to Bruce and Charlie on the *Cape*.

CHAPTER 25

Having found a film for Georgie to watch on Disney Chanel, Charlie went up to the pilot station where Bruce had been making phone calls. Bruce gave Charlie the outcome of the calls, finally saying. "I have asked Mike to start putting together a package for a seven-year-old girl. Would you make a list up for me, you know what I mean? No expense spared, I would love for this kid to have everything she can for as long as she can."

Charlie hugged Bruce. "On it, my Captain."

Bruce held on to the hug, luxuriating in the feel of the proximity of their bodies and the continued growing bond of love they felt for each other. Georgie, seeing the adults having a brief discussion and then engaging in what seemed like a mutually loving hug, was novel to her and so she inquisitively joined them at the helm station. "Do you guys always hug like that?" She asked innocently.

"Yes, of course. Why do you want to join in?" Charlie extended her arm in invitation. And Georgie did.

"Bruce?" Georgie asked hesitantly. "What's going to happen to me now?"

Bruce disengaged from the hug with Charlie, bent down and lifting her under her armpits, swung her up onto his left hip. "Well, for the next couple of days, you are going to be right here with us. So, we'll be swimming, sunbathing and cleaning the boat. How does that sound to you?"

"Really!" Georgie sounded incredulous.

"Really!" Bruce and Charlie echoed.

"But then what will happen?" She enquired miserably.

Bruce pondered the question continuing to hold onto her. He sat down at the chart station and sat her on his lap. "Georgie, the one thing no one can do is to see into the future. I know that earlier I promised you, that I wouldn't send you home and I will try as hard as I can to keep that promise to you. But you know as well as I do, that because you are seven years old, you have to be the responsibility of an adult or adults. If your parents aren't available or can no longer take care of you. Then you are made a ward of the state, that is to say, you will have to go into a home of sorts where you can then be properly looked after, pending being fostered or adopted. Now we have an even bigger problem where you are concerned and none of this is your fault at all. Do you understand so far?"

Georgie nodded. "I think so."

Charlie sat on the helm seat and Bruce continued. "Because you are English and you have no passport or documentation to say who you are and now, through no fault of your own, you have found yourself in a situation where you are miles from home and in a different country. What is even more complicated, is that we are now in the middle of a pandemic. As a result of this pandemic which has been caused by Covid 19, a lot of people have lost their lives and now most of the sensible world are isolating as we are here. Do you know what that means, Georgie?"

"Yes, we had to do it at home. We couldn't go to school or see our friends or anything."

"Georgie, did you say that your mother went to live with another man. Do you know where she went?" The glimmer of an idea had begun to form in the back of Bruce's mind as he digressed.

"Yes, I went there once. The man had some big lorries, I think it was near Reading."

"So, to carry on!" Bruce smiled inwardly, as he picked up his train of thought. "You see, the authorities, that is the law, say that every person under the age of eighteen, that is you." Bruce pointed to Georgie still sitting on his lap." Are required to be under parental supervision or have a legally appointed guardian. Up until now, your father has been your legal guardian." Georgie started to stir uncomfortably, gently Bruce continued. "The last thing that we will do is to send you back to your father. Or to anyone where we think you won't be happy or safe. Okay?" Georgie nodded in confirmation. "Technically, I suppose that we should give you up to the Spanish authorities because that is where we are now. However, I don't think that would be fair on you. So, I think that if you want to, you can stay with us for a while until we can get everything sorted out. Would you be happy with that?"

"Yes, but why can't I stay with you forever?" Georgie looked up at Bruce. She remembered when he had taken her in his arms and held her tight and had known then in her heart of hearts, she was in the safest place ever. As long as she was with him, no harm would ever come to her.

Charlie moved from the helm seat and squatted in front of Bruce and Georgie. "Sweetheart, that would be lovely, we think you are a very special, little girl. But there are complicated procedures to have to go through where we would have to get consent forms and involve social services. These things take an absolute age to sort out and not only are we in Spain but we are also in the middle of pandemic. However, in the meantime, we will try to keep you with us for as long as we can. How about that?"

"Yes, please." Georgie nodded her head. Charlie circled her arms around her man and the girl.

"Just one more question, sweetheart." Bruce addressed Georgie. "Do you know your mother's name at all?"

Hesitantly, Georgie answered. "Lorna Kowalski."

"Thank you! You have been fantastic." Bruce smiled at her.

Charlie looked at him quizzically.

"And now, I think that we should go and get your bed made up ready for tonight. What do you think?" Charlie added.

Bruce put Georgie back down on her feet.

Bruce and Charlie moved all the sewing stuff into the double cabin opposite but left the first aid kit secure under the outboard bunk and made up the inner bunk for Georgie. Charlie had made two outfits of knickers and dresses and a bikini bottom with ties at the sides. She showed Georgie where her clothing was to be kept and where her laundry basket was. Charlie had also fashioned a makeshift nightdress from one of her older ones.

"Right." Charlie announced. "I am going back up to the galley to finish off the vegetables, you, my darling." She pointed at Bruce. "May pour me a nice glass of Chablis and you two darlings." Charlie pointed at Georgie and Bruce. "Can set the table for me, please."

Almost straight after dinner, they managed to get a very tired Georgie into bed and settled for the night. They didn't anticipate her settling easily for the first night, but fifteen minutes after they had switched off her cabin lights, Charlie went back below to check on her. Thirty seconds later, Charlie emerged with a satisfied smirk on her face. "Lights out and absolutely dead to the world." She settled back on the sofa, cuddling up next to Bruce.

"Right you, what is it that you have got up your sleeve? I saw that look on your face earlier when you quizzed Georgie about her mother."

"I am not sure. I don't even know if we can legally do it yet." Bruce turned to look at Charlie more directly. Charlie reciprocated turning towards Bruce on the sofa. "What would you say to having a daughter. If we could? This would be a very big 'if' though and a whole lot of circumstances would have to drop into place for that to happen."

Charlie's mouth opened in disbelief at the question and she shook her head. "Bruce, do you mean Georgie?"

"Yes of course. Who else?"

Charlie gasped in surprise and paused, turning slightly away from Bruce. "Yes!" She turned back towards Bruce. "Yes, oh my God! Really? But how? Yes, yes and yes again." Again, she paused, turned slightly away from Bruce and then turned back towards him. "But Brucie what about you my darling?"

Bruce looked at Charlie, the blue and the hazel eyes met. "What about me? There is something about Georgie that makes me believe that she deserves more than she has to look forward to at this moment. I happen to think that we may be able to provide that." Bruce recalled the unspoken bond that had been formed between them earlier on the shower floor. "Besides which, I have sort of taken to her, in a strange sort of way. But it is early days as yet."

Charlie had also remembered the bonding of the child with her husband earlier in the day on the shower floor. Once again, feeling the unnecessary pang of jealousy. Charlie gently massaged Bruce's shoulder in empathy. She reached forward and gently kissed his lips in understanding.

It had been a long day for everyone and emotions had been high so, it wasn't too long afterwards that Bruce and Charlie went below. They had left Georgie's door open with a night light on. Once Bruce and Charlie had finished their showers, Charlie checked on a sound asleep blond-haired girl and returning, left their cabin door ajar as well. It was just after half-past five when Bruce was aware of the small body climbing up onto the bed next to him. Gently he pulled her over the top of him and settled her between Charlie and himself. Charlie turned in her half-sleep and put her arm over both of them. Georgie was almost instantly sound asleep.

Bruce was awake at seven o'clock. The two girls were still asleep, taking up most of the bed between them. Gathering his clothes, Bruce used the spare double cabin heads and got dressed. Knowing that Miguel would be casting off from Malaga shortly, if he hadn't already. Bruce also thought that it would be a very good idea to disassemble the booby trap at the cove entrance before the *Rio-Jenil* arrived. So, launching *Willie*, Bruce made his way over to disarm the flare. He was just in the process of doing so when he saw what he assumed to be the *Rio Jenil* slowly making her way down the coast. They were still some distance away, taking the flare and the fishing line with him, Bruce returned to the *Cape* and a cheerful greeting from the girls. Breakfast was on the go and life felt wonderful. Once he had stowed the flare with the others in the workshop area, Bruce made his way up to the salon where he was greeted with a hug from Georgie. Kissing Charlie and picking up his first mug of tea, he said to Georgie.

"And you, young lady, who was the little tinker that snuck into our bed in the early hours of this morning?" Bruce admonished her with a grin.

Charlie laughingly spoke to Georgie. "Don't you worry honey, Brucie has a seven-year-old granddaughter that does it all the time and he loves it, so don't you worry about it."

Bruce laughed and made his way up to the flybridge and fully raised the two VHF antennas, briefly admiring the view of the cove from the raised position of the flybridge. Once again, it was one of those warm late spring Spanish mornings, the blue water of the Mediterranean cove sparkled in the warmth and brightness of the rising sun, the forthcoming challenges of the day almost seemed inconsequential. A black-headed gull wheeled overhead, calling to its mate that answered it from somewhere towards the mouth of the cove. The sound of the one-foot swells gently breaking on the distant beach and the calm reaction of the boat to the easy swells filled Bruce with a sense of peace and wellbeing. Bruce returned to the main deck and the lower helm, where he switched on the VHF radios, there was a brief crackle and the brief hiss of squelch, but nothing else. They all heard the *Rio Jenil* cruise past the cove, the sound of those big marine diesels was unmistakable, but she sailed on passing the cove entrance until the sound of her engines diminished in the distance. They decided that they would have a leisurely day in the sun and breakfast in the cockpit. Georgie got smothered with sun cream only after Charlie had put her long blond hair into two plaits.

Following breakfast, Bruce got on the sat phone and called Brian Stone back in the UK, leaving the girls in the cockpit enjoying the sun.

"I have had a unit from the Basingstoke 'nick' make enquiries at the address you gave me." There was the sound of papers being rifled on the desk surface as Brian paused momentarily. "The outcome is that there is no one there. There is an irate property owner who is owed three months' worth of rent and no one has been seen there since the 27th of March. That was when at about 15:00 hrs, the father, one Ardy Taylor and Georgina the daughter were seen getting into the family car and driving off. The picture you sent me has definitely been confirmed as Georgina Taylor." Bruce grunted an acknowledgement before Brian continued. "Ardy Taylor's vehicle has been found abandoned at the Reading, East Bound Services. CCTV footage has him getting into a Lithuanian registered truck, no sign of Georgina though. Hang on." The sound of more papers being shuffled on the desk. "Ahh! Here we are. The truck passed through Folkestone just after 22:00 on the night of the 27th. No record of Taylor was indicated, but that means nothing. Hope that helps Bruce?"

"Thanks, Brian, that just about confirms everything from this angle. Has anyone filed a missing person's report?"

"No nothing at all."

"Brian, I need a big, big favour, please?"

"Bruce, anything I can do at all. Me and the boys more than owe you for what you did." The memory of the bomb at the safe house in Northern Ireland and the heroic action of Bruce armed only with a Browning nine millimetre pistol taking on the four UVF terrorists armed with two Armalite AR15 rifles and two Uzi submachine guns returned to the forefront of his mind. "What do you need?"

"Firstly, you and the boys owe me nothing at all. If the circumstances had been reversed, you guys would have done the same for me. So big favour, please, mate. Can you trace Georgina's mother, I think she is of Polish origin and is living with a Polish bloke who may have a transport company of sorts, somewhere near Reading. The only name I have got is Lorna Kowalski for the mother. She apparently left Georgina in the hands of her father some two years ago. So now it sounds as though Georgina's father has probably skipped the country, which for his sake I hope he has. Because otherwise, he would be facing some very, real allegations of child abuse and rape."

"Oh my God! Really? Is she alright now?"

"Yes well, as well as she can be under the circumstances, I suppose, poor kid. Apart from everything else she has been sold, shipwrecked, nearly drowned and now she has ended up on our boat with us in Spain with no paperwork and no passport. Quite frankly, right now, her future is looking really fuckin' bleak."

Bruce turned around as Charlie brought him a fresh mug of tea. She kissed him lightly on the cheek and gently squeezed his arm in encouragement. He pursed his lips in a kissing action, noting that Georgie was well out of earshot down in the cockpit.

"I guess that the Spanish will probably want to take charge of her now as an illegal immigrant?" Brian's voice came back over the phone.

"Yes, that is the one thing that is worrying me, but the OIC out here is a fairly good friend of ours and I am hoping that he can cut us a bit of slack. I am sort of depending on you for that. If you can find Georgina's excuse for a mother, apply some pressure to her and get her to sign adoption papers naming Charlie and I as the adoptees."

"Whoosh! That's a bit of a tall order Brucie boy." There was a pause and the line was silent for five seconds. "Actually, that is doable. I have a friend who is very high up on the Social Services ladder and owes me one. And especially as this is for a very, very special cause."

"Brian, just to help matters along, yesterday afternoon, Charlie and I had a lengthy chat with Georgie. I am going to send you a recording of that conversation attached to an email, with a few more pictures of her and her bruises."

"What are we talking about here Bruce?"

"I am only going to say child abuse at the moment. I will let you make up your own mind from what you can see and hear from what I am going to send you."

"Oh! Okay then Bruce, every bit helps I guess."

"Great, cheers, mate. I really appreciate the help. Brian, do you still have any contact with MI?"

Brian was hesitant before replying. "Yes. sort of. Why?"

"I think that I am going to need to talk to someone very soon."

"Would you like to give me a clue?"

"Yes, sure. It's about suspicions regarding Alpha, two, three, two."

"Okay, I don't know what that means, but someone will call you in due course."

Bruce placed the phone back into its holder and remained at the helm station. He swiftly emailed the recording that he had made during the course of talking to Georgie. This was accompanied by some photographs that he had taken of Georgie's bruises.

It was about an hour and a half later when the *Rio Jenil* cautiously came into the cove, turned around and facing the cove entrance dropped her anchor and shut down her main engines. Bruce and Charlie waved to the crew, all five of the crew and Miguel waved back. Noticing that the Spanish crew were launching their tender, Bruce collected his Crewsaver, got into *Willie* and headed towards the beach to meet with Miguel.

Once on the beach, Miguel was accompanied by Alphonso, the young man who had shot Van de Niekerk a few weeks before. They greeted each other warmly, retaining their two-metre distances apart. Miguel had with him two large shopping bags, which he placed on the beach explaining. "When I told Clarissa about the young girl, Georgina, she gathered up as many clothes and things from her friends that she thought may come in handy. Have you heard anything back about where she has come from yet?"

Bruce briefed Miguel on what Brian had been able to unearth to date but conveniently left out the subterfuge that they were planning.

Miguel shook his head. "Bruce, I understand. Is it possibly better that you let me take her into Spanish custody?"

"If you took that little girl into custody now, that would be another trauma to put her through She has been sold into slavery, nearly drowned after being shipwrecked. Now she is with people that speak her language and care very much about her. Of course, you would be perfectly within your rights to do so but think also of the paperwork and the international complications that you would have to cope with. Let alone the Covid restrictions and isolation. Let us have a few days and see what we might be able to discover. After all, she isn't exactly going anywhere, is she?" Bruce smiled at Miguel, who laughed back. Bruce continued. "She trusts us now and slowly, between Charlie and I, we can start to get the information out of her that we would need. And don't worry, my friend, I will keep you in the picture. I am probably keener than you are to get hold of the bastards that are responsible." Bruce concluded.

"Where exactly did you find her, Bruce?" Miguel asked.

There was a murmuring of slightly raised voices from the remainder of the crew of the *Rio Jenil*, causing Bruce to look out into the cove. Wading out knee-deep into the water, Bruce pointed to the right-hand side of the cove entrance. "She was over there, clinging onto the rocks."

"But Bruce, there was a storm, how could you have seen her from that distance?" Miguel asked watching Bruce with incredulity as one of the dolphins came right up to Bruce. Clicking and squeaking, she raised her head to Bruce in greeting.

"Hello, Daphne." He stroked her head. Turning to Miguel he said. This is Daphne and the big bull out there is Dougie." Turning back to the dolphins, he said. "Go on guys, go and play." He slowly raised both his arms in a go away motion. They went out into the cove and started jumping, tail slapping and doing their own little displays. As Bruce started to leave the water, he said to Miguel. "They attracted my attention to her." Bruce continued to tell the story of how the humans and dolphins had become friends.

"You know Bruce." Miguel started. "If I hadn't seen that with my own eyes, I wouldn't have believed you." Miguel shook his head in virtual disbelief and looked out to the cove where the dolphins were now playing around the stern of the *Cape,* much to Georgie's delight. "I think that you are extraordinary. I also think that I should follow my heart and let you continue with what you think is the best course of action, mi amigo."

"Thank you, my friend, look, here are Brian Stone's contact details, I have already passed yours onto him, so he will keep you in the loop from his end as well." Bruce said handing over the piece of paper with the details neatly printed. "Have you spotted any signs of a wreck or wreckage at all?" Bruce asked.

"No nothing at all, still no boats are reported missing at the moment." Miguel shook his head.

There was a shout from the radio operator and a rapid exchange in Spanish between the *Rio Jenil* and Miguel. Miguel turned to Bruce. "Bruce, I am sorry, I will have to go. A fisherman has found a body in the water just up the coast about three kilometres from here!"

"No problem, listen, give our love and thanks to Clarissa." Bruce said to Miguel as the main engines on the *Rio Jenil* burst into life with black smoke belching out of her exhausts. "Adios Alphonso, nos vemos luego." (See you later.)

Bruce put the shopping bags into *Willie* and returned to the *Cape* handing the bags over to Charlie and a curious little girl. Opening the bags, Charlie gasped in astonishment. "I think that we ought to take these down to your cabin and sort them out on your bed. What do you think Georgie?"

"Oooh! Yes, please. Are these all for me?" Georgie's eyes were wide with surprise and excitement.

Bruce returned to the chart table and got out a detailed chart for the immediate area, then checked online for the way that the currents ran. Again, returning to the chart table, he re-examined the chart and although it wasn't immediately obvious, there was an indication of a rise in the ocean floor which, typically, during a storm could cause the water to shoal. Georgie's words returning to Bruce's mind 'and then I saw a big wave'. That must have been a shoaling wave that hit the boat that Georgie was on. If they had been sailing close to the coast in the area of Dolphin Cove, that would explain it. Between the coast and the bar that Bruce had just identified, the water depth went down to twenty-five metres that was the equivalent to just over eighty feet. That was dive able. More so, there was a strong probability that the body that Miguel was investigating could have come from the area outside of the cove they were in. Bruce put the charts away and shut down the laptop, deciding that for the moment he would keep the information he had to himself.

Going below, Bruce was just in time to see Charlie and Georgie putting away a quantity of clothing and underwear suitable for a seven to eight-year-old, including a swimsuit and a bright pink buoyancy aid. Collecting the list that Charlie had compiled for him, Bruce made his way back up to the pilot station and back to the bat phone.

It rang promptly at one o'clock, Bruce picked it up on the first jarring ring. Again, the number was withheld. "Hi, Mike. How are you doing?"

"Hi Bruce, I am on a secure link and I know your sat phone is secure." Mike replied. "I understand that you need to talk to someone. Can you confirm the subject of your conversation please?"

"Yes, it is regarding alpha, two, three, two."

The ether remained silent for some five seconds before Mike continued. "I have absolutely no idea what that is, I am going to pass that up the line, could we possibly resume this conversation tomorrow?"

"Yes, of course, in the interim period I will email you the list that I need for my guest if that is still okay with you. Just let me know when you need some card details or let me have some BACS information if that is better for you."

"Absolutely no problem at all, just stay safe, all three of you." Mike closed the connection.

To some extent, this was good news for Bruce as it gave him a bit of an extension to put his plan into action.

CHAPTER 26

Apart from taking *Willie* ashore where they spent some time on the beach gathering up the driftwood in preparation for their next bonfire/braaivleis and just generally stretching their legs in the sunshine. Bruce's mind was never far from whatever it was that Brian Stone was up to back in the UK.

Immediately following on from his conversation with Bruce, having received the email and attachments, Brian left his Southampton office heading for the car park and his black Land Rover Discovery. As soon as he had got into the vehicle and was on his way up the M3 heading in the direction of Basingstoke, Brian embarked on a series of telephone calls. The first was to a colleague of his in the Thames Valley Police based in Reading. The second was to a senior welfare officer based in Winchester. This was the longer of the calls, as it took quite a bit of explaining and one or two veiled threats. One of which included an oversight, which may have resulted in a possible negligence offence. The third phone call was to a senior Families Court Judge who lived in Stockbridge, Hampshire. This conversation was on a first-name basis. The Judge, a former Captain in the Royal Signals, had been one of the four trapped in that house in Northern Ireland. As soon as he heard of Bruce's situation and intentions, he was more than happy to give up on his days fishing on the River Test to assist Bruce and Brian's request to formerly home a little girl. Brian was just approaching the M3 exit for Basingstoke and Reading when his phone rang. It was his colleague from the TVP at Reading. They thought that they had located the transport company concerned and Lorna Kowalski as well. There was a local Police Officer on his way there to assist Brian when he got there. Once the location details had been passed on, Brian fed the information into his sat-nav system and that was where he arrived twenty minutes later.

At first, Lorna Kowalski denied even having had a daughter, despite the evidence provided by the records office. Then she was told about the disappearance of Ardy Taylor and her connection to him, again supported by information from the records office and then the mystical appearance of her daughter in Southern Spain. She was subsequently arrested on suspicion of complicity in trafficking her daughter for immoral purposes and taken to Basingstoke Police Station. After two hours in a cell, she provided all the information required, made a statement and signed all the necessary documentation giving over her daughter for adoption by a Mr and Mrs Williams with an address in Hayling Island.

Brian then drove to Winchester where he received the necessary signed adoption papers from the welfare officer he had spoken to earlier. Then it was on to Stockbridge where he sat down for a late lunch with the senior Families Court Judge whence the adoption papers were duly authorised and finalised. From that moment, the former Georgina Taylor was now Georgina Williams with an address also in Hayling Island. By the time Brian had got back to his office in Southampton, it was a quarter past five. Spanish time and time on the *Cape* was one hour ahead of the UK.

It wasn't long after six in the evening, Bruce, Charlie and Georgie were sat in the cockpit enjoying the last of the day. It was a warm evening and the resident bats from a fissure high up on the cliffs providing the three humans with a performance of intricate flying as they fed on the local insects. The bat phone up at the lower helm shrilled and Bruce reluctantly got up to answer it. It was Brian.

"Hello, sailor." Greeted Brian. "I have got some brilliant news for you boyo. I think that we must have conducted the fastest legal adoption in history. I have just attached all the necessary paperwork in an email to you." Brian's Welsh accent was very strong that evening.

"That's fantastic news, Brian. Were there any problems?"

"No, none at all. Douglas sends his regards by the way and said that you and your new family should visit him the next time you are in the UK."

They carried on comparing the weather and Covid restrictions in the UK and Spain and exchanged a few other pleasantries before terminating the call. Returning to the cockpit, Charlie glanced at Bruce inquisitively.

"It's a go, honey." Bruce volunteered, settling himself back into the cockpit lounger next to Georgie and picking up his glass of wine. Bruce and

Georgie were sat opposite Charlie who was impossibly trying to hide an enigmatic smile that was almost turning into a smirk of satisfaction. Bruce smiled back at her.

"Boy, you guys are really acting strangely again." Georgie sat up and looked from one adult to another.

Charlie looked directly at Georgie. "Georgie, do you remember Bruce said to you that he would not send you back to your father or anywhere that you didn't want to go?"

"Yes." The reply was hesitant.

"Do you also remember that you said you wanted to stay with us forever?"

"Yes." Georgie swivelled and looked up at Bruce, who was leaning back in the sofa with his hands clasped behind his head and a grin from ear to ear.

"What?" Georgie enquired.

"Georgie, come over here, please, sweetheart." Charlie offered with a smile holding her arms out to the child. Georgie obliged and was lifted onto Charlie's lap. Charlie lovingly wrapped her arms around her, pulling Georgie into her bosom. "Georgie, this may be a bit sudden and seem complicated. But how would you feel about us adopting you?"

"What does that mean, exactly?" The question was cautious.

"Well, basically, what it would mean is that Bruce and I would be your legal parents, you would no longer be Georgina Taylor but Georgina Williams, you would live with us for as long as you wanted. There would be papers to say that we have sole custody over you and that no one can take you away from us.

Georgie was silent but looked at both Bruce and Charlie in turn as she considered this turn of events. Bruce wordlessly got up and sat down next to Charlie, placing his right arm around Charlie's shoulder.

"But yesterday you said it would take forever and you would have to talk to Social Services and that it was complicated?"

"Yes, you are right. But I have low friends in high places and it is quite surprising what can be achieved in a very short space of time." Bruce answered her.

"Does that mean that you will be my Mum and Dad and I get to call you that forever?" Georgie looked directly at Bruce's smiling face into those wonderful blue eyes, not daring to think that this man could ever possibly be her Dad and the beautiful woman who was holding her so lovingly, would be her Mum.

"If that is what you would like." Bruce answered her, almost matter of factly, taking in the look of disbelief on her face, he added. "No sweetheart, I am not joking. This is for real Georgie. If this is what you would like to happen, then I will make it happen."

"But how?"

"All you have to say is yes, if you want to, then it is done, it as simple as that." Bruce concluded.

Georgie looked from one face to the other for some five seconds, then burst into tears. Charlie hugged Georgie tightly into her and rocked her gently, Bruce reached across and gently rubbed her arm.

"Is this a trick she snuffled?" as the tears started to subside.

"I promise you, Georgie, this is no trick." Bruce squeezed her arm in reassurance, Charlie with tears streaming down her cheeks with the emotion of the moment, also smiled a reassurance as she gave Georgie another loving squeeze and kissed the top of her head.

"Yes, yes, please." Georgie nodded her head in agreement.

"Well, my little one." Bruce choked back on his own emotions. "Welcome to the Williams family. I have never had a daughter till now."

Georgie was still sat on Charlie's lap with her arms wrapped around her. "Mum?" Georgie almost whispered.

"Yes, my darling." Charlie hoarsely replied, tears of joy streaming down her cheeks.

"Please don't cry."

The rest of the evening was spent discussing the immediate future. Bruce wasn't sure whether or not to call Miguel to inform him of the change of circumstances in respect of Georgie's adoption. Deciding against the idea until there was documentary evidence available. He now knew how he was going to get it.

After the emotional part of the early evening, the meal and subsequent period leading up to Georgie's shower and bedtime seemed relatively subdued. It wasn't until after Georgie's bedtime that Bruce and Charlie sat down on the sofa in the lounge, both nursing their first whiskies of the evening. Charlie put her feet up on the sofa, lying back and placing her head on Bruce's leg with a satisfying smile. "You are just so full of surprises, Bruce Williams and I just love you so much." She whispered up to him.

Bruce smiled down at her and gently stroked her temple with his thumb.

It was half-past seven the next morning and Bruce had been dozing, Charlie was spooning him and he could hear and feel her gentle breathing on the back of his neck, the sensation of her breasts pressing tenderly into his shoulders and her hips against his bottom. With her right arm casually over his torso, her hand carelessly just over his navel, was giving him what felt like the erection of erections. A full bladder meant that he would have to get up soon to see to that necessity. Thank goodness Georgie hadn't come in yet. Bruce stretched and turned over pressing his erect penis between Charlie's hips. Charlie kissed his forehead and pulled his head down into her breasts, almost purring like a cat. Bruce was in seventh heaven. It lasted all of two minutes. "It's no good." He murmured. "I really need to take a wee."

"Maybe that's a good thing right now, don't forget that we have a seven-year-old daughter on this boat as well." Charlie whispered in his ear, the warm breath sending a tremor down through his body. Charlie chuckled at the reaction she had gained.

Bruce spent the morning preparing for his telephone call. He had hoped that the mentioning of the code for the Novichok would produce some reaction from high up in MI. Promptly at one pm. the bat phone again shrilled in the lower helm, Bruce picked it up during that first ring and listened.

"Hi, Bruce. How are you doing?"

"Fine, thanks. Did you receive my email by the way?"

"Yes, thanks. Bruce, I have another two interested parties listening in to our conversation, if that's alright with you?"

"Yes, that's fine by me. Okay, Mike, here is the situation." Bruce started. "When we first met in Gibraltar, you knew very little of me and I knew even less about you. Before we left for the UK you were aware that we had been having some problems with, shall we say for want of a better term, the local nasties."

"Yes." Replied Mike. "I now know that you are ex 'D' Squadron and several people speak very highly of you. How can we help?"

Speaking quickly and concisely, Bruce had rehearsed the conversation a few times. "There are a couple of things, the first and probably at this moment the most important is that I am going to refer to two people who were in Salisbury in 2018 and were responsible for the use of Alpha, two, three, two. One of them, I now believe is deceased. The second one was responsible for the placing of a charge under our boat in Malaga Marina. You were on board at the time and I have no idea where he is at the moment. There were a series of four charts secreted on board this vessel that I believe at least two factions were interested in recovering. I further believe that these charts relate to the whereabouts of the containers of the product that were not used in Salisbury. So, if that product were to fall into the wrong hands, this world would be a worse place to live in. Are you with me so far?"

"Yes." the reply sounded a little hesitant. "How do you come to know of the other two containers?"

"There was a degree of speculation at the time and now you have just confirmed it." Bruce smiled to himself.

Non-plussed at having had the truth discovered, Mike continued. "Okay. So, what now?"

"I need to get this information to someone in a secure manner and have it verified. I am unable to be seen to leave my current location given the circumstances. Would a clandestine RV at sea be acceptable, it would mean that I would be in a very, small open boat?" There was another pause in the conversation, Bruce was sure that he could hear muted voices in the background.

Charlie and Georgie came up into the pilot station, Georgie went to the chart table and used that to rest a piece of paper with a picture on it. Georgie was happily colouring in the picture which looked remarkably like the *Cape*. Charlie kissed Bruce on the forehead and made an eating sign as she went into the galley to prepare lunch. Bruce responded by giving her a thumbs-up sign.

The senior intelligence officer that had been monitoring the phone call, initially out of interest, suddenly became very interested when the Novichok code came across from a known and reputable ex-Special Air Services operative. He also knew of the Russian agent currently being detained on board *Astound*, who was the surviving half of the Salisbury poisoning duo. If this ex-soldier knew anything about the missing Novichok, then Her Majesty's Secret Intelligence Service wanted to know as well.

Mike came back on the line again. "Okay. And the second thing on your mind is?"

"From our conversation of yesterday, you will be aware that we have a guest on board. I have copied you the legal documentation, I now need a passport with our surname for the guest. Come to think of it, whilst you are doing one, you may as well do the other persons' passport as well. I have already emailed you a list of goods for our guest, no expense spared please, also the photographs for the passports.

"Nine, one, zero!" This was a strange voice.

"Affirmative!" Bruce responded immediately. Nine, one, zero were the last three digits of Bruce's former Army number.

"Where and when?" The question was direct.

Bruce replied without hesitation. "Zulu is now minus five-eight hours at November, three, six. Two, six. Two, three, two. Whisky, five. Zero, three. Eight, two, three." This meant that they would meet in fifty-eight hours at the grid reference where November was north and Whisky was the westerly coordinates. The grid reference was just over five nautical miles out to sea in a straight line south from the cove. Because an RV had been requested and accepted, Bruce knew that the passports and official adoption certificate would be in a diplomatic bag and in Gibraltar within the next twenty-four hours. It might take longer to source some of the other requirements though.

Mike came back on the phone. "Okay, Bruce. That is a go from this end, stay safe. All of you!" The call was terminated.

Georgie had stopped colouring and was staring at Bruce probably because of the strange way that he had been speaking on the phone, she was now wearing a nice pair of girlie shorts and a colourful pink top.

Bruce got out of the helm seat and walked over looking at her colouring. Kissing the top of her head he said. "That is a really lovely picture Georgie, you are doing a great job there." Then pointing to the jolly roger, Bruce said. "What's this then, are we pirates now?"

"I guess so." Georgie replied a little shyly.

"Well then, I guess that I am going to have to make you walk the plank then." Bruce chided the child.

"Noooo!" Georgie screeched, smiling at him knowing the words to be spoken in jest.

"Okay then, shall we go and get some lunch instead?" Bruce smiled, picking her up by the arms, he swung her up so that she was riding piggyback as they headed towards the galley and Charlie.

"Well?" Enquired Charlie. "What did they say?"

"It was a yes from him and a yes from him as well so, that was two yesses." Bruce mimicked a well-known judge from a well-known international talent competition which was also held in the UK.

"Oh, Brucie darling, that's wonderful news. When?"

"About two and a half days." Bruce smiled at her.

"Boy, you guys are really talking funny again today." Georgie quipped, still riding piggyback on Bruce.

"Don't worry, we will tell you all about it." Charlie assured her. "Now do we all want some squash with our sandwiches?"

CHAPTER 27

Two nights later and it had just gone half-past eight in the evening, Georgie was in bed and asleep, *Willie* was in the water with a full fuel tank and two flares tucked in the storage compartment. Bruce and Charlie were in the aft section of the *Cape* as Bruce got dressed into his wet suit, booties and a hood. Once he had completed that, he then secured his red Seabob, *Bobbi* into the passenger seat with a quick-release strap. If needed, the Seabob would be able to tow him a lot further than he could swim. Bruce's insides were churning. His plan to rendezvous five nautical miles out to sea in the dark was to all intents and purposes, not the best idea he had had. It struck him that he had probably had better plans in the past. It was, however, a necessity to get the information that he had to the right people. Sailing the *Cape* into Gibraltar harbour was not an option during the lockdown and then there was no guarantee that he would be able to get in front of the right person. This way, he was certain that no expense would be spared.

Bruce set off from the *Cape* just after nine o'clock in the evening, he planned to motor the Williams 435 as slowly as possible out to the rendezvous point as such minimising any wake, the Rotax four-Tec 150 petrol engine at just over tick over was virtually inaudible. At night sound travelled considerably and at sea even more so. The brightness on the screen of the chart plotter was minimised so that Bruce could hardly see it. Even before the tender had got to the mouth of the cove it was invisible and inaudible to Charlie who was standing in silence on the aft deck of the *Cape*.

Bruce found himself at the rendezvous point at a quarter to eleven, fifteen minutes early and settled down to wait for whatever vessel he was going to meet with. In all honesty, he anticipated some small vessel that would then take him offshore to a waiting naval destroyer or possibly a disguised fishing vessel. Switching off the engine, he took in his surroundings. Much further out to sea, he could see two other very large ships, both of them with all their deck lights on and heading in a westerly direction towards Gibraltar. They were a good two to three nautical miles further out to sea and separated by a similar distance. Looking back towards the distant shore, he could see all the lights of Marbella, Fuengirola and towns and villages. Subsequently, Bruce found himself beginning to wish that he had chosen a coastline that wasn't so well lit up. With the help of the ambient light, Bruce poured himself a cup of coffee from the flask that Charlie had prepared. Thinking of her, he knew that she would be at the pilot station on the *Cape* listening to the silent VHF radio. Bruce continued to keep a lookout for other boats. As he wasn't showing any lights, the last thing he wanted was to be run down by a ship sailing in close to the shore. Checking the plotter, he noticed he was drifting a little to the southeast of his rendezvous point, he decided to let the drift continue and to correct his position nearer the time for the RV. At ten fifty-five, Bruce started the engine and gently steered the tender back onto the rendezvous position.

Then it happened, taking Bruce totally by surprise and scaring the living daylights out of him. Bruce hadn't discounted the use of a submarine, but the top of the conning tower mysteriously, silently and terrifyingly appeared in the gloom next to *Willie*. Almost immediately, two soldiers appeared on the wet deck of the conning tower, which was only three feet above the surface of the ocean. Both were wearing night-vision goggles and were pointing weapons at Bruce. Slowly he reached down and placed the engine in neutral and then, turning the key, switched it off. Then very slowly, Bruce raised his arms above his head, open palms of his hands facing towards the two soldiers. Quietly, one of them spoke. "Identify yourself." It was a female voice.

Almost croaking Bruce replied. "Bruce Williams, ex Sergeant, two, four, zero, eight, six, nine, one, zero." Out of bravado and nerves, he continued. "So, take your fingers off the triggers and lower your fuckin' weapons. Who else do you think you are going to find out in the middle of the fuckin' oggin. Dick heads!" Inwardly he was disgusted with himself for being so momentarily terrified as the submarine had surfaced.

The weapons were lowered "Apologies, pass me your painter and come aboard."

Stiffly, Bruce got to his feet, picked up the line from the bow and threw it across towards the two soldiers, it was deftly caught and Bruce found himself alongside the conning tower. Picking up the dry bag containing the charts, Bruce awkwardly stepped onto the wet tower deck, close enough now he could identify the weapons as Heckler and Koch submachine guns with suppressors fitted. 'Special Forces kit'. Bruce thought.

The female voice curtly said. "I am just going to take your temperature." She pointed an Infra-Red pistol thermometer at his forehead, there was a pause of three seconds, then she continued. "Put this on." It was a harness with a length of rope on and a carabiner at the other end. She indicated where to attach the carabiner, gradually they descended the sail passing through a watertight housing. There was the constant hissing of air in the vaguely red illuminated sail. After the fresh natural air of the sea, the air inside the vessel smelt almost clinical. The deck was lit with night vision saving red lighting. Once the watertight door leading up through the sail was closed the standard white light was restored. Bruce looked around him blinking in the harsh light, there was no one that he recognised.

A man wearing a plain navy blue boiler suit with the name 'Smith' on it stepped forward. "Williams, I am from Military Intelligence, it doesn't matter what my name is. What have you got for me?"

Bruce turned away from the MI man and having identified the Commander as being the senior officer on deck he said. "Commander, thank you for allowing me aboard your boat. I am going to address you and not this jumped up little prick with no manners." Bruce had felt offended by the MI man's approach towards him. After all, it was he who had the information that the MI man wanted.

The Commander smiled and stepped forward, extending his right hand in formal greeting. "I am Commander Hammond, welcome aboard Her Majesty's Submarine *Astound*, Mr Williams."

Bruce was led to a space on the bridge which supported a chart table where he was allowed to make his presentation without interruption. He started with the discovery of the charts and the pinholes. Continuing with then finding out about the former owner of the *Cape* and subsequently the identification of both Singleton and Donaldson. Then their connection with the attempted assassinations of Yuri Akiripal and his daughter in Salisbury and finally the joining of the pinpricks with them crossing in Sardinia.

Hammond addressed another officer. "See what you make of those coordinates, Navs."

Less than a minute later, Navs replied. "I have that as an intersection just to the south of the village of Sedilo. Nicely done, Mr Williams."

"Thank you, Navs." Bruce replied. "What do you think, Mr Smith?" Bruce addressed the man in the coveralls who had been examining the photographs which Bruce had printed out. There was also a full statement of events, the discoveries and conclusions that Bruce had made.

Smith looked up in surprise, his face turning pink. "Well, I think that there is a lot of supposition to what you have just said and those charts, they were made in 1947, for heaven's sake."

"No, they are current modern charts, made to look as if they were printed in 1947."

Even as Bruce was speaking, Navs was checking the charts, moments later he said. "I concur with Mr Williams." Hammond smiled at his navigator.

"Right." Said Bruce. "I need to be getting back ashore. Commander, I understand that you may have a package for me?"

"Three actually, they will be topside and in your tender by now, Mr Williams."

"Oh please, Commander, it's Bruce. And thank you for your hospitality." Bruce shook hands with Hammond then with the Navigating Officer. Ignoring Smith, Bruce joined his escort to the surface.

Re-boarding *Willie*, he thanked his escorts, noticing the outline of three dry bags the size of kit bags that had been stowed in the bow of *Willie*. Bruce started the engine and moved a short way off from the submarine, waiting for his eyes to fully adjust to the dark. Checking his watch, he saw that it was five minutes to midnight. Switching on the handheld VHF, Bruce checked the frequency and briefly keyed the transmit button twice. Very shortly after that, he received the sound of a microphone button being briefly keyed twice in response. He had just let Charlie know that he was fine and on his way back. Bruce responded by keying his transmit button briefly just once. Bruce watched in awe as the conning tower and short mast that he presumed to be a periscope, literally, just silently disappeared beneath the swell of the Mediterranean Sea. 'I guess that is why they are called the silent service'. Bruce thought to himself. He sat quietly for the next three minutes and gathered his thoughts, continuing to listen to the sounds of the night on the ocean. He poured a full cup of coffee from the flask, brought up the waypoint for the centre of the cove entrance. Bruce then set *Willie* in gear, continuing back to shore and ensuring that he was approaching from directly south of the waypoint to avoid an outcrop of rocks just to the east of the cove entrance.

Bruce heard them well before he could see them. The muted chatter of foreign voices and the straining sound of the outboard engine, then he got the distinct oily smell of a two-stroke engine. Bruce realised that he must have just crossed behind them. Instantly Bruce switched the Rotax engine off and let *Willie* drift away from the boatload of illegals. Waiting for them to get far enough away from him, Bruce was just about to start the engine when suddenly the sea was lit up with searchlights and shouted commands in Spanish. A burst of three rounds from a fifty calibre machine gun was fired over the heads of the illegals into the black waters of the sea beyond them. Unseen to the Spanish gunner, those rounds exploded into the water perilously close to Bruce. Bruce needed no further encouragement. He started to get as far away as possible from the trigger happy Spanish sailor that was manning the fifty calibre machine gun. As fast as he could and without alerting anyone to his presence, he moved away to a distance of about five hundred yards when Bruce stopped again. He switched off the engine and waited to see if anyone on the Spanish boat was aware of his existence. He hoped not. The Williams 435 could easily outstrip most of the Spanish naval boats, but he couldn't go faster than a bullet. Re-considering his situation, Bruce decided to head back out to sea and away from the Spanish Navy. What he didn't want to do was to allow himself to be backlit by the lights on the shore. Continuing to keep a close eye on the Spanish boat Bruce headed due south until the Spanish Navy cutter was just within sight. He just about heard the throb of the big marine diesels as the ship got underway and headed away on a westerly course.

He could see her silhouetted against the shoreline and was thankful that he had taken the course of action he had. The Spanish ship would probably head to San Fernando, which was possibly the nearest Spanish Naval station. Deciding to remain where he was for a full fifteen minutes, Bruce switched everything off and allowed the boat to drift. The Spanish warship was well and truly gone when he powered *Willie* up. It seemed, however, that he had drifted considerably further out to sea than he had anticipated. It wasn't long before he got himself back on course, ensuring that he was again approaching the cove entrance from the south to avoid the rocky outcrop.

It was just before five o'clock as Bruce manoeuvred *Willie* back through the entrance to the cove and saw the dim red light coming from the pilot station. Switching the handheld to low power, Bruce keyed the transmit button. "Don't reply, but I am home." Bruce saw her silhouetted against the upper works as Charlie exited the pilot station and made her way to the stern and the submerged swim deck.

"Oh my God! I am so glad to see you. You were a long time getting back." Charlie wrapped her arms around him as Bruce stiffly got out of *Willie* with the end of the mooring line in his hand.

"I am afraid that I ran into the Spanish Navy picking up a boatload of illegals." Bruce stated matter of factly.

"Did they see you, honey?" Charlie asked with concern in her voice.

"Nah! I should have been in the bloody Special Boat Service." Bruce laughed with her. "C'mon let's get this stuff aboard and sorted. I need to get out of this suit, I sweated my nuts off when I was on that submarine."

"Submarine?" Charlie exclaimed.

"Yep, a submarine. I'll tell you all about it later."

One of the bags was exceptionally heavy. Bruce carried it up to the main salon and then returned to *Willie* to get the last bag, which was full but relatively light by comparison to the first bag. Bruce showered in the dive station and rinsed out his wet suit at the same time. Using one of the swimming towels to dry himself with, he briefly contemplated his night's activities. Wrapping the towel around his torso, he locked down the access to the dive station and engine room and went into the salon, closing and locking the door behind him. Charlie was on her knees sorting through piles of brand new clothes. There was underwear, nightwear, shorts, jeans, swimming costumes, a dressing gown and a teddy bear. There were ribbons and things to hold her hair back, a brush and comb set for her hair and amongst it, an A4 reinforced package envelope addressed to Bruce. Before Bruce sat down, he went to the sideboard and poured two large whiskies added a small amount of water to each of them and handing one to Charlie, he sat down on the sofa and opened the envelope. In it were two brand new UK passports. One in the name of Georgina, Samantha Williams and the second was Charlie's in her new married name. There was also a certificate to say that Bruce and Charlie were the legal adoptive guardians of Georgie.

Bruce, still with a towel wrapped around his midriff, picked up the large teddy bear, sprawling himself onto the salon sofa with his whisky in his hand. He leaned his head back and closed his eyes summarising in his mind the activities of the night and the achievements gained. Still kneeling on the salon deck carpet, Charlie continued to sift through the clothing and hygiene items, stacking the items into appropriate piles. She looked up at Bruce, he looked tired and the anxieties of his clandestine activities of the last few hours showed clearly on his face. Sitting back on her heels, she asked. "You tired hun?"

"Knackered, I feel I could sleep for a week. But just think of what we have achieved, very probably the fastest legal adoption in UK history. Ever!"

Charlie got up stiffly from the deck and sat next to Bruce on the sofa. Taking his drink from him, she put it on the coffee table and wrapped her arms around him, pulling his head into her shoulder. "You are my absolute hero and I can't wait for us to tell Georgie the news."

The sleepy voice came from the head of the stairs. "Can't wait to tell Georgie what news?" Then Georgie took in the sight of all the clothes and the near nakedness of Bruce. "What on earth just happened here?" She asked sleepily, rubbing her eyes.

Charlie smiled at the sleepy child at the top of the stairs and held her arms out to her. "Brucie darling, why don't you go and put some clothes on before you scare this lovely little girl to death."

Bruce got up a little self-consciously, took a sip from his drink, making sure that the towel was well wrapped around himself just as Georgie replied.

"It's alright, Mummy, Daddy darling doesn't scare me, especially when he is holding a teddy bear. Is that for me?" Georgie asked sleepily.

"It certainly is." Bruce handed it to an approaching Georgie that stopped her in her tracks. "And don't forget to say a thank you to Mum as well." Bruce finished and handed the bear over to Georgie as he departed for the companionway below. He quickly dressed in a pair of slacks and a clean T-shirt with a lightweight hoodie and returned to the salon, where he finished his whisky and poured a second one. A very excited Georgie, now wide awake, was sitting next to Charlie.

"I have never had so many clothes. Where have they come from?" Georgie questioned Charlie.

"Maybe it was an early birthday present from Santa Claus." Bruce volunteered.

"Nooaw, silly! Santa Clause only comes at Christmas." Georgie turned to Bruce.

"Well, that just goes to show how much I don't know." Bruce quipped.

"And anyway, what is it that you haven't told me yet and what is in those bags over there?" Georgie asked, looking at Charlie and Bruce alternatively.

Bruce resumed his seat on the sofa, picking Georgie up as he did and placed her on his lap. "Well, young lady, it's like this. Your new Mum and I reckoned that we couldn't have our new daughter needing anything, so we did a bit of shopping online and I went to collect it last night."

Georgie looked at Bruce quizzically. "So where did you have to go and collect all this stuff from?"

"Seriously?"

"Uh-huh!"

"I took *Willie* out about five nautical miles to the south of here and met up with a Royal Navy Submarine called *Astound*. I had some information I needed to pass on in person. So, at the same time, I picked up the stuff that we had ordered for you and also your new passport and formal documentation that says you now officially belong to us." Bruce leaned forward to the coffee table as he was speaking and picked up Georgie's new UK passport. He opened it up to the page with her photograph and name on it. "So, can you read the name in this passport?" Bruce held the passport open at the appropriate page.

"Georgina Samantha Williams."

Bruce felt the tears through his shirt as her little arms wrapped themselves around his chest. Murmuring through her emotions Georgie asked. "Does that mean I get to call you Mum and Dad forever now?"

"You can call us what you like within reason, sweetheart, but yes." Bruce said as he leaned forward and kissed the top of her head.

Charlie reached over and took Georgie over onto her lap. "Now I really hope that those are happy tears?" She asked.

Georgie looked up at Charlie and again over to Bruce. "I have never been so happy in all my life. I think that I am going to burst with happiness." The tears poured out of her, Charlie hugged her into her bosom with tears of joy pouring down her cheeks as well. Even Bruce's eyes were moisture-laden.

CHAPTER 28

The remainder of the day was a confusing mixture of sorting out Georgie's new wardrobe. Telephone calls to the UK and Gibraltar and attempts to catch up on some sleep. Neither Bruce nor Charlie had had any sleep during the previous night. The other two dry bags had contained a mixture of a Crewsaver, wet suits, mask, snorkel, fins, swimming goggles, a Faber seven litre dive cylinder, regulator, BCD and last, but not least, a Yamaha DPV scooter. Finding homes for the new equipment and of course, trying to contain a very excited little girl became a bit of a challenge. There were a quantity of little girls games, a couple more teddy bears, drawing and colouring books, colouring pencils and reading books.

The safety aspects of when and where everybody wore Crewsavers had already been taught to Georgie and now it was just a matter of swapping the buoyancy aid for her new Crewsaver, reinforcing as to when and where she was to wear it. The new passports and other documentation joined the very pistol, cartridges and Bruce's and Charlie's original passport stored in the safe next to the chart table. Going to bed that night, Bruce had just finished cleaning his teeth and got into bed, when Charlie snuggled up to Bruce putting her head on his shoulder, she said. "Brucie, thank you for giving me something that I thought that I would never have."

Turning towards her he asked. "And what pray tell, would that have been?"

"A child silly." Charlie smiled.

Bruce kissed her on her lips and cuddling up together he was then almost instantly asleep. It wasn't until the following morning that life seemed to stabilise into something that could be called normal.

The next week followed on as spring continued towards the end of April of 2020, with the mornings dawning warm and sunny, life on board the *Cape* continuing on. Georgie had started to lose some of her scrawny looks and had started to tan nicely. Charlie brushed her blond hair every morning and evening until it glowed, she had remained nervous of the dolphins but was becoming very competent and confident in the water, although whilst in the water, she never ventured further than an arm's reach from Bruce. As the days got warmer, the standard daytime dress code on the *Cape* became almost as few clothes as possible. Georgie had set up her outdoor play area in the cockpit of the main deck but had to clear everything away before meals or when she had finished playing. Two days previously, they had started some schoolwork with her which consisted of arithmetic and times tables, spelling and writing. She loved the concept of learning and it was Charlie that took on the role of teacher. That left Bruce free to carry on with the basic chores on the *Cape*, the constant cleaning of the decks and upper works, ensuring that the solar panels remained dirt and salt-free. Checking oil levels in the two generators, it was coming up to time to having to carry out fuel filter changes on both generators and changing the filters for the water maker. Bruce also made time to take a sweeping brush and clean off any algae that had started to build upon the hull, cleaning off the underwater lights at the same time. Although life was idealistic, Bruce started to begin to feel a little stagnated, the fact that they were stuck in the cove in isolation. There were places that he and Charlie wanted to explore, there was family they wanted to see and hug and introduce Georgie to as well.

One thing that crossed Bruce's mind was, where was the wreck of the boat that had been transporting Georgie. He had spoken to Miguel a couple of days earlier and there were two boats reported missing, there was no trace of them or the owners. The body that Miguel had been sent to investigate was thought to be that of an illegal immigrant. Bruce decided that he needed to investigate the trough on the seafloor that he had discovered on the charts a few days previously. Bruce was in the pilot station on his computer at the chart table and had been in contact with an English couple who owned a Hans Christian. They had been caught out by the Coronavirus, just outside Cartagena, unfortunately, trapped in the Mer Menor off the coast of La Manga. Bruce had replied to their email and was in the process of shutting down his laptop computer when there was the sound of scampering bare feet on the deck behind him. "Daddy, Daddy darling, can we go swimming this afternoon? Please, please?" The skimpily clad little body landed on his lap.

"Yes, I guess so, once we have let our lunch go down." Bruce responded laughingly at her. It hadn't taken her long to pick up on Charlie's 'Brucie Darlings'. "I think I'll have you for lunch, you skinny little urchin." Bruce picked her up in his arms and pretended he was going to eat her.

Squealing with delight she wriggled in his arms trying to get away from him.

"I'll tell you what." Charlie put her arm around Bruce. "I'll make you a nice juicy sandwich, then you wait until I have fattened up this skinny waif, then we can both eat her." Charlie joined in with the game.

Noticing the open chart on the table, Charlie asked curiously. "What have you got here hun?"

Bruce started to explain his theories about the wave that Georgie had seen, just before the boat she was in at the time, sank. Georgie had taken in what the adults were talking about and followed the conversation with interest. "I reckon that if we have a good look down in this area over here, this is where, if we are going to find anything at all, then that is where it will be." Bruce indicated the area on the chart that was about one hundred and seventy-five to two hundred yards in length.

"How are we going to do this?" Charlie inquired.

"We both take gear out with us and Seabobs. One of us will have to remain with Georgie but monitor the other from the surface. I think that we should also pick up some scallops and see if we can catch a fish and then have a braai on the beach this evening. What do you think girls?"

"What is a braai Dad?" Georgie inquired.

"A braai is like a BBQ Georgie." Charlie replied to the question. "And yes, I think that would be a perfect idea, sweetheart."

"Yeah!" Georgie exclaimed with delight.

After a light lunch, they loaded the required equipment that they needed into *Willie* and finally got into their wet suits. As usual, Charlie got to drive with Bruce and Georgie sitting up in the bow. It wasn't long until they got to the point where Bruce thought that the trough started. Sitting on the edge of *Willie* Bruce got his BCD on, did his final check and somersaulted backwards with *Bobbi* held to his chest. Bruce returned briefly to the surface, gave the international sign for okay and started for the ocean floor seventy feet below him. Moving slowly and allowing *Bobbi* to tow him, Bruce started to carry out a zigzag search.

Bruce found her. She was lying on her starboard side in seventy feet of water, the visibility wasn't good, only about thirty feet at best and she was partially lying under what appeared to be a bit of a ledge. She would have been impossible to see with a sonar detector, let alone visually from the surface. Bruce recognised her as a Prestige motor cruiser. As he swam around to the stern, he saw her name and port of registration. If it were possible with a large mouthpiece in, Bruce would have gasped with surprise. A cold shiver ran down his spine and the hairs on the back of his head stood on end. He overcame the primal instinct of kicking for the surface and re-regulated his breathing. The boat wreck was the *Annabella* and Puerto de Banus was her port of registration. Remembering that it had only been a few weeks previously that he had been on that boat with Charlie, Mike and Sheila Dunn as well. He hardly recognised the boat, the Bimini, aerials, sat dome and radar had all gone completely, she really looked a mess. Looking at the boat it seemed very eerie the only sounds that he could hear were predominantly of water and the sound of his exhaled bubbles of air rising to the surface. Bruce took in the current that was causing the kelp to wave in the water, checking his dive computer he saw that he had another twenty minutes of bottom time and at the moment a five minute stop at fifteen feet. Telling himself that there was nothing in the wreck that would harm him, he tethered *Bobbi* to a rail, removing the LED flashlight from his belt. Bruce willed himself in through the stern of the main deck and cast the torch around in the gloom. Cautiously he then pulled himself into the forward VIP cabin and came literally face to face with a corpse. After having got over the initial shock, he divested the corpse of the bag that it had around its shoulder but left the AK 47 around the dead person's neck. He then cast around briefly for anything else of interest, it was then that he spotted an ammunition box. Removing his finds with him, Bruce thought to check the master cabin, fully expecting to find yet another corpse, he was, to say the least, utterly relieved not to have done so. He did however find another AK 47 and a briefcase, removing the briefcase out beyond the stern of the *Annabella*, Bruce considered his next move. Deciding to leave the heavy goods, the two assault rifles and the ammunition box behind. Bruce went in search of rope or line, he found exactly what he was looking for in one of the forward storage bins, there must have been a good seventy yards of mooring line. Removing the mooring line, he discovered the body of the owner of the *Annabella*. He had been stabbed in the chest. Pushing the body back down into the storage locker, he secured it again. Bruce attached one end to the stern rail and after he had retrieved *Bobbi* he started slowly for the surface, making sure that his ascent did not exceed the speed of the smallest air bubble. Stopping at fifteen feet, he noted that he still had a five-minute decompression. Bruce could hear the gentle murmur of the Rotax engine and the sound of the impellor drawing water through the thrust system of the tender above him on the surface.

After Bruce had disappeared beneath the surface, Georgie with a mask on, stuck her head over the edge of the boat to watch Bruce fade into the depths of the sea. Charlie created a waypoint from their current position and slowly continued to follow the trace of bubbles Bruce left behind. As Bruce descended further, it became more difficult to trace his progress from the surface. Charlie had calculated that Bruce would probably only have enough air for a forty-five to fifty-minute dive, depending on the final depth that he was going to be working at. Charlie was fully confident that Bruce was a more than competent diver and had fully and swiftly embraced the new technology.

"Mum! There are bubbles over there." Georgie indicated with her arm to a point some fifty yards from *Willie*.

"Well done, darling. Charlie exclaimed. She continued to watch the bubbles, they weren't moving, which was a sure sign that Bruce was static in the water and very probably decompressing. She edged the tender a little closer remaining twenty feet from where the bubbles were breaking on the surface, not wishing to intimidate him by parking *Willie* directly over him. Georgie had her mask on again and with her backside stuck in the air and her head just under the surface, twenty seconds later, spluttering she lifted her head out took another breath of air and stuck her head back under the surface of the water.

After a further ten seconds. "I can see him, I can see him. Daddy is coming up, he waved to me." An excited, very nasal voice announced from the bow. Sure enough, five minutes later, Bruce's head broke the surface just at the stern of the tender. Bruce handed the recovered man bag and briefcase to Charlie then handed over the free end of the line.

Removing his face mask Bruce asked. "Do me a favour please hun, punch this location in as a waypoint on the plotter for me."

"You found it then?" Charlie asked.

"Yes and you will never believe it either, it was the *Annabella*, the boat that we looked at with the Dunns." Bruce replied. Shucking his gear and stowing it in the bow. Swiftly he recovered the end of the rope and attached a buoy to it to mark the position of the wreck. "I need to get hold of Miguel as soon as possible as well and he doesn't need to know anything about this stuff." He indicated the results of his dive.

"I agree." Charlie accepted.

The production of the two bags had immediately quietened Georgie. Noticing this Bruce asked. "Are you alright sweetheart?" He placed an arm around Georgie.

"Those are the same bags that the men had on the boat when the big wave came and we sunk."

"I know sweetheart. But now I have them and those men won't be able to hurt you or anyone ever again." Bruce hugged her into him. "Georgie, how many men were on that boat?"

"There were three in all." She stated matter of factly. "There was one driving the boat and there was one in a room at the front of the boat and there was one guarding me near the back door. I was outside being sick when the big wave came."

"Thank you for being so brave my darling. I think that you having been outside when that big wave came was probably one of the reasons that you are still alive today." Bruce hugged her and kissed her forehead. "C'mon darling let's go home." Bruce said to Charlie who was still at the helm. It was a good three hundred and fifty yards from where the *Annabella* had sunk to the entrance of the cove and a further seventy-five yards to the point at where Bruce had found Georgie.

Bruce made the phone call to Miguel as soon as they got back to the *Cape*, then returning to the tender, he removed the two articles and placed them in the workshop. With the help of Charlie and Georgie, Bruce rinsed off his dive gear, placed his cylinder on charge. Fish was going to be off the menu tonight, Bruce mentioned this to Charlie who had agreed and also to the sharing of the discovery of the bodies with Georgie. Just over an hour after the phone call to Miguel, Bruce could hear the big marine diesels up the coast. Jumping into *Willie* and leaving the two girls on the *Cape*, Bruce sped out of the cove to meet the Guardia Civil. Two divers were already prepared when the *Rio Jenil* approached the tender. Bruce gave Miguel as much information as he could, also passing on the new information that he had gleaned from Georgie earlier in the afternoon.

Within a half-hour, Bruce had returned to the *Cape* picking up his little battery-powered chain saw and the BBQ bucket. He put them in *Willie*, then went to look for Georgie.

"I think she went below." Charlie volunteered as she continued to prepare some Rib Eye steaks and defrost some asparagus.

The cabin door was closed, Bruce knocked. "Georgie, may I come in, please?" Bruce respectfully waited for her reply.

"I suppose." Georgie replied from behind the door.

He found her sitting on her bunk, looking through a book, seemingly withdrawn. "Hey, what's up with my little tinker?" Bruce asked in an upbeat manner. "I thought that you might like to come ashore with me and gather up some wood for our braai this evening?" Bruce sat down next to her on the bunk.

Almost dejectedly, Georgie started. "I felt that my life only started when you rescued me, it was almost feeling like being born again and you and Mum have just done so much to help me and I just thought that we had been all together for all of my life." She turned and put her arms around him. "And then this afternoon, I remembered that it wasn't true and that I had lived a life before and it hadn't been a very nice life at all."

There was a gentle knock on the open cabin door. "May I come in, please?" Charlie asked as she entered the cabin and sat down on the opposite bunk to the one that Bruce and Georgie were sitting on.

"Well, the thing is, sweetheart, we know that you didn't have a nice life before, but you see it is also very important that we catch these people who did what they have done to you. I have to say that you have been very lucky. If there hadn't been a storm, heavens know where you would be by now and just think how easily you may have drowned or died from hypothermia." This remained a mystery to Bruce, currently, Georgie's ability to swim was only for a distance of twenty yards and that was an improvement from what she had initially been able to swim. The question remained as to how she had managed to get across over four hundred and twenty-five yards in a storm-tossed sea. Bruce had his suspicions.

Continuing, Bruce added. "These people have used children to benefit their cause and they will continue to exploit other young children in the future." Bruce explained quietly and matter of factly to Georgie. "Your real life did start just over a week ago or however long ago it was, but remember that it has also changed our lives forever as well. What you also need to know my little darling, is that for Charlie, now your Mum, you are a little miracle and one day, I am sure that she will explain that to you." Georgie squeezed Bruce as she nodded her head against his chest. "Yes, there are going to be times like this afternoon when you will remember the distant past and it will hurt you, but you will have to learn to take it on the chin so to speak. The best part about it though, is that as time goes by, it will get easier and for what it's worth your Mum and I will be here for the foreseeable future to keep you safe." Sitting up and drawing Georgie onto his lap and kissing her cheek he continued. "Now are we going to have a braai tonight? Because if so, then we need to go and gather some firewood so that we can go and cook some steaks and some mealies."

Turning to face Bruce, Georgie asked. "Dad, what are mealies?"

"Corn on the cob, with lashings of butter and salt and pepper and I am going to eat them all up like I am going to eat you all up right now." Bruce pretended to eat her and reduced Georgie to a giggling, wriggling and squirming wretch. "C'mon then, let's go gathering wood." Bruce gathered up the child into his arms and gently squeezed her into his chest. "No one is ever going to hurt you again. No one!"

All three of them piled into *Willie* and as usual with Charlie at the helm, made for the beach. Once on the beach, Bruce showed Georgie the type of wood and kindling that they would need to start the fire. Once they had collected sufficient wood, Bruce demonstrated to Georgie how to set the fire before finally allowing her to light it. Once alight, Bruce showed Georgie how to carefully feed it with the larger pieces of the driftwood that they had collected. This was a skill that had been taught to Bruce when he was only five years old, by a Matabele warrior in a country which was then called Rhodesia. Then using a single burner gas stove, which amongst other things, had been brought over from the *Cape*, Bruce prepared to cook the sudsa in a heavy-based pan. In the interim time, Charlie, having defrosted some cobs of corn prepared these as a starter to their feast. Once cooked thoroughly, Bruce showed Georgie how to skewer the cob at either end and then put butter, salt and pepper so allowing the butter to melt over the corn cob. Then munching the corn directly off the cob. The process was then concluded by finally soaking up what was left of the butter onto the bare cob and sucking it clean. The eating of the corn on the cob was concluded with much hilarity as Georgie ended up with as much of the butter and corn smeared around her face and dripping down her front as went into her mouth. Following this, Bruce took a very happy Georgie down to the water's edge and with much laughter, did his best to remove what was left of the corn on the cob and butter from her face.

As the flames of the fire died down and the embers glowed, Charlie put the steaks on to cook, turning them only once after a few minutes. Allowing the steaks to rest, Bruce and Charlie served the bredie and sudsa onto the three plates and then accompanied them with the steaks. They had taken out a bottle of The Guv'nor with them and although Georgie had seen Bruce and Charlie drink wine on numerous occasions before, it was with some surprise that on this occasion she appeared curious, so Bruce allowed her a sip from his beaker. This resulted in her making a face and saying that it tasted sour. Georgie, followed up by rinsing her mouth with two big swallows of squash from her beaker.

Bruce commented to Charlie. "Well, I think that we can safely say that our wine stocks are safe for the foreseeable future, darling." Between them, they gathered the dishes and pan, ready to put back into *Willie* in readiness for the return to the *Cape*.

Allowing their meal to digest before they made their way back to the *Cape* Bruce and Charlie were sitting on the beach blanket, Georgie was down by the water's edge drawing shapes in the wet sand with a stick, her full belly a little distended showing through the bikini bottom and butter streaked T-shirt that she was wearing. She appeared utterly absorbed in what she was doing, humming away to herself. Bruce was trying to interpret what the tune was when he caught sight of the dolphins slowly coming into the calm waters of the cove. "Georgie." Bruce called quietly over to her. She looked up to where Bruce and Charlie were sitting on the blanket. "The dolphins have just come into the cove sweetheart." Although Georgie had been introduced to the dolphins before, she had been very nervous about them and had never been in the water with them. Bruce got up and walked down the beach, taking Georgie's hand in his, he looked down to see what she had been drawing in the sand. What he saw made Bruce gasp in amazement. As plain as day, the drawing in the sand consisted of the outline of a dolphin with a smaller 'stick person' on the dolphins back and there were other dolphin drawings around the main one. Charlie realising that something wasn't quite right, had also got up off the blanket and was on her way down to join Bruce and Georgie.

"You really need to see this, Charlie." Bruce exclaimed as he picked Georgie up.

"Oh my God!" Exclaimed Charlie. "Does this mean what I think it means?" Addressing Georgie, she continued. "Sweetheart, did the dolphins rescue you on the day that the boat sank?"

By this time Georgie had Bruce in a headlock with her arms around his neck and her head on his shoulder. "I think so, I held on to a big fish, it came up under me and then I saw the rocks where Daddy found me and I got off. But I was really scared and didn't remember until now, I guess."

"That's all right sweetheart. That doesn't matter." Charlie put her arms around the child and Bruce as well. "The dolphins are our friends. Daddy helped one, the one we call Daphne. We were swimming here in the cove one day when they came into the cove and Daphne came right up close to Dad. It was then that we could see a fishhook stuck in her fin, so he took the hook out of her fin for her and now every time we go swimming, Daphne doesn't leave his side."

Bruce gently put Georgie down on her feet but continued to hold her hand. As Georgie got knee deep, she stopped, however, Bruce continued into the water until he too was knee-deep. Daphne didn't need any encouragement, she came straight up to Bruce for a tickle. Lifting her head out of the water, she emitted a series of clicks and squeaks then nodded her head up and down in a greeting to Bruce. The main bull in the pod, Dougie was not quite so forward as Daphne, but on this occasion, he came in very close to Bruce, closing to within about three feet. This was the closest that he had ever been to Bruce, he lifted his head out of the water and looked directly at Georgie. Bruce stood up and his suspicions were almost confirmed as he spoke to Georgie. "Georgie, this is Dougie and I think that it was Dougie who gave you a ride from where the boat you were on sank. I think that it was Dougie who really saved your life. Would you like to come and say hello to him?" Bruce reached back towards the nervous child. "I'll hold you all the time, all you need to do is just pat him gently on his head, you see just the same as I am doing for Daphne."

Georgie extended her arms up towards Bruce for him to hold her. Bruce picked her up easily and clutching her around her waist leaving her arms free. Dougie, almost sensing that the child was nervous, approached slowly and then raised his head. Gingerly, Georgie reached forward and timidly patted the dolphin's head. A lifetime of friendship was cemented at that moment and a giant step for this little girl, who had never even been to the seaside before until she had found herself washed up on the south coast of Spain. Dougie raised his head, gave a little squeak and two clicks and then backed off from the shore. The next thing they saw was that Dougie had charged out into the middle of the cove jumping out of the water to a height of more than twice his length, five seconds later he repeated the jump. Following a further five seconds after the second, he again repeated the jump, but this time with a somersault thrown in. They were all surprised at the display that the dolphins produced, Georgie with her arms held up in the air squealing with delight. Daphne nudged Bruce's leg, he bent down still holding Georgie and patted her raised head and following Bruce's example Georgie also patted Daphne's head. Daphne emitted a single squeak and two clicks and then went storming out into the cove to join the other cavorting dolphins.

Returning to the *Cape*, a tired and elated Georgie was sent straight below to her cabin for her shower and hair wash. Charlie organised the galley and the washing up while Bruce went down to the workshop area to inspect the contents of the briefcase that he had removed from the *Annabella*. The briefcase wasn't waterproof and the first thing that caught Bruce's attention was the Russian Makarov pistol and moderator. This had just made his day, the downside to it was that the ammunition would probably be ruined. Carefully Bruce cleared and stripped the weapon placing all the parts in a container and sprayed them all with WD40. Then unloading the magazine, he stood the seventeen nine millimetre rounds on a piece of cotton cloth and sprayed them with WD40 as well. To some degree, this was probably a futile exercise as the ammunition didn't look as though it had been waterproofed in the first instance. Bruce then turned his attention to the sodden pieces of printed paper in some sort of Arabic language. Sourcing a length of thin nylon from the stores he rigged a line, on this, he hung the four sheets of paper, securing them in the corners with clothes pegs. He would complete the drying process in the morning with the hot air blower, should it be necessary and when he had more time. It had already been a very long day.

Returning to the salon, he found Charlie putting the finishing touches on Georgie's blond tresses, wearing one of her new nightdresses she looked really tired. "How's our little urchin then?" Bruce addressed Charlie.

"I think that we have a very tired little girl here." Charlie replied.

"I am not really that tired." Interjected Georgie with a yawn.

"Oh, really and who do you think you are trying to fool with that huge yawn?" Bruce responded with a smile, sitting down on the sofa.

"Oh, Daddy darling." Georgie started. "Would you read me a story, please?"

"Mmmm!" Bruce cupped his chin in his hand, with his forefinger extended up to his cheek. "Let's see now. I'll tell you what I'll do is this, I will tell you a story instead. How's that? But only and only if you promise that you will be a very, very good girl tomorrow. Okay?"

"Okay!" And with a couple of skips and a giggle, she hopped up onto Bruce's lap. "What's the story about?" Georgie asked.

"It's about a little boy, a long, long time ago." Bruce started, settling Georgie on his right knee and laying her back in the crook of his right arm with her head against his right bicep. "There was a little boy and he was born in a land far from here, where there were people of different colours, there were black people, brown people, yellow people and white people as well and they all lived happily together. This little boy was very lucky because he had two mothers and two fathers." Bruce continued for another minute then he felt as much as heard Georgie's change of breathing pattern as she fell asleep, her head lolled into the slight gap between his upper arm and his chest.

Bruce looked over and just grinned at Charlie, who smiled back in return, remembering the conversation she'd had with Ron and the photographs on the wall of the study at the bungalow on Hayling Island. "Would you like me to take her down now?" Charlie asked getting up off her seat.

"No, it's fine." Bruce replied softly. "It just goes to show what a boring storyteller I am. I'll let her get a bit deeper first, then I should be able to manage her. But a drink wouldn't go amiss, please."

Charlie smiled and went to the sideboard where she poured the two Glenmorangie's with water. "You know, it was only a very few weeks ago that someone here said that they had done their bit of parenting and now it was his time to enjoy life." Charlie handed Bruce his drink, which he took in his left hand.

Bruce smiled at Charlie remembering the incident well. "Cheers!" He said, taking a sip of the whisky. "Anyway, who could have foretold that this little bundle of joy was going to get washed up in our cove." Bruce looked down lovingly at the sleeping face.

Charlie stroked Bruce's cheek with the back of her right hand. "So, what were you up to in the workshop?" She enquired.

Bruce told her about the find and the documents written in what appeared to be Arabic and then explained his intentions to photocopy them and then save them as document files. From there he could cut and paste the documents onto any one of several free websites that carried out Arabic to English translations. It might or might not give them a clue of some sorts as to what had lain in wait for Georgie's future.

Determining that Georgie was well and truly sound asleep, Bruce got up from the sofa holding the child in his right arm and with Charlie preceding him, took her down to her cabin. Charlie had pulled the covers back and Bruce gently laid Georgie down on the bunk, kissing her on the cheek. Georgie instinctively, still sound asleep, rolled over onto her left side. Pulling the light covers up around Georgie, Charlie also kissed her goodnight on the cheek and followed Bruce out of the cabin, leaving the door just ajar. The dimmed blue LED night light just gave sufficient light for her to see by, should she awake in the night.

Bruce decided that he would shower, so he carried on into their cabin. Charlie went back to the main deck and closed down all the lights and made sure that accesses were secured for the night.

It had been a warm evening and Charlie was still wearing her skimpy shorts and a thin T-shirt when she returned to the cabin. This was just as Bruce was exiting the shower, towel in hand. It was very evident that Charlie wasn't wearing a bra, her nipples seemed huge as her breasts stretched the fabric of the T-shirt. She took the towel from Bruce and turning him around started to dry his back, then still facing his back, she slowly moved the towel around and started to dry his chest, the thin material of the T-shirt not doing much to mask the feeling of her breasts pushing into his back. Charlie moved the towel down across Bruce's abdomen and then down to his genitals, caressing them gently with the towel. Bruce's penis very quickly became erect and he turned within her arms deftly removing the T-shirt and then engaged willing lips and tongues. The towel and Charlie's shorts seemed to drop to the deck at a similar time, Bruce tenderly pushed Charlie backwards out of the bathroom until she caught the back of her legs on the side of the bed, causing her to fall backwards onto it. As Charlie tumbled backwards, Bruce neatly removed Charlie's last vestment of clothing and getting between her parted legs lay down on top of her. Willingly Charlie raised her knees allowing Bruce's penis full access to her womanhood. Their passionate lovemaking continued urgently and silently for a further five minutes. With both of them more than aware that they now shared the boat with another soul, finally reaching their mostly silent climaxes together. It was the first time that they had made love since Georgie had joined them on the *Cape* and they lay still, panting with the exertion of their lovemaking, letting their sweat and love juices mingle. Relieving Charlie of his 'dead weight' on top of her, Bruce propped himself up on his elbows. "I love you, Charlie Williams."

"I love you too, Bruce Williams." Charlie lifted her head and kissed him on the mouth. The slight abdominal effort of lifting her head caused Bruce's penis to slip out from her vagina. "Oops! I hadn't meant for that to happen." Charlie looked disappointed. Rolling sideways, Bruce gave Charlie a brief kiss and went into the bathroom, returning with some tissue following which he then took a second very brief shower. Ten minutes later Charlie joined Bruce in bed and with Charlie spooning Bruce, they were both very quickly sound asleep.

CHAPTER 29

Going back to the 19th of April, the *Star* docked in the small port of Kaslik to the north of Beirut. A very unhappy Abadi had received news that not only was the one piece of merchandise that he really wanted and that was extremely valuable to him hadn't turned up, but now his contacts in Spain had disappeared off the face of the earth as well. He had contacted Krawiec, the Polish couple, that had first picked up Georgie, by email in the usual fashion and had been assured that the girl had been dropped off with Abdullah on the 9th of April. That was in plenty of time for them to make the meeting with Van de Niekerk on the 12th of April. He found this very strange, especially as Van de Niekerk joined the *Star* on the 10th of April, looking for a passage to Lebanon.

Breaking his own rules completely, which was to distance himself as far as possible from the *Star* and its crew, Abadi needed to speak to Azil firsthand, agreeing to meet him and Van de Niekerk at the Paradox Restaurant, just off Seaside Road. Abadi was not on his own. One of his private security guards discreetly accompanied him, another was at the wheel of the Range Rover that had stopped at the front door of the restaurant and was now discreetly parked where the driver had a good view of the restaurant door and its approaches. Abadi ensured that he was at the meeting point well before the arranged time, thus ensuring that he retained command of the situation. Speaking to the manager, he ordered coffee and instructed him that he would be having a short conference with two men and that they were not to be bothered. The other two men would not be wanting any refreshment and were not to be approached, under any circumstances.

When Azil and Van de Niekerk arrived at the meeting, Abadi did not rise from his seat, nor did he offer to shake hands. Van de Niekerk looked pale, despite a Mediterranean cruise aboard the *Star*. Abadi invited the men to sit, then turning to the master of his ship, he asked. "So, Captain Azil, how is that you have not managed to bring me the English girl from Spain?"

Azil had rehearsed the speech he was about to deliver to Abadi and did so meticulously accounting for every minute of time. Abadi did not interrupt him once. However, the loss of that particular piece of trade was worth seven hundred and fifty thousand dollars US. She had been promised to an oil-rich Sheikh in Djibouti who had a special penchant for young English blonds, even though she was only seven years old she would be groomed, until the time of her first period. Once Azil had finished, he turned to Van de Niekerk.

"So, Mr Van de Niekerk, how is it that you have come to require passage to Lebanon on my ship?"

Van de Niekerk inadvertently scratched at his crotch as he came to explain the circumstances of his wounding, arrest and subsequent necessary urgent departure from Spain. Abadi listened, again not interrupting. When Van de Niekerk had finished, Abadi, pondered what he had been told, then putting his first question to Van de Niekerk. "So, why was it that you were trying to rob the Englishman and this Amazon woman?"

Reluctantly, Van de Niekerk recounted the information that he and Pedro had uncovered regarding a powerful weapon and the possibility that the charts would lead to the location of said weapon.

"So, do you think the charts are still on this boat?" Abadi questioned.

"It is possible." Van de Niekerk replied. "The verdamte English man gave some charts to the police, so I was told. But I also know that he had copies made."

Abadi considered his next question. "Do you know where this Englishman and his boat are now?"

"Yes." Van de Niekerk replied. "During my passage here, I was able to make some discreet telephone enquiries. I believe that he is in isolation at someplace to the west of Marbella on the south coast of Spain."

"In your absence, would this man Pedro have continued your business for you?" Abadi enquired.

"Yes, Sir." Van de Niekerk thought that it might stand him in better stead so, decided to show him some respect. "My enquiries regarding my boat and Pedro say that he sailed from Puerto Banus on the evening of the 9th of April, since then neither he nor my boat have been seen." Van de Niekerk wriggled, trying to ease the itching around the base of his penis and rectum. "Three nights after the disappearance of my boat, the night that I was due to meet your representative Abdul Abdulla, it appears that another boat and its owner also disappeared. The Spanish police have apparently recovered some bodies and have related this to the disappearance of the second boat."

Considering his next question carefully, Abadi then asked. "If I were to promise you a good deal, would you be prepared to return to Spain, with my trusted servant Azil, locate this Englishman and his boat and deliver me these charts that you have mentioned?"

Van de Niekerk pondered his reply, Abadi could be a very useful friend and he certainly needed some sort of shelter and an income. "Yes, Sir." He replied. "But I would ask that I need to see a doctor as a matter of great urgency. I will need a passport to be able to go ashore in Spain and I will also need some Euros to loosen the tongues of my informants." Van de Niekerk concluded.

Abadi considered the request and then replied. "So be it." Turning to Azil. "My friend Captain Azil, you will take on a cargo of cloths and spices and deliver them to the Spanish port of Motril. This will allow you, Mr Van de Niekerk, to go and make some further enquiries to satisfy our end requirements. You will now both return to the ship and will remain aboard. You will sail as soon as all requirements have been met. Go now."

Bruce woke when Georgie crept into bed with them. He pulled her over his body and settled her between them, then turned over so that he was lying on his back. Georgie settled herself into the crook of his arm and almost straight away was sound asleep. It was six o'clock according to his bedside clock and the chronometer on the far bedroom wall next to the television. He continued to doze for the next hour and a quarter. Finally, deciding he couldn't sleep anymore and certainly with a whole lot of variables going through his mind, the lovemaking from the previous evening and of course how did Georgie come to be here and the circumstances of her arrival. Quietly, Bruce got out of bed, retrieved his clothes from the wardrobe and used the bathroom of the spare double cabin for his morning ablutions.

Bruce's first stop was the galley, where he quickly got the kettle on and made ready for his first brew of the day. Whilst waiting for the kettle to boil, he opened the blinds and the rear salon door and went and stood in the cockpit. He knew that the sun was well up, but as yet, it wouldn't have reached into the cove. The sky was a beautiful azure blue with not a single cloud in it. A gentle swell was running in the cove and a couple of the small black-headed Mediterranean Gulls were being a little vocal. Generally, they were nowhere as much of a nuisance as the Herring Gulls in the UK, added to which there was also the sound of the water lapping gently on the beach. It appeared to Bruce that the world was at peace with itself or, certainly as far as this little cove was concerned.

Bruce returned to the galley and finished making his tea, stirring it and leaving the spoon in the sink. Taking his tea, he made his way aft and into the workshop area. First, he carefully examined the flimsy Arabic typewritten pages it was very fortunate that the typescript didn't seem to have run very much at all. They were almost dry, finding his hot air blower, which would normally be ideal for stripping varnish, he selected the lowest heat setting and proceeded to give the four sheets of paper a blow-dry. The process only took about fifteen minutes to complete, after which he carefully removed them. Gathering them up with his now empty tea mug, he went back up through the salon to the chart station, where he switched on his computer and the printer/ scanner.

Placing the first page onto the scanner glass, he returned to the computer, selected to scan as a document and to save it as a word document. The scanner whirred and the progress bar continued until the scan was completed. Whereupon the document opened automatically. Selecting all the script, Bruce right-clicked and selected the 'copy' option, then opened his Google browser and started typing in Arabic to Engl. The browser automatically completed Arabic to English Translator, selecting this, the web page opened and right at the top was a box inviting him to enter the text. With the cursor on the box, Bruce right-clicked the mouse button, selected the 'paste' option and the Arabic text was entered. Almost immediately, the translation appeared in the box opposite. Bruce copied this and pasted it into the word document below the Arabic transcript. It was an email and read along the lines of.

Date: 03/04/20
To: abdul.abdullah@gmail.com
Copy To: ben.azil@gmail.com
Subject: Meeting for Disposal of Goods.

My Faithful Servant.

Proceed to the town of Puerto Banus on the south coast of Spain near Marbella. There you will meet with the infidel Van de Niekerk. We have used this man before and he is to be trusted. At 21:00 on the 12th day of April. The boat is called 'Esmeralda'. You will pay him the agreed sum of €2,500 and you will ask him to convey you to the following grid reference N36° 23.988' W4°54.023'. There you will hand over the blond merchandise to the Captain of the ship 'Star'. Upon approval, you will then return to the shore and await further instructions.

May Allah be with you.
Ben Yousif Abadi

Bruce repeated the exercise with the two other documents which again looked as though they were emails.

Date: 08/04/20
To: ben.azil@gmail.com
Copy To: abdul.abdullah@gmail.com
Subject: Collection of Merchandise.

My faithful Servant.

You are to proceed to the following coordinates. N36° 23.988'
W4°54.023'. There you will rendezvous with the motor yacht
'Esmeralda' at 01:00 hrs on the morning of the 12th day of April after
you have disposed of your alternate cargo from Algeria at a safe
distance away from the co-ordinates above.

You are to ensure that this merchandise is in pristine condition and
it is to remain that way. You will then make all haste to the Port of
Kaslik where you will disembark all goods. We will hopefully see you
approximately on the 19th day of April.

May Allah be with you.
Ben Yousif Abadi

Date: 24/03/20
To: krawiec.m@gmail.com
Copy To: abdul.abdullah@gmail.com
Subject: Collection of Human Merchandise.

My Faithful Servant.

You are to proceed to the town of Basingstoke in Hampshire, England.

To the south of the town of Basingstoke on the A30 road, there is
an area for parking where there are no cameras. On the 27th of this
month, at 19:00 hrs local time you will meet with a white European,

he will have some merchandise for you. You will pay him £5,000 after you have examined the goods, you will convey the merchandise to Spain where you will deposit the goods at the usual meeting point with Abdul Abdullah. The money has been forwarded to your business account. Further instructions will follow.

Thank you, my friend.
Ben Yousif Abadi

Bruce was just about to start putting the emails into chronological order when he heard her before he saw her. Georgie came pounding up the stairs in her bikini bottoms and a T-shirt, spotting Bruce at the computer in front of the chart desk, changed direction and without diminishing her speed jumped onto Bruce. She started by nearly strangling him and then pulling away slightly took hold of the whiskers on the side of his cheeks and pulled his lips onto hers. "Morning Daddy!" she said with excitement. "Isn't it a lovely day. What are you doing with those things?" Georgie pointed at the documents on the chart table.

Charlie followed at a little more sedate pace, over Georgie's head, he could see that she was wearing one of those enigmatic smiles that just said. 'I am on top of the world. Again'. She encompassed both Bruce and Georgie, kissing Bruce on the top of his head and then pulling it into her bosom.

Georgie protested. "You two are really weird again this morning." Slipping off Bruce's lap, she turned and with her hands on her hips and watched the adults hug each other.

Charlie turned to her. "C'mon honey, you can join in too." Georgie didn't need another invitation. Looking over Bruce's shoulder, Charlie could see exactly what Bruce had been doing. "Any luck?" She whispered in his ear. Bruce just nodded his head gently against her bosom. "Right, let's go find some breakfast then." She spoke to Georgie.

Breakfast completed, dishes washed, dried and put away, Charlie got Georgie started on some arithmetic which she had printed out for her and then came forward to where Bruce had resumed work at the chart table.

"So, what have you got, my lover?" Charlie asked.

"It seems that Georgie was sold off by a person, possibly her father, on the 27th of March. On the 12th of April, she was supposed to be met by none other than our Van de Niekerk who was supposed to convey her out to sea, to meet with a ship called the *Star*. Van de Niekerk was going to be met by a person or persons who weren't her initial abductors. Van de Niekerk's boat the *Esmeralda* is mentioned. But as far as we know, Van de Niekerk is in custody, having been shot in the leg. The other thing we know is that it wasn't the *Esmeralda* that conveyed Georgie. It was the *Annabella*." Charlie nodded her head in understanding. Bruce continued. "There is a hell of a lot going on here that we don't know about."

"What about this piece of paper here?" Charlie asked, picking up the fourth page. "Hang on, this is in Spanish, it is a receipt with a Spanish address on it."

"Charlie, we need to get this information to someone who can do something about it." Bruce started to stand up. "Problem is I can't go to Miguel and say. 'Oh, by the way look what I have just found.' Can I?" Bruce paused. "Got it! I'll fire this off to Brian Stone. He can say that it came from GCHQ, then he can feed it back to Miguel and the Spanish authorities. I'll do it as a report and send off copies of the originals as well as the translations."

"Great idea." Charlie remarked. "I'll get back to her ladyship back there." She indicated Georgie, who was ignoring the adults and was concentrating on solving the problems that had been set for her.

Bruce had a brief conversation over the sat phone with Brian before sending off the report via email. Then he phoned Mike Dunn, informing him of the discovery of the copies of the emails of which he agreed to send him as well. At the same time, Brian updated Bruce on what had happened to Mitch. She had mystically turned up in court and had been sentenced to a minimum of five years in prison, where it seemed that she had unfortunately taken her own life. All the manufactured evidence against Charlie's parents and a half dozen other people had been recovered and destroyed. All parties concerned had been duly and very mysteriously notified. Bruce's next phone call was to his very grateful father-in-law.

Bruce spent the remainder of the morning on the computer sending out various emails with regards to his discoveries and the translations. Then caught up with his own and family correspondence. Shortly after Georgie's adoption, Bruce and Charlie had notified all their families with regards to the addition of Georgie to the family and had sent them pictures. One in particular, that he had added into the current correspondence was of the three of them in a selfie on the foredeck sunning themselves. Bruce had also included a head and shoulder close up of a smiling, slightly freckle-faced Georgie wearing Bruce's 'Captains hat'. The background was the flag that Charlie had created.

Bruce had just finished his correspondence when he said. "I know you are there." He turned around in his seat and there she was, about four yards back from him. Right at the back of the salon, Charlie was standing with an 'I told you so' smile on her face. Bruce had had some quiet music on in the pilot station at the time and couldn't possibly have heard her sneaking up on him.

Georgie turned around to look at Charlie and then turned back to look at Bruce. "How do you do that?" Georgie adopted her latest stance when she was puzzled or being her seven-year-old going on seventeen, that was to stand with her feet apart and her fists on her hips, just like a little wonder woman.

"Come here." Bruce beckoned her towards him. As she approached, Bruce leant forward and picked her up and sat her across his lap. Bending his head forward he loudly sniffed at her body. "Yep! That was definitely you."

Charlie had ventured forward and was leaning against the helm seat, legs crossed. "I told you that he can smell us. He can smell me from the top of the stairs." Charlie laughed.

Georgie had gone off to do some colouring and was down at the table where she did her schoolwork in the cockpit. Bruce and Charlie were still up at the lower helm and it was Charlie that started the conversation. "I don't get it, Bruce. It is men that have hurt her in the past and yet it is always to you that she comes to first."

"Sorry, I don't really follow." Bruce looked at Charlie as he started to close down the computer.

"Well, when she sneaks into our bed in the mornings, for instance, she will always get into your side of the bed until you put her between us. Also, if something scares her, it is always to you that she runs to first. Then yesterday evening on the beach with the dolphins, she placed her entire trust and faith in you. She knew that she was safe with you. I mean, it has only been, what a little over one week now?"

Bruce pondered the question. "Numerous possibilities, I guess. One I suppose is that I was the one that got her off the rocks and saved her life and it was me that the little body was hanging onto and maybe for the first time in her mind an adult that she could trust. But then don't forget who was it that for the first time in however long, did she have a nice warm motherly body to cuddle up into. Like on that first day. So, who was it when she stubbed her toe, did she run to for consolation and because she had hurt herself? Who is it that she goes to for help with her colouring and to have her hair fixed and all the other 'mumsy' things? I think that she looks to us as any other normal child would do, parents with their strengths and abilities."

"Wow!" Charlie looked astonished. "I hadn't thought of it like that. I suppose you are right."

"Not that I feel that it is necessary at the moment. But to be frankly honest, it would take one hell of a 'trick cyclist' to get into her head and unfathom things. On the other hand, of course, it might just be that our girl is of such a mental disposition, that she has just put her past in the background. It is almost as though she has deleted all those 'cookies' and has reset her 'home page', or she has just done a 'Ctrl. Alt. Del.' In her mind."

Glancing back down the boat to make sure that Georgie wasn't aware of their discussion, Charlie replied. "I guess that there is that to consider as well. I am just wondering if, in this modern-day world, we just refer people to psychiatrists because it is the norm. That if someone undergoes a traumatic experience, they automatically have to have their lives reviewed by someone else." Pausing briefly, she checked Georgie again and then turned back to Bruce. "So how do you really feel about all this? A few weeks ago, you were all set to sail off around the world, all done with parenting. Now you are married and have an adopted daughter." Charlie smiled at him.

"I know, what a mess I have got myself into." Bruce smiled ruefully. "But right now, I wouldn't change it for the world. Anyway, I had always wanted a daughter." Bruce got up from the chart table and put his arms around Charlie and gently and longingly kissed her on the lips. On the parting of their lips, they both looked down the boat at Georgie who was staring at her adopted parents. Hand in hand they walked down the boat to the cockpit.

"Were you guys talking about me?" Georgie enquired.

"Yes, as a matter of fact, we were. We were saying what a beautiful daughter we have got." Charlie replied.

A very serious looking Georgie got down and ran around the table and hugging both of them, burst into tears. Bruce picked her up. "Hey, hey, hey! There is no need for tears now, not unless they are happy tears of course."

"They are very, very happy tears, Daddy and I have never called anyone Daddy or Mummy before now." Georgie sniffled. Charlie held out her arms and Georgie willingly went into her arms, wrapped her legs around Charlie's waist and buried her face in Charlie's neck. Bruce stepped away and smilingly just held his arms outwards and shrugged, as if to say, 'point proven'.

Once lunch was over, Bruce scanned the news channels, it was still doom and gloom over the coronavirus. President Trump was threatening the Chinese for having introduced Covid 19 and was saying that an anti-malaria drug kept the virus at bay. Bruce switched the TV off.

"It is such a lovely afternoon. Shall we go for a swim?" Bruce suggested. "Or better still, I think that it is time that Georgie learns how to drive *Willie* and the jet ski."

The expression on Georgie's face was priceless. "Do you really mean that?" Georgie had jumped up, not believing her ears. Even Charlie sat up in surprise.

"Yes, why not? You are part of this boat's crew and you should know and understand how all the equipment works. What would happen if there was an emergency and Mum and I couldn't do anything and you were the only one who could operate most essentially *Willie*?" Bruce questioned the two females.

"I think that is a great idea." Charlie responded, putting her Kindle down.

"Right, let's hop to it then, crew. Crewsavers on and let's go. Whoopee!" Bruce's enthusiasm caught on. Georgie and Charlie did a quick dance around together and then shot off to the lower helm to pick up the Crewsavers.

The instruction started with the release of *Willie's* straps, plus the removal of the cover, the lowering of the swim platform all the pre-start checks. Then the exciting bit about venting the engine bay before starting the engine. Bruce and Charlie spent an hour and a half letting Georgie get used to the handling and the driving of the Williams 435 in the cove and repeated attempts at lining back up onto the submerged swim deck in preparation for recovery. Georgie turned out to be an extremely fast learner and a natural sailor. To end the lesson, they took *Willie* out of the cove and let Georgie have some experience of driving the boat at speed and then finished off with doing some fast manoeuvring. Then it was back to the *Cape*. Once back, the coaching continued with the recovery of the tender and then the final re-fuelling and rinse down with the freshwater hose. It was at that point that the period of instruction disintegrated into mayhem with Bruce being the instigator of a water fight with the hose pipe. It was such a warm afternoon, Bruce picked up Georgie and jumped into the cove with her across his chest, Georgie squealing with mock terror as they landed in the water. Charlie had picked up the hose pipe and continued to squirt it at the two in the water.

Georgie had moved around behind Bruce and was lightly holding onto his shoulders when suddenly she changed her position and wrapping her legs around Bruce and moved her hands from his shoulders enfolded his neck in a bear hug with her arms. "Daddy, Daddy look dolphins." She whispered loudly in his ear.

Daphne raised her head out of the water and gave a squeak of greeting. Bruce reached out welcomingly and patted her head gently. "Hello, Daphne."

Turning back to Charlie, he asked. "Honey if you wouldn't mind getting our swimming goggles, we could swim to the beach and let Georgie have a play in the shallows."

"On it, Mon Capitain." Charlie replied with a mock French accent and a salute.

Whilst Charlie had gone to look for the three pairs of goggles, Bruce gently encouraged Georgie to relax and to move around in front of him, which she cautiously did, saying. "Dad, I am nervous."

"I know, sweetheart and they know as well." Bruce gentled her and encouraged her to pat Daphne as he had done.

"How do they know?" She stammered, her face six inches from his face as she looked into those blue eyes.

"Animals and especially dolphins, because they are mammals as well, are very sensitive to the type of vibes that we as humans give off. Animals also have a way of giving us humans signs if they are nervous or shy. Right now, you have Daphne and Dougie about three feet from your back and because they realise that you are nervous and unsure, they are keeping their distance from you as a matter of respect. They will also pick up on the love that I have for you and that I am also here to protect you."

Standing on the swim deck, Charlie handed down Bruce's and Georgie's goggles to Bruce then took off her top and bra, before sliding into the water. "Mum, you have gone topless." Georgie exclaimed, turning and looking at Bruce with a smile.

"You can take your top off as well if you want to, honey." Charlie replied matter of factly. Georgie didn't need a second invitation. Bruce supported the squirming child as she pulled the wet T-shirt off over her head and threw it, surprisingly accurately, onto the swim deck. Bruce again supported Georgie whilst she put her goggles on and once, he had his on, he spoke to Georgie.

"Okay Georgie, we are going to swim to the beach. Now I know that you can't swim that far, so what I need you to do is just hold on to my shoulders with your arms straight and kick gently with your feet. Okay?"

Georgie nodded her head in response and moved around behind Bruce putting her hands on Bruce's shoulders. Bruce started to swim in a slow breaststroke. Charlie was keeping pace with Bruce, on the other side of him, Dougie was keeping pace as well, but almost so close that Bruce had to swim one-handed.

"Georgie." Bruce instructed. "Very carefully reach over and take gentle hold of the base of Dougie's fin." Georgie did as she was asked. "Good girl." Bruce encouraged her. "Now move your other hand onto Dougie." Georgie did so but looked apprehensively at Bruce. "Good girl. You are now one of the very, very few people who have ever swum with a wild dolphin." And not for the first time either, he thought to himself.

Maintaining pace with Bruce but having moved far enough away from Bruce to enable him to continue the breaststroke with both arms, dolphins and humans swam towards the beach. Bruce glanced across at Georgie, her beaming smile spread from ear to ear, her long single plait of blond hair streaming out behind her. 'I should get her a mermaid suit'. Bruce thought as he turned and looked at Charlie, their fingertips brushed as they were swimming in absolute harmony. Charlie was keeping precise pace with Bruce, almost synchronised swimming, then she pursed her lips as though kissing Bruce, he returned it twice.

At five yards out from the beach, both Bruce and Charlie could stand on the firm sand, Dougie continued until they were at a point where Georgie could stand where she was waist-deep in the water. The adults were a good four yards from her when she let go of Dougie's fin and waded to the front of the dolphin and gently put her arms around his head. "I love you, Dougie."

Dougie lifted his head, gave two little squeaks, moved backwards to Bruce and nuzzled him for attention. Bruce put his left hand under Dougie's chin and with his right hand gave the dolphin a gentle scratch on his forehead. Charlie came up behind Bruce and hugged into his back, pushing her body against him and flattening her breasts into his shoulders.

They stayed on the beach for a further forty minutes playing in the shallows with the dolphins, two older mature females with their calves close to them, also started to trust the humans and were coming in closer but not quite to touching distance. Charlie noticing that Georgie was just beginning to shiver, decided that was enough for one day and they still had to swim back to the boat. As they started the swim back, Georgie was on Dougie's back, holding onto the front of the dolphin's dorsal fin, with her elbows bent and her feet streamlined out behind her. Georgie, grinning like a Cheshire cat encouraging Dougie with yells of. "Go on Dougie! Giddy up!" During the swim back out to the *Cape* Dougie took Georgie in four complete circles around the adult humans, never going any further than ten yards from them. When they got back to the swim platform, a shivering Georgie fussed Dougie kissing him on the top of his beak and gave him several hugs. Reluctantly leaving the dolphins, she got out of the water to face a quick warm freshwater rinse off that Charlie was waiting with, then divested of her bikini bottoms and wrapped around in a luxury size swimming towel.

Bruce said his goodbyes to the dolphins and lifted himself out onto the swim platform. Georgie was sat on the steps leading up to the main deck and was drying her hair.

Wrapped in their towels they sat on the steps and enjoyed the warmth of the sunshine. Wearing the towel like a sarong, Bruce finished tying down and putting the cover over the tender.

"That's really quite an inhibitive feeling." Bruce observed.

"What is hun?" Charlie asked, halfway through drying her hair.

"Wearing a sarong." Bruce finished as he completed the tie-down on the weather cover for the tender.

Charlie paused. "Yes, I can imagine." She said with a smile that created little dimples, beautifully framed by the black hair she was drying.

The afternoon passed into the evening, it was when they had finished their evening meal that Charlie inquired about plans for the next day.

"I am thinking that we should consider a 'dump day' tomorrow, the grey tank is getting pretty full again and I guess that the engines would probably benefit from a run as well."

"What's a dump day?" Georgie chipped in.

Charlie patiently explained about the necessity of disposing of their rubbish and also about having to empty the waste holding tanks on the boat and how they had done it previously some two weeks before.

"Gosh, that's a relief." Georgie said with a sigh. "I thought that everything just went straight out into the sea. That's why I couldn't understand why we went swimming around the boat."

The adults laughed, Bruce took Georgie by the hand. "Come with me sweetheart and I'll show you where the tanks are." After having had the sewage and wastewater explained to her how the system operated, Georgie then had a really good idea as to how everything worked and why it was referred to as a dump day.

CHAPTER 30

Charlie had taken Georgie down to her cabin and was saying her goodnights she was then going to go for her shower and wash her hair, leaving Bruce to finish his glass of wine.

Bruce contemplated the conversation that he had earlier had with Charlie and at the same time mentally reviewed his situation. Yes, it had been nearly some three months earlier when this beautiful young woman had come into his life. The fact that she had done so in a deceitful manner had really never mattered to him. They were now very happily married and God forbid, they even had a seven-year-old daughter.

Georgie was a bright button, she had picked up on the running of the *Cape* very quickly and life on board during the time that they had been anchored in Dolphin Cove. There were certain things that she could do on her own and certain things that she was allowed to do but under adult supervision and the one place that she was totally banned from was the engine room. She kept her bathroom clean and tidy, she kept herself hygienically very clean and could wash and dry her hair without supervision. At first, it had been apparent that she had not been taught to eat properly with a knife and fork. This was soon rectified and her table manners were now impeccable. She loved learning and was so quick to pick up on arithmetic, English and reading, she helped Charlie in the galley and could make soda bread on her own. Bruce had constructed a little wooden step that she could stand on to reach the work surface safely. She loved her long blond hair and when Charlie insisted on trimming the split ends, there were tears at first. However, following the lengthy explanation that it would help her hair grow, she readily agreed. Georgie doted on love and the sense of belonging, which she shared with her adopted parents. She enjoyed being able to touch Charlie and Bruce or ask a question at any time without rebuke and in turn thrived on the adult response that they gave in return.

She had very quickly adapted to her new life on the *Cape* and her desire to have adults that she could refer to as a Mum and Dad, this was apparent because of the speed at which she started to use the terms.

Charlie was a perfect mother and so quickly found that bond that a mother and child have. The one thing that Charlie would never have been able to experience, was that of having carried a child to term in her womb. To have gone through that very special tearing pain of giving birth and to experience the warm slippery bundle between her legs. Watching Charlie and Georgie interact was gratifying and none more so than when Charlie did Georgie's hair. The styles would vary daily. Her favourite was to have her hair plaited as per Emilia Clarke when she played the part of Mother of the Dragons in the TV series, Game of Thrones. It really did give Georgie the image of being a very young Khaleesi and it really suited her. They would sometimes sit on their own and talk quietly between themselves. It would usually be Charlie that was doing the talking and Georgie the listening, interspersed with the inevitable questions that a child would have. It was following the last of these conversations, that Georgie had approached Bruce who was sat at the computer editing photographs and put her arms around him. Bruce had lifted her onto his lap.

"I am sorry Daddy, now I know." Georgie just hugged him tightly.

Quizzically Bruce asked. "What is it that you know, sweetheart?"

Charlie, who had followed her, leaned against the helm seat and speaking quietly had said. "I have just told her about your past, I am sorry, but she did ask." A tear had rolled down her right cheek.

Bruce had given Georgie a gentle squeeze, stood up and holding Georgie in his right arm, had kissed the tear on Charlie's cheek. "That is absolutely fine." Bruce had choked back on the emotions that were welling up in his chest. 'I must be getting old and soft with all the emotions that I have been experiencing recently'. He had thought to himself.

His memory had then briefly flashed back to his early days with Sheba and Saba. The happy memories that he had shared with his sisters and parents, the special love that he and Sarah, his eldest sister, had for each other. Not forgetting the very special life that he had shared with Themba and Andiwe, his Matabele parents. The tragic losses that he had experienced, the most recent being two years ago when he had lost his first wife, Lucy, in the tragic road accident in Germany.

Continuing with the reminiscing, Bruce thought about what his original intentions had been. Okay, so Charlie had come into his life and they had got married but if this damned pandemic hadn't hit when it did, they would probably have been halfway to Greece by now and with no Georgie. In truth, he was so happy that his life had turned out the way it had, otherwise, what would have happened to Georgie. Would she have been doomed to live her life as someone's sex slave? So, now what of their future? At some time, the pandemic would pass and life would then return to some normality of sorts. What would they do? Bruce considered that he would possibly berth the *Cape* in Gibraltar for a month, then fly back to the UK to visit friends and family and introduce Georgie. He would have to consider a family car now, of course, they wouldn't be able to get the three of them into the TR6. He did like Ron's Range Rover so he thought that he might consider one of those. God knows he could certainly afford it. Should they now consider settling back in the UK and getting a proper house and seeing to Georgie's schooling? What do they learn in schools these days? When will the UK schools open again? What if the predictions of a second wave of this Coronavirus pandemic hit again? Boris Johnson had been hospitalized on the fourth of April and then discharged on the twelfth of April, he was still convalescing at Chequers, the Prime Ministers country residence.

Charlie came up the stairs and saw Bruce nursing the empty glass in his hand, obviously miles away. "Brucie baby, have you been down to say good night to Georgie yet?"

"Oh my God! No." Bruce got up from his reverie, noticing Charlie in her shorty pink robe, her hair wrapped in a towel.

Taking his wine glass from him with a knowing smile, Charlie said. "I'll have this filled up for you by the time you get back, darling."

Bruce made his way down the companionway and cautiously entered Georgie's cabin, she was almost asleep. Bruce sat on the edge of her bunk as she turned over onto her back and lifted her arms up for a hug. Bruce gently lowered his head onto her chest as Georgie wrapped her arms around his head and pulled him down to her. Bruce savoured the smell of the fresh milky almost puppy-like smell of the child. He lifted his head and gently kissed her on the lips. "Goodnight my little one, sleep tight and tomorrow we will have more adventures." Georgie turned over onto her side with a beautiful little smile and was almost immediately asleep. It brought a lump to his throat as he sat on the edge of the bunk, looking at the sweet little face in slumber. Who could ever want to hurt her?

Dump day arrived with another beautiful morning, Georgie under the watchful eye of Charlie, got *Willie* launched, Bruce got his rubbish sheet prepared and the garbage loaded into the tender and with Georgie at the helm and Charlie sat next to her, they set off for the bins. Once the rubbish bags had been humped up the beach and put into the dumpsters, Charlie decided that she would prefer to shop on her own and that Bruce and Georgie should wait with *Willie*. As soon as Bruce saw Charlie exit the store, he went and helped her with what looked like two very heavy bags. As he took the bags from Charlie, he spotted them. Carrying the bags back and placing them in the tender, Bruce returned to the store, picked up two of the beach balls and went in and paid for them, then returned to the girls waiting with *Willie*.

"Why do you want those for?" Georgie asked, her voice full of curiosity.

Charlie corrected her grammar. "It is what do you want those for, or why do you want those balls and I bet that they are for the dolphins to play with. Right?" She turned to Bruce.

"Absolutely! Correctomundo!" Bruce replied, casually tossing the balls into the boat with a smile from ear to ear.

Returning to the *Cape*, Georgie and Bruce stowed *Willie* whilst Charlie put away the shopping and made teas. After having done the checks on the engines, Bruce secured the engine room door and the access to the workshop area. Going back up to the main deck, he took Georgie up to helm with him and said. "Right, now you are going to hear sounds and motions that you are not going to be familiar with once we get underway. If at any time you feel seasick, do not worry about it, because we will slow down and Mum will get you a tablet to help settle your tummy. Okay?" Bruce started the two engines on the keys.

"I'll be alright, Daddy, I promise. I was fine in *Willie*." Georgie was determined that she wouldn't be seasick. "Oh wow! Is that the main engines running?" She asked as she felt the slight tremble through her bare feet on the deck and heard the muted burble of the big Caterpillar engines from the still open back doors.

"That certainly is" Bruce replied. "Okay, crewsavers on he instructed her as he put his own on and handed hers to her. "Georgie, I need you to stay right here for the moment. Okay?" He picked her up and sat her on the helm seat.

"Okay, Daddy darling." She grinned at him. Bruce went aft and closed the back doors of the salon, then joined Charlie and Georgie at the helm station.

"All secure?" Bruce asked.

"All secure." Charlie answered.

Bruce put the two big Cats into forward after three seconds he put them back into neutral and started winding in the anchor chains, lifting the starboard one first, then the port anchor. As the chains were being wound in, Charlie had been on the bow rinsing the chains off with fresh water. She was just finishing the starboard anchor as Bruce manoeuvred the big boat through ninety degrees to starboard and very slowly made his way across the cove. Then he turned her a further ninety degrees to port. As the bows faced the open sea, he then opened both throttles marginally and for the first time took the helm wheel. Charlie who in the meantime had returned to the pilot station stood behind the helm seat with her arms around Georgie.

"That was clever, Daddy. You turned the boat without using the steering wheel once." Georgie quipped.

"Your Dad is a very, very good boat driver, my little one and maybe one day he will teach you." Charlie commented. "How are you feeling?"

"Great!" Georgie turned slightly towards Charlie. "Daddy called me that last night."

"What, sweetheart, what did he call you?"

"He said, goodnight my little one, sleep tight and tomorrow we will have more adventures. Didn't you Dad?"

Bruce turned to look in bewilderment at her. "I certainly did, but you were almost asleep, or you were two seconds later. So do you always listen to everything I say then?"

Grinning like an imp, Georgie replied. "I always listen to everything you say, Daddy darling."

Charlie was grinning silently behind her. Once the *Cape* was out of the cove, Bruce turned her easterly for about one mile before heading her south and into deep water. Once the engines had both come up to operating temperature, he gradually opened the throttles until they were doing twenty-five knots. The *Cape Agulhas* felt like a thoroughbred beneath his feet, the engines almost sang in a bass tone, there was probably a three-foot swell running but the boat just ploughed through. Bruce glanced backwards through the stern at the perfect white V of the wake contrasting with the beautiful sea blue of the Mediterranean. Right now, he was in just the most wonderful place in the world with his two most favourite people in the world. Glancing backwards again he could see the Spanish coast was rapidly beginning to disappear behind them. Then, glancing at Georgie, who seemed to have a grin fixed from ear to ear. A bit of spray flew backwards from the bow and landed on the screen. Then a bit more and in next to no time, they were ten nautical miles offshore. Bruce started to ease the throttles back until they were at about six knots, then changed his course south-east into wind, checked the radar, there was nothing within ten miles of them and with a depth of nearly 3,000 feet under the keel.

Turning to Charlie, Bruce said. "Right, my love, you have the helm, just keep us on this course whilst I go and do the necessary." Picking up one of the portable VHF radios, he let himself out of the rear salon door and then closing it behind him, Bruce made his way down to the control panel just outside the engine room. The first thing he did was to top off the freshwater tanks with the desalination plant, twenty minutes later that was full, the next thing he did was to pump out the sewage and the greywater from the holding tanks. The whole process took nearly thirty minutes. Checking the tank levels and satisfied that he had pumped out everything, Bruce returned to the pilot station and let Charlie take the boat back to the cove, guiding her through the final delicate manoeuvres, more or less to their original position.

The next days in the cove were spent with the mornings involved with schoolwork and the afternoons with swimming, snorkelling, introducing Georgie to scuba diving. On Sunday, the 26th of April, all three were sat at the breakfast table. Charlie had got up and was just going to get Georgie's schoolbooks out when Bruce realised what day of the week it was.

"Whoaa! Hang on, girls. Today is Sunday, so no schoolwork today." Bruce exclaimed.

Charlie turned around. "Good grief, I hadn't even realised what day it was." Addressing Georgie, she said. "I am so sorry, hun, it didn't dawn on me that it was Sunday." They spent the rest of the morning lounging on the foredeck, sunbathing and reading and then went for a cooling off dip before their lunch of fresh baguette sandwiches, which Charlie had baked. After lunch, they layout in the cockpit in the shade of the flybridge overhang. Bruce and Charlie had resumed their discussions on where to spend the upcoming winter, notwithstanding they still had the summer to get through. Georgie, who had been lying next to Charlie asked. "Dad, can I have a diary on the computer, you know, one that I can write in every day, please?"

Charlie turned to Georgie. "Darling it is may I have not can I have."

Georgie looked at Charlie and said. "Daddy darling, may I have a diary on the computer, you know one that I can write in every day, please?"

The adults burst out laughing even Georgie sniggered at her own humour. When the mirth died down, Bruce said. "Yes, of course, you may my little one."

"You have called me that again Daddy, you have called me my little one again."

Concerned that he had offended her Bruce turned onto his side, lifting himself up on his elbow. "I am so sorry, sweetheart, I didn't realise that you didn't like it."

Georgie stood up from where she was kneeling on the sunbed and stepped over Charlie. "But I do Daddy. It is so special to me. It is hard for me to say how it makes me feel."

Swallowing hard, Bruce sat up and encompassed the cool little body in his arms. "Well, I suppose that we had better go and get you sorted out on the computer then."

Ten minutes later, Bruce returned to Charlie on the cockpit lounger. Charlie turned to him. "That was lovely little speech from Georgie." Charlie commented. Pausing and looking away briefly, she continued with a look of concern. "Brucie baby, just recently you seem to have been miles away at times. Is everything alright?"

"Oh, God! Yes!" Bruce replied in surprise. "Actually, I had been thinking as to just how happy I am here in our own little bubble. But then I have been considering the realities of life and to be honest, we haven't really been able to discuss our lives for the future. Mostly because we don't really know what this bloody pandemic holds for us or for our future."

"Well, to be honest, I have been thinking along the same lines." Charlie paused briefly before continuing. "I know that you relish joint decisions but if I may, I would really like to continue homeschooling Georgie."

"I don't see as to how that would be a problem. I can see the pleasure you get when you teach her something and the willingness with the way that she absorbs it. That little girl totally adores you. To send her away to school would be unkind at the moment but it isn't something we have to consider right now. The question is do we give her a choice in the matter when the time comes?"

"Oh, yes, I think so, but at the same time, we have to point out the pros and cons of making that sort of decision." Charlie smiled at Bruce.

"I have had some experience with teenage boys and granddaughters and my goodness, they are sweet and lovely up to about ten. After that, they change their spots and become totally different animals. What about you when you were starting to develop spots and hormones"?

Charlie laughed. "Oh, I was just pure sweetness and light as you would expect."

It wasn't long before Georgie arrived back with the adults. "Mum, can you come and help me, please?"

Bruce interrupted. "Georgie, how about you and I do a braaivleis tonight and give Mum the evening off. In the meantime, why don't we see if maybe I can help?"

"Oh, okay, Dad, but this is like, girlie talk." The look on her face said it all and Charlie saw it as well. Without a moment's hesitation, Charlie was on her feet. "C'mon, sweetheart, let's sort out this girlie talk thing then." The two of them made their way forwards towards the helm position. Bruce continued reading his new kindle book, two minutes later he was aware of the two girls going below to the accommodation area. 'Okay.' He thought. 'Something very girlie is going on.' When the girls re-joined Bruce some ten minutes later, he sensed Georgie's shyness at being asked the inevitable question but he chose not to ask it. "Right you are girls, what are we going to do for the rest of the afternoon?" At this point, the music on the AV changed and the Girls Aloud number Jump came on. Bruce started to simulate the dance performed by Hugh Grant in the film Love Actually. That reduced Georgie into hysterics. Charlie laughed as she joined in with Bruce performing the dance, so they started the music again from the top and Georgie joined in. Ice broken.

The rest of the afternoon was taken up with sunbathing and preparing the braaivleis for the evening and it wasn't until after Georgie had gone to bed that Charlie volunteered the information surrounding the mystery of the girlie chat from earlier. It appeared that Georgie had developed some sort of mild vaginal infection, probably caused by a grain of sand that had caused some irritation. Georgie was so concerned that it had been caused by her not keeping herself clean that she was mortified at the thought as to what Bruce and Charlie would think of her. It had, however, allowed Charlie to perform a full examination of Georgie's vagina which led Charlie on to say that there were evident signs of a brutal assault. Her hymen had been broken and that there was a lot of scar tissue. There was more than enough medical evidence to convict for rape. It was Charlie's opinion that following the assault, she must have bled a lot as well and would have been very sore for a long time. Bruce had seethed inwardly and he spent a good portion of the evening trying to work out how he could obtain retribution on Georgie's behalf.

During the next day, Miguel and the crew of the *Rio Jenil* visited the cove, and again it was Alphonso who accompanied Miguel to the beach and waited on the sandy shore for the arrival of Bruce. Bruce and Charlie decided that it was time for Miguel to meet Georgie personally, so all three of them boarded *Willie* and made for the beach. Bruce made sure that he had Georgie's passport and adoption papers with him. Maintaining their social distancing, they greeted each other warmly, Bruce introducing Georgie to the two Spanish officers.

"Miguel, we need to walk a little." Bruce invited. As they set off slowly up the beach, reaching a point just out of earshot of the others, Bruce continued. "Please don't take this the wrong way and incidentally I am not taking the piss out of you or the Spanish Government, however, an opportunity arose and it was just too good to miss." Bruce recounted the entire story relating to the charts and his subsequent discoveries. The circumstances around Georgie's appearance in Spain and her swift adoption. "Just think of the paperwork I have saved you." Bruce concluded.

They had both stopped at the far end of the beach. "I have so many questions, for you, I don't even know where to begin. You actually met with a British submarine in the middle of the night in the middle of the ocean. Who are you, Bruce, James Bond?"

"No, I used to be with the British Special Air Service Regiment." Bruce concluded modestly. "James Bond wouldn't have got through our selection process."

Slowly they made their way back towards the others on the beach, Miguel asking questions and Bruce answering them truthfully. Having got back to the other three on the beach, Bruce stood next to Charlie, with Georgie between them facing Miguel.

"So, Miss Georgina Williams." Smiling, Miguel addressed Georgie. "How are you enjoying our glorious Spanish weather so far?"

Georgie who had spent the whole time clinging onto Charlie as closely as she could shyly returned the smile. "It is lovely and warm, thank you, Sir."

Miguel knelt in the soft dry sand in front of Georgie. "Do you know Georgie? I think that you are a very lucky young lady and I wish you every happiness because I think that you really deserve it." Miguel stood back up, brushing the sand from his trousers. They carried on chatting for a further five minutes, the main topic of conversation being the Coronavirus and Van de Niekerk's escape from custody at the hospital.

CHAPTER 31

The following four days of idyllic living in the warming sunshine of Southern Spain continued aboard the *Cape Agulhas* the little family continued to cement their relationship. Bruce and Georgie shared Bruce's Kindle, the family were sat in the cool salon, Georgie was sat next to Bruce on the sofa, barely touching each other. Charlie had been sat opposite them engrossed in her Kindle, Bruce was mildly aware that Georgie was surreptitiously staring at Charlie, a puzzled look on her face. Charlie finished the chapter she was reading, put down her Kindle and made excuses about going to the galley to make preparations for their evening meal.

Once out of earshot, Bruce gently asked Georgie. "What is it that you find so interesting about Mum that you need to stare at her?"

Georgie turned and looked up at Bruce, marginally surprised at the question. "I don't know. I can't put my finger on it. It's like I recognise her from somewhere in the past, but I can't ever remember meeting her. Maybe she reminds me of someone I once knew."

Bruce smiled knowingly. "I am surprised that it has taken you so long and you still can't place her?"

"Noaah! Please help me, Daddy?"

Without a word, Bruce picked up his iPad and immediately went to the Pinterest app. In the search bar at the top of the page, he typed in 'Gal Gadot'. Numerous images of Gal Gadot in various guises of Wonder Woman leapt onto the electronic page. Georgie's mouth opened in wonderment at the revelation. Getting up from the sofa, Bruce went into the galley. "Honey, I need to borrow you for a moment please, our daughter has just worked out who you are." Charlie's bra strap length jet black hair was pulled back tight into a ponytail and finished with a single plait, revealing all the wonderful features of her Grecian goddess-like features. Her breasts were fuller than those portrayed in the image, as were the tops of her thighs and buttocks.

"Wonder Woman is my Mum." Georgie clapped her hands in delight.

"You are not quite right there Georgie, your Mum is better than any Wonder Woman. If you think about it, Wonder Woman is a comic book character, your Mum is the real deal." Bruce was stood behind Charlie pulling her into him with his arms wrapped around her waist and very conscious of the feel of her buttocks pressing into his groin.

"Aaahh! Thank you, honey." Charlie pushed gently backwards into Bruce, realising the effect it was having on him. Then turning around, she kissed him lightly on the lips.

One hundred and twenty nautical miles to the east of the Williams family and two days earlier, the *Star* was entering the port of Motril. Van de Niekerk was feeling very uncomfortable. The rash around his genitals and anus was even more painful, he was suffering attacks of diarrhoea, sweats during the night, muscle aches and the wound in his right thigh had inexplicably become infected. The 'quack' that had come aboard and examined him while they were in the port of Kaslik had taken one look at him and correctly diagnosed syphilis. There had been no necessity to take a blood sample as the patient was departing imminently. He gave Van de Niekerk a shot of Streptomycin there and then, but also supplied him with two further shots to take with him, should he require them. Had the Doctor taken a blood sample, he would have made a far more chilling discovery. Not only had Van de Niekerk contracted syphilis from the Ghanaian woman he had raped, but he had also contracted a virulent form of HIV, causing his immune system to rapidly fail. He had also used the two backup shots of Streptomycin and he still wasn't getting any better, nor would he.

He had contacted Manuel, the carpenter at Boats.co.uk, who Boshirov had used to monitor the *Cape* and to plant the tracking and listening devices. Unbeknown to both Boshirov and Tockalov, Manuel was also a friend of both Pedro and Van de Niekerk. Manuel had informed him that the *Cape Agulhas* was self-isolating in a cove to the west of Marbella, but he had also heard a rumour that they had rescued a blond English girl who was on the boat with them. Excitedly Van de Niekerk passed on this information to Azil, making his day as well.

It was Sunday, the 26th of April as the *Star* arrived in Motril, she wasn't allowed to dock, because in Spain nothing happens on a Sunday. So, they had to drop anchor one nautical mile outside the port. No one would be allowed ashore until customs and health requirements had been met, having arrived from Lebanon. Lebanon was a country that remained rife with the Covid virus, yet very little had been done, despite the announcement of a lockdown in March and then an extension in mid-April. The corrupt officials of the Lebanese Government had singularly failed to do very much to contain the pandemic. However, the Lebanese Army and Police got to practice their counter-demonstration techniques and to fire tear gas daily.

Van de Niekerk was anxious to progress with his search for the Englishman and the woman. He was subsequently strongly advised by Azil not to risk anything. Azil was more than aware that the Spanish authorities would be keeping a very close eye on the *Star* and the one thing that he could not afford to do, was to have the ship refused entry, then being sent away without discharging his cargo. In the interim period, Van de Niekerk contacted Manuel again and promised him a thousand Euro's if he could find the exact location of the *Cape Agulhas*. Manuel didn't have access to a boat, but he did have a Peugeot scooter and so with the promise of a thousand Euro's Manuel fell to his task willingly. He started at Torremolinos and began making his way westwards towards Gibraltar, diligently inspecting every cove and every inch of the coastline. By the end of Sunday, Manuel had got as far west as Puerto Banus. He resumed his search in a somewhat leisurely manner on Monday morning and towards the end of the day he had to drive into an urbanisation that was overlooking a large cove. Being rather nervous of heights, he crawled to the edge of the cliff and looked down. There he found the *Cape Agulhas* anchored in the cove. He spent five minutes watching the boat but didn't see any movement in or around her at the time. The tender was still on the raised swim deck, covered up and no lights were showing. Making a note of the name of the urbanisation, Manuel headed back home and got out a large scale map of the area and from that, he calculated a grid reference and wrote it down.

At nine o'clock on Monday morning, the *Star* was radioed to expect a boarding party of medical assessors and customs officials. Van de Niekerk was hastily hidden in the secret compartment reserved for people trafficking and was told to remain there while they were in port. The *Star* was finally allowed to berth at midday. The stevedores started to unload her and then stopped work at one o'clock, not returning until five o'clock in the evening. By the end of Monday, she had only had half her cargo unloaded. All this time, Van de Niekerk was kept in the humid airless compartment, almost justifiable really. At ten o'clock that evening, he was allowed to leave the compartment and to return to his cabin where he was instructed to remain for the remainder of the night. Van de Niekerk's mobile telephone burst into life. It was Manuel, he had found the *Cape Agulhas*, the coordinates were given to him and already the ordeal of the past twelve hours seemed to pass behind him. He summoned Azil and together they hatched a plan of attack for the next afternoon.

Onboard the *Cape*, Tuesday followed on from Monday and in the afternoon it was decided to start Georgie in her training with the 310LX jet ski. Subsequently, it was lowered into the water from the aft flybridge deck with the crane. This was a task that Bruce and Charlie accomplished on their own, not wishing to involve Georgie in crane operations just yet. Once they had the jet ski in the water and alongside the swim platform, it became apparent that Georgie was going to have difficulty in reaching the steering bars and controlling them, sitting Georgie on Bruce's lap wasn't comfortable for either of them, so they found a small cushion and sacrificed it to the purpose. Georgie spent the first hour getting used to the relative weight to power ratio that the 310 horsepower 1500cc engine produced. To be fair, not only was Georgie a very fast learner, but she had a natural ability to recognise how the mechanics of operating the machine worked. She admitted a deep respect for the machine and was reluctant to increase the speed to a point where she couldn't control it. Bruce didn't push her and continued to let her progress at her own pace, making suggestions and infrequently having to resume control. Georgie was thrilled but quickly admitted that it wasn't her favourite, only because she was too small to be able to control it adequately. Changing drivers, Charlie took over and Bruce sandwiched Georgie between them as Charlie gave them a white knuckle ride out of the cove. Returning to the cove, Bruce reset the booby trap at the entrance just as the pod of dolphins came into the cove, tying up the jet ski to the stern of the *Cape* they spent the rest of the afternoon frolicking off the beach with the dolphins and the newly acquired beach balls. The dolphins loved the balls and amazingly picked up on flicking the balls to the humans in the shallower water and to themselves. If Bruce hadn't known better, he would have said that they had been circus trained. Exhausted, they returned to the *Cape* for the evening, leaving the balls in the cove for the dolphins. Bruce decided to leave the jet ski in the water at the stern of the *Cape* until he could refuel it and stow it properly in the morning.

At Motril, it was six o'clock on Tuesday morning when the stevedores returned and completed their offloading by midday and by one o'clock in the afternoon, the *Star* was steaming west by south-west following the coast of Spain. At a little after seven o'clock in the evening the *Star* stopped her engine approximately one nautical mile from the entrance to the cove. Van de Niekerk, one of the eunuchs and a deckhand boarded a small inflatable with an outboard motor. They slowly motored their way down the coast. The antique outboard could only manage about four knots at best, so that it had gone eight o'clock in the evening when it entered the cove. Their stealth approach came to an abrupt end when there was a loud whooshing sound followed by an explosion and a flash which must have drawn the whole of the world's attention to the cove.

To the Williams family on the *Cape*, it certainly did. They had been sitting in the main salon with the doors open and a warm evening breeze blowing through the boat when the booby trap went off. They all jumped at the unexpected sound. They took in the dinghy approaching from the cove entrance towards the starboard side of the *Cape*. Bruce was the first to react. He disappeared into the workshop area and grabbed two of the flares and returning to the main deck, shouted. "Stop where you are or I will fire." Bruce threatened. The dinghy had now closed to less than one hundred yards and he could see that a European male, who looked vaguely familiar, was holding a pistol in his right hand. Bruce saw the muzzle flash and heard the crack of the bullet fly over his head, dropping one of the flares onto the deck. He struggled with the firing mechanism of the flare he was holding, finally, it fired off unexpectedly and hit the water next to the inflatable, ricocheting off the water and flew off across the cove, finally exploding with a deafening crack and a red flash. By now, the dinghy was twenty metres away from the *Cape*. Bruce bent down to recover the second flare, which had rolled away towards the port railing, he bent picking it up and turned towards the would-be pirates. Bruce's world went blank as he tumbled over the rail and fell into the water inert.

Charlie screamed as Bruce fell backwards into the water, rushing to the rail she was just about to jump in when she was seized by the pestilence smelling Van de Niekerk.

"Now! I have you, amazon bitch. You are going to suffer with me and from whatever it is that I have."

Georgie had started to run up towards the pilot station. "Get her!" Van de Niekerk shouted at the eunuch. Georgie ran into the lower helm position and was going to take the keys out of the ignitions and was surprised that they weren't there, she glanced around for them, the delay cost her her freedom. The eunuch grabbed Georgie by her hair and then picked her up around her waist and carried her effortlessly back down the salon, despite Georgie kicking and screaming.

In the meantime, the crewman had hold of Charlie, forcing her arm up behind her. Van de Niekerk shoved the muzzle of the pistol painfully up under Charlie's chin. "Okay bitch, I want to know where the charts are. Now! Don't fuck me about because I would just as soon as kill you right here. Right now!"

Trying to ease the pressure on her arm and the discomfort from the muzzle jammed under her jaw, she replied. "I am afraid that you are too late. As soon as my husband realised what their significance was, he contacted British Military Intelligence. The Royal Navy met him offshore one dark night about two weeks ago."

Dumbfounded by the reply, Van de Niekerk released the pressure on Charlie's chin. The reply had been so preposterous, it must be true. "How did he meet with the Navy?" He asked, replacing the pistol under Charlie's chin.

Again, lifting her head backwards to avoid the pressure from the pistol she answered. "He met with a submarine called *Astound*, her Captain is called Commander Hammond."

Above them in the clifftop urbanisation, when the first rocket had gone up, two of the occupants of the dwellings overlooking the cove wondered what the hell was going on. They knew that a large cruiser was in self-isolation in the cove and that the onboard occupants caused absolutely no problem at all. As far as the male residents were concerned the very attractive woman made for some wonderful eye candy through their binoculars. They almost simultaneously exited their homes and made for the viewing platform, which, incidentally, could not be seen from the beach below. Then came the sound of shots and they saw another flair had been fired, this time from the stern of the cruiser. From their vantage point, they were able to watch the drama unfold below and saw Bruce being shot by the long-haired European man in the dinghy, causing Bruce to go over the port railing and into the water. One of the gentlemen carried a mobile phone about his person and dialled 112. This is the Spanish emergency number and the equivalent of the English 999. Within two minutes, a BO105 helicopter of the Guardia Civil was winding up its rotors on the tarmac at its Malaga base. Two minutes later and fully crewed, it lifted off bound for the cove.

Onboard the *Cape*, still trying to get over the absurd answers the woman had given him and confused, he removed the pistol from under Charlie's chin and moved away from her. It was Charlie's left arm that was being pinned behind her. She reached behind her with her right arm taking hold of her left wrist and pushed down with all her strength, at the same time she stamped down on the midfoot of the crewman's right foot crushing the bones in the top of his foot with her heel, he screamed in agony, Charlie then took him in a headlock and twisting him around knocked Van de Niekerk to the deck. The pistol went flying from his hand as he tried to save himself from hitting the door stanchion. Charlie finished off the crewman by twice driving her right knee into his chest with every ounce of strength she had. That shattered five ribs and badly punctured his right lung. She turned and kicked Van de Niekerk in the chest and then straight-armed the eunuch in the throat, which caused him to drop Georgie. Struggling to catch his breath, the eunuch rubbed his throat and then produced a wicked-looking knife with a broad wide blade and took up a stance ready

347

for a knife fight. He was a big man and looked completely at ease with what he was doing, a smile of confidence crossed his face as he showed an immaculate set of white teeth which contrasted with his dark brown face. He opened his mouth and licked his lips in anticipation, the inside of his mouth was a very pale pink, almost like that of a hippopotamus. He switched the knife to his left hand then back to his right in the blink of an eyelid. He was going to enjoy cutting this western bitch. He was going to leave her with her entrails bleeding on the deck while she was still alive to feel his last act of cutting out her clitoris. She would never need it again and it would make a fine trophy. She would scream as she died, he knew this because he had done it before.

Not looking at Georgie as she backed away from the eunuch, Charlie's legs came against the edge of the sofa, crouching she took hold of a cushion in her right hand. "Georgie, cabin run!" At the same time, she flicked the cushion in a deft underhanded flick, as it left her hand she ran. The cushion had flown under the knife and caught the eunuch right in the face. It bought Charlie sufficient time to get down the companionway towards the master stateroom. Unfortunately, the eunuch again managed to grab a handful of Georgie's hair. She screamed. Knowing the value of the girl, he knew that his master would pay him well for this night's work, but he would need to keep her safe.

Van de Niekerk had regained his feet. "Where is the woman?" He demanded of the eunuch, who responded by pointing at the access to the cabins.

Charlie had turned around to go back to rescue Georgie from the eunuch when she saw Van de Niekerk heading up the main deck towards her. He levelled the pistol and fired. The crack of the shot in the confined area was deafening. The round crashed into the woodwork above Charlie's head. She ran for the master cabin and locked the door as she heard Van de Niekerk get to the bottom of the companionway.

Helping the crewman to his feet and speaking in Arabic the eunuch said. "Come, my friend with the little cock, let us return to our ship with this excellent merchandise. The pestilent infidel can stay here with the infidel bitch and this cursed boat." The crewman struggled into the bow of the dinghy, coughing painfully, as he spat blood from his mouth. His lung was collapsing and he would die before he got back to the *Star*. The one person who could have saved him and had the equipment to do it had locked herself in the master cabin and now he was just about to sail away from potential salvation.

Van de Niekerk hammered on the cabin door with the butt of his pistol, chipping the wood and causing ugly indentations "Open the fucking door bitch and I will let you die quick like your English bastard." He was about to fire a bullet into the door lock mechanism, just like they do in the movies when he heard the outboard start and the dinghy begin to move off from the *Cape*.

Moving as fast as he could up the stairwell, he went straight out onto the aft deck and yelled at the top of his voice. "Come back here, you fucking sons of Satan, you quisling deserters, Azil will hear of this." He fired three shots at them which went well wide of the mark in what was now near darkness.

Below in the master cabin, Charlie had heard the dinghy departing as well. She had heard Van de Niekerk disappear up the companionway and make his way to the rear of the boat, his shouts, insults and the shots that he had fired. Her realisations started to come to reality, Bruce was dead, Georgie had been kidnapped and she was trapped below by a madman with a gun. But she and Georgie were still alive, she had seen her in the dinghy. While they were both still alive, there remained some form of hope.

Van de Niekerk stood briefly on the aft deck and realised that he had been deserted by Azil's crew. Would Azil send them back for him? He doubted it. Then further considering his situation, he realised that he was on board this fine vessel, she would fetch a pretty penny on the black market in North Africa. Looking forwards, he spied the decanters of whisky and port on the starboard sideboard. It had been a long, long time since he had been able to have an alcoholic drink and the temptation then was just too overwhelming. Making his way to the sideboard, he put the pistol down, turned over a tumbler, removed the decanter stopper and carelessly splashed whisky half filling the tumbler. Picking it up, he swallowed half the contents of Glenmorangie. Van de Niekerk choked and spluttered as the fiery liquid set fire to the back of his throat and then it hit his near-empty stomach, he retched violently, bending over and clutching his stomach.

"That is my fucking whisky you are wasting, you callous bastard." The voice was loud and slightly guttural.

Van de Niekerk looked up in alarm, reaching for the pistol, at the same time, he started to back away towards the stern. He recognised the voice as being the same one that had threatened him some eleven weeks earlier. Looking up through tear streaming eyes, he saw Bruce Williams standing just past the companionway, he was advancing slowly towards him. In his right hand, he recognised the bright orange menacing barrel of a flare gun. Blood was oozing from the wound on the left of his head.

When the nine-millimetre bullet had grazed Bruce on the side of his head, it had thrown him backwards and over the port railing, he had hit the water on his side. As he sank, instinct had taken over his body in survival mode and he had regained a semblance of consciousness, that instinct made him swim towards the stern of the boat. There he was able to surface out of sight under the raised swim platform. Whilst floating under the swim platform Bruce slowly began to regain some of his senses. His first realisation was that his two most precious people in the world were in serious danger. Bruce moved cautiously to the port side of the sheltering platform and had quietly brought the steps down it was at this point that he had heard Georgie scream as the eunuch had grabbed her hair the second time. He heard the crack of the pistol shot that Van de Niekerk had fired at Charlie and watched the eunuch with Georgie under his left arm and supporting his crewmate climb down from the aft cockpit onto the swim platform. Then subsequently into the dinghy that they had arrived in. This was Bruce's opportunity to get back on board the *Cape*. He did so, as quietly as he could, streaming water onto the deck, his head aching with the worst headache he had ever encountered. Bruce cautiously made his way along the port deck and entered the galley through the access door. He heard Van de Niekerk come back up the companionway and run back down towards the rear of the boat, seizing upon that opportunity, Bruce slunk out and into the pilot station and the chart area. He punched in the four-digit combination and removed the very pistol and the five shells with it. Breaking the pistol, he loaded the first shell into the breach. Now he was armed, the first person that was going to die was that Dutch bastard with the pistol.

Bruce continued to advance on the retreating Van de Niekerk and closed to within nine feet of him as he got to a point just past the rear access for the salon. Pulling the hammer back, he cocked the weapon. "I warned you before what I would do to you." Bruce was as focused as he could be and saw Van de Niekerk start to bring the pistol up. It was almost as though his actions reverted to slow motion as Bruce squeezed the trigger. In the confined space of the cabin, the shot was explosive. Bruce had aimed at the targets chest but being wildly inaccurate as a weapon of defence the flare hit Van de Niekerk high in the stomach. This knocked him backwards into the table in the cockpit, causing him to then collapse to his knees, dropping the pistol and with both hands clutching the wound to his stomach. Bruce had seen and had caused many men to die in the past. But none like this, sulphurous smoke poured from the wound between the man's fingers and similarly from his mouth as he coughed blood.

Dispassionately, Bruce lowered the weapon. "I missed your arse you cretin and now I hope that you are having a very painful death."

Wide-eyed, and in excruciating pain, it took Van de Niekerk a total of another fifty-five seconds to die as Bruce impassively watched on. It ended when his body slumped forward onto his face. The destruction of the man was witnessed by Charlie from the top of the companionway. Slowly she approached Bruce and when she reached him, she reacted to the wound on the side of his head.

"Oh, my God! Brucie. I thought that you were dead." Tears were streaming down her cheeks. "Come here, sit down." Charlie gently guided Bruce to the sofa in the salon. "I need to get a dressing on that wound, sweetheart. Wait here."

Bruce started to stand up. "Where is Georgie?" Bruce asked.

Charlie got Bruce to sit down and explained that Georgie had been kidnapped. "I really need to get a dressing on that wound, darling."

Bruce stood up again. "There isn't enough time, we need to get to Georgie. Fast! Quick the jet ski, the key is in it." Charlie needed no further encouragement, as she jumped on starting the machine, Bruce got on behind her. Hanging on to her waist as Charlie sped the machine out of the cove and just picking up the outline of the dinghy in the last light of the day and as it was highlighted by the lights from the *Star*.

The two Spanish residents had kept up a constant commentary of events as they unfolded, keeping the 112 operator updated. She, in turn, relayed the information to the pilot of the responding helicopter. From what they could see, there was a jet ski that had been put out from the cove at high speed and was now seemingly in pursuit of the dinghy. This appeared to be heading towards a freighter that was possibly about two kilometres up the coast.

Going through periods of nausea and dizziness, Bruce hung onto Charlie as they pursued the dinghy at just over thirty-five knots. The 310LX was capable of almost twice the speed but Charlie didn't want to alarm the pirates. She was also aware of Bruce's condition hanging on to her and resting his head on her back. The eunuch at the tiller of the noisy, smoking outboard was facing forward and was sat on the starboard side of the dinghy. This was the same side as Georgie was, only she was slumped down on the floor with her legs straight out in front of her. Had the now dead crewman still been alive, he might have seen the jet ski closing quickly from the stern of the dinghy. As the distance diminished between the two vessels, Bruce's plan was simple. Hit the fucker hard. Bruce gave Charlie a brief idea of his plan. Coming out of the wake of the dinghy, Charlie made her approach towards the rear quarter on the starboard side of the dinghy and increased her speed. Bruce put both his feet on the seat of the Kawasaki with his hands on Charlie's shoulders in readiness to pounce. Some sixth sense alerted the eunuch and he twisted his body around to face the rapidly incoming jet ski. Drawing the knife at the same time he pointed it at the figure that was now literally flying towards his head with a face wearing a terrifying mask of absolute hate. A moment later and his life was extinguished as his neck snapped with a loud crack caused by the impact of the arm that had wrapped around his neck.

Bruce had been on the point of launching himself from the speeding Kawasaki at the big man at the helm of the dinghy, when the man had turned. It was too late, Bruce had already launched himself, his target was the man's neck. As Bruce's left arm coiled around the neck of his target, he didn't feel the knife penetrate his body, entering just below his left rib cage and travelling up through the back of his chest cavity, just as the blade snapped off inside him. Nor was he aware of the fracture of both his radius and ulna bones in his arm and the dislocation of his left shoulder. The resulting impetus that Bruce had gained from the jet ski's speed had sent Bruce's feet flying around over Georgie's head and slammed into the already dead crewman's chest. The result of the pendulum action of Bruce's arm around the neck of his victim, not only snapped the neck but caused both men to sail over the opposite side of the dinghy and into the ocean.

To Bruce it felt like an eternity, his body had just gone through too much for one day and now he just wanted to sleep. Some instinct told him that he couldn't give up now, there were people who now depended on him and especially that sweet child, Georgie. Bruce tried to kick for the surface, he couldn't move his left arm. Why couldn't he move the bloody arm? What was wrong with him? There was a numbness in his left side. Push your fuckin self, Williams. Don't give up now, you pussy, fuck my head hurts. C'mon Williams, you wanker get up there. He screamed at himself. There was a bright light above him, he swam with all his remaining strength towards it. 'I must be crossing over to the other side now so, this is what it is like to die. Fuck!'. He thought. Bruce's head broke the surface of the water into a maelstrom of wind and whipped water. Overhead, the BO 105 helicopter hovered with its searchlight concentrated on where the pilot had seen Bruce and his victim disappear into the water. The diver was already in the water and making for where Bruce was not only struggling against the sea but also the turbulence caused by the downdraught of the helicopter.

When Bruce had taken his dive at the eunuch in the dinghy and the eunuch's hand had come off the throttle, the ancient and unmaintained engine of the dinghy had stopped. Charlie had taken the 310LX in a fast, tight three hundred and sixty degree turn and had come back alongside the drifting dinghy. They were only one hundred and fifty yards from the hull of the *Star*. The crew had lined the side of the upper deck and were shouting insults at Charlie.

"Georgie!" Charlie had almost screamed, waking Georgie from the surreal events that she had been subjected to. "Georgie, now! Come on, get on the jet ski." Charlie had picked her up out of the dinghy and placed her on the saddle in front of her, just as the helicopter arrived overhead and lit up the ocean with its searchlight. Charlie saw Bruce's head break surface and immediately got the Kawasaki alongside him. Bending over she grabbed a handful of his T-shirt. Bruce did not look good. He was very pale. Bruce groaned as she started to pull him around to the stern of the jet ski, then she saw the broken hilt of the knife embedded in him and noticed his left arm waving limply in the water.

"Brucie!" She screamed. Stay with me, stay with me, don't leave us. C'mon baby, you'll be alright now." Charlie sobbed.

"Daddy, Daddy!" Georgie cried. "Oh Daddy, please don't die, please don't die, I love you. Please don't die. Mummy, please save him."

The diver, frogman rescuer from the helicopter arrived on the scene and already a stretcher was being lowered from the helicopter. Charlie explained quickly what had happened and pointed out the latest injuries that had occurred to Bruce. The diver understood and radioed the pilot. The stretcher was floated under Bruce and as soon as he was strapped on it, the BO 105 was lifting him into the belly of the aircraft. As soon as the stretcher was inboard the aircraft, it wheeled away and was heading for the Hospital de Santa Maria in Malaga.

No sooner than the BO 105 had left, than an AS355 Eurocopter, belonging to the Cuerpo Nacional de Policía (CNP) arrived and took over control of the area. The *Star* was ordered to stop engines and all hands were ordered to kneel on the foredeck with their hands behind their necks. A burst of machine-gun fire from the side-mounted door gunner gave them some encouragement to comply. Georgie was sobbing inconsolably into Charlie's arms, who was herself in bits but trying to keep it together for Georgie's sake. At the same time, Charlie tried to explain to the diver what had happened during the course of the traumatic evening. The diver radioed the circling CNP helicopter and relayed the information back to them as his aircraft was now out of range. A major incident was being declared and another BO 105 was already on route to the scene as were a naval fast patrol boat, a destroyer and two Guardia Civil launches which had been scrambled too, one was going to the cove. In the interim period, a second CNP helicopter was now circling the cove but had nowhere to land. They would remain overhead until the Guardia Civil launch arrived. The *Rio Jenil* with her Captain, Miguel Garcia, had also been scrambled and would take charge of the investigation when they arrived.

The second EB 105 arrived overhead and winched Charlie and Georgie aboard and then re-lowered the winch for the diver. Charlie with Georgie clinging to her was wrapped in blankets.

Charlie constantly reassured Georgie that Bruce would be fine. "He is a tough nut to crack, your Dad is. He used to be in the SAS, you've heard of them, haven't you? Who dares wins and all that."

The diver understood some English and had picked up on the reassurances that Charlie was passing onto Georgie. He spent two minutes on the radio and then came over to Charlie and Georgie, addressing the child, touching her gently on the shoulder and over the noise of the engine and rotors said. "Your daddy, very brave man, save you life, he be fine, he go operation now." Then in Spanish, he spoke to Charlie and told her that Bruce had started to respond positively to the infusion of the isotonic fluid, oxygen and sedative pain killer that he had been given and would shortly be on his way into theatre where he would be operated on by one of the country's top trauma surgeons. They were now on their way to the same hospital and would be given a private room when they got there. Charlie, somewhat relieved, but by no means convinced, thanked the diver profusely for the update. She had seen a few men die after they had shown initial signs of progress. It was almost as though their will to live had abandoned them, however, to be fair, these hadn't been her Brucie baby and he had everything to live for.

CHAPTER 32

Some fifteen minutes later, the EB 105 helicopter landed on the roof of the hospital where a nurse was waiting to escort Charlie and Georgie down to the private room that had been allocated to Bruce pending his release from theatre. It was a pleasant room with an armchair, a three-seater sofa as well as a TV and all the accoutrements of a trauma recovery room including a private toilet. Georgie, exhausted, was wrapped in a blanket and was sound asleep on the sofa. During the next three hours and forty-five minutes, whilst Bruce was in theatre, Charlie received two visitors.

The first was Clarissa. In total rejection of social distancing, the two women hugged, Charlie in tears being comforted by the Spanish woman. Clarissa had been informed by her husband of the major incident and the attempted kidnapping of Georgie as well as the shooting of Bruce. Comforting Charlie she assured her that she would visit during the following day. But before departing, she made a phone call to her husband asking that he should collect the laptop and charger from the *Cape*. At the same time, giving over the four-digit safe combination, he was also asked to collect the contents from the safe that included passports and credit cards. Clarissa took her leave when the second visitor arrived.

The second visitor was a clerk from the admin department. The hospital had obviously realised that the Williams weren't Spanish but needed to know if they had their NHS European Health Insurance Cards with them or a credit card. Charlie, to say the least, had a sense of humour failure. She took the clerk out into the corridor so as not to disturb Georgie and in her perfect Spanish, explained to the unfortunate clerk exactly what their circumstances were and where their passports and other valuables were. Charlie told her that they would definitely be going private and that as soon as she had what was required, she would make suitable payment.

It was just before one o'clock in the morning when two orderlies entered the ward and took the bed away. Charlie was told that they needed the bed as Bruce was just about to come out of theatre and would be put into a post-operation recovery room. At the same time, she was also informed that the surgeon would be visiting her very shortly. Ten minutes later, the surgeon, still in scrubs, entered the ward and seeing Georgie asleep, motioned Charlie into the corridor.

She was a tall woman almost the same height as Charlie, with ash grey hair who spoke perfect English. She introduced herself as Maria de Santiago. She had studied in Cambridge and served as a volunteer in Afghanistan. In the first instance, she was very interested in Bruce's obvious past history, Charlie explained, using the technical medical terms, which caused the older woman to ask how she was medically qualified. Charlie briefly explained her past in the British Army, which brought nods of understanding. Bruce appeared to have been very lucky. The bullet had taken a small part of his skull out, he would have a headache for a few days, but they would keep an eye on that. The knife wound had missed most of his vital organs apart from having nicked his spleen. It had, however, caused quite a bit of damage to the interior of his chest cavity, this had been repaired and that would recover faster than the fractured radius and ulna bones of his left arm. These had now been pinned together as well as relocating the dislocated shoulder.

Charlie sobbed with relief, tears cascaded down her cheeks. "Thank you!" She stammered.

Feeling Charlie's anguish, she offered her a tissue. "Wait here for a moment. I will find a nurse to sit with your daughter, then you can come with me to see your husband."

Overcome, Charlie replied. "Please, thank you so much."

When they entered the darkened ward a nurse in full anti-pandemic kit was talking gently to Bruce in Spanish. There was a brief exchange between the surgeon and the nurse. Going to Bruce's side, Charlie started trying to persuade Bruce to wake up. Taking his right hand in both of hers.

"Brucie baby. Come on, darling, wakey, wakey now, sweetheart. Just open your eyes for me please, just a little then you can have a drink and go back to sleep. Brucie, sweetheart. Please!"

Bruce opened his eyes marginally and groaned. That was enough. The tears welled again as she leant forward and gently kissed him on the lips.

Two weeks passed, during which Bruce continued his recovery under the constant watchful eye of Maria de Santiago, Charlie with Georgie, who never wanted to leave Bruce's side, visited frequently. He had received numerous visits from Miguel and Clarissa, Sergio, José and Senata with food (the hospital food was atrocious) and before, it had become public, the families of the two murdered Police Officers. Grateful for the justice that Bruce had dispensed. His night-time nurse was the same nurse that the late Van de Niekerk had kidnapped during his hospital escape so that when Charlie and Georgie weren't there to fuss over him, Sonya and her doctor husband were.

The jet ski had been recovered and had been re-patriated with the *Cape*. The morning after the incident and once the body of Van de Niekerk had been removed, Sergio and one of his helpers had been taken out to the *Cape Agulhas*. She was then put on a berth at Boats.co.uk where during the following weeks, the damaged cabin door and the bullet damaged woodwork had been expertly repaired. The damaged teak decking on the rear of the after deck was replaced, as was the blood-stained and soiled carpet in the salon. In the interim period, Charlie had secured a suite at the Hotel MS Naasranga with superb views over Malaga and the marina. In between the twice-daily and sometimes three times a day visits to the hospital, Georgie and Charlie did some home schooling. Georgie insisted that she wanted to learn to speak Spanish, with which she progressed very rapidly.

On the afternoon of Friday the 8th of May, the *Cape Agulhas* was once again moored on berth 144, the keys were handed back to Charlie, enabling her and Georgie to move back onboard the boat. On Sunday the 10th of May, the Spanish government relaxed their restrictions, on the following day, Charlie had a phone call from her mother, would Bruce and Charlie mind if they came out to visit and help support them, they had a flight booked for the following day.

It was an emotive occasion for Bruce when he was discharged from hospital on the afternoon of Wednesday the 13th (always a lucky day) of May. The staff came in to say their goodbyes, Maria de Santiago was the last one and accompanied him to the waiting CNP cruiser. (The Police had insisted that it was the least they could do in view of their fallen colleagues. As far as they were concerned, Bruce was their hero.) Maria had already met his parents in law and knew that no one could possibly have any better post-op medical care than Bruce. As Bruce got up out of the wheelchair, he embraced his surgeon with his right arm.

"Maria, you will please come and visit us. I, we, owe you so much I can't begin to put it into words." Although Maria was only two years older than Bruce, she had almost taken on a strange fondness of him over the past two weeks. He was well aware that she had spent far more time with him than she ever needed to and had joined in with family conversations when Charlie and Georgie had been visiting. Being regaled with stories from Georgie of dolphins, underwater adventures and cloudless starlit nights when they were lying on their backs on the foredeck of the *Cape*. To Georgie, she became Tia (Auntie) Maria.

Returning back to the *Cape* on berth 144, was an emotional homecoming. The Police cruiser stopped on the quay next to the pontoon, James was on hand to help him on board. Bruce thanked the two Police Officers profusely. Then he waved a greeting to José and his family as he cast an eye over the immaculate boat. James and Charlie had been very busy, Bruce thought.

He entered the salon through the open rear cockpit doors and was greeted by Charlie, holding Georgie's hand. "I couldn't do this outside." She sobbed as she gently enfolded him. Georgie was hugging him equally gently around his waist. He looked down at her as she turned her face up, tears were cascading down her cheeks.

"Listen, girls, I really hope that these are happy tears." Bruce felt his own emotions close to the surface. He kissed Charlie longingly on the lips. Seeing Mary looking on from the galley entrance, he extended his right arm out to her in an invitation to join in the group hug.

Having enjoyed his first real cup of English tea in just over two weeks, Bruce relaxed into the sumptuous luxury of the sofa, his left arm still in a sling was covered in an open splint which allowed access for the area where the wound was and where the bones had been pinned. Georgie was in the galley helping Charlie getting things ready for the evening meal.

Addressing James and Mary, who were sitting opposite him, he asked. "So, what do you think of our houseboat?"

James replied. "She is bigger than I thought she would be and absolutely gorgeous."

"Are you okay in the forward cabin?" Bruce asked.

"Oh! Heavens, yes." Mary replied. "When Charlie described it to me, I had thoughts of it being a little claustrophobic. It's bigger than our cabin on the Hans Christian."

Charlie and Georgie had finished up in the kitchen and came out to the main salon. "Oh good." James said as he started to get up. "Mary and I thought that we would take Georgie out for a short walk and explore some of the sights. If that's alright with you, of course?"

"Fine with me." Bruce replied. "But it's entirely up to Georgie. What do you say, honey?" Bruce looked at Georgie.

"Okay!" Georgie replied.

Once the three had departed, Georgie holding hands with her adopted grandparents, Charlie had made a second cup of tea and sat down next to Bruce.

"Do you like Spain?" Bruce asked Charlie.

Charlie turned and looked at Bruce inquisitively. "Yes, I do, very much. Why do you ask?"

"I wondered if you might like to have a home here in Andalusia?" Bruce nonchalantly asked.

"That's come a bit out of the blue, but yes. I would." Charlie replied. "You aren't thinking of giving up the *Cape*, are you?"

"Oh, good grief no." Bruce sounded horrified. "I just figured that it might be nice to have a permanent family base out here in Spain. The world would still be our oyster, so to speak, we could keep the bungalow in England as a Pied de Terre."

"Brucie, I think that would be a lovely idea, sweetheart. What are you going to do for the next couple of months while your arm heals?"

"I have been thinking about that." Bruce paused. "I think that I should write my memoirs. Bruce looked at Charlie with a sardonic grin.

Charlie stared thoughtfully at Bruce for a moment before she replied. "I love you, Bruce Williams."

"I love you too, Charlie Williams."

GLOSSARY OF TERMS

1 Mile	0.86897624 Nautical Mile.
Aft	To go to the back or rearwards.
Alexa	Cloud based instrument for music and information.
BCD	Buoyancy Control Device.
Bow	Front of a boat or ship.
Bredie	A tomato and pepper based vegetable stew.
Clear a Weapon	To remove a bullet in the chamber. Make safe.
CNI	Centro Nacional de Intelligencia (Spanish Secret Service).
CNP	Cuerpo Nacional de Policía.
Cockpit	The open aft end of a cruiser.
Fender basher	Time waster.
Hammer and tongs	Working at maximum rate.
Heads	Toilet on a boat or ship.
Kawasaki 310LX	1 or 2 person scooter for use on water.
Legged it	Removed, stolen.
Makarov	Russian 9 mm pistol.
Mealie's	Corn on the cob.
MI	Military Intelligence.
Moderator	Device fitted to the end of a firearm. Silencer.
Navs	Nick name for the Navigation Officer.
Nick	English slang for Police Station.

Painter	Line attached to the front of a small boat.
Passerelle	Narrow gang plank used mostly in stern on docking.
Pings	Nick name given to operator of a submarine sonar.
Port	Left side of a vessel marked in red or red light.
Quack	Rude term for a doctor, or one that is not qualified.
Rhodesia	Currently called Zimbabwe.
Sat Phone	Telephone operated via satellites.
Seabob	Powerful electrically powered personal 'tug'.
Sig Sauer	Standard issue German 9mm semi-automatic pistol.
Starboard	Right side of a vessel marked in green or green light.
Sudsa	Maize meal. Staple African diet.
The Guv'nor	A popular Spanish produced red wine.
Thrusters	Propellors to push a boat sideways.
Tia	Spanish for Aunty.
Tio	Spanish for Uncle.
Tomatie Bredie	A mixture of stewed tomatoes and peppers.
Trick Cyclist	Slang for Psychiatrist.
TVP	Thames Valley Police.
Tyre kicker	Time waster.
Urbanisation	Community or residential development.
Wake	Shape of the water behind a boat.
Yamaha DPV	Childs Underwater Tractor.

International Maritime Law Quote

1. *Article 22(1) state that, a warship which encounters a foreign merchant ship on the high seas is not justified in boarding her unless there is reasonable ground for suspecting:(a) That the ship is engaged in piracy; or (b) That the ship is engaged in the slave trade; or (c) the ship is of the same nationality as the warship. [There is no Piracy if any action is not "committed for private ends"].*

Mediterranean Sea Depth

The Mediterranean Sea is a large sea or body of water that is located between Europe, northern Africa, and southwestern Asia. Its total area is 970,000 square miles (2,500,000 sq km) and its greatest depth is located off the coast of Greece at around 16,800 feet (5,121 m) deep. The average depth of the sea, however, is about 4,900 feet (1,500 m).

Nick Names

1. Seabob. Red   'Bobbi'
2. Seabob. Blue   'Blue'
3. Williams Tender   'Willie'
4. Sat Phone   'Bat Phone'
5. Quad   'Quincy'